SOMETHING IN THE WATER

Fish jumped in the shallows. Birds sang in the woods. The sun climbed toward midday. The temperature soared with it, too.

"It's getting too hot to do this much longer," I told Ben.

He smiled. "Well, I know a place where we can find some cold beers."

"Show me that place, Ben." I grinned. "It sounds like a good place to be."

Ben reached down into the water's edge to grab a hefty branch that divided itself off into a mass of twigs.

"Leave it," I told him. "We've got enough for today."

"Kindling," he panted as he hauled it in. It must have been heavier than it looked. "It'll make good kindling."

I laid the hooked pole down on the beach, ready to give him a hand, when he let out this cry of shock.

"What's wrong?" I saw that he was staring into the mass of twigs. His eyes had turned big and round in his face. His body had fixed into the same position, as if he couldn't bring himself to move.

"Oh, my God . . ."

Other *Leisure* books by Simon Clark:

VAMPYRRHIC
DARKER
DARKNESS DEMANDS
BLOOD CRAZY
NAILED BY THE HEART

SIMON CLARK

STRANGER

LEISURE BOOKS NEW YORK CITY

For Janet

A LEISURE BOOK ®

October 2003

Published by

Dorchester Publishing Co., Inc.
200 Madison Avenue
New York, NY 10016

ISBN 0-8439-5076-5

The name "Leisure Books" and the stylized "L" with design are trademarks of Dorchester Publishing Co., Inc.

Printed in the United States of America.

Visit us on the web at www.dorchesterpub.com.

To the man on the train
To the girl in the library
To the family on the beach
To lovers asleep in their beds

For strangers everywhere

STRANGER

One

"Where did you find him?"

"Down in Lime Bay, right at the water's edge. He'd made it across in one of those fiberglass canoes."

"All that way?"

"He's a lucky man. There's a good westerly blowing today. He said it carried him across in less than three hours."

"How is he?"

"Tired. Got a little burned by the sun, but—"

"No, has he spoken?"

"Don't worry, he's a blue-eyed boy. He's one of us."

"Are you sure?"

"Right down to the accent. He says he used to attend school in Lewis before the shit piled into the fan."

"Your people are looking after him?"

"They're feeding him coffee and sandwiches. He looks as healthy as a horse to me."

I'd tagged along with the crowds who were eager to see what that big, dirty old lake had washed up on our shores. The old boys and girls tried to look as if they

1

were in control and taking this in their stride. But you could tell different. You see, a stranger was in town. A stranger was big news. They were excited. They wanted to feast their eyes on a fresh face.

Ben looked at me. "Greg, there's no need for you to come." He grinned, happy as a kid on his birthday. "He's one of us."

"There's no harm in me checking then, is there?"

"Suit yourself. But he's local. They say he's from across the water in Lewis."

"Lewis is deserted."

"Maybe he was already out of town," crowed an old dear who I can never fix a name to.

"Or maybe he got away before it happened?"

"Maybe," I agreed.

"Yeah." A kid scowled at me. "So you leave him alone, right?"

"OK." I shrugged. "No problem."

Come to that, they all looked like a bunch of kids on their birthdays. Eyes bright, all eager-beaver smiles, rushing down the road that led to the beach. Where no doubt more smiling residents of this sweet little town of Sullivan were giving that hungry—and once hunted—kid nice fresh sandwiches and hot coffee.

If you ask me, the people of Sullivan were rehearsing for the day when a convoy of national guard, or regular army, or even the residents of fucking Disneyland turned up on the edge of town to tell them that everything was back to normal. That America was exactly how it was ten months ago. Yeah. Some hope. Some fucking hope.

Don't get me wrong. These weren't people who'd spent the last year crying over spilt milk. No, to me, they were all pretending the milk had never actually spilt in the first place.

It had, of course. It had spilt big time. BIG TIME.

I watched the crowd go jigging and arm-waving and

talking and smiling at one another. They thought this was the first sign of a return to normality. Me? I went to perch myself on the hood of a Mercedes that sat gathering dust in the shade. The sun burned good and hard that morning in May. It was a day to catch you out. A stiff one blew off the lake making it feel cool. But the sun would broil six inches of skin off your face if you stayed out in it too long.

I sat there as blobs of sunlight slithered like drunken spiders across the ground. Ben calls it "dappling" when light falls through the branches. Crap on that. To me, it's drunken spiders made of light dancing all over the place. I drew doodles in the dust. Mainly gallows with hanging men. But more than anything I burned to stand on the car and shout at that bunch of happy townspeople.

IDIOTS!

Most of them were old. At least the tomb side of fifty.

IDIOTS!

That sheer goofy optimism did it for me. They were too damn optimistic. Even though they'd seen most of their children leave town to head for cities where they believed in their heart of hearts that everything would be as it once was. With bright lights, busy stores, theater shows, and men, women and children crowding the sidewalks. Those territories out there beyond the hills had sucked those young people in, of course. Only it hadn't spat them back out again. They were (in the words of the song) *gone, gone, gone. . . .*

And without a spit of doubt, hearts chock-full of hope beat in those chests of men and women scuttling down to the beach as they asked themselves: *Has my Petey come back?*

Or:

Please God, make it my dear son, Ben. Please make it be him that you've brought safely back to me after all this time. . . .

3

Keep praying. Because it won't be him. None that left after the big BAD June the freaking first ever came back. All we got in the last few months were strangers. And you can paint that word bold and you can paint it black: **STRANGERS**.

Speak of the devil.

I watched as the crowd returned. They walked with a guy of around seventeen. And, yeah, he was a blue-eyed boy. With neat blond hair, too, like he'd just turned up for his sister's wedding. Clothes tidy. Shoes clean . . . fairly clean, that is. Maybe he'd broken into a store on the other side of the lake to help himself to a new pair. He walked, drinking from a paper cup full of coffee. He seemed tired. But his blue eyes were bright enough. He chatted with the townies who guided him toward the house at the edge of Sullivan where strangers lodged until we placed them with a family. He looked catalogue friendly. The kind who'd ng bamodel clothes your mom would like. The kind you wouldn't be seen wearing on a morgue slab. As they passed, the kid who'd warned me off earlier stared at me. A few townies glared as well. Hell, you could read the warning loud and clear. *Leave him, Valdiva. He's one of us. He's OK, Valdiva. Leave him be . . .*

I watched him pass surrounded by this bodyguard of sorts. As he sipped his coffee he said something complimentary about the town church. The old folk smiled. They were pleased and proud that this *nice* young man said something *nice* about their town.

Then the guy looked at me. I sat drawing hanged men in the dust on the car and looked him back in the eye. Bright blue eyes, remember. The kind that made you think of Jesus eyes in stained glass. People glared at me, daring me to speak out as they headed for the lodging house. Ben smiled at me, then shrugged. *Don't let them bug you,* he seemed to be saying. *They're excited, that's all. They're like excited kids with a new playmate. They want to keep him all to themselves.*

I waited an hour before walking up to the lodging house. I had to wait a little while longer. The sun burned hard enough against my neck to push me into the shade of the trees. There, I listened to the sounds of Sullivan. Someway off the sound of a piano. Light sparkling notes that matched a day full of sunshine. I heard a dog barking farther in the distance. Children called to each other as they tossed a ball into the sky. Bees buzzing in blossom. Birds calling to each other. An old man sawing wood in his yard. They were the normal sounds I heard every day.

And I stood there, looking up at the face of the lodging house. Its windows stared right back at me.

At last the stranger came out. He wasn't alone. More than a dozen men and women were with him. Maybe they were going to show him something of the town and to meet the civic leaders—maybe even the chamber of freaking commerce—before they'd leave him to rest in his room. I watched him come down the steps onto the white concrete path that led to the sidewalk. The guy looked relaxed. He smiled the friendly smile.

I looked hard at him. I looked until my eyes watered from the effort. At first it didn't come. In fact, I was ready to walk away. But then that little knot came inside me. I don't know how to describe it. A knot of anxiety? A knot of tension? Almost the kind of feeling you get before jumping off the highest board at the pool for the first time. It gets tighter and tighter inside me. Muscles in my neck and legs become hard as they tense so fiercely you'd think they'd rip apart. Even the muscles in my back writhe like they're infested with a life all their own and are trying to worm out of my skin.

The townsfolk walking with the stranger stopped. Stopped dead. Just as if I'd pointed a gun at their heads. But there was this single expression on all their faces. It was sheer disappointment. They could have

5

been kids who'd got up on Christmas Day to find that Santa Claus hadn't called after all.

As I'd waited there I'd leaned the big ax against the tree. Even though I'd chopped wood for months to earn my keep the ax still made my arms ache if I carried it too long. Huge son of a bitch it was. With a half-moon blade that glittered like silver. And a long, thick shaft stained dark from my sweat. I know I haven't mentioned the ax until now. Maybe I hoped I could skip this bit. But I won't do that. I've promised myself to tell you everything—warts, blood blisters and all. Right? You follow?

So.

I picked up the ax.

Stepped out into the sunlight.

Then I hit the stranger.

First blow. To the head. Knock him to the ground. I struck so hard that it sliced off his bottom jaw. The chin full of perfect white teeth plopped onto the path.

Second blow. To the center of the back as he falls. Cut the spinal cord. Arms might flail; head might flip; but without two working legs he's going nowhere.

Third blow. Fourth blow. Fifth blow. As he lies there, strike chest, belly and groin. Open up the rib cage like a bunch of celery. Split the belly to free his intestine. Bloody snakes all over the floor. See how they run, my man. Oh, see how they run!

OK. How did he take it? He may have screamed. He may have tried to run. Or did he know what I'd do? Did he just stand there and wait for the ax to bite into him?

I don't know. Something comes over me. Afterward there are only freeze-frame images. Ribs protruding from raw meat. Blood, certainly. Lots of blood painting the path this brilliant, brilliant red.

As the stranger lay dead at my feet I remember

shouting at the stupid stone faces of the men and women.

"You fucking knew it! You knew he wasn't one of us. Why didn't *you* kill him? Why did you wait for me to do your own fucking dirty work?"

When I first arrived in Sullivan nine months ago someone gave me chocolate cake. I was so hungry I told them chocolate cake was my favorite. That's the kind of code you use when you want more. If they'd fed me an ass's head I'd have told them that was my favorite food. I was *that* hungry.

As I sat later that day on the bench that overlooks the lake to what's left of Lewis, Mr. and Mrs. Angstrom brought me chocolate cake. They said nothing. They just set the cake down. Then quiet, even stealthy, as if leaving a sleeping baby, they went.

Chocolate cake. I wasn't its biggest fan really. I couldn't eat that piece turning all glossy in the sun beside me any more than I could sprout big feathery wings and fly up to heaven.

They always give me chocolate cake afterward.

I wonder: Is it supposed to be an offering? A way of saying, *Sorry, son. Sorry you had to go through that.* Comfort food? Or just the executioner's fee?

If it is, I come pretty cheap.

No one else came near me for the rest of the day. My face started to blister in the heat, but I didn't notice. I just sat until the sun went down and the stars came out one by one.

Two

Like it was diseased vermin, they burned the blue-eyed
stranger on the shore, then buried the ashes with the
others. Later there was this big meeting in the hotel. I
didn't go, but I knew what they were talking about.
This was no south-of-the-border bread bandit who had
washed up in Sullivan this morning. This was a regular
blue-eyed guy from the next town. Somehow he'd got
the Jumpy. That meant everything was changing. And
changing for the worse. How long before the men and
women of Sullivan would be watching me with their
big frightened eyes just in case I got the telltale twinge
when I looked at them?

I walked out of town around Lime Bay. There on the
headland is a pile of white rocks. Every night I added
another dozen to it. It's now perhaps the size of a
truck; a near-perfect square that glows milky white
when the moon comes up. Rocks there are all shapes
and sizes, but if I stand and look at them for a while I
can start to see them as pieces of a puzzle. Originally
I'd only meant to build a platform maybe the size of a

bedsheet and about knee high. But the thing had just grown bigger and bigger.

Once when Ben got drunk and was sore at me for some reason he called it my "goddam obsession." He apologized afterward.

But yeah, *obsession*. I guess that's what it was. Now I build it a little higher every night. I take pieces of that white rock that might be the size of a cigarette carton or as big as a shoebox, that are either square or broad and flat like a book. Then I stand and stare at what I've built so far. It might take a while, but eventually I see where the piece fits, just like when you're doing a jigsaw puzzle. Somehow my brain manages to perfectly match the shape of a rock in my hand to the same shaped space in my neat heap of stones.

I work either at night when there's a moon that's bright enough for me to see my *obsession*. Or I work at dawn or at dusk. Here, it's far enough from the town for me not to be stared at like a freak in a cage. There are no houses on the headland. Precious few trees either. It's just a bald finger of land poking out into the lake. So, as the clock in the town hall chimed midnight, I worked. My rhythmic ritual. Select stone. Stand. Stare at my "goddam obsession." Stare at the stone in my hand. Then slot it into place on the pile. Repeat the procedure. Stand and stare. Listen to the rhythm of my breathing. The chirp of crickets. The night birds calling across the water. Do it all over again. That night I split my finger sliding a rock into its socket. But that wasn't going to spoil the rhythm. Blood got onto the stones. Juicy red paw prints. But it didn't look out of place. It looked right.

"You shouldn't be doing this tonight, Greg."

I looked up to see Lynne standing there. She fingered the flare of her cotton skirt. This was the first time I'd seen her really nervous. As if I frightened her. Nine months ago she'd worn the skirt and I'd told her that it was my favorite. Tonight she was wearing the same skirt to please me. More chocolate cake syndrome, huh?

She repeated the line as near as dammit. "Don't do this tonight, Greg. You don't have to."

"It gives me something to do." *Yeah, it's my goddam obsession.* "Where's William?"

"Asleep."

"How are the kids?"

"They're fine. The dogs are fine, too, just in case you ask." Lynne laughed. I hadn't heard her laugh like that before. It was nervy . . . tight-sounding. Sure, she was frightened. She was frightened of me. But here she was, only she wasn't paying me in chocolate cake.

"Greg," she said. "Why don't we walk down to the beach?"

"I can't yet." I picked up a rock that was the size of a skull. It even had dark shading where the eyes would be. "I haven't done my regulation twelve stones."

"You don't have to do this anymore, you know?" Her eyes glinted at me in the moonlight. "They're . . ." She hunted for the word. "They're safe now."

My throat tightened the way it does when you know you can't speak. I found the perfect slot for my skull-shaped rock and slid it into place. Blood smeared the skull stone where the mouth would be.

It took a while before I freed the words from the back of my throat. "You should go home to William. He'll wonder where you are if he wakes up and finds you're not in bed."

"He'll know where I'll be."

"You haven't been here to see me for a while. What brought you?"

"I've been busy with Adam and Marsha. Marsha's been difficult for weeks, not sleeping and messing the house. The doctor says it's the terrible twos."

"I've seen William taking them down to the beach.

You know, you've a good husband there, Lynne?"

"I know."

"Then why come up here to see me?"

"I was thinking that—"

"You were thinking? Or did the Caucus call on you tonight and suggest it's time everyone worked a little harder to keep Greg Valdiva sweet?"

"Greg, no, they didn't." She looked hurt. "I know full well what happened today. I thought you needed someone you could talk to."

"Or someone to fuck?"

She smiled. "If that's what you want. I'll be more than happy to—"

"To turn tricks like a whore?"

"Anything you want, Greg. I'll do—"

"Anything?" My voice had risen louder. My heart beat furious against my chest like an angry fist. Yes, she would do anything. I could be brutal. I could hurt her. Beat her with my fist as I filled her with my cum. And she'd smile and say, "Thank you, Greg, I'm delighted to be of service." She'd say the words in that polite hotel receptionist voice of hers. Her smile wouldn't falter. I could insult her, foul mouth her husband, trash her kids to hell and back. That's why I felt myself getting angry with her. Because she was willing to sacrifice so much of herself to keep me sweet. As if I was some fucking hairy-assed god or something. The whole of Sullivan would bust their spleen to keep me sweet. Because I'd recognized a stranger for what he REALLY was. I'd saved their skins again. Only I didn't feel good about it. I didn't feel good about being offered the chocolate cake. I didn't feel great about being offered a good man's wife.

Let me tell you this: It ain't pretty. I ain't proud. Once, soon after I arrived here, when I felt lonely as hell, I'd fucked Lynne. The great and good of the town recognized the value of me forming an emotional attachment to Lynne. That fucking her every once in a while would keep me sweet. Maybe I would even fall ass-over-tit in love with her; then she'd have a hold over me and, in turn, Sullivan would have me in its grip. Then I wouldn't leave. I would be the town's guardian angel forever.

But their plan didn't work. Not exactly. Yes, Lynne is beautiful. She has the willowy body of a supermodel. She's a gold medal–winning lover. But I'd fucked her because I was lonely and I wanted to sleep with my arms around a woman. Only it wasn't an addiction. Because I felt a great heap of guilt burning inside me. Her husband was a nice guy. Very softly spoken and always shot me a friendly smile, like I was doing him a HUGE favor by humping his woman.

So, as Lynne began to speak sweetly, as she began to move toward me with that hip-swaying walk of hers, and shoot me those love-me-tonight looks I found myself wanting to make me, Greg Valdiva, ugly from the soul outward to the tip of my sunburnt nose.

But I couldn't be deliberately cruel. She was a sweet-natured person. Instead I kept saying to her in a voice that came to my ears as a hoarse whisper, "Go home, Lynne; it's late."

"But I want to stay here with you, Greg."

"You belong at home, Lynne. Your kids and your husband are asleep. Go back to them, Lynne."

"Greg—"

"Lynne. Please. What I really want now . . . what would make me really happy . . . is to be left alone." I looked at her, knowing right then how good it would be to see her naked and to be able to kiss her breasts, stroke her legs. But guilt tore through me like a burning stake. "Lynne, go home."

She sighed. "OK, Greg." She spoke lovingly. Her voice just so sweet I felt the blood tingle in my veins.

"But if you need anything, you know where I'll be." She smiled. "Call me, right?"

"Right. Thanks, Lynne." I said it as if I meant it. What's more I realized I *did* mean it.

For a second she paused. I thought she'd kiss me. A sweet, good-night kind of kiss. But if she did that, I don't think I could stop myself from kissing her right back on her soft mouth. Once I was on that track I'd be on the old animal roller-coaster ride. I'd have her for sure. But not there. Not where I built the block of stones that I'd keep building I guess until they touched the sky. Or I died first. One of the two.

But she smiled a bright smile, wished me good night. Then lightly she walked back along the headland path in the direction of home and family. After that I stood looking out across the lake. At the way the moon filled it with lights that seemed to swell then shrink like a million beating hearts. With Lynne gone she no longer filled the night air with her perfume. I smelled lake water. Eventually the thump of my heart receded and I could hear the crickets again, riding with the ghostly call of a night bird.

At last I finished placing the final stone of my regulation dozen. It gleamed there in the moonlight. A block of white stone close on six tons. Just for a moment my mind raced through the rock, down into the soil. There was an irrational kind of eagerness to see what nine months lying in the ground had done to them.

It required physical effort on my part. A real wrenching back to stop myself picturing them.

Even so, one memory came back clearly enough. The week after I'd buried my mother and twelve-year-old sister here up on the headland I'd visited them. Some wild animal had opened up the single grave they shared. Strands of Chelle's lovely dark hair lay pasted around the sides of the hole. Somehow it looked like

13

the way seaweed looks on the beach. The paws of the animal had clawed it all in the same direction. The thing's teeth had messed their faces, but it was the hair I remember so strongly. Dear God, that memory's a hard unforgiving shape inside my head. Chelle liked playing with that hair. Not in an aren't-I-so-pretty kind of way. She'd fool around with it. Of course my mother would go nuts when she saw the way Chelle would gel it in spikes or braid it with fuse wire. What really detonated the Mom bomb was when Chelle shampooed this paste they use at school to glue paper (it's kid-friendly glue; not the kind you'd inhale to get so high you jump off the school roof or torch the principal's car—a kind of flour and water mixture); anyway, she mixed this gloop into her hair, then molded it so it stood on end like a unicorn's horn. It made her a good foot taller. What's more, the thing set concrete hard.

Mom exploded. But she saw the funny side of it later. A good six weeks later, that is.

So, it was seeing her lovely hair smeared like seaweed in the dirt by some slobbering raccoon that really sent me over the edge. That was the birth of my GODDAM OBSESSION. I refilled the hole. Then I placed a layer of rocks over it so nothing could disturb the grave. As I worked I saw that you could interlock the different shaped rocks like a jigsaw puzzle. I kept going. Outward and upward. I keep adding to it. You see, I don't think I could stop myself if I tried.

It's a monument to my mother and sister. A good one, I think. In a hundred years' time people will stop on the headland, look at that big cube of stone, and even though they might not know who lies there they'll tell each other that those people were important. They weren't forgotten.

The day the stranger died—the one with the Jesus eyes—I decided to build another kind of monument. It would be to the people I've met. To the people I

14

found myself killing. Hell, it might even be some kind of monument to me. One that people can look at a hundred years from now and know what life was like the year the entire world went wrong. That monument, I decided, would be the story of what happened to our world and about what happened to me.

And this is it.

Three

Do you understand people? Can you guess what's going through their minds? I used to date a girl who would be nice as pie with me all day, then turn 'round in the evening and say the day had been total crap. If she was nice to me one week she'd be one hell of a bitch the week after. As if she'd overspent from her good-nature account and needed some back.

Three days after I killed the blue-eyed stranger pretty much the whole of Sullivan was like that. That mood pendulum swung from gratitude to one of hatred. OK, so it was concealed hatred. But they hated me when they said their *Good morning, Greg*s. When I delivered firewood it pained them to be so ingratiatingly *nice*. Though nothing would be said to my face, I knew from the stiff bits of conversation that they were only being nice because they thought it mandatory. Well, that was the usual routine after I'd gone and done their bloody work for them.

This time it wasn't going to be exactly the same.

I drove the truck along the same old route, dropping

16

off bundles of sticks and baskets of logs at those pleasant suburban houses with their double garages and
swimming pools out back.

"Thank you, Greg."

"Have a nice day, Greg."

"See you Friday, Greg."

"Here, help yourself to a cold soda, Greg."

Yeah, that was the same old song they sang . . . they
sang it all day as I hefted the firewood to the wood-
burning stoves they used for cooking now that the electricity supply was down to six hours a day. And I was
civil in return. I wished them good day. Thanked them
when they offered food or a drink. But you could read
the minds of those townspeople, all right.

*You're a weird one, Greg Valdiva. What makes you tick?
How do you know when a stranger has bad blood? Do you
get some kind of porn thrill hacking out someone's brains with
an ax? Weren't you disgusted with yourself when you hit the
bread bandit so hard he shit blood all over the sidewalk?*

You're a disgusting son of a bitch, Valdiva.

For two pins we'd make you leave town.

*Hell for one pin, Valdiva, we'd shoot you dead, you mon-
ster . . .*

Yeah, that's what they were thinking.

But isn't that what you are deciding?

Maybe. But then I am some kind of monster. But I
was Sullivan's own pet monster. I kept the more dangerous monsters from the outside world at bay.

Today, then, it was the old routine. Nice salutations.
Disgusted stares. Except for when I reached a house at
the end of the street with cherry trees overhanging a
kind of cute rustic picnic table and chairs. Eight or
maybe nine teenagers clustered 'round it smoking cigarettes and drinking beer out of these big, oversize
plastic bottles. Most of them I'd pass the time of day
with now and then, except for a snotty-nosed guy who
always looked at me as if I was something hot and filthy

he'd just stepped in. His name was Crowther. His family had something to do with the battery factory over in Lewis. Crowther was pissed. Pissed as in angry. And maybe pissed as in being drunk. One day he'd have inherited Crowther Electrical and become a millionaire 'round about a hundred times over. Only ten months ago the battery factory, along with most of Lewis, became nothing but a pile of burnt brick. That gave the guy a well-I've-got-nothing-else-to-lose kind of quality.

"How're you doing, Valdiva?" Crowther shouted this in a friendly way. But the way he was looking down his nose at me, you could tell he was getting all juicy with contempt.

"Fine, thanks," I replied.

"I see you've got wood?" Crowther grinned at his people. "Have you got wood for me, Valdiva?"

"I've got wood for anyone who wants it," I replied.

The others laughed in a good-natured way. They saw I'd got the joke and was easygoing enough to run with it.

"How much wood have you got for me, Greg?"

I looked at the girl who'd spoken. She was pretty. And she was smiling a nice smile.

That got up Crowther's nose. It killed the superior grin on his face. "Valdiva, why d'ya do that crap job?"

"Delivering firewood?"

"Sure. Why do you moonlight, delivering sticks, when you know you're the main man 'round here?"

"I don't know about that." I pulled bundles of wood from the back of the truck and set them down in the drive.

"Sure you are, Valdiva. You've got a *real* profession. Being the firewood guy, well . . . it must be so demeaning for you."

"Got to pay the rent somehow."

"They'd give you a fucking mansion if you asked."

He jerked his thumb back at the house behind him. "They'd give you my fucking house, come to that. And they'd throw me out and I'd wind up living in your old hut down by the lake. What do you think of that?"

I kept it light as I began stacking the logs beside the stick bundles. "I don't need a big house, Crowther. Not one as big as yours, anyway."

"It's a nice house for entertaining company." Crowther stroked the bare knee of the girl sitting beside him.

"I imagine it is," I said. "By the way, I got a note from your father asking for an extra gallon of kerosene. Where shall I put it?"

"Let's see . . ." He playacted thinking about the question. "I know . . . how about somewhere where the sun doesn't shine?"

He laughed at his own joke, but this time his cronies didn't. They looked shocked and glanced at one another in a way that oozed pure discomfort.

Maybe the beer had lubed Crowther's tongue. "Say, Valdiva, how does it feel to—to, you know . . . do it to one of those bread bandits? You know . . ." He made chopping motions with his free hand. "You know, slice and dice?"

"Crowther." The girl at his side hissed his name like he was making a big social gaffe at a cocktail party.

He didn't listen. "You know, I've seen what you did to them. Man, those guys were mincemeat. I mean, you don't hold back, do you? You really fucking cream them. Wham! Off go their faces. Wham! Off go their hands. You really mess those wops up, don't you?"

His drinking buddies were getting agitated by Crowther's spiel now. They pulled at his arms, hissed his name. I heard one whisper pleadingly to him, "Hey, come on, man. Cool it; you're going to get him annoyed."

"Why shouldn't I get him fucking annoyed?" That was

19

the indignant drunk's voice. The one that gets louder and more penetrating with every word. "Why shouldn't I get the bastard annoyed? Who the hell does Valdiva think he is? He walks in here last year and suddenly he becomes the town hero. But all he does is turn some filthy bread bandit into jelly every few weeks." He was on one now. Crowther was moved by the spirit, as they say. The spirit of what, God alone knows, but he lurched to his feet, then rolled up to me before throwing himself down to his knees. Hands together like he was praying, he made his eyes go all big and adoring like he was talking to Jesus. He started crying out. "Oh, my Lord God Valdiva. Forgive me if I spoke out of turn. Do not smite me. Do not turn thy back upon my miserable face. Do not withhold your bountiful gift of wood." He started laughing as he remembered the joke. "Please, please, oh mighty Valdiva. Please give me your wood. For thy wood is a beautiful thing to behold. Give me wood, master. Give me *great* wood!"

Crowther's friends made as if they intended to scurry across to drag him away, but they only came a few feet, then they stood there in a huddle, looking nervous and unhappy. They shot little glances at one another as if to ask, *Oh, shit, what do we do now?*

Drunk, but with a glittery kind of anger, Crowther still knelt on the floor pretending to plead for forgiveness.

I froze my expression into a neutral mask. "I'll put the can of kerosene right here next to the wood," I told him. "The next delivery's Friday. But if your father needs more kerosene I can drop a gallon off tomorrow afternoon."

Like he'd been pulled up by the hair, Crowther snapped up onto his feet. "Yeah, and we're expected to be grateful for that, are we?"

"Look, I don't want any trouble. I only—"

"You don't want any trouble. You *are* trouble. Did

you know that? Everyone's shit scared of you, Valdiva."

"Remember what I said about the kerosene." I shut the flap of the truck.

"But I'm not scared of you, Valdiva!" His face had been red. Now the color drained, leaving it waxy white. "I'm not scared, d'ya hear?"

"Crowther." I compensated for his yelling by talking in a whisper. "Take it easy, all right?"

He stopped shooting his mouth off now. His eyes bulged at me from that white face. As I turned away to climb into the truck he grabbed one of the cut logs from the pile and swung it at me. A numbness spread down the side of my face. At that moment there was no pain. I just said to myself, *OK, turn back and stop him from doing it again.* Only the blow had been harder than I thought. I found myself rocking back on my heels. When he raised the log again I didn't defend myself. . . . Christ, I couldn't defend myself. I just remember seeing Crowther's face blaze with fury. The eyes blazed pure fury, too. Maybe this was the same expression I wore on my face when I killed.

Four

OUTSIDER. At school that was me. That's what I felt, anyway. Somehow I never seemed part of a group. No gang invited me to join. Don't get me wrong, I had friends. But there was always this sense of being apart from the rest of the kids in school. Sometimes I'd catch them looking at me in a certain way, as if they were thinking, *Hey, that Greg Valdiva, he's different somehow.*

Somehow?

How?

Search me.

I don't know what it was then. Or what it is now. I had no weird hobbies like collecting a million candy bar wrappers or had a thing about learning comic strips by heart. I didn't form romantic attachments to farmyard animals. Nothing like that. No one would even describe me as nerdy. Although I'd never get into fights. When other kids fought I'd never get excited like the rest who'd gather 'round chanting *"Fight, fight, fight!"* And who'd cheer when the first lick of blood appeared on a guy's nose. Instead I'd get a sick feeling in my stomach. So some other guys did take to calling me yellow. For a while I got a reputation for being a coward. Some would push me around. Nothing heavy. It was just a bit of swagger to show off in front of their friends. *Go give Valdiva a push when he's carrying his lunch tray. Trip him up in the hallway. In class take his book and scribble "Valdiva faggot ass" on the front.*

I didn't react to this. I just let them do it. I just kind of blanked it out. It seemed to be happening to someone else, not me. They never hurt me physically much. If at all.

Then it all changed.

I remember heading home from school one day. I'd have been fourteen. I cut through the park, carrying files and books under my arm. As I passed by the swings Chunk and his posse were there. Chunk earned his name by the quantity of muscle that enfolded his arms and thighs. Muscles even seemed to bulge out of his shaved head. He was a big cheese on the school football team. He boxed, too. And his reputation as a nose-breaker spread far and wide. Once he thumped a bunch of kids who'd turned up at his door trick-or-treating on Halloween. School legend had it he busted their noses while shouting, "Is Halloween scary enough for you now? Is it?" Yeah, lovable guy, isn't he? Now it was my turn.

"If it isn't Miss Valdiva," he called.

There were a few girls with him, as well as his old roughhouse buddies. They laughed this giddy laugh, egging him on.

"What ya got there, faggot boy?"

I carried on walking. The thing is, keep your head down when kids toss out a few experimental insults. If your local neighborhood bully realizes he's getting under your skin and sees you reacting to his torments, then it only gives him that taste in his mouth for hurting you a little more. Be impassive as a block of wood. Don't react. Don't show pain.

It works sometimes.

Maybe not that day in December, though. Seeing the girls giggle and sort of get turned on by his insults, Chunk turned up the menace. "Don't ignore me, Valdiva. Come here."

This time I stopped. He slipped easily into bad boy mode. He came up behind me and pulled my head back by my hair. "In a hurry to scrub your mommy's back in the bathtub, queer boy?"

"I'm going out tonight, Chunk."

"Ooohh . . ." Smirking, he looked back at his posse, who laughed and hooted, encouraging him to crank up the bad boy persona. "Oooh. You're coming out, are you? It's about time, faggot boy."

"I'm going out."

"No, you're not. You're *coming* out of the closet, aren't you, Valdiva? Admit it. Say: 'I'm a pervert and I'm coming prancing out of the closet tonight.' Say it!"

I didn't let my impassive expression slip. "I'm going out. It's my sister's birthday. I've got—"

"Did you hear that?" Chunk laughed. "Mr. Queer of the year loves his sister, too. Man, you're a bigger fucking pervert than I thought."

He pulled my hair harder. I could hear a crackling sound as hair started to snap from my scalp.

"Valdiva's got to get home in time to share the tub with his sister."

I saw the girls giggling more. Their eyes glittered. Man, those juices were really starting to flow. They were getting high on Chunk roughing me up. Chunk swung me 'round to face a wall that came up to my chest, pushing me toward it so I'd be pinned face forward. He was hyperventilating. Psyching himself up to wade into my face with his fists. This was better than sex for him. A real gutsy one-on-one beating. All the time he was panting insults at me. Really getting himself steamed up. "Little freak; little worm . . ."

He pushed his face right against the side of mine, telling me how he was going to hurt me so badly my own mother would have to donate DNA so they could identify me. He was so close I could smell fried onions on his breath. From the corner of my eye I could see the black, clogged pores in his nose. A sheen of sweat glistened on his eyelids. He grunted like he was getting turned on. Then he *really* shoved me against the brick, pushing harder and harder, all the time grunting insults with that stinking onion breath of his that damn near choked me.

It's happened enough times since. But there was no sense of me having done anything. One second Chunk was crushing my belly against the wall so hard I couldn't breathe.

The next I heard the girls screaming, "Leave him, he's had enough! Leave him, you bastard, you're killing him!"

I swear I don't remember what I did. But the next thing I know, I've got Chunk's shaved head in my hands and I'm bouncing it down against the wall. There's blood everywhere. Chunk's eyes were open, but they were dead-looking. And the strange thing is I felt no anger, no rage, no emotion, no nothing. And there was no physical effort on my part. None that I could sense. It was like bouncing a big beach ball onto the bricks.

The guys in Chunk's posse just stared in horror. It was the girls who were trying to do something. Screaming at me to stop. Trying to pull me back. And the strangest thing: I still had the books and files tucked neatly under one armpit. Like I was doing nothing more than bouncing a ball on a cold afternoon in December.

Only this beach ball pumped living blood all over

me and all over the wall in thick, juicy red squirts.

Chunk had a head of solid bone. He was back at school after Christmas. The upside was he didn't touch me, or even make eye contact again. The down side? There has to be one, doesn't there? His mother and father were big shits in a lawyer's practice. They might as well have nailed that assault charge to my head. They couldn't have made it stick there any more tightly.

I got probation as well as newspaper headlines with my photograph hollering loud and clear IS THIS THE MOST EVIL TEENAGER IN TOWN? Well, words to that effect. In a formal way, all *nicely* legal, I was thrown out of school. Neighbors and co-workers crucified my mother in that *nice,* civilized way responsible adults employ on former friends. They stopped talking to her. She was no longer invited for coffee. Some kids beat up my sister. She was seven years old. Other stuff, too. Dog turd smeared in the mailbox. The kid across the road fired his air gun at the kitchen window. Someone ran a screwdriver down the side of our car to achieve that *nice* customized scratched-to-hell look.

You know the sort of thing, don't you? Really neighborly stuff. Christ.

And then there was the Halloween that followed the ruckus with Chunk. It wound up trick-or-treat night for us, all right, with OUT, OUT OUT! aerosoled across the garage door. Mom wept. I mean really wept: Her tears left big damp splotches on her sweater and her eyes were puffy and sore for days afterward.

You think I'm angry? You bet I'm angry. She didn't deserve that. Or the fact that the guy she was seeing dumped her because of all this. Yeah, but what's new about this kind of crap? This stuff happens in every street. Every neighborhood. Every town. Happens damn well everywhere.

I wound up writing about Chunk and all that shit because I was angry about what happened the day I delivered wood in the truck and Crowther tried to crack open my skull with a log I'd just taken the trouble to saw the day before.

No. I'd set out to write everything properly. Everything with a beginning, a middle and an end. Instead, I found myself jumping 'round, describing stuff when I was fourteen, then going back to when Crowther battered me with the log. Like that pile of rocks I was building as a memorial to my mom and my sister, I intended this as a kind of memorial. A great pile of words in a book that would, somehow, all neatly fit together to tell you what happened and what it was like to live in a world that had gone head over tip.

But to write a book? How do you start? When I sat down that night of the Crowther attack I began. There I was, in the cabin by the lake, trying to write the first line. The right-hand side of my face was a mess of reds and purples where the log had gone about making a big impression. A scab the size of a quarter clung to my forehead. One eye was closed. My neck ached like sin itself. But I was determined to crack this thing open.

No words would come. Instead there were these brilliant images. They didn't just sidle into my head, they crashed, exploded, BOOMED like bombs inside my mind. There was no order to them. I saw them as clearly as the day we saw it all on TV. When they took the White House and burned it to the ground. There were thousands of bread bandits running over the lawn. A guy with hair that somehow made me think of ice cream, all white and wavy, came out to talk to them. The reporter said he was some senator who once helped those guys who were now trashing the place. He stood there with his hands outstretched like he was trying to halt a tidal wave. But the bread bandits just dove on him. They had no weapons, so they ripped him apart with their bare hands. One even tore off the senator's scalp and tossed it into a tree. His white hair hung there from a branch in one piece. That image returns to me a lot.

Here comes another memory bomb. Pow! It's completely out of chronological order. Boom! Here's the image exploding inside my head right now. I remember killing the first stranger. He turned up in town, totally normal-looking. But instinctively I knew he was lousy with Jumpy. I grabbed a wrench and, well, there I go again. Hitting you with this helter-skelter of images. Yes, I killed him. A guy with a thick black mustache. He had a mole on his left cheek like a brown thumb print. And he wore a leather belt with a dog's head buckle. On his feet, neat shoes with a Cuban heel. And he had this red-checked shirt with a button badge that said SMILE. I'M A FRIEND. Yeah, it all comes back. Every detail.

So I sat there with my beat-up face, just gazing out the window not really knowing how to begin. Across the lake squatted the remains of Lewis. They say when you're writing a book you shouldn't use flashbacks. But what the hell? Here's a flashback for you, because I can't get it out of my head. I remember the first time I walked into Lewis. I saw burnt buildings; wrecked cars littering the streets; a dog starved down to its ribs turning over a human skull with its paw, searching for a mouthful of brain fresh enough to keep body and soul together. Like some ghost, I saw myself gliding through the shattered window of a KFC, where I found a box of ketchup packets. Was I hungry? Jesus Christ, I'd run out of belt holes. I had the waist of a starved wasp. That's how hungry I was. Sitting there on a fallen cash register, I *oooohhh*ed and *aaaaaah*ed as I tore away the foil corner and squirted blob after blob of spicy red ketchup into my mouth. Shit. In my mind's eye I can travel in time, too. I can see myself roaming the town, breaking into any garage that was still in one piece. At last I'd found a car with air in its tires and enough gas in the tank to drive back the fifty miles or so to pick up my mom and sister where they'd hidden in a church. Both were sick then, only I didn't know how sick.

With my forehead buzzing, the grazes stiffening my face into a mask, I pictured myself gliding back across the water to Lewis again. Past the cinema with its heap of human bones in the foyer. With spiders in the popcorn maker. Bats have colonized the projection room. Woolworth's is burnt to the foundations. Wal-Mart survived as a structure, but it's been cleaned of everything. Not a single can of beans, not a bottle of beer remains.

I can glide through the deserted houses. There's a mess of something in the bathtub where Grandma fell and broke her hip when the rumpus began. And no one came to pull her out. Some dogs ate babies before they starved. Swimming pools are slick with pond slime. And as for the local high school? Boy, oh, boy, there are tombs noisier than those classrooms now.

I reeled my mind's eye back in. I saw myself gliding past the ruined stores, across the road, through the ruined ferry station, down along the quay . . . faster, faster, faster . . . then I'm flying out across the water to Sullivan. It's evening; townspeople quietly going about their business like they've always done. Mrs. Hatchard is giving a piano recital at Brown's Hotel in the square. A bunch of kids are hurrying down Central Way to where the Millennium cinema sits in the center of town.

Whoa! And there I am sitting in the cabin (well out of town, I should stress. Welluvva way from the good people of Sullivan). *Still sitting there with a pencil in your hand, Valdiva? Still figuring out how to say it? Where to begin?*

Well . . . where do you begin, Valdiva?

At the beginning, chirps the clever tyke that lives in

the back of your head. The one always ready with the smart cracks that never help you one little bit. OK, wise guy. I'll try at the beginning. Right at the beginning of what I remember. So, what is my earliest memory? Well, that one's easy.

My mom driving me to get my hair cut. I must have been three years old. And the last place I wanted to go was the barbershop. I hated it so much I'd scream the place down. I hated the way the barber would push my head forward, then backward, then sideways as he cut my hair. I hated the way he'd stare at my hair like there was a circus show taking place among the follicles More than anything, I hated the hair clippings that would creep down inside my shirt and prickle my skin, making me itch like crazy.

"You're going to get your hair cut whether you like it or not, young man." That's what my mother said for the tenth time. Normally, she was relaxed and fairly cheerful. Now her lips had pressed together into a hard line. She tugged the steering wheel hard. I was being a brat. Believe me, that irritated the hell out of her.

Then I had one of those lessons in life that surprise you as a child. Adults don't always get their own way. For no real reason the back wheel of the car fell off.

Now that's my first memory. Sitting behind my mother as she drove the car. We're both watching this wheel go rolling down the road. And it's going faster than us and keeps on rolling into the distance. My mother looked shocked at first, but then, as she stopped the car (which must have been throwing up sparks and smoke from the rear axle as it plowed the blacktop), she started to laugh. She laughed like a loon. I laughed, too, as that wheel carried serenely on. Rolling clean across the state as far as I knew.

There! That was my first memory. Now it's easier to

write what comes next. And how everything fell apart. And how I come to be sitting here with the blood of strangers still dried to the laces of my shoes. You couldn't tell knots from blood clots.

STRANGER

Five

There was a Valdiva in the theater the night Abraham Lincoln got shot. My grandparents tell the story that Morton Valdiva helped carry the blood-soaked president out of the theater box. It seems Morton Valdiva had served as a ship's surgeon. So he tears off a great chunk of his own shirt as a dressing and tries to stop the president bleeding out there and then onto the theater rug. But Lincoln's people didn't know old Mort Valdiva and dragged him away, thinking this stranger might cause Lincoln more harm. My grandparents insist that my ancestor could have saved Lincoln's life if only they'd let him do his job.

OK, so it's a family legend. But once, a long time ago, I was shown a cotton shirt that had been framed like a picture under glass. If it had once been white it had now turned deep gray. Sure enough, there's a strip torn out that Morton Valdiva had planned to use to plug the bullet wound and maybe save the great man's life. What's more, there's a stain down the shirtfront that Grandpa said (in the awed tones of a believer showing me a piece of the True Cross) was the blood of Lincoln.

Every family has its own legends. You'll have your own. That your ancestors were on the *Mayflower,* that they're blood descendants of Pocahontas or that they shook Neil Armstrong by the hand the day before he blasted off into space, or that they were dancing in the streets of Berlin the night the Wall came down.

To bring the Valdiva story more up-to-date, my mother and father met at college. He neglected his studies in favor of DJ-ing on student radio. He got good at it, too. A local station hired him for the late-night slot, playing soft rock ballads. But he made that show his own. Like a prospector he panned the import bins at local record stores, or made on-air pleas for kids to send in tapes of their own music. Soon he was what they called a cult figure. Soft rock oldies went out the window. Within weeks he had the raunchiest, most cutting edge music show in the state. Teenagers stayed home just to hear him play this great new music. A bigger station poached him. He married my mom. A year later MTV called. Great things awaited my dad. But then he died. I'd have been eighteen months old.

You know, nature can play tricks. For no real reason people are born with harelips, or a finger short of the regulation ten pack, or with birthmarks like a strawberry on their chin. Nature monkeyed around with the electrical signals that regulated the rhythm of my father's heart. One evening my father went to bed, a healthy twenty-four-year-old man. Sometime in the night a blob of neurons sent a message to the nerves that control the heartbeat. *OK, guys, time to pull the plug on this one.*

As simple as that. His heart stopped. He never woke up in the morning. This may sound cold on my part, but I can't get sentimental about my dad. He sounded like a great guy and all. Only I never knew him. Later, when I was around eight or so, I started thinking about him a lot. I couldn't remember a face or the sound of his voice. I was a baby when he died, for Chrissakes. If I did try hard to remember him I heard music in my head; a powerful music that went soaring upward; in my imagination I'd see a shadow that sort of filled the room. For a while I'd imagine this was my father returning as my guardian angel.

Well, things moved on. My mother went on to enjoy other relationships with men, but nothing lasting. One of these resulted in the birth of my sister. I never associated her as the daughter of another man. He'd moved on, never to be seen again. Nor did I kid myself that this was a virgin birth.

Chelle was noisy as hell. I have to say that. For a long time I wasn't bowled over with sharing a house with a sister. But within a few years we learnt to get on well together. And so we grew up—Mom, Chelle and me in a small house in a small New Jersey town. Mom worked long, loooong hours for a marketing company. Cash tended to be on the scant side. The cars we owned always had a nice rust bloom running 'round the wheel arches. Life ran to normal enough schedules—school, vacations, Christmas, birthdays. Nothing earthquaking. Apart from the Chunk episode that I mentioned a while back.

In fact the whole world ran to its normal schedule. Of course it wasn't a fairy tale of peace and prosperity. Worldwide there were the usual wars, famines, floods, hurricanes, droughts, stock market implosions, political assassinations, revolutions, treaty signings—you name it. You've seen all that stuff on TV. It wasn't pretty, but for Planet Earth and humankind it was business as usual.

As all that stuff happened I quit school, flipped a finger at college and found work at the local airport (yes, brothers and sisters, I was the guy who tossed your suitcases onto the conveyor belt that fed the carousels). As movie stars partied on Oscar night, as farmers worked their land, as politicians cut their deals and as people like me and you ordered pizza in time for our favorite medical drama, or shopped, or ground away at homework or at our day jobs, or slept in our beds, something unusual was happening. Something so unusual, something so out of the ordinary, nobody noticed at the time. Or at least if they did they shut it out of their minds.

My job here in Sullivan is to make sure everyone's got enough firewood for the cooking stoves they've now got sitting out in their backyards. Part of that job is to collect all the old newspapers I can find, so they can light their fires in the first place. During the winter nights I found myself reading them. At first it was just something to do; then for no real reason I started hunting down news stories that described the early stages of . . . hell! Let's make no bones about it, the disaster. And I should spell the word in great, menacing black letters:

DISASTER

So I clipped reports from newspapers as blizzards turned the world white outside.

I've only started putting them into some kind of order. At the time they didn't point to any kind of global disaster or apocalypse (yeah, *apocalypse* is a good word). They were the kind of thing you glanced at, thought, "Well that's pretty strange," then turned to the TV pages and forgot all about them. But it's there, all right. Like the little drops of blood in your handkerchief. That's nothing, you tell yourself. A few drops of blood. I only blew my goddam nose too hard, didn't I? But if only it was true. Those few specks of red in your tissue are the start of something BIG. A *something* that could be a freshly budding tumor in your lungs that will eat you alive.

These clippings were whispers of events just around the corner. As the man said: "Coming events cast their shadows before."

Take this one. It has a nice, cheesy title: GENESIS OF CALAMITY. Another Bible-sounding title could have been HERE COMES THE FLOOD. There are plenty like this that hint at what was on its way.

I'll copy out here in full:

Miguel Santarrez followed the well-worn path down the mountain to the little Colombian town of Carallaya. The young man had made this journey on foot every month since he was a boy when his family brought the sheep down to market. He knew every switchback turn, where to ford the river now in flood from the spring rains. Always he'd made the journey by day, only now he followed the dangerous path at night in the teeth of a gale that howled with pitiless savagery along the ravine. In his arms he carried his infant son. The fever that wracked the little body had reduced the baby's cries to a whimper. Miguel knew the only chance for the boy's survival lay with the doctor in town.

Two hours later Miguel walked along the windswept streets of Carallaya. He passed through the deserted market square by shuttered stores and cantinas. With the time long past midnight he no longer expected to find the doctor awake, but the sight that met his eyes was enough to stop him dead in the street. A house lay with its front door swinging back and forth in the storm. Lights still burned, but there was no one home. Miguel saw it was the same with the neighboring house, and the next, and the next. The once bustling town of twenty thousand lay deserted. Not a living soul remained. And when the desperate Miguel Santarrez telephoned the city hospital in

Barranquilla, his call went unanswered. When he switched on a radio in an abandoned home all he heard was static. . . .

Get the picture? The article tells it like a mystery story, or a weird piece of Forteana—an abandoned town hidden in the mountains of South America. All exotic-sounding, all faraway and, when all's said and done, not a blind thing to do with us.

Only it started to get closer to home. Creeping north through South America men and women began to abandon their towns and cities. Nation governments down there worked like fury to contain the news and stop the panic. But it was a case of "Here comes the Flood." Once it started there was no way of turning back the flow.

You'll know about rabies. You know dogs, bats, even people foam at the mouth and die. But did you know a symptom of the disease is hydrophobia? A victim of rabies becomes terrified of water. There's no way you can sit the person down and say, "Look, this is only a glass of water. It can't harm you." No, show a rabid man a glass of water and he'll go crazy with fear. He'd jump through a tenth-story window rather than have that glass near him. Throw the glass of water in his face and pure fear would kill him stone dead.

Something like that got into the air or water system in South America. No one knows exactly how it was transmitted. But that bug moved *fast*. From what they could tell it began with symptoms like gastric flu, triggering bouts of stomachache, diarrhea and low-grade fever. Nothing life-threatening. At least not what they thought was dangerous. But scientists reckon the virus . . . if it was a virus . . . moved into the brain after the initial bout of the craps. Like hydrophobia in rabies or aversion to light in meningitis, people developed a morbid fear of illness. And I mean *real* fear. A fear so large and so overwhelming and so God almighty powerful that people were terrified to visit a relative in the hospital in case they inhaled bacteria and became sick themselves. There's footage of sufferers being carried into hospitals for treatment, but they're so terrified they hold their breath to stop inhaling disease bugs and just pass out right on the floor. Some stopped breathing altogether. Terror jerked their throat muscles into spasm, sealing the airway, and good-bye, Earth.

You can read later news reports, when medical experts started to understand this plague. It seemed there was something like a 90 percent infection rate. And those patients completely recovered from the physical effects of stomachache and diarrhea (*exploding underpants syndrome* was how Bart described it in a "Simpsons" episode that spoofed the whole epidemic). The colony of bugs in the brain was the real problem. I mean, you only have to think it through. A town is hit by the plague (called Gantose Syndrome after the smug asshole that first identified it—if you saw his photograph you'd know why I used those words); as people recover from the physical illness they're gripped by the phobia. Your neighbors are still going down with it. They have fevers; they're clutching their bellies. And in the meantime you are going out of your mind with fear. Like the man with hydrophobia killing himself to escape the glass of water, you can't just tell yourself, "OK, my terror of illness is all in the mind. I'll just ignore it." You can't. What's more, all your family are the same. So your fear feeds their fear. So you tell yourself, "I'm getting the hell out of here. I'm going where I'll be safe." But where will you be safe? Go north, your instincts tell you. "America will help me. They've got the best medicines. The best health care. Go north."

And did they go north?

You bet.

What must have been three quarters of the fucking

entire South American continent walked out of their houses and headed north. You can imagine millions choking roads in cars, buses and tractors as they drive northward. Jesus, just look through your mind's eye. People who are desperate with terror get hungry and thirsty and tired. Cars break down. They beg lifts. They steal cars. They kill the people in the next car for a bag of apples because they're so hungry. Highways turn into stinking mortuaries with thousands of corpses rotting at the roadside. Flies swarm so thick in the air they become a black fog through which car lights can't penetrate.

Flies. Shit-filled ditches. Corpses going rotten in the sun. What does that spread?

Disease.

What do the people infected with Gantose fear?

Disease!

So in terror they move faster. They infect country after country as these refugees pour north.

As I said earlier, Nature likes to play tricks. Remember years ago, when there was that panic about a flesh-eating tropical disease? And how scientists said it would rampage across the world? Then (red faces all around) they realized it couldn't spread naturally outside the tropics. Well, the Gantose bug wound up being cut from the same cloth.

The plague ran northward like a tidal wave. Then north of the Panama Canal when you hit the drier territories of Mexico suddenly there were no new cases. OK, so a few people came down with it, but these had contracted the disease in places like Brazil and Peru. They'd incubated the disease as they'd grabbed a flight north. What's more, they didn't infect Mexicans. Those South Americans who reached the States, even though they went down with the screaming meanies whenever they saw a hospital or an ambulance, didn't pass the bug on to a single American.

* * *

There was a race issue here. One prominent medical expert announced that it was all a question of blood. That most of the South American population had a little native Indian blood in them; maybe a dash of Inca or Aztec, I don't know. This professor guy was frozen out of his university post pretty quickly. But there were many who believed him. They used it as an excuse to exclude anyone with a Hispanic face from restaurants and bars. Even those whose grandparents were born here.

The bottom line was that all those months ago the disease appeared to have run out of gas. Those infected with Gantose even stopped going into a mindless panic when someone sneezed across the street. But you can't dump hell knows how many million people into Mexico without the place exploding at the seams. Massive global aid programs worked for a while, but there were still too many people to feed. Distribution networks collapsed. Even though grain piled mountain high at ports it didn't reach the refugees deeper inland. Hunger drove them farther north, as far as the U.S. border with its walls and fences to keep illegal immigrants out. There, as the saying goes, the irresistible force met the immovable object.

Here's another cutting. It contains an interview with one of the American patrol guards on the Mexican border the day of the Breakout.

"It's all gone to hell. But how can you stop them? There must have been a million men, women and children. And there were kids holding babies in their arms." The harrowing memories were enough to render the man's face ugly, and he'd just lit his third cigarette in the ten minutes I'd been speaking with him. *"They tore the border fence apart with their bare hands. . . . I mean, what am I supposed to do? Shoot them? Shoot kids and babies, for*

STRANGER

Chrissakes. All we could do was climb on top of our cruiser as they came by. They weren't people; they were a whole flood. So we just hung on to the roof light and watched them pour by."

The flood that engulfed America began that dry-as-a-bone May morning. "Refugees sometimes turn into invading armies," prophesied one commentator, but millions of Americans contributed food parcels and volunteered to help avert a humanitarian disaster. We, as a nation, labored to do the right thing.

Soon every state accepted a given number of refugees. And that flood kept coming. Empty hostels, hotels, army camps, redundant cruise liners were crammed to capacity. You could visit your local supermarket one day, everything normal. The next day you drove into the parking lot and there'd be five hundred Brazilians living in a shanty town of cardboard boxes. It got like that in the city parks. Tents made of sticks and carrier bags became home to millions nationwide. Of course they were all hungry. They all needed clean water. Medicines. Clothes. Shoes. And, goddam, we did do the *right* thing. We did our best to feed them. But there were too many. These half-starved bastards—and I don't mean that in an insulting way, believe me—filled the streets begging for food. They weren't violent or intimidating or anything. Of course, hardly any spoke English, and it seemed the only word they did learn was *bread*. So you'd walk downtown and there would be beautiful young Brazilian women or Mexican women (helluva lot of Mexicans seemed to get carried with the northward flow) and they're all holding out their hands; they've got beautiful brown eyes that overflow with pleading, and they're all saying one word as you pass:

"Bread."

"Bread."

"Bread."

You might give them every penny in your pocket and still know you hadn't done enough. Because between you and Blockbuster, or Barnes & Noble, or McDonald's, or wherever the fuck you were going, is another ten thousand people all saying this one stupid word as you pass. Bread, bread, bread, bread . . .

And you find you start getting angry with them, because deep down you're angry with yourself. It's human nature to help a person who comes to you for help. Only you can't do it. You can't help them all. And this one word comes in a soft pulsing chant as you walk on by.

Bread

Bread

Bread

Bread-bread-bread-bread-bread-bread . . .

As one refugee stops saying it the next starts. Bread, bread, bread . . .

Shit. After that you couldn't swallow a piece of bread without it sticking in your throat like a stone.

It wasn't long before the people from South of the Border who became our sudden guests got a new name. Forget refugees. Or the "displaced." Or even "victims." They became bread bandits. I don't think the name started on TV or radio. It was probably some word-of-mouth thing. A kid called a refugee a "bread bandit" one day. Within a week or so the name had spread. It wasn't intended to be cruel, but it seemed apt. So it stuck. We still use it today. I've killed bread bandits.

Diseases often develop in cycles. Good old syphilis is the classic example. It takes years to run its course. Mostly it might disappear for ten years or more and the infected person has no symptoms, nothing. Then back it comes out of the great blue yonder. The sufferer suddenly finds pus squirting from his ears. His hair falls out. His skin gets all blistered and a dirty great crust of scabs forms on his face. Madness gathers up his wits and hurls them from the window.

The funkily named Gantose Syndrome was something like that. When experts told us the condition had run its course what seemed to have happened was that the Gantose bug merely submerged itself into the bones and muscle tissues of the victims, where it mutated into something even more sinister. After the first real heat wave of the year that was enough to knock an elephant off its feet Gantose 2 flared up again.

Here's another headline:

tet!
USA

This explains everything in the word. Like the surprise attack by the communists in Vietnam, in what were supposed to be safe cities hundreds of miles away from the front line, so America was torched. I mean literally torched. On Sunday, June 1, refugees ran amok in towns and cities across the whole of the U.S.

Afterward, there were all kinds of theories. That it had been a coordinated attack. That the bread bandits all had little radios with them, that the order was broadcast in code and WHAM! They rioted in their millions, turning over cars, looting stores, burning houses, killing American men, women and children with their bare hands.

It wasn't quite like that. Everyone agrees now it was that bug in their blood. It burrowed into their brains and made them do that. Just like a man with rabies'll jump from a window rather than permit a glass of water to come near him. But why did it all happen on that Sunday? The doctor here in Sullivan will tell you it was the heat wave that fired up the dormant bug, pushing it into its next phase of the condition.

Still things don't add up. A mystery the size of Texas's still hanging over our heads. Sure there were millions of bread bandits here. To carry on the disease image, they'd infiltrated and infected the entire body of our country from one end to the other. But there still weren't enough of them to make the whole nation implode. But that's what happened. Our society, which seemed solid as the rock you stand on, just disintegrated.

One problem was the lack of food. Huge, HUGE problem. Bread bandits looted everything down to the last candy bar from supermarkets. They torched cars on the highways. Roads blocked everywhere, and the image blazing in my mind right now is that big antique vase in a cartoon. The one that gets just a gentle tap and a little crack appears . . . that crack in the china leads to another one, then another, and another, until with a low crick-crack sound the vase becomes a mass of fractures before the whole thing collapses into dust. Our country was like that vase. Suddenly there was no food. Thousands of families were burned from their homes. Bread bandits torched food warehouses. Food couldn't be delivered to where it was needed through gridlocked roads.

American citizens became refugees, too. Only they headed for cities that had no food either. What takes your breath away was the SPEED it all happened. I'm not talking weeks, but four, maybe five, days. Panic-buying at service stations meant gasoline vanished. No new stocks could be brought in because roads were a mess of burnt-out trucks. The guys who were to clear the routes into town with bulldozers didn't show up to man the vehicles because they were working their guts out to find food for their families. Can you blame them? Any more than you can blame the cops for choosing to guard their own homes, rather then standing guard at city hall to stop some bread bandit trashing the Xerox machine? It's human instinct. Family first.

Freakish things happened. Marines protected an IRS office while bread bandits butchered kids in kindergarten half a mile away. One state governor fled to Hawaii, then flew back again and hanged himself in his office. Another died rescuing patients from a hospital. Bravery, cowardice, confusion, terror, panic—we saw a lifetime's worth inside a week.

The other Freak Event was Sullivan. Somehow the wild flood that engulfed the nation missed this chunk of suburban life as it sat there on the lake. Life went on as normal. In fact, it became so normal it became a freakshow in its own right.

So there I sat as dusk fell. I wrote down everything I knew on this block of paper. I pushed myself so hard to explain what happened I stopped feeling the pain in my face. The water was still now after the breeze of the day. Bats dipped to take insects from just above the lake. Uphill, electricity still fed the town. People burned more lights than were necessary. But then, nighttime had taken on a more sinister edge of late.

It wasn't quite dark when I saw the procession of people heading toward my cabin. There must have been twenty of them. I didn't like what I saw. Because the first person I recognized was the guy who tried to break that log over my head earlier in the day. Crowther's face wore a grim expression. Anger burned in his eyes.

There was nowhere to run. So I put down my paper and my pencil and went outside to see what they wanted from me.

Six

If looks could kill . . . That's a phrase you'll know well enough. When someone who hates you can't physically touch you but the look in his eye screams, *I'm going to rip your fucking head off!*

Crowther's hate-shot eyes burned right into mine. The crowd that walked with him were mainly middle-aged or older. This was no lynch mob. They were the ruling committee of Sullivan, who were known as the Caucus. The youngest there was Lynne's husband. He was thirty-one. I recognized Crowther's father, looking the picture of misery.

I came down the steps from the cabin's veranda and waited for them to speak. They'd walked purposefully enough. Now, however, they slowed to a kind of shuffling approach, as if suddenly they no longer wanted to be here. Rose Bertholly had been a corporate lawyer before the fall. She glanced back at the others, took a breath that seemed to say, *Ok, I guess it's up to me,* then: "Greg. How are you?"

Stupid question. I'd been slammed by a hunk of maple wood.

"How's your face?" she asked when I didn't answer.

"OK. Considering." I looked at Crowther junior. Meanwhile, Crowther senior shuffled his feet in the dirt like he wanted those feet to carry him away.

"I won't beat about the bush, Greg."

Nice choice of words, lady lawyer.

"The Caucus met tonight. We discussed Mr. Crowther's assault on you. We consider it unwarranted. . . ."

That mean he didn't have a good enough excuse to crack my skull bone?

"It was cowardly, and we deem it a serious infringement of the rule of law in this time of national emergency."

Well, said, Miss Bertholly. You must have been sharp as a blade in court.

"Greg." She gave me a look that was seriously lawyer-like. "The Caucus has agreed unanimously that Mr. Crowther is guilty of the crime of actual bodily harm against you. We feel very strongly, also, that he shouldn't go unpunished." She paused. "How do you respond to that, Greg?"

"My response would be, why do you call me Greg and the guy who tried killing me, Mr. Crowther?" I looked from Crowther junior to Crowther senior. "It seems strange to me. Or is it because I crawled in here on my hands and knees just a few months ago? While the two Mr. Crowthers here are old Sullivan blood and the local neighborhood millionaires?" I jerked my head in the direction of the burnt piece of crap that Lewis had become. "See how much you can buy for a dollar across there."

"Greg . . . Mr. Valdiva. I apologize." Her voice was polite, but the words came out with a glint of ice on them now. "This isn't a court of law."

"Isn't it?"

"I was merely trying to be informal."

"Oh."

"I can't blame you for being angry."

"Me? Angry?"

"You suffered a physical assault today. It was unprovoked."

"Assault? If you took the hard end of the wood like I did you'd call it attempted murder."

"Mr. Valdiva. Mr. Crowther had maybe a few more drinks than he ought. He didn't mean to—"

I couldn't stop the snort of pure disbelief shooting out of my nostrils. "Oh, I see. You're closing ranks. It was just a bit of fun that got out of hand. See?" I tilted my head to the light shining from the cabin so she could see the crazy paving of grazes and bruising. "That's Crowther's little bit of fun."

"Hey, Valdiva." Now it was old man Crowther's turn. Disgust came oozing through his voice as he spoke. "Valdiva. My boy would not harm anyone without just cause. He must have been—"

"Jim." An old man beside Crowther senior held up a hand. "Jim, the Caucus has made its decision. Your son is guilty of assault. There's no debate about that."

"The question is," Miss Bertholly said crisply, "what will the punishment be?"

I shrugged. "OK. So why have you come down here to discuss that?"

There was a pause long enough to hear the cry of night birds shimmering across the water. Those men and women shifted uneasily, as if they heard the sound of ghost children calling to them from the ruins of Lewis.

"Why have the Caucus meet here outside my house? You'll have made up your damned minds about Crowther anyway. You going to stop ten dollars from his allowance, Mr. Crowther? Are you going to ground him for a week?" This slice of crappola had become a joke. I turned to go inside.

"Mr. Valdiva," Miss Bertholly said. "We—the Caucus, that is—have also decided that as you are the victim you must decide the punishment."

"Get away . . ." I shook my head. "You want me to fix a punishment for Crowther? Why?"

"Because if we chose a punishment you'd only say . . ." She took a breath and selected more diplomatic words, "If you chose the punishment you would know that an adequate redress had been made."

"OK." I nodded. "OK. That sounds fair enough." I reached back to the veranda rail to grab a coil of rope that hung from a nail there. Underarm, I tossed it at old man Crowther. He caught it as it slapped into his chest.

"I've decided the punishment," I told them. "Hang him."

There was a silence you could have carved with a blade. Even the call of the night birds died. All I could hear was the lap of water out there in the darkness.

"There's a lighting rig down at the jetty. It's a good ten feet tall. You can string him up from that."

Jesus, their faces. They looked as if I'd thrown a hand grenade at them. Crowther junior had arrived with a look of defiance pasted across his face. Now his eyes seemed to race from one person to another, finishing with a pleading look at his father. I looked into the eyes of the others there, especially into the eyes of Miss Bertholly the lawyer.

"What did he say? Dad, what did Valdiva say?" Crowther's voice came stammering out of his mouth. "Dad?" His eyes had morphed into big rolling white balls that locked tight onto the rope in his father's hands. *"Dad? D-der-does he want to hang me?"*

Gritting my teeth, I lunged forward to snatch the rope from the old man's hands. "Go home," I told them, angry. "Go home; it's late."

With the rope in my hand I went back to the cabin,

punched open the door, then crashed it shut behind me.

I stood there with the door pressed shut by my back. Jesus . . . my hands were trembling. Sweat poured down my face, its salt getting onto my tongue. I balled my hand and rubbed it across my mouth with the back of my fist.

"Christ. Idiots . . . You crazy idiots . . ." I looked at the rope as if it had burst into a mass of bloody tumors, then threw it from me. Because I'd read that look in their eyes. They'd have gone along with what I'd asked for. They were going to hang Crowther junior, the poor bastard.

Sweet Jesus Christ.

What was happening with these people?

Seven

"You're kidding me, Valdiva."

"No, I'm not."

"Straight up?"

"Straight up."

"You told them to hang the Crowther kid and they were actually going to do it?"

I nodded as I hooked the log before pulling it out of the lake onto the beach.

"But you say his own father was there?" Ben's eyes were huge. He couldn't get his head 'round this slice of news. "He was just going to stand by and watch his own son be killed?"

"He'd have put the noose 'round his own son's neck if I'd demanded it."

"Jesus."

"I tell you, they looked weird. If you ask me the . . . what do you call it? Trauma . . . the trauma of what's happened to these people over the last few months has gotten to them. They're getting desperate."

"Why? We're safe enough here."

"For the time being."

"We're damn lucky, Greg, The Caucus is publishing a report next week. They say we've got enough gasoline in those big storage tanks in the interchange to last ten years."

"Yeah, I know, and enough juice for the power plant for twenty years if they ration the electricity supply to six hours a day."

"And five warehouses crammed with canned foodstuff."

"And close on a hundred thousand gallons of beer, truckloads of whiskey and about ten million cigarettes." I hooked another hunk of wood and started hauling in. "Yeah, everything's peachy."

"Not peachy, Greg. But everything's OK. What with the dairy herds and the poultry farms, fish from the lake and fruit from the orchards." He sounded enthused now; words came tumbling out. "And the crops on the south end of the island, we're self-sufficient. We can sit here for a decade and still not have to break sweat to feed ourselves. That's going to be more than enough time for the country to get back to . . . oh, hell."

The "oh, hell" indicated that the piece of timber I'd been hauling wasn't a piece of timber after all. Instead of a three-foot hunk of firewood I saw a fraying head linked to a torso. The face and eyes had gone. Whether it was a man or woman I couldn't say. All I could say for sure was that fifty pounds of human flesh had seen better days. I pushed it back out into the lake with the pole. Gas from inside the body bubbled out, making it sink slowly out of sight.

"Now you know why the fish get so fat these days," I told Ben. "So you're telling me the Caucus master plan is that we all sit tight here waiting for the government to announce that society is back to normal?"

"There's no point in doing anything rash."

I nodded across the lake at the distant hills. "You mean nothing rash like going out there and finding out for ourselves whether the country's getting back on its feet again?"

"You know it's too dangerous to leave the island."

"You mean guys have left, but they never came back?"

"Sure, so why risk it?"

"Why risk it?" I hooked more wood—this time it was a window frame—and pulled it out of the water. "I figure we should satisfy ourselves that America, probably the whole world, has bellied up good and hard; then we can stop this pretense that one day the radio and TV stations will come back on air, and that the president's going to announce everything's hunky dory."

"You don't think it's going to happen, Greg?"

"Do I hell. There is no president anymore. There is no government. They're all dead."

So we carried on. Ben being bright-eyed and optimistic. Me? Well, I was cynical as hell. Our nation, and every other nation, without doubt, was well and truly busted. Only the men and women of Sullivan, population 4800, were still locked down with a tungsten-hard case of denial. USA's A-OK? No way, *amigo*. USA's DOA.

I liked Ben. He was one of the few guys in the town I could talk with. He was a year older than me at twenty. He liked the same music. He had the same sense of humor. When I first met him he seemed one of those super-intelligent people who towered over you and made you feel prickly, as if he were going to put you down the first time you opened your mouth and let slip you're no Einstein. The first time we met was when the Caucus ordered him to show me 'round the island. I'd have been in Sullivan just a week at that point.

"Of course 'island' is a misnomer," he'd told me as he drove through town in a Ford.

Misnomer? Christ, what kind of guy uses the word *misnomer*? I decided this bright-eyed student type with arms and a neck as thin as wires would only be my best buddy when hell developed icicles. And did you see that? I told myself as he fiddled with the car's CD player. His hands shook like someone was running a couple of hundred volts through him. He could hardly push the buttons. His jerky fingers were all over the damn place. If he aimed to pick his nose he'd wind up with his finger in an eye. Probably not even his own.

"Calling Sullivan an island is a misnomer," he was saying while prodding the buttons. "You probably saw as you came in, it's connected by a narrow strip of land to the mainland. The only road into Sullivan runs along that. If anything, Sullivan is shaped like a frying pan, with the handle forming the isthmus connecting us to the mainland. Across there is the Crowther distribution center. All those warehouses used to supply Lewis—that's the big town, over the lake. You see, in years gone by it was easier to transport food, gasoline and general goods into Sullivan by railroad, than ship them across the lake. The terrain around here's pretty bad for a decent road system . . . across there is the power plant. There, the building with the tall silver chimney. We're so isolated we've got our own generators."

"They still work?"

"Absolutely. Years ago they found pockets of orimulsion under the island."

"Orimulsion?" That was a new one on me; sounded like something to do with house paint.

"Orimulsion." He tried flicking a bug away from his face. Those trembling fingers fluttered with the speed of batwings. "Orimulsion is a naturally occurring gas that's highly inflammable. It's no good for domestic

54

use. Too corrosive. It'd rot your stove to crud inside twelve months. But it's great for industrial use. What they did was bore down into the orimulsion pocket, then simply build the power plant over the top of it. That gas is good for twenty years yet." The bug buzzed back and his damn fluttery fingers jerked up. He was steering with one hand now, and boy, those shakes. The car started flipping side-to-side on the street. A couple of kids on bicycles were pedaling the other way. "The Caucus . . . that's the committee that governs Sullivan . . . they ruled that in order to eke out the orimulsion stock we shouldn't squander electricity, so . . ." He tried flicking the insect from his face, only those trembling fingers were going all over the place. He even knocked the rearview mirror. And, Christ, those kids. They were going to be road meat in ten seconds flat. I flicked the bug against the windshield, where I crushed it under my knuckle.

"Good shot," he said, then carried on, happily talking about what a brilliant job his hometown was making of what must have been the biggest disaster this side of Noah's flood. "So they decided to ration electricity to six hours a day, running from six in the evening until midnight. You see, dark evenings are bad for morale, so if we keep the power going for lighting and home entertainment people can watch movies on tape and disk and so on."

At last his trembling finger hit the play button. At that moment electric guitar sounds soared from the speakers. A driving bass pumped loud enough to shake the car.

"Hendrix!" He nodded to the rhythm as he drove. "This is gold . . . pure gold."

We drove out of town and past fields where cows chewed their cud. He waved to a woman walking her dog. A rat-sized thing on the end of a leash that wore a tartan coat.

"That's Miss Bertholly. She's a big cheese on the Caucus." He looked at me. "She's a real iceberg in pants; don't let her order you 'round."

Then he flashed me a wide friendly grin. Something gave way inside me. I don't know what. Because for the last few days I'd been wearing a face engraved out of granite, or as good as. I'd not cracked a single smile since I'd buried my sister and mom out on the bluff. Suddenly I felt this big object moving through me and didn't know what the hell it was. Then it came out, and I was making this weird braying sound.

Jesus. I looked at myself in the rearview mirror that Ben's jerky hand had knocked to face me. There I was with my black hair sticking up in wild spikes, my dark eyes glistening, and I realized I was laughing. It wasn't as if Ben had said the wittiest line in the world. But it uncorked a hell of a lot of emotion pent up inside me. Now I was laughing so hard I thought my guts would rip out through my skin.

Ben looked at me with a grin. Before you knew it, he was laughing, too.

So roaring like a pair of madmen we cruised around the island that wasn't *really* an island, while all the time Hendrix's guitar blazed from the speakers like the cosmos itself had found its own voice and begun to sing.

After that I'd go out for a beer or two with Ben, or we'd hang out with a few like-minded souls.

Ben had one of these brains that people describe as lively and inquiring. He'd been hot as biology student. For months he speculated about the real cause of the "disease" that infected the bread bandits.

Often he'd air his ideas as I made my daily round, using a hook on the end of a twenty-foot pole to haul driftwood from the lake. I'd leave it there on the shore in piles, then either me or old Mr. Locksley would roll up in the truck and haul it back to my cabin, where I'd cut it up for firewood.

"Greg," Ben once said to me, "you know that scientists never did find bacteria or a virus that could be attributed to the disease?"

"What?" I said, half listening as I hauled branches out of the water. "You mean old Jumpy?"

"Jumpy." He grinned. "That's it, give a terrible disease a comical name and it doesn't seem half so bad, does it?"

"Well, Jumpy seemed to sum it up well enough. Once those bread bandits had a full-blown case they nearly jumped out of their skin. They got so they were terrified of their own shadows."

"Sure, the disease was named. Officially it was Gantose Syndrome, then it became corrupted to Jumpy. But they don't know what caused it, or what it actually is, never mind the question of how it could be cured."

"Does it matter now? No . . . it's OK, Ben. I'll pull it out of the water." Good-natured Ben would sometimes try and help, but his hands would shake so much he'd shake the wet wood and spray water into our faces. He was good company, though, when I was out fishing for wood, so I always encouraged him to walk with me 'round the shoreline.

And so he'd tell me his latest theory. "If you ask me, Greg, even if Jumpy is a disease it's not caused by bacteria or a virus."

"It has to be one or the other, Ben. Even I know that you don't get sick without some kind of infection."

"That's not true. Your body can be invaded by something called a prion."

"A prion. What the hell's that when it's at home?"

"A prion can't even be described as being alive as such. Usually it's referred to as an agent, but it seems to be capable of reproduction. What's more, it's far smaller than a virus. Even worse, it's virtually indestructible and can't be destroyed by heat. Prions have been transmitted using scalpels that have been sterilized."

"Then why haven't these prions killed everyone off in the past?"

"Because the diseases they cause are rare. And prions tend not to be harmful as a rule. We've all got them swimming about inside us, but as I said, they're rarely dangerous. They just lie dormant all our lives."

"What's the problem then? Don't we all have benign bugs inside us?"

"That's true. Normally prions don't bother us. But if they do turn nasty . . ."

"I could see that big BUT coming."

"But if they do turn nasty," he said, getting enthusiastic again, "they produce a substance called amyloid, which always forms in brain tissue, not in any other part of the body."

"Ah." I saw where he was going with this. "If it attacks the brain, then it's going to affect behavior."

"Bull's eye. And prions are transmissible."

"You mean that these prions may be responsible for Jumpy?"

"I do. And that it caused millions of people in South America to act in such a bizarre and unusual way."

"But simultaneously?"

"Some diseases spread fast. You've ridden a bus in winter when half the passengers are sneezing and coughing."

"Have prion diseases spread as fast as this before?"

"Not to anyone's knowledge." He gave a grim smile. "A tad worrying, isn't it?"

We talked on the beach as I collected wood that lake currents delivered to us with all the regularity of the old-time mailman. That had been my job of work for the last few months. For that I lived rent-free and took a weekly wage. Dollar bills in the outside world might only be good for starting campfires, but here in Sullivan they were still legal tender.

STRANGER

Never going out farther than their statutory two hundred yards were half a dozen rowboats, each with two or maybe three guys fishing. They'd never go beyond the orange buoys that marked the two-hundred-yard boundary offshore. If you ask me, they'd die of a heart attack if you even suggested they fire up the outboard motors and ride the four miles or so across the lake to Lewis, which now sat there like a crusty black scab. Those old guys'd tell you they didn't believe in ghosts. But get this: They were still scared of them.

Fish jumped from the shallows. Birds sang in the woods. The sun climbed toward midday. The temperature soared with it, too.

"It's getting too hot to do this much longer," I told Ben.

He smiled. "Well, I know a place where we can find some cold beers."

"Show me that place, Ben." I grinned. "It sounds like a good place to be."

Ben reached down into the water's edge to grab a hefty branch that divided itself off into a mass of twigs.

"Leave it," I told him. "We've got enough for today."

"Kindling," he panted as he hauled it in. It must have been heavier than it looked. "It'll make good kindling."

I laid the hooked pole down onto the beach, ready to give him a hand, when he let out this cry of shock.

"What's wrong?" I saw that he was staring into the mass of twigs. His eyes had turned big and round in his face. His body had fixed into the same position, as if he couldn't bring himself to move.

"Oh, my God . . ." he gasped, then lost his balance to fall back onto his butt on the shingle.

"Ben?" I bent down to look into the tangle of sticks that still dripped water. "What's the matter, it's only a head. So what's the problem, buddy? You've seen three of those today."

"Not like this one I haven't."

"Why, what's so different about it?"

"Take a look for yourself." He swallowed hard, as if his breakfast threatened to come storming back. "And while you're about it: Count the eyes."

Eight

****
THIS IS A
WARNING
****

Following a meeting May 15, the Caucus has implemented the following emergency ruling with immediate effect:
STRANGERS
No more strangers are to be admitted into Sullivan.
Report any outsiders you see approaching the island by road or by boat.

If you see anyone on the island you suspect might be a stranger REPORT IT!

Be aware that anyone giving food or shelter to a stranger will be punished.

Any such punishment will be severe. Be warned.

OFF ISLAND TRAVEL

All travel off island is strictly forbidden.

TAKE THESE MEASURES SERIOUSLY

THEY HAVE BEEN MADE TO KEEP OUR COMMUNITY SAFE.

Caucus Order 174, May 15

We read the notice stapled to the post by the jetty. I saw more of those yellow sheets of paper fixed to trees on the road that lead up to the town.

"The Caucus is getting jittery," I told Ben.

"They're not the only ones." He still looked pale after seeing the severed head caught up in the branch he'd pulled from the water. "The whole world's in meltdown."

I'd only seen the head for a moment before it slithered from the fork in the branch and sank out of sight. Hell, it looked weird. Sickeningly weird. I was happy to see it vanish again, believe me, but Ben had shouted to me to pull it out with the hook (but on no account to touch it with my bare hands; something I wouldn't have done for all the tea in China anyway). Showing as a gray ball through the clear water, the head came to a rest on pebbles on the lake bed. I must have disturbed it as I splashed into the shallows because in a moment it rolled away. Soon I couldn't even see it, never mind hooking the thing out. Ben had called me back, telling me that the lake bed plunged down a good fifty feet there into an underwater ravine. The head was gone. Sweet Jesus, I was pleased to no end it had gone, too.

Even so, I still had a sharp mental image of it as it lay there wedged into the fork of the branch. A man's head, it had only just started to decompose; that meant it had to have come from someone who'd been alive and well until a few days ago.

I use the word *well* loosely . . . very, very loosely. Because there was something about the head that just wasn't right. The hair had been long, the face heavily bearded. A bread bandit, I figured. The eyes were closed. You could have fooled yourself that the guy was only sleeping (if it hadn't been for the strings of raw meat hanging down where the neck should be). But what took your breath away, and what horrified Ben so much that he cried out, was that a sickening bulge of brown flesh came out of the side of the face where the cheek should be. Set in that were two wide blue eyes. And those eyes seemed somehow *alive*. They stared right into mine. Then a second later the head slipped from the branch and back into the water, where it now lay fifty feet beneath the surface. Thank God.

Usually Ben would be full of ideas about anything new or unusual. This time he kept silent. As we walked back all he did was swallow in a queasy way.

This piece of yellow paper at least took his mind off what he'd just seen.

"It's because of the stranger. . . ." I thought for a moment he was going to say *that stranger you killed*. Instead he said, "It's because of the stranger who arrived recently." He wiped his mouth, as if the taste of his own vomit was still on his tongue. "The Caucus decided that because he wasn't a bread bandit and he was from this part of the country, the disease must have infected North Americans."

"They believe he really was infected?"

"*You know,*" he said firmly. "You saw it in him. God knows how you do it, but you knew he'd got it in him."

I sensed a creeping cold in my blood. "I might have been wrong."

"You've not been wrong yet."

"Yet."

"The town's put their faith in you. You've got some instinct that tells you when a person's infected."

"And so they turn a blind eye when I hack some poor bastard to pieces. I don't want to kill, Ben. I just find myself doing it, but it's like I'm watching it all happen from across the street. Why don't they just put anyone arriving in town in quarantine until they're sure? They don't have to wait until I've passed fucking judgment on some poor fucking stranger." I began to feel angry again. That anger always lurked below the surface . . . as soon as I started to think or talk about what I'd done it came shooting out of me in flames of bloody red.

Ben was quick to try and calm me. "Greg. We're lucky to have you. You've saved our necks."

"Lucky?" I gave a sour-sounding laugh.

"Sure. Before you turned up we'd let anyone in who came to town, bread bandits as well as our own countrymen. But we didn't know what was in the blood of the bread bandits or what was in their brains. We'd give those people food and lodging. They'd be completely normal, completely sane. But then . . ." He clicked his fingers. "One day, they'd snap. One Chilean guy said he was a doctor. He was polite, charming even. But one night he went downstairs, grabbed a carving knife and cut the throats of the family he was lodging with. Now you're here, Greg. You've got a nose for who's infected. Somehow you can see it in them, but we can't. You're our best early warning system."

"Yeah, right . . . but now I've killed a guy who's an American. Who might have been born just down the road."

"And that means the disease has spread. We know it can infect our people." Ben nodded back at the yellow notice. "That means the town has got to be more security conscious. From now on nobody comes onto the island. No one leaves."

"And that means suddenly our world has gotten a whole lot smaller." I looked 'round. "We've turned the place into a prison."

He shook his head. "Not a prison. A fortress."

"Either way, nobody's going anywhere, are they?"

We headed off to Ben's apartment, where he'd left some beers in the icebox of the refrigerator. Even though the electricity had been cut at midnight they were still cold enough to raise the hairs on the back of your neck. He also maintained a store of rechargeable batteries. So we sat there listening to Hendrix hurl those amazing guitar sounds out into the cosmic hereafter while we poured the beautifully cold beer down our hot and thirsty throats.

For a long time we didn't say much. Suddenly a whole army of question marks had come marching over our mental horizons. They were dark, menacing. And I found myself thinking: Why had the disease suddenly spread to our own countrymen? Had it infected us here in Sullivan? If it had, when would we see the first symptoms? Or would it be only me who recognized the disease in people? If that was the case, how long would it be before I used the ax on a neighbor? Or even Ben, sitting there on the sofa, listening to Hendrix's guitar calling out to eternity?

I swallowed the beer in big, hard gulps.

There was another question, too. A weird, twisty one. One that lurked in the background but seemed every bit as sinister as the rest. What had gone wrong with that human head we found tangled up in the branch? How could it bud an extra pair of eyes? Questions, Valdiva. Questions. Questions.

We'd been in Ben's apartment barely an hour before the siren started. Its phantom wail cut into the room like the bad news it was.

When the siren called, able-bodied men and women were expected to collect weapons, to assemble at certain points in the town, to be ready for Trouble with a capital *T*. On account of his shaky hands, Ben wasn't in the guard—the idea of him handling a rifle with those twitchy fingers put the fear of God into the guard sergeants. Even so, he came along. He often wrote articles for Sullivan's (increasingly) slender newspaper; with a change of hats he moved from stock clerk to reporter. In ten minutes I was sitting in the back of the a pickup barreling with half a dozen others in the direction of the wall. Which was a "misnomer," as Ben would have said, for a twenty-foot mass of steel fencing and barbed wire running the entire width of the isthmus and cutting the island off from the outside world.

A guy in an engineer's hard hat shouted to the half dozen or so of us in the back of the pickup that outsiders were aiming to break in.

Hanging on to the sides, slipstream zithering his hair, Ben looked at me. "It looks as if we've got our first invasion," he called.

Nine

Some invasion. The trucks skidded to a stop fifty yards from the gate in clouds of dust. We climbed out with the guard sergeants telling us to take it nice and easy; to stay back until the "threat had been quantified." Jeez. Why don't those guys speak so you can understand them?

There, under a cloudless blue sky, the wall ran from left to right, cutting across the highway and single railroad track. Both ends of that mountain range of barbed wire ended in the water at either side of the land bridge. The guards' officers—in real life a butcher, a cinema manager and a retired police chief—moved toward the gate. Someone handed me a shotgun and a handful of shells that I stuffed into my shirt pockets. I squinted against the glare of the sun. Through the monster of a steel gate I saw the invasion force.

Hell. Misnomers were thick as dog shit in a municipal park. Well, let me tell you, the invasion force consisted of a family in a sedan. The car was glossily clean.

It couldn't have come far. Two of the car's occupants climbed out, leaving a young woman in the passenger seat. She stared out at us, her eyes pumped full of anxiety.

The two who came forward to the gate were a man in his thirties and a boy of around eleven. Like the car they were clean; the man had shaved recently. Both were unarmed.

The stranger talked to the officers at the gate, though I noticed the three officers hung well back—*you don't know what filthy little microbes are peeling themselves from the strangers, do you, boys?* I even saw one of them take a glance at the flag to see which way the breeze was blowing. The truth of the matter was, there was no breeze today. The lake was as flat as a mirror.

Curiosity got the better of us. We moved forward to hear the conversation.

"You've got to," the stranger was saying . . . hell, not saying, *pleading*. He wanted something so bad it hurt.

"I'm sorry." The cinema manager indicated a sign painted on a five-by-five board. "No one's allowed in."

"But my wife's pregnant. She needs to be where she can get medical attention."

"What's wrong with the place you've just come from?"

"We've been living in a cabin up in the hills."

"Go back there. You'll be safe."

The man shook his head. "There's no one else there. She needs a doctor to look at her. Besides, we're running short of food."

"Got a rifle?"

"Yes, but—"

"Hunt, then. Catch food. The woods are full of wild game."

"But don't you understand?" The man sounded angry now. "My wife is seven months pregnant. She's not been well lately. She needs a doctor."

STRANGER

At that moment the woman pulled herself from the car, using the door to lever herself upright. "Jim, tell him about my brother."

"OK, Tina, just you take it easy." He looked at the boy. "Mark, go look after your Mom while I talk."

"I'm sorry, sir," the retired police chief spoke now in that polite but firm voice he must have used a million times before in his career. "You're going to have to turn your car around and leave the island."

"What goddam fucking island?" The stranger's patience had reached burn out. "It's not an island. It's a fucking town at the edge of a fucking lake. . . ."

"Jim," the woman pleaded, "Don't get mad at them. They're just being cautious."

"Tina, OK. Sit back in the car."

"They don't know us, Jim. For all they know we might be—"

"Bread bandits? Hey, guys. Do we look like bread bandits?"

"No," replied the old police chief, "but you can't—"

"Then let us in. Please."

"Sorry."

"But you can see my wife isn't well."

"We're taking no chances."

"But do we look South American? We're from a place that's three hours' north of here."

"What place?" asked the ex-chief.

"Golant, just off Route 3. Look, I've got a driver's license that—"

The ex-chief gave a regretful sigh. "Sorry. No can do. We've reached a decision to seal this town off from the outside. We can't risk contamination."

"Contamination! Do you think my wife and my son and my unborn child can contaminate you?"

"Jim," called the woman from the car. "Tell them about my brother."

Jim turned back to us. "My wife's brother owns a vacation home here."

"He's living here now?"

"No. He was in New York with his family when the crash came. We haven't heard from him since." His voice softened into those pleading tones again. "Don't you see? We wouldn't beg a place to stay, we could move into my brother-in-law's cabin. I know how to weld . . . look!" Suddenly eager, he gripped the gate bars with his two hands and gave it a shake. "I could make this even stronger. I could make it so strong it would keep an army out. You need to weld reinforcing bars diagonally across the—"

"Sorry." The ex-chief spoke gently. He sounded genuinely regretful. "I truly am sorry. I can't permit you to enter the town. You look like good people, but we just don't know if you're carrying the disease."

"So you're going to turn us away, and leave us to starve?"

The officers looked at each other; then the ex-chief spoke again. "We can give you food and medicine if you know what your wife needs."

"I don't know what drugs she needs. I need a doctor to see her. Hey, listen . . . listen!"

But the three officers moved back to our group. I glanced at Ben. His expression revealed that the incident sickened him. He had a good heart. If you ask me, he'd have allowed the family in.

The stranger returned to the car, spoke in an agitated way to his wife, then came back to the gate to yell, "We're not moving, do you hear? We're going to sit outside these gates until we starve to death or you let us in. Did you hear me? Did you?"

The ex-chief spoke to a couple of guards. "Bring them some food, boys. Pack it in fish crates so we can shove it through the gap under the gate."

Sergeants dismissed us from guard duty; the idea was

we'd return to our own jobs, but most of us hung 'round, not enjoying what we were seeing but feeling as if we somehow had to see it out.

Returning to his car, the stranger sat on the hood. Inside his family must have cooked in the heat of the car's interior, but they weren't quitting the standoff yet. Clearly, the guy thought we'd cave. That we wouldn't stand here and watch the pregnant woman suffer.

After a while a truck returned with the wooden fish crates into which dried foodstuff and cans had been packed. Using broom handles so as not to get too close to the strangers and so risk possible infection, a couple of guards slid the crates through the gap under the fence in the direction of the strangers' car.

We sweated it out for hours. At one point the guy tried to climb the gate, but there was so much barbed wire coiling 'round the bars, he didn't make it halfway to the top before he had to slither down again. The boy came up to the gate to call at us, "Let us in. Let us in. My mom's sick. Let us in!" And so on for a good twenty minutes. The woman looked tired and a kind of quiet resignation rotted the expression on her face. Later the guy cried. They sat in front of the car hugging each other. It was about that time the woman started saying something to the guy. For a while he shook his head, then he started to nod.

When next he climbed out of the car he never even looked at us. Nor did we look directly at him. There was something embarrassing about the situation now. No one made eye contact. No one spoke. For the next ten minutes the boy and the man loaded the car with food, then quickly they climbed back in, and the engine fired into life. Without even so much as a reproachful glance the family drove off into the distance to whatever hazardous future waited for them out there.

A shame-filled silence hung over us. It took a while,

but eventually we returned to the trucks for the drive back to town.

Some invasion.

That night after the heat of the day it felt good to work on my mother and sister's tomb. Cool air. Cool stone against my palms. It was good to be alone, too. As I worked on my three-dimensional jigsaw puzzle—my goddam obsession, as Ben had dubbed it—I couldn't help but think about the family we'd turned away. I guess the woman might wind up losing the baby. She might even lose her own life with it. There'd be the man and the boy with the screaming woman in a lonely cabin in the woods. I slotted a cube of rock into the tomb structure. It fitted as neatly as a plug into its socket. I patted it down the final inch or so with the palm of my hand.

I immediately picked up another chunk of rock. This had a more complicated shape, with seven sides. With luck it would stop me thinking about the family.

But it wasn't easy. What if we'd relented? Let them in. What if a few hours later that knot of tension came into my belly? That alarm signal at some deep, deep animal level that said: *Beware, Valdiva, you've got yourself a batch of Jumpies here. Kill them before it's too late. . . .*

So what's worse, Valdiva? Turning the family away to maybe die a lingering death out in the woods? Or finishing them all with a few savage blows with the ax?

Some cousin of that instinct that gave me the ability to divine when a person was infected with Jumpy also identified the perfect-shaped void in the wall for the lump of rock I rolled 'round in my hands. In it went. *Snick.* Perfect fit.

I stood back to look at the tomb. There it was, the size of a truck, a perfect square, gleaming like cream in the starlight.

An old woman once walked down here as I worked.

STRANGER

She complimented me on my labors and said the structure reminded her of an ancient Egyptian tomb called a Mastaba. Mastabas, she said, were used to entomb Egyptian dead long before they built the Pyramids. I don't know anything about that. Instinct told me to build it that way. Like instinct told me when a person was hot with Jumpy. I didn't think or plan what to do. I only acted on instinct. And if God or the Devil shaped that instinct, I don't know. That's just the way it was.

Stars shone brighter than diamonds. I sat with my back to the tomb, feeling the cool stone through my shirt back. Even though it was close on two in the morning I didn't feel like sleeping. That cabin of mine could be a lonely place; somehow it felt less lonely up here on the bluff by the graves of Chelle and Mom. Here, I counted shooting stars. "Wow, Chelle, did you see the size of that one?"

I bit my lip. It was so easy to believe they were sitting beside me, alive and breathing and singing out "Oooh" and "Aaah" when a fiery blue meteor came crackling through the atmosphere sixty miles above our heads.

Still biting my lip hard, I looked out across the lake. It had a silvery look tonight, yet somehow mixed with a lot of darkness. Glints of starlight reflected on the water before slowly vanishing, to be replaced by a great gulf of blackness that looked as dark as death itself. I imagined myself running to the end of the bluff and diving the twenty feet down into the water. Down, down, down . . . swimming through clouds of bubbles, through swarms of fish that would move with a metallic glitter. In my mind's eye I saw myself swimming across the rocks, around clumps of weeds, over the rotting bones of sunken boats. I imagined swimming right away across the lake underwater on one gulp of air. There I'd climb out onto the harbor wall at Lewis.

Suddenly it seemed the most desirable thing in the

world to get away from this claustrophobic town. The stores and cinemas and supermarkets across the lake might be smashed to crud, but it would be a real taste of freedom. There was an aura about Sullivan these days that pushed my mood down into a dark place. It was the same kind of feeling you got when you walked into an old folks' home. You sensed it was a place where life hung by a thread. That, there, all the people looked backward to the past. That they had no future. No fun. Nothing but the slippered creep, creep of death getting closer and closer.

Maybe I wasn't far from the truth. Most of Sullivan's population was elderly. They'd only survived because they'd stayed put in this out-of-the-way place. And stay put they did. The poster warning people not to leave the island was a joke because no one had been away from it in the last six months. Fishermen never went past the orange buoys that market the two-hundred-yard line from shore. No one went hunting in the forest that stretched out into the mainland proper beyond the isthmus. Hell, no one had looked over the nearest hill for months. Someone could have built a new Disneyland there and we'd be none the wiser.

I'd been half asleep as I allowed those thoughts to run through my head. The grass was soft there; the night air could have been an all-enveloping comforter. So when I saw the light it didn't register.

I watched it in that disconnected mental state. Not even asking myself who the hell was shining a light across the lake in that ghost town.

The yellow light showed as nothing more than a spark. It could have been a star that had somehow tumbled from the sky to rest in one of the ruined buildings.

It moved.

This did bring my head up. I stared, feeling a tingle spread across my skin.

Someone was across there in Sullivan. He was shining a light; a small lamp or even a candle, I don't know. But it was steady enough. It didn't look like starlight reflected by a window. It moved again. Now it disappeared, then reappeared, as if someone unseen carried the light through what remained of one of the buildings.

Sure. There were people out there. We'd seen strangers today. But this was the first time I'd seen a light in Lewis. Normally even strangers stayed away from the ruined town. It was as if people had a gut feeling that told them the place was contaminated, or even that it was lousy with ghosts.

The light moved higher. Disappeared.

Gone.

It's not coming back, I told myself. They've left.

But then the light reappeared. This time it was at a higher level. I pictured the ruined waterfront buildings I'd seen through a 'scope. They'd stood up to six stories tall. Now it looked as if someone had set a light in one of the shattered windows to burn there as a signal to us across the lake. Not that anyone from Sullivan would take a damn shred of notice of it, never mind dare making the trip across to the ghost town.

Then I thought something insane. I decided to take a boat over there myself. It didn't make sense. All I might find was a pack of bread bandits who'd break my skull. Or maybe I'd be find someone who'd infect me with Jumpy. But that insane notion blazed inside my head. *Go there, Valdiva. Anything to get out of this hole for a few hours.*

At this time of night there'd be no one to see me slip one of the cruisers from its mooring. I'd be in Lewis in twenty minutes. By starlight I followed the path down from the bluff, through the trees to the jetty. There, the boats sat so still on the water you'd swear that the lake had become as hard as onyx. There were cruisers with big hunky motors that could fly me across the lake in minutes. But the noise they'd make at this time of night would wake a skeleton.

I opted for the smaller tourist cruisers. These harked back to the time that the town council started taking green issues seriously and encouraged boat rental businesses to bring in boats with electric motors rather than the old internal combustion engines. They weren't fast, but they were whisper quiet. I knew the batteries would be charged because Peter Gerletz and his daughters used them as fishing boats. I even borrowed one every now and again to collect driftwood where it beached on a sandbar a hundred yards offshore.

Taking careful steps, I moved down the jetty, hearing the mousy squeak of timbers shifting under my feet.

"That you, Gerletz? It's OK, I'm not stealing your precious boats." It was the voice of the old police chief coming from the shadows. I stepped forward to see him sitting on the jetty boards with his back to a mooring post. He looked relaxed. No wonder; I saw a bottle of whiskey on the boards beside him. Well, a third of a bottle, to be more precise. A shot glass sat neatly beside the bottle.

"Gerletz, don't worry. Go back to sleep. I'm guarding your damn boats tonight."

"It's not Peter Gerletz," I said.

"Who then? Not one of my ghosts come to haunt me?" I heard a soft laugh as he poured a splash of whiskey into the shot glass.

"It's Greg Valdiva."

"Oh, the outsider?" He swallowed the shot in one. "But it's not fair to call you an outsider now, is it? You've been here . . . what? Six months?"

"Eight."

"Eight? As long as that?"

He groaned a bone-weary groan as he made himself

more comfortable against the post. "So, what brings you down here? A midnight swim?"

"No." I could hardly say I intended to break one of the Caucus's shiny-new laws. Instead I shrugged. "Couldn't sleep."

"Ah, Valdiva, you're one of the guard, aren't you?"

"Yes."

"So you saw that sorry spectacle today?"

I nodded.

"You know, that really works against my grain, Valdiva. I swore to uphold law and order and protect the innocent. I've still got my badge and I still clean it with complete and sincere pride."

"We had no choice. We had to refuse them entry."

"Especially after last week. When that blue-eyed American boy..." He merely gestured with the glass instead of finishing the sentence. "It seems that damn bug can get into our blood, too. No one's immune, isn't that so?"

"I guess."

"You guess right, my friend. But even so. What happened today just didn't seem right. That pregnant lady? She needed our help. But we just told them to shove off. That sticks in my craw. I say if we're going to go down with a case of Jumpy we might as well get it over with, because we're only postponing the inevitable by hiding away here."

"You're going to tell the Caucus that?"

He looked up as if seeing me properly for the first time. "Valdiva. You speak your mind, don't you? As well as being our town executioner.... Pardon me, you didn't need reminding of that. Jack Daniel's always did loosen my tongue past the point where my diplomatic side becomes a mere speck on the horizon..." He seemed to lose the thread for a while. He charged his glass again, then downed it in one. "Here I am like some old wino. I busted plenty of those when I first joined the force. Hell, the smell of their pee followed you home. It got so Mary made me change out of my uniform in the garage. We even had a shower installed in the utility room there. 'Get out of those clothes,' she'd say, 'you've been hauling in drunks again. I can smell the pee on your jacket.'" He chuckled. "That's why I refuse to drink this whiskey out of the bottle like a bum. I'm drinking it out of a glass like an officer and a gentleman." He poured another shot. "The answer to your question, Valdiva, is no. I won't be telling the Caucus that Sullivan here is a hopeless case . . . a terminal patient waiting for the inevitable. That we're all going to contract that damn disease one day. We are, but I won't tell them that. I have what you might call such a strong sense of duty it's pathological. So I'll do my hardest to do the right thing for our community. Even if I sometimes think—privately, mind—it stinks . . . stinks of something brown and wet. Now, sir, can I interest you in a glass of this?"

"No thanks. I just needed some air. I'm going to turn in."

"Good night, Valdiva. I hope you sleep better than I will."

"Good night, Mr. Finch."

I'd started walking back along the jetty when he called out again. "Valdiva, do yourself a favor." I looked back at him sitting there, pouring himself another whiskey. "Get away from here. It's useless advice, I know. But this town is going to start getting unhealthy. And I'm not talking about any disease here. I don't know what it is, that's the funny thing. But when I walk 'round and look in my neighbors' faces I start getting a bad taste in my mouth."

"What do you think might be wrong?"

"I don't know. Something just isn't right. So if I were you, I'd get right away from here . . . as far as you can. Call it cop instinct." He picked up the bottle as if to read the label. "Aw, what do I know?" He smiled and seemed to step up the amiable old drunk act, as if he'd suddenly had second thoughts and didn't want me to take what he'd said at all seriously. "Forget it, Valdiva. It's just the whiskey talking. You get yourself a good night's sleep. There's nothing to worry about."

There's nothing to worry about. I tended to believe everything the old cop told me. But I didn't believe that last comment. *There's nothing to worry about.*

With the man's lie echoing inside my skull I walked home.

Ten

The smell of bacon woke me. Lynne had slipped in early to cook breakfast. She did this every week or so. When I pictured her husband making breakfast for their two children at the same time I pulled the sheet higher over my head.

As I heard her singing lightly to herself I imagined her moving 'round the kitchen to pour orange juice, or spoon coffee into cups. That lovely swaying walk of hers that made me think of Hawaiian dancers in grass skirts. After cutting bread she'd push her long hair back away from her face, or maybe move it with a flick of her head.

I knew if I called down to her to forget breakfast she'd come upstairs, peeling off her T-shirt as she came, exposing those firm, perfectly shaped breasts. She'd slip down the tiny skirt she wore. I'd admire those long golden legs, then pull back the sheet so she could slide into bed beside me.

That ache of longing twisted me up inside. All I had to do was take a breath, then say her name out loud. *Lynne.*

Instead I lay there not moving as the ritual continued. It was one of those sweeteners. Hot tasty breakfast
for the town executioner. An idea cooked up by the
Caucus months ago. Of course, they'd suggested it
would be Lynne's civic duty to provide anything else
that I might want along with bacon, scrambled eggs
and golden pancakes.

Just had to click my fingers. She'd be there naked in
the doorway. Smiling sexily, she'd ask, "How do you
want me? It's your choice, Greg—anything. Just command it."

A couple of hours later she'd walk up the hill to
town, maybe a little on the sore side, so she'd discreetly
carry her panties in a bag.

As I warred with my own conflicting emotions—part
of me craving to call her upstairs, the other part ready
to order her back to her husband—I suddenly realized
that things might be set for change. Now that the town
had slapped a prohibition on strangers entering the
island, where did that leave me? Before they let me
screen newcomers in (as the man said) my own inim-
itable fashion. When that monkey instinct inside a dark
corner of my mind made me kill they'd accepted that
it was a necessary evil. They cleared away the bloody
aftermath and rewarded me with chocolate cake and
sex.

But it was different now, wasn't it? Now that they'd
sealed themselves from the outside world they didn't
need my services anymore. What's more, they'd always
been suspicious of me. They tolerated me because I
was essential to their own survival, that's all. The old
ex-cop's warning came back to me from the night before. *Valdiva, do yourself a favor. Get away from here . . .
as far away as you can. . . .*

Maybe right now they were discussing the proposal
on the agenda: Get rid of Valdiva . . . oust the monster.
I could see all those gray heads nodding 'round the

table as Miss Bertholly agreed: "Valdiva's surplus to requirements now. Can anyone nominate a hunter who's good with a rifle?"

"Get him before he figures out he's redundant," old man Crowther would say. "Make his whore girl go down to cook him breakfast. I know a guy who'll blow him to pieces with a twelve-gauge while he's still in bed. Better still, why waste good bullets? Wait until he's screwing her and kill the pair of them with one shell."

That mental movie of my blood hitting the bedroom wall was clear enough, I can tell you. At the sound of the door opening downstairs I bounced out of bed and went to the top of the stairs. Lynne looked startled as she opened the screen to the veranda.

"You gave me a scare, Greg," she said, seeing the expression on my face. "What's wrong?"

I looked at the plate full of breakfast on the table. "Where are you going, Lynne?"

"Nowhere. Well . . . I was just throwing out this bread for the birds. You should get in the habit of checking it. It's so stale you could crack rocks with it." She threw the crust out onto the grass, then came back into the kitchen, smiling. "There's chilled juice, and I made fresh pancakes. Coffee?"

"Yeah." I looked through the window at the top of the stairs. Outside there was no one about. No Crowther narc anyway, with a shotgun. Maybe my imagination had gotten overripe. Even so . . .

"Greg. Relax. You look as if you've seen a ghost."

Yeah, my own.

She played with her hair a little in that sexy way of hers. "Say . . . do you want breakfast in bed this morning?"

I thanked her but declined. I said I needed to make an early start cutting wood out back. She was thoroughly pleasant, even flirty, but all we did was make small talk.

STRANGER

The old cop swilling whiskey on the jetty had pre-
vented me from taking the boat across the lake to Lewis
to find out who it was burning the lamp up in the
ruins. But now I was more than ever determined to
take that trip. What's more, this town seemed even
more claustrophobic—dangerous, even—now that I realized its people didn't need me anymore. When I
walked down Main Street I knew I'd get an itch between my shoulder blades just where a rifle bullet
might find a home.

Lynne nibbled toast with me as I ate her breakfast.
It was good, and the temptation to suggest half an hour
up on the bed took some time to quit. But eventually
she said her good-byes before heading back up the hill
in the direction of home. I hauled the chainsaw from
the shed, topped up the tank, then fired her up.
The logger's chainsaw was muscular enough to loosen
the fillings in your teeth, but it made short work of the
heftier pieces of driftwood. I cut the timber into disks
maybe eight inches long. Soon a blizzard of sawdust
filled the air, turning the sunlight misty and golden.

I worked through the pile of timber the lake had
given up (along with its more grisly fruit). I thought of
the severed head with its extra set of eyes. Suddenly I
could taste the scrambled egg in my mouth again with
that extra spice of bile.

Revving the chainsaw motor, I forced the image out
of my skull. Instead I concentrated on the blurring
teeth that bit through the timber. The world was getting stranger by the day. No doubt about that. Hell, I
just wondered what strange turn lay around the corner
to take us all by surprise.

Later I made my deliveries in the hot sun. With the
pickup piled with firewood I drove through town.
Everything looked rock-solid normal. People waved at
me. If anything their mood seemed lighter now that a

goodly number of days had passed since I killed the outsider. Normal rhythms reasserted themselves. The supermarket had its usual quota of customers pushing shopping carts of groceries to their cars. The McDonald's just across from the cinema boasted a few people chewing the fat over coffees and cake (the old Ronald McDonald menu had varied through necessity over the last few months). Cars cruised by. A cop on a motorbike gave me a thumbs-up as I made a left into the residential area. Here I found the few children who remained in Sullivan playing on skateboards, riding bikes. A couple of toddlers were running in and out of a lawn sprinkler shrieking like crazy. Even when I at last reached Crowther's house all he did was shoot me a sullen look before sloping indoors. I piled wood on the drive for him to collect at his own sweet leisure, then pointed the nose of the pickup back into town.

I'd just helped myself to a Swiss cheese sandwich and a jug of iced water in the supermarket coffeehouse when Ben saw me and hurried in through the door. "Help yourself," I said nodding at the iced water. "It's hot as hell outside today."

"Yeah, it's getting more like hell every day." He pulled a grim smile. "Take a look at that." He pushed a book across the table at me.

I checked the title. "*Secrets of the Arcane.* Whatever lights your lamp, Ben."

"After we saw that head yesterday I did some reading."

I gave a heartfelt groan. "That head? Do you have to remind me? I'm still eating."

"But what the hell was it, Greg?" This was more like the old Ben. The proto-scientist Ben who enthusiastically searched for answers. "Every now and again you hear of four-legged chickens and two-headed lambs. But have you seen a human being with an extra set of eyes?"

STRANGER

I groaned again and pushed the uneaten sandwich to one side. "I asked you not to mention it. I can feel eyeballs in the cheese with my tongue now."

"You find people with genetic defects and mutations, but have you ever see anything as . . . as severe as that?"

"Listen, Ben . . . here, let me get that for you." He made as if to pour water from the jug into a glass, but with those shaky hands he splashed liquid over the tabletop (and my now unloved sandwich).

"Thanks." He took a thirsty swallow.

"Ben. You see weird mutant stuff in the *Fortean Times* and *Ripley's*. Men covered with hair like apes. Women with three nostrils. Kids with paws instead of fingers."

"But that head was nothing like I've ever seen before in a book."

"It was probably some poor devil who'd spent his life locked in the attic being fed a pail of fish heads every Thursday. He escaped after the crash, then wondered 'round until he wound up in the lake. End of sad story."

"I don't know. Maybe. Maybe not."

"You really think it might be something else?"

"Who knows? You might have noticed, but the world's taken a weird jump out left of field these days." He smiled. "Now listen to this." And he started to read from the book. " 'Long ago the alchemist Thomas Vaughn wrote the hermetic treatise *Lumen de Lumine*. He described a process where animal and human bodies can be made to descend into primal matter, the *tenebrae activae*, as he termed it.' No, Greg, don't shake your head, just listen, will you? It says here that Vaughn believed this was a kind of melting pot into which you can feed human beings and from which new life could be created."

"You're saying that's what happened to old Johnny Cluster Eyes you found in the lake?"

"Maybe."

I leaned forward. "Ben, listen to your buddy. You need to find yourself a girlfriend, you really do."

He shot me a kind of startled look, then he read something in my face. For a second I thought he'd be insulted, but he started laughing with that breathless bray of his. Right from the first time we met I'd found the laugh infectious, and now I started laughing, too. The other customers in the coffeehouse looked at us as if we might have gone half crazy.

Come to think of it, they might have been half right at that.

Eleven

Days slipped by in that breathless heat. In the cool of early morning I hooked driftwood from the lake. Sometimes I'd find human corpses in the shallows. Most were so far gone that you couldn't tell if they were male or female. Young or old. Bread bandit or Yankee. They were mushy things resembling old leather satchels with ragged holes where the fish had picked away the soft tissues. They always went for the eyes, too. Fish must find eye meat the sweetest. Every so often Lake Coben would offer up a fresh specimen that proved to me that there were still people out there in the forests and hills beyond Sullivan. For reasons unknown to me they sometimes wound up dead in the lake. Maybe bread bandits hunted them down like wild dogs out there, beat them to death, then tossed them into a stream that fed the lake where they eventually floated here.

As the days passed there were no more outsiders showing up either. What's more, I didn't see any more of that light in the ruins of Lewis, so the urge to take a boat across there sort of went off the boil.

The rest of my workday was taken up with cutting the wood and delivering it in the pickup. With electricity rationed to those six hours in the evening, anyone wanting a hot drink or a cooked meal used wood stoves, which were nothing grander than barbecues out in their backyards.

Every night I fitted more stones to the tomb and made it that much larger.

Hey, it wasn't all work. We went to the cinema to see a movie that we might have seen a dozen times before. After all, with the world in pieces there'd be no new features coming to town. It wasn't as bad as it sounded. There was something magical about seeing the world as it once was, before the crash. Most nights the cinema was a good half full. Then there were the bars, the pool hall, bowling, or maybe just a tub full of beers swimming in a gallon of water and ice. A few of us would gather on a porch to sip beer while chewing the fat beneath starry skies.

To say the whole world had gone shit-faced sounds idyllic, doesn't it? I remember the beach barbecue when we must have eaten a whole hog, grunt and all. There weren't a lot of young people in Sullivan, but we made a real party of it at night. We emptied a few cases of wine while the empty beer bottles rose in a glittering pyramid on the sand. A kid with a Jeep that boasted the mother and father of all sound systems drove it down to the shore. The music boomed across the lake. If the 50,000 ghosts that must surely haunt Lewis had ears they'd have had a feast of music that night.

But there I go, remembering the good times. A kind of golden six weeks after the arrival of the pregnant woman and her family. There was no trouble. Unless you can count the underpants bunting that some drunken kids strung across the town hall. Or the Caucus complaining that certain work quotas weren't being met. Like who cares that ten thousand tins of baked beans in warehouse A should have been moved two hundred yards to warehouse B? Or that some of the residents grumbled that the music was getting too loud? Or—horror of horrors—those young people were actually enjoying themselves and laughing in the streets at night? If you ask me, I say to hell with the whiny complaints. Those young people were taking a vacation from the cold, brutal reality surrounding us.

And yeah, you've guessed right. It was too good to last.

One Sunday in July a storm came down on the town like a landslide. Thunder. Lighting. Torrential rain. The lake turned to cream. Surf broke over the jetties. One of the fishing boats tore loose and went rolling away through the waves, never to be seen again.

The Gerletz family were the boat experts. They raced through the storm tying extra lines to the lake cruisers and fishing craft to stop them being carried away. They had their hands more than full taking care of all the island's boats as well as their own fleet. Soon they called in more help. I found myself with Ben and one of the Gerletzs' daughters, a big-boned twenty-one-year-old, along with half a dozen townspeople. We hauled small boats out of the water high up onto the beach, away from the pounding surf. Everyone was soaking wet. The temperature plummeted so much our bodies steamed as we worked our way along the shore, tying more lines to the big lake cruisers in the hope they wouldn't be torn out into the lake where they'd be lost for sure.

And all the time we stumbled through lightning flashes, deafened by thunder that threatened to bring the entire sky crashing down.

That was the afternoon the whole world turned rotten again. It happened fast.

*   *   *

This is how fast.

We moved away from the main harbor area to a stretch of coast where free-floating cruisers were moored. These were simply roped to concrete anchors in the shallows or to three or four rickety jetties that clearly weren't going to withstand this storm-force punishment.

Ben and a couple of middle-aged guys waded into the water to haul at a rowboat that had water sloshing 'round up to the seat planks.

"Leave that one," Gerletz called over the thunder. "Get the big lake cruisers secure first. This wind's going to rip them from the moorings."

Quitting the rowboat, they waded to where a big white cruiser bounced on the surf. Miss Gerletz must have had muscles in her spit. She plunged into the water, reached up and grabbed the big boat by the guardrail post and dragged its prow to face the beach. "Tie that line to the cleat, then run it up to the concrete block on the beach."

This we did, but the boat bucked crazy-horse style. Even with three of us holding onto the rope it buzzed through our fingers, dealing out friction burns right, left and center.

The boat was a real millionaire's toy. I could see white leather upholstery in the cabin and gin and whiskey decanters rattling in their holders. You might wonder why we worked so hard to save these vessels. The truth of the matter is, they made useful workboats now. More than one millionaire's cruiser was used to ship gasoline barrels 'round the island to the part of Lime Bay that was inaccessible by truck. Even so I couldn't resist a grim smile. The boat I wrestled to save that gleamed as white as a cheerleader's grin had the name *Crowther* painted on the stern in gold. No doubt

Crowther junior would thank me for saving his family's boat.

Yeah, right: some time never!

There wasn't time to dwell on it. The Gerletz girl finished tying off the mooring to the concrete slab firmly anchored into the beach. "Next," she panted, then hurried to another boat.

With waterspouts rearing up like goosenecks out in the lake and rain slamming into our faces, we moved forward. Inside forty-five minutes we'd secured extra mooring lines on a dozen lake cruisers. Some of these were hefty twenty-tonners that boasted galleys, cabins and bars. So far we hadn't lost a single one on our stretch of coast. Some of the rowboats were a different matter. Several had sunk; one had been smashed into two clean halves across a rock. But they weren't a real concern. There must be a good couple of hundred rowboats on Sullivan; plenty of those were pulled high and dry on the beach.

A real cause for concern was a big cruiser tethered to the jetty at the far end of the beach. This was the farthest from town, the least used, certainly the most poorly maintained. Even from a hundred yards away I could see the whole structure rock under the pressure of the huge cruiser that had broken loose at the stern. The winds caught the boat, swinging it out first into the lake then back and—CRASH!—against the jetty. By the time we'd reached the thing the jetty's planks had started to pop off the timber frame with every knock of the boat.

"Hurry up, you guys!" the Gerletz girl yelled through the storm. "We're going to lose this one if we don't work fast."

"Someone's all ready up there," Ben shouted.

"See who it is."

I looked at the figure that wrestled with a rope, trying to tie it to the iron ring set in the jetty.

"It's Charlie Finch," one of the men said, using his hand to shield his eyes from the stinging rain. "He's got the front line tied."

Gerletz moved up the plank. "We need to get the aft line secure, otherwise she's going to smash the jetty to pieces." The boat underlined what she'd just said by swinging back into the jetty again with enough force to make the whole thing shudder. Ahead another plank popped off the frame. "It's coming apart at the seams."

We were halfway along the jetty, all set to help the old cop tie down the boat, when he saw us. Then he did a weird thing.

He waved us back. "It's OK," he shouted. "I can handle it."

"Don't worry, Mr. Finch," Ben called. "We'll give you a hand."

"I'm fine!"

But he didn't look fine.

"I can handle it," he repeated. "Go see to the other boats."

"They're all tied down," Gerletz said. "This is the last one."

The last one. But it was the big daddy of them all. This was a multimillionaire's yacht with what must have been half a dozen cabins and a couple of bathrooms. In the near darkness the thing looked like a big, angry bear that swung from side to side to butt the jetty with those crashing blows.

"Go back," Finch bellowed. "I'll have it tied in a minute."

"You'll never manage it by yourself." Gerletz shook her head in disbelief. "I'll climb onto the boat and throw another line."

"This is good enough." The ex-cop looked furious that we were trying to help him. His eyes blazed at us through the spray.

"The line's not strong enough," she said. "You need thicker rope."

"It's not safe out here," Finch insisted. "The surf will wash someone into the lake."

"Don't worry, I'll make it." With that, Gerletz bounded from the jetty onto the boat. The girl must have been scrambling across boats in all weathers since she could walk. Even though the boat bucked under her, she ran from one end of the deck to the other without touching the guardrail once. In seconds she'd pulled a hefty orange rope from a locker, uncoiled it, tied it to the deck cleat, then hurled it at us. The thing nearly got away from us into the surging water, but Ben got a grip, and soon we were all hauling the rope. It was like trying to pull a house from its foundations. For a while I didn't think we'd bring the pitching boat under control, but at last it moved. Soon it lay hard against the jetty. It still rose and fell with the waves, but at least it no longer battered the wooden structure like a gigantic hammer.

"It should hold," Gerletz shouted from the deck. "But I wouldn't put my shirt on it."

She returned partway down the deck, but instead of returning to the jetty she opened a cabin door.

Finch shouted at her. "Where are you going?" The alarm in the man's voice startled her.

She looked back at him. "The boat's too low in the water. She might have a leak."

"It doesn't matter," Finch cried. "Leave it until the storm's dropped."

"But it might—"

"It's not safe on there. The damn boat might sink with you on it."

"Don't worry," she said, puzzled by his manner. "It won't sink yet."

"Get off the boat; you can't be certain." Lightning lit up his face. There was something terrible about his

93

expression. Like he'd seen a room full of corpses. "Just get off the damned boat, OK?"

"No." This time she sounded annoyed. "I'm not leaving it like this. You can wait on the beach, but I'm going to pump out the bilges."

She'd ducked her head to go into the boat. Thunder crashed across the lake so loud that I saw Ben wince at the sheer volume. I also saw Finch. He was tense and staring at the boat. The man's reaction to Gerletz entering the boat just didn't make sense.

Or at least it didn't make sense then.

Because five seconds later Gerletz came scrambling out of the boat onto the deck like she'd been thrown there. She looked through the dark maw of the cabin door, then called back to us. This time her voice was high, anxious-sounding.

"Greg. Come up here quick."

With the boat securely tied I had no difficulty in climbing up onto its broad deck. I shot a questioning look at Gerletz.

"You better take a look at what's in the cabin," she said.

With the electric storm lighting the boat like a strobe I took a single cautious step through the doorway.

I stopped dead and whispered, "Oh, Christ."

Outside Finch was groaning, "No, no, no, no . . ."

There in the gloom, lit only now and then by the flicker of lightning, were a group of faces. As I looked at them, they looked back at me, their eyes seeming to glow in the storm light.

"Valdiva," called one of the men back on the jetty. "What the hell's going on?"

I stepped back onto the deck. "There's a bunch of kids in there." I took a breath. "They're outsiders."

Twelve

This is when the impossible happened. When the town of Sullivan learned that the old ex-cop, Finch, had been hiding outsiders on the boat, it exploded. There's no other word for it. As far as the public was concerned Finch became enemy number one. Not content with arresting him and locking him in the town's four-cell jail, they wrecked his house and smashed up his car. Someone even went down to the bottom of his yard, where he kept his dog. They burnt the kennel, then shot his animal as it cried for its master. Man, you could have taken a knife and carved the mood of savagery that hung over the town.

Just twenty-four hours after the outsiders had been found, Finch stood trial in the courthouse. It sickened me. OK, Finch had risked infecting himself and thereby others on the island, but it was that volcanic eruption of public fury that got me. I know the people were scared, but it was how they dealt with it that turned my gut. As I sat on a patch of grass outside the courthouse that Monday afternoon I told myself there'd be a lynching. Hundreds of people seethed like a boiling lake outside the doors. Already some children had thrown stones. One cop wound up with a busted cheekbone. The fury had infected everyone from ninety-year-olds down to toddlers.

Ben sat beside me. He looked restless, uneasy. "They want Finch's blood, don't they?"

I nodded. "I think they're going to get it, too."

"So what's the point of a trial? They're going to find him guilty anyway."

"They already have," I told Ben. "Now they're deciding the punishment."

"Jeez . . . he was only trying to help the poor devils."

I knew Ben had been down to the boat where the outsiders had been secretly hiding out and that had now become their prison that morning. I asked him what was going to happen to them.

"It's already happened," he replied. "The Caucus didn't waste any time."

I shot him a questioning look. The mood the townspeople were in, I wouldn't put it past them to shoot the strangers dead just like they killed Finch's dog.

Ben noticed the expression on my face. "Don't worry, they haven't been harmed. At least not yet. Old man Gerletz took the boat to the far end of the lake. They've been put down on the shore there."

"Where they'll be left to starve, no doubt."

"Gerletz dumped some food with them. So they're OK for now."

"*For now* being the key phrase. Jesus, there might be bread bandits out there."

Ben shrugged. "Orders from the Caucus."

"Yeah, orders from the Caucus. What will they end up deciding next?"

"They've already ordered that the boat they were using be burnt out in the lake so as not to risk contamination."

"But Finch could be contaminated. What's the point in going to all that trouble when it might already be too late?"

Ben just shrugged again. "People are frightened; they've got so desperate they'll do anything if they think it will save them."

"From what I saw of the outsiders, they just looked like a couple of ordinary families. They had kids with them."

"But you don't know that. What would happen if you got that sixth sense of yours going? And you knew they were infected? You'd have waded into them with an ax, wouldn't you?"

I looked at him, burning with anger for a moment; then it passed. "I guess you're right, Ben."

"This way the town has at last done its own dirty work instead of leaving it up to you."

He was right again. Even so, it seemed so unfair. Those outsiders might have been free of the virus or whatever. They might have lived here and never developed Jumpy in twenty years. Just then, over at the courthouse, shouting rose into a roar. The doors opened and a bunch of cops and Caucus members left the building. They climbed into cars and screeched away.

"I guess they've made their decision," Ben said, looking as if an unpleasant taste had found its way onto his tongue. "My guess is they've passed a death sentence."

It turned out they had. But not in the way you might have thought.

I said to Ben, "Are you covering this story for the paper?"

"No, the editor's handling this one himself."

It was one of those times when you're curious to find out what's happening, but deep down you just don't want to know. Finch had been found guilty. Whatever punishment they were going to impose on the guy, you knew it was going to be bad. Ben had used the word *draconian*. I wasn't all that sure what draconian meant, but it sounded like a hard, evil word.

The crowd's agitation infected Ben. He stood up, began to pace 'round, running his hands through his hair.

The crowd . . . no, for crowd read MOB . . . was beginning to yell. "Bring him out! Bring out Finch!"

I guessed they'd made up their own minds to tear him to crud there and then.

Then something started happening. A *something* that made me uneasy. I stood up to watch. Outside the courthouse is an open area. It's called the Peace Garden. There are sculptures of children holding hands, a fountain, fenced areas of grass with flowering cherry trees. There's also a kind of raised stage made from brick that probably is around waist high. In the past it's been used for music recitals. Last Christmas the local children performed a carol service there. Standing in a tight pack, perhaps it would accommodate a choir of around twenty. There were concrete steps leading up to the stage at both ends where processions, or orchestras, or bands, could enter and leave without having to clamber up onto the thing.

Until a few minutes ago some kids had been there shouting abuse at the courthouse; now the cops came out of the building and cleared the stage. Then they formed a cordon around it to keep people off.

Ben swallowed. His hands were shaking worse than ever. "Jesus, I guess they're going to bring out Finch and shoot him there."

"Maybe we should go somewhere else," I suggested. "This isn't going to be pretty."

"No." His voice had a trembling quality to it, but he'd made up his mind. "No. I'm going to see this out.

Then I'm going to write a story for the newspaper. I'm going to shame Sullivan for this."

But the people of Sullivan had no symptoms of shame, or even second thoughts. A cheer went up. The crowd began to applaud another group of guys who'd emerged from the courthouse. For some reason they carried a table. By the time they reached the raised stage in the Peace Garden I could see it was a hefty antique piece of furniture. A good eight feet long, it had six legs that looked nearly as thick as tree trunks. With some sweating and cussing they managed to lift it up onto the stage. Moments later a couple of other guys appeared with a board, or what appeared to be a board, but then I realized it must have been a door that had been removed from of one of the offices inside the building.

"What on earth are they doing?" Ben shook his head.

"I don't know, but my guess is they've got something unpleasant planned."

The crowd milled, shouted. There was a sense of excitement now. A sense of *revenge*.

Over the next half hour the eager crowd saw plenty more activity. All of it mysterious, if not downright weird. A truck arrived piled with house bricks. After that an ambulance pulled up right by the stage where the table now stood.

OK. I'd got the picture now. Finch would be marched up onto the stage. A firing squad would assemble. Bang, he's dead. His corpse gets dumped into the ambulance. Show's over folks. There's nothing more to see.

But they'd got something far worse planned.

Miss Bertholly neatly climbed up the steps onto the stage. She went to stand by the table. As if ready for the funeral that would take place any time now, she was already dressed in black. Another member of the Caucus (who I recognized as Crowther senior) handed her a microphone that was attached to the bullhorn he carried.

There was still a buzz of voices in the crowd. It fell silent the second she began to talk.

"Listen to me, please . . . may I have everyone's attention? Thank you. Today is a black day for Sullivan. It's going to become darker still. But this afternoon we must perform an act that will be burnt into our memories forever. Because we must have no repeat of the crime Charles Finch has committed. If it happens again, if strangers are admitted into this, our place of safety, it will probably spell the end for us all. We can't allow this to happen. No one wants to see their wives, their husbands or children die. Let this be recorded, then. Finch has been found guilty of endangering our lives by bringing threat of the disease into our community. Those strangers might have been infected; there was a clear risk they might have infected us. Fortunately they never left the boat, so the chance that the disease will manifest itself here is slight. At a meeting of the Caucus in which the presiding officer, Justice Abrahams, was present, it was decided that the penalty for this terrible crime against our people could only be the most severe at our disposal. Death." She paused to scan the crowd with her cold eyes, perhaps looking for any dissenters. There were none. People nodded. A man shouted, "Hear, hear."

"However," she continued, her amplified voice echoing from the buildings, "for Finch to be executed has been deemed insufficient punishment. After all, if Finch dies this afternoon he has in effect escaped the remorse he should feel for his crime."

Ben and I looked at one another. What the hell was she talking about? Had she gone crazy?

"Therefore—" Her voice rang out loud enough to scare the doves from the rooftops. "Therefore, the penalty of death will be applied to the daughter of Charles Finch, one Lynne Margaret Wagner."

The madness had started. I moved toward the stage, my heart pumping like fury, my fists clenched.

"It is the will of the Caucus that the penalty be executed now."

I was hearing the words . . . I heard them loud and clear, but somehow they no longer made sense. I felt as if I'd broken loose from the real world. That this was some vicious nightmare that had erupted into wide-awake daytime.

The woman continued to speak in that ice-cool lawyer voice. "It is also the will of the Caucus that each person here will be a party to the execution." She looked down at one of the police officers within the cordon. "Sergeant Marsh, please discharge your duty."

The crowd packed in toward the stage. I felt myself hemmed in by men and women who strained to see what was happening there. The heat from their bodies came through their clothes; they panted, their eyes blazed. The smell of their perspiration spiked my nostrils—hell, they were so close I could smell unwashed hair. There was something feverish about them. Like they'd been gripped by sheer passion. Something they had no control over.

Something like the passion that gripped me when I killed. But I was immune to this. Their hot bodies pressed hard against me from every direction, but all I felt was this cold, cold vacuum inside me.

"Lynne . . ."

I saw Lynne brought from the back of the ambulance to be led up the steps. For the first time I thought of her as "my Lynne," the beautiful woman who'd slip into my cabin to make breakfast once in a while. The same woman with the hip-swaying walk who I'd once held in my arms.

Blinking at the sudden sunlight, she shielded her

eyes. Then she looked 'round as if confused, or maybe wondering if this was anything more than a weird practical joke. A moment later she saw her father. He'd been brought from the courthouse to watch.

The cops sat her on the table. Then, before she even seemed aware of it, they pushed her down; there was something gentle about the action . . . they pushed her until she lay flat on her back, like it was some kind of weird outdoor operating table.

More men moved forward with the door, which they placed across her chest. From above it must have looked like the figure of a cross, like so: + Lynne's head and throat lay clear of the door, as did her legs. Two guys held each end of the door so it formed a seesaw across her chest, with her torso as the pivot.

"No . . ." I heard her voice plainly enough. Like she was waking up from a dream, she started to struggle. "No, let me go. What do you think you're doing?" She turned her head to see her father, who stood cuffed to two security guards. The man's face had an engraved look to it. As if his head and face had been carved from granite that had the word HORROR written all the way through it.

Cool as ice, Bertholly explained. "Each adult man and woman will be handed a house brick. Once you have the brick you will form a line at this end of the raised dais, where Mr. Crowther junior is standing. When instructed to do so, you will walk up here and place the brick on the door. This will continue until the door cannot contain any more bricks."

An electricity of excitement crackled through the crowd. They surged forward, eager to be first. No way did I want to go, but I was carried along with them. As the tidal wave of people shoved me forward I saw Lynne begin to struggle, her head twisting from left to right, her legs kicking. In a second men and women pounced on her to hold her still.

I yelled. In some way I thought I'd yell myself awake. This had to be a nightmare.

But with remorseless momentum events rolled forward. Men and women were handed bricks, they stood in line, they climbed the steps, they walked up to where Lynne lay on the table, her long hair hanging down. There, they placed the bricks on the door that the two men balanced on her chest.

To me, in that shocked state, the procedure didn't make sense. Why were they doing that? Why weigh the door down on Lynne's breast?

By the time the tenth brick had been placed there I heard her scream. "Take it off! It's heavy. You're hurting me. Do you hear? *It's hurting!*"

So, that was it.

Brick by brick, the door lying across her chest would become heavier. Neighbor after neighbor would play his part in her death.

My God, yes. Miss Bertholly the lawyer would be right. Everyone would remember this. They'd remember when bit by bit they crushed the life out of the mother of two children. The beautiful woman whose crime it was to be the daughter of Charles Finch.

Shouting in fury, I forced my way through the crowd to the stage. Lynne's face had flushed red. Her eyes narrowed with pain. Her head turned, slowly now, from left to right as the crushing pain made her squirm. She was no longer screaming; she was whispering. "No . . . please . . . stop it. Stop it." Already she found it hard to inhale. Her lips appeared to swell with the pressure. I saw her tongue emerge to lick the dry skin.

"Stop it!" I yelled. "Let her go!"

By this time the bricks had formed a neat stack a foot high and occupied a good half of the door area. The downward pressure must have been immense.

Finch stood between the two guards looking down

on his daughter's face. His expression tore something in my heart.

"Let her go," I yelled. "You don't know what you're doing!" I shouted this at the people laying those three-pound bricks on the door balanced on her chest—and now balanced with difficulty by the two guys who had to sweat to keep the door level.

But of course the people *did* know what they were doing. They lusted for revenge. Here was revenge in a huge meaty heap. And, Christ, were they going to gorge themselves stupid. The good folk of Sullivan eagerly collected their bricks, climbed onto the stage, then placed them on the woman who lay squirming and panting on the table. Her face had a dark, congested look to it. Her facial muscles contorted beneath the skin. Her limbs writhed so much it took all her captors' strength to stop them thrashing against the table.

Suddenly I was free of the crowd. One of the cops in the cordon reached out to grab me, but I swung a punch hard enough to knock him clean off his feet. Another cop lunged at me. I got ready to slam him, too, but I saw the canister in his hand. A second later a stream of pepper spray hit me full in the face.

Instantly the sensation that two white-hot spikes were being plunged into my eyes slammed through me. I went down choking. Blinded. My hands were pinned roughly behind my back. I felt steel tightly encircle my wrists. Hell, my eyes burned so much I wanted to claw them out with my fingernails but, now handcuffed, I couldn't even touch them.

More hands pushed me. I felt myself shoved up onto the stage where I stood gasping, blinded, my hands manacled behind my back.

"Lynne," I shouted. "Lynne, I can't see you!"

Then I heard her voice through the swarming voices of the mob.

"Greg, I'm here. Help me." The weight must have been crushing down on her chest. Constricting her lungs and heart. But I heard her all right. Spinning blindly, eyes burning, I began this sheer idiotic search of the platform to somehow find her.

"Greg. Please, help me, I'm—"

Simultaneously I heard a popping sound. Muffled yet frighteningly loud. "Greg, please, it's hurting so much, I don't think I can . . ." A loud crunch. *Really loud.* The sound of some delicate structure giving way under pressure.

"GREG!"

The force of that final shout of hers exploded inside my head. I stopped spinning 'round, blindly laboring to find her. I dropped down onto my knees, my head bowed. I was shaking through and through.

I knew Lynne was dead. The good people of Sullivan had their sweet justice.

Thirteen

My turn. The weight pressed down on my chest so hard I couldn't breathe. My heart began to crush, forcing the dark blood that pools there out through ruptured arteries. When my ribs collapsed with the sound of snapping sticks that's when I woke.

The dream left me dripping with sweat and panting so hard that it had dried my tongue like an old leaf. For a moment I wondered why my bed had become so hard, but as I reached out for the blankets I felt wooden sides.

Coffin walls.

They've buried you alive, Valdiva. Those smiling men and women of Sullivan with their polite manners, their big houses and swimming pools, have drugged you, stuffed you in a coffin and buried you six feet down. *They wanted you out of their lives, Valdiva.* Now you're going to choke on your own dirty air in this box. Choking in a lungful of air, I punched up into the darkness at the coffin lid.

Only air, Valdiva. You're punching air, my man. I

turned my head, and the whiskey bottle rattled against my forehead. When I sat up the earth tilted under me.

Christ. That whiskey had tasted like water. It seemed as alcoholic as water, too. Shit . . . My mouth tasted like I'd been licking a dead ass for the last twenty-four hours.

My world tilted again. Then turned slowly. But this was no funky special effect courtesy of a hangover. I remembered now. I'd done what I'd be promising myself for days. I'd taken one of the battery-powered cruisers across the lake.

Even with a gutful of whiskey I'd not been so dumb as to make the trip in daylight. I'd untied the boat in the dead of night; then, with the electric motor humming softly as a purring cat, I'd slipped across here in secret. I'd be back before dawn. No one'd ever know. Of course I'd never even climbed out of the damn boat. I must have slithered down to lie on the duckboards, where I'd slept like a dead thing for God knows how many hours.

This was the first time I'd slept since Sullivan's smiling bastards had killed Lynne. Good grief, was the whole town crazy? That had been two days ago. After macing me, then piling the bricks onto Lynne until her ribs caved in, they'd cleared every sign of the execution. . . . No, it was no execution; they'd simply murdered the woman out of sheer revenge because her father had taken in a bunch of refugees.

The day after the killing had been like a dream; everything seemed unreal. Even my cabin, where they'd dumped me, seemed a place of odd angles and weird dimensions. The kitchen looked bigger than it had before. There were more stairs, a whole mountain of them to climb. All the color had leeched from the walls and rugs and drapes. Maybe that was the effect of the chemicals that had been sprayed into my eyes (sprayed with vicious pleasure, no doubt). I figure, also, it was the shock of not only knowing Lynne was dead, but the aftermath as well.

Now that was weird.

Like I said, they cleared the Peace Garden where they'd killed her. I took a walk up there as soon as my stinging eyes would allow. And with my eyeballs burning like a couple of baked rocks in my head I saw that all the bricks had gone, as had the table on which they'd laid her. And they'd put tubs of flowering plants on the raised platform. The entire area smelled of disinfectant, too. They must have sloshed gallons of the stuff all over the damned place. And get this: No one would talk about what happened. No one.

Even when I spoke to Ben about it he changed the subject. When I tried to mention it again he kept saying, "Put it behind you, Greg. You've got to forget it."

I began to wonder if the Caucus would make another of their sinister announcements, ordering that no one must utter Lynne's name or even allude to her murder in any shape or form.

But it didn't stop there. Townsfolk didn't actually ignore me, but they wouldn't make eye contact, or they'd suddenly be interested in a tree or study their watches when I passed by. Any excuse so they didn't have to look at me, never mind actually passing the time of day. When they had to speak to me for any reason there'd be this cool kind of politeness, as if it was *me* who'd done something I should be ashamed of—not them, the bastards. They'd killed Lynne, not me. But they were treating me like they did after I'd done their dirty work for them and hacked up some stranger.

Even when I started delivering firewood again, people would go indoors when they saw my truck pull into the neighborhood. In one street a gang of children threw eggs at the truck. Hardly the crime of the century, but when I had to get out to clear the windshield of yolk that the wipers couldn't shift I saw the kids' parents in a garden turn their backs. If you read body language you knew full well that they'd encouraged their nice, well-mannered boys and girls to hurl those eggs.

For the next few hours I moved in a kind of vacuum. The violence against the woman that *they* had pressured into sleeping with me shook me badly. So much so that the trees and houses and stores looked distorted somehow, which I guess must be an aftereffect of the trauma. I even lost my sense of taste and smell. Another sure sign of shock. It didn't help, either, that people treated me like I was rotten with leprosy. They slid away from me whenever I was near.

You want to see how quickly you can empty a diner? Just picture me walking through the door. And it was all done so politely. No one said anything; somehow they just slipped discreetly away. Leaving the waitress there with a fixed smile that was warm as ice.

No wonder I had to get away.

First: I tried to hide away in the whiskey.

Second: When that didn't work I took the boat for a midnight trip.

That brought me to the good old ghost town of Lewis.

It took a little while to get all my senses back one by one as I sat there in the boat in total darkness. There were no sounds except for the kissing noises of waves lapping against the ferry terminal quay where I'd tied the boat.

Only I don't remember mooring it there, of course. That whiskey had been more powerful than it had seemed at the time. For a good ten minutes I sat motionless while my brain reacquainted itself with the cold reality of being awake. Presently my eyes adjusted a little to the dark. I could see the empty bottle in the bottom of the boat, the jacket I'd draped over the seat.

After that my eyes followed the pale line of the mooring rope, then ran up the concrete steps to the harbor wall.

Now was as good a time as any. Time for a little walk. I climbed out of the boat and made it up the steps without stumbling in the dark. At the top I looked across in the direction of Sullivan, now sleeping as innocent as a baby. With it being after midnight the electricity would have been cut. No streetlights or house lights indicated that the fucking lunatic town even existed.

Hell, that's what it had become, an insane town. But it masked that insanity with a terrible, glittering sanity. It was like a drunk who does everything with absolute precision in the hope no one thinks he's juiced out of his stinking mind. Sullivan was like that. Everyone pretended to be so perfectly sane it sent a great blazing message into the sky. The words might have crackled above the rooftops: WE'RE INSANE. WE KNOW WE'RE INSANE. ONLY WE'RE PRETENDING WE AREN'T.

So tomorrow life would continue normally in Sullivan. People would make believe that the world outside continued as normal (even though all they need do was switch on a radio or a TV to find nothing but dead channels). Residents would wash cars, have lunch by their pools, take in a movie, dine out, play tennis, walk the dog, chat to their neighbors about little Joey or little Mary's school show.

So you see, I had to get away from the place. It would send me crazy, too.

Now I walked along the harbor into the ghost town.

Or what was left of it. Most of the downtown area had been burnt to the foundations. Elsewhere buildings had become skeletons. And everywhere it was dark. The more I walked through that silence, smelling the rot and the still sharp reek of burnt wood and plastic and human skin, the more I sensed that this wasn't

110

the kind of darkness you'd experience at night. This wasn't so much a case of there being no light. This was dark, dark, *dark*. Dark . . . as if a black fog had crept out of the lake. Darkness that poured in through doors and windows, or swept like floodwater along a street. Black dark. Wet dark. As they say, "a darkness to be felt." You could reach out and run your fingers across that cold, damp darkness like you could run your fingers over the cold, still face of your dead grandfather.

Outside a Burger King that was now as dead and cold as any corpse ever was, I found a wooden bench. I sat there to breathe in the darkness. This is what it was like to be in a ghost town alone in the middle of the night. SILENCE and DARKNESS. They were twin phantoms that haunted the lonely roads.

Junk littered the streets. Cars thick with rust. Broken glass. Dollar bills mushed by rain. A broken rifle. Lumps of concrete. Cardboard boxes. I even saw a diamond necklace trailing over a woman's shoe. There were human skulls, too. Hundreds of them. And long thighbones, some with strands of boy and girl meat stuck to them. Maybe the rats didn't have enough appetite for all that carrion.

I sat there feeling the darkness of the town wash over me. It came in crushing waves. I found myself being pressed down by the weight of it. Images bloomed out of the dark of Lynne lying there, breathless. The bricks piling up on her breasts. The crushing weight.

My own heartbeat thudded inside me. The darkness seemed to be changing, becoming even more intense, even *darker*. I breathed it in. I sensed that velvet dark filling my lungs like black lake water. It oozed through lung tissue into my blood. I sensed it mingle with my blood to coil through my veins. A dark purple tide that poured into my heart.

These were the ghosts, I told myself. These were the ghosts of all those men, women and children who were slaughtered when our nation crashed and burned last year. They were envious of me being alive. Here they were to suffocate me with that liquid darkness.

Thud, thud, thud . . . my heartbeat grew heavier and slower.

I gazed up at the dead bones of buildings. Empty windows like eye sockets stared back at me. Darkness swirled and coiled inside them. Pulsing with purple blooms. All around me pockets of an even deeper darkness exploded.

Black lightning. I repeated the phrase inside my brain as darkness pooled there, too, thickening like congealing blood. This is black lightning.

Black lightning's going to kill you. Black lightning's going to strike.

Darkness pouring out of the ruins. The ghost town looming over me. It's gonna swallow me whole.

Ghosts emerging from the buildings. They're coming for me at last. They're here to take me down to hell, where I will go on suffocating in darkness forever.

Shadows move slowly out of the doorways. They have tumors for heads. Stones for eyes. Toadstools for tongues. They have long dark arms to wrap around me. Mouths that are wet wounds to suck on my lips.

Time's spinning like a falling plane . . . turning in slow motion forever and ever . . . never reaching the ground . . . never crashing . . . never exploding . . . but always—AL-WAYS—feeling that terrible sense of falling. . . .

Black lightning is erupting all around me. How long before it detonates inside my head? How long, Valdiva . . . how long?

I opened my eyes.

The ghost of a boy stood there just in front of me. He looked about ten years old. His face had the white waxy look of a candle. His eyes burned with a luminous glow, a bluish light that made you think of phantoms.

He reached out a long bone of an arm, his fingers stretching out toward my face.

I moved my head back to stop the ghost boy from touching me with his tomb-chilled fingers.

His mouth snapped open, exposing the hard white glint of teeth. I recognized the expression. That was the look of shock. The boy turned away, tripped over the broken rifle, then recovered his balance and ran.

I snapped to my feet and shouted after the running figure. *"Stop!"*

He didn't stop. If anything he ran faster, his arms windmilling like he was running in terror.

Or to warn his own kind that a stranger was in town.

At that moment I knew I couldn't let him escape. I raced after him through the darkness. One thought pumped through my mind: *Catch him. Catch him. Catch him . . .*

Fourteen

Ghost be damnned. That kid was meat and bone.

"Wait!" I called as I ran after him. "Stop. I won't hurt you!"

Wouldn't I, now? That kid might be dirty with the Jumpy virus or whatever the hell it was.

"Wait!"

The kid didn't wait. He ran hard, kicking aside human skulls, scrambling 'round torched cars, raising dust with his flashing feet.

He was in a hurry all right. Maybe in a hurry to tell his own people that he'd found a weird-looking stranger who'd sat on the bench staring into space. His own kind might be just a bunch of survivors who'd wandered into town. Or they might be bread bandits. If that were the case they'd do their darnedest to rip me to pieces. Either way, my gut instinct told me to catch the kid.

So we ran through the dead streets. Our footsteps came thudding back to us from the ruins like a heartbeat. The walls had a gray bone look to them now as dawn began to leech up over the city.

STRANGER

For a ten-year-old he was a fast runner and had gotten a good start, but I was gaining on him now. Another twenty seconds and I'd catch him.

What then, Valdiva?

I felt my stomach muscles get a little twitchy. Now, if I did get that knotting sensation in my guts; if instinct yelled loud and clear that the kid had Jumpy, then I knew what I'd have to do.

The kid was slowing. He'd got a hand pressed into his side where the stitch jabbed him good and hard. He couldn't run for much longer. I closed in fast. Now I was maybe thirty yards away.

He took a sharp left. A wrecked school bus stood nose to nose with a truck. I saw the kid pull up sharp when he saw he couldn't run any farther. He glanced back at me. I had a vivid impression of a white face framed with a shock of wild, dark hair. When he saw me barreling toward him he began to climb through the bus's ripped-out flank. There was a chance he could scramble out the other side. Then he'd have the advantage.

I checked to see if I could squeeze 'round the end of the bus, but, no, it had been rammed up tight against the wall of an apartment building. Maybe people here had used it as a last line of defense before the bread bandits overran them months ago.

With the kid out of sight I began to suspect I'd lost him. Then he'd be free to tell his people that they'd got a stranger in their midst. I piled into the bus after the kid, scattering the bones of a skeleton still wearing a silver sheriff's badge. This had been a fortress, all right. The windows on the far side of the bus had metal plates welded across them. That meant the kid couldn't get out that way.

Just when I thought I'd got him cornered I saw him climbing out the front where the windshield had been.

What's more, the way led straight through a window of the apartment building.

Damn. That kid's a slippery fish.

"Wait . . . just wait; I only want to talk to you . . ."

But all I saw were the soles of the kid's sneakers disappearing into the building as he scrambled out of the bus.

I paused, thinking. That might be the bread bandits' lair . . . He might have led me into an ambush. There might be twenty guys waiting in there. I listened, trying to pick up any sounds that weren't drowned out by my own panting as I caught my breath.

As I stood there my muscles gave a twitch in my stomach. It might be nothing but the sudden exertion. Or it might be instinct kicking in, twisting my stomach into knots. That's the way it always started. A moment later the shutter would come down inside my head. Then that overwhelming, overpowering urge to kill would come. I killed strangers with that evil little bug in their veins. As simple as that. And believe me, it got bloody. Bloody as hell. But that was the way it was. Amen. There was nothing I could do about it.

As I moved down the bus, pushing aside empty ammo crates, I felt my own blood turn cold. The muscles in my stomach twitched, twisted. My back muscles clenched. That *feeling* came into me, coiling with a reptilian slowness inside my stomach.

The boy was in the building. I sensed him running up the stairs. In my mind's eye I could see those pale sneakers flickering up the darkened stairwell. I flung empty boxes aside as I ran to the front of the bus. Automatically I scanned the vehicle for a weapon. A pair of revolvers and an Uzi lay on a table behind the driver's seat. They were rusty as hell. They weren't even any use as a club. Instead I reached down to the skeleton of a guy who must have had the build of a heavyweight boxer. I shook the army uniform he'd been wearing until one of his thighbones fell out. I tested its weight in my hand. This made a formidable baton. If need be I could break heads with this knuckley, bulbous joint.

I climbed through the gaping front of the bus into the building. Furniture had been arranged to make a canteen. Tables covered with plates and stone-hard slices of bread dominated the room. Again I realized this must have formed part of a defensive position. The people of Lewis had built a fortress here to keep out their attackers.

They'd failed, of course. Skeletons covering the floor with smashed skulls proved that.

With the huge thighbone in my right hand I moved into the hallway. And, yeah, sure enough, I could hear the whispery echo of the kid's feet as he climbed the stairs.

I began to climb, too, taking stairs two or even three at a time. I glanced up to see the kid's hands hauling him up by the stair rail. He was exhausted. And Christ, yes, I'd got the Twitch. My stomach muscles coiled themselves into knots. Back and neck muscles turned into rock-hard slabs. My fist tightened around the bone club so hard veins strained out through the flesh like a bunch of purple-skinned worms.

"Wait!" I shouted. I knew why I needed him to wait now. Sweet Jesus Christ, that blood lust had come roaring down on me in an avalanche of sheer fury.

"WAIT!" I bellowed the word. The kid gave a frightened gasp. Then he slipped onto his hands and knees on the stairs just fifteen feet above my head. He looked down through the stair rail at me. His brown eyes locked onto mine. Whether they burned in fear or hatred I don't know.

I heard my own voice come sliding through my lips with an ice-cold power. *"Wait there."*

Not running now, I climbed the stairs one deliberate

step at a time. My fist tightened around the bone club, forcing muscle to bulge against the skin of my forearm.

"Don't move," I told the boy. "Don't you move."

With a sudden cry he scrambled away on all fours. Instead of climbing the stairs he made off down a hallway. I paused to hear the scuffling sound of his hands and knees against the floor. I heard his whimper, too. He was scared. Because now he knew my plan.

Suddenly, with shocking clarity, I saw myself as he must have seen me. A huge shadowy stranger; ugly and beastlike. A monster from a nightmare was chasing him. There was cold fury in this terrifying man's eye.

By the time I reached the next floor I heard a door slam shut. He'd hidden himself in one of the deserted apartments. I moved slowly now. It still might be a trap. Who knows—his own kind waiting for me in those gloomy rooms? A door opened partway. I pushed it farther open with the end of the thighbone. A curtain sealed off the rest of the hallway. Using the club I slashed at it, bringing it down in a cloud of dust.

My muscles had tangled themselves into a million knots. My whole torso ached. He was close. What's more, I could near as dammit smell Jumpy in the air. The boy must have it bad. I burned to use the club now. I could feel the tension building inside me like a bomb.

I walked back into the hallway, moving fast, allowing my own instincts to track the boy. I needed to kill. I needed to kill fast and bloody; smash this diseased carcass from the face of the planet.

Hell, I'd never felt it as strong as this. It seemed the walls themselves were alive with the disease. I kicked a door open. Unmarked dust on the apartment floor sang out that he hadn't scurried in there. I moved onto the next, my teeth grinding with rage. God, I was in the grip of this thing now. Instinct rode me like a howl-

118

ing demon. Child or no child—nothing could stop me now. Nothing on this fucking planet.

A door moved an inch across the hallway. In three paces I reached it. With a snarl in my throat, I kicked it open. Footprints now. I saw the chevron pattern left by the sneaker soles, moving deeper into the apartment. I followed them into a living room. A TV had been toppled from its stand. Long-dried blood stained a couch. Pictures hung at crazy angles on the wall. People had fought and died here.

One more, I told myself . . . there'd be one more. Dirty bastard . . . dirty little diseased bastard. Getting a firm grip on the club, I followed the footprints in the dust to the far side of the room.

Waves of revulsion flowed at me. This was strong. I'd not felt it like this before.

I reached a door and put my hand on the handle. Because without a shadow of a doubt the Jumpy-riddled carcass of the boy must be cowering inside. I'd break that skull open. I'd paint the wall with his brains . . . I'd wear his blood on my face as a glistening red mask. I couldn't stop myself now. I was in the grip of this thing now. I'd—

Then I froze. Slowly . . . slowly . . . I looked back down to my right. The boy crouched on the floor behind an armchair. His chin was tucked down into his knees, his arms around his shins as he tried to compress himself into a tiny ball. Only his eyes looked huge and terrified as they stared up into mine.

"I told you to wait." I breathed. Although that wasn't important now. I took a step forward and raised the heavy bone over my head.

The kid made an easy target. *That skull would scrunch easily as eggshell. Go on, Valdiva, break open the head; plunge that bone like it's a big old wooden spoon . . . Stir his brains to cream. Do it, Valdiva. Do it. Do it!*

Easy, easy target. He was too scared to run, only . . .

119

Only something wasn't right.

Something about the kid, but I couldn't identify it.

I told myself to get the job done. But somehow it didn't *feel* right. Instead, that hairy old instinct of mine turned my head back to the door that I'd been drawn to. Just an ordinary apartment door made of wood. No window. It might lead to the kitchen.

Ambush?

I looked down at the dust on the carpet. Possibly an ambush, I told myself, only there were no footprints leading to the door. As we were on an upper floor, it seemed unlikely there'd be another way in.

The kid sat there frozen. He merely watched me with those big glistening eyes that were scared as hell.

"What's in there?"

He just stared at me, saying nothing.

I repeated the question, my voice harder. "What's in there?"

This time he just gave a shake of the head. Either that was an *I don't know.* Or an *I do know, but I'm not telling.*

Slowly I reached out to touch the door. The moment my fingertips touched the wood the twitches came back into my stomach so strong I nearly doubled up. A poisonous loathing oozed through the door panel into my fingers. Jesus, what was with this place?

For a second I stood there with every muscle in my body quivering like electricity ran through them. Then I moved. I raised the club and snatched open the door.

I'd expected an explosion of movement from inside the room, but there was no movement. Instead, someone had done something strange to the room. *A strange, strange something that made me stand and stare.*

There, hard up against the door, was a wall of what I can only describe as Jell-O. A pinkish wall of the stuff that stood quivering from the floor to the ceiling.

No . . . this didn't make sense. I touched it gently

with the end of the thighbone. It wobbled, just like a bowl full of Jell-O would wobble if you lightly pressed your finger against it. Whatever the stuff was, it formed a smooth membrane that bulged out slightly now the door that had supported it had been removed. Stunned, I couldn't drag my eyes off that pinkish wall.

I looked more closely. Like a big bowl of Jell-O, you could see through it. I saw objects suspended in the stuff like pieces of fruit in a dessert. Irregular in shape, they ranged from the size of a strawberry to as big as a basketball.

Behind me the kid whimpered. I shot a look back to see him give a frightened shake of his head as he stared at me . . . or stared at that pink block that filled the room as completely as water in a fish tank.

It wasn't pleasant to see. It made me think of blood that had set into a translucent gel. And yet it was compelling. I found myself looking not just at it but into it, like I was searching for something I knew would be there. Something hidden . . . and for some reason it was important that I find it. And the smell of it? Boy, did it stink! Jesus H Christ, it did. A kind of raw blood smell that's disgusting and kind of interesting all at the same time. The pink stuff was hot, too, like touching someone's face when they're running a fever.

I peered at the objects suspended there. Damn. This stuff had a glossy surface; I could even see my own face reflected there. Only distorted, until the mouth looked too big for the head and—

Hell, that wasn't my reflection.

One second I registered a severed head floating there.

The next a pair of eyes suddenly blazed from the head as the eyelids snapped open.

The next second the head lunged forward at me. The face pressed hard against the membrane, splitting the skin, exposing a slime-covered nose and eyes and a wide-open mouth that lunged at my exposed throat.

Fifteen

The boy stood at my side as we watched the apartment building. Whatever that thing in the room had been I don't know. But it was gone now. Flames jetted from the windows of the apartment on the seventh floor. Black smoke coiled against the sky, painting a grim smear there.

I waited for a good hour, half wondering—hell! half-fearing—that somehow the pink mass would escape. But it stayed there, to be cremated by the fire I'd started. What's more, it was hard to dislodge the image of the face lunging from that godawful red muck at my throat. A sheer reflex action had spared me from its champing jaws.

All I could say for sure was that the head had once belonged to someone human. What it was now, God alone knew. The head looked as if it had belonged to a man of around forty. The features were distorted. The mouth had somehow grown out of proportion to the face. Its eyes were swollen things that bulged grotesquely from the sockets. Yet the skin had a slick new-born look to it, covered with a pink gel.

From the fire came popping noises as timbers caught hold; windows cracked with a sudden *snap!* Later came another sound. It might have been simply air escaping from a confined space, but I swear I could hear a thin-sounding cry. You could believe it came from someone burning up with pain. The cry grew louder. More agonized. Higher in pitch. Then as quickly faded.

Once I was sure the fire would consume the building—and what it contained—I turned and walked away. The boy followed.

"Are you alone?" I asked him.

Not replying, he trudged along the street with his fists pushed down into the pockets of his jeans.

"Do you speak English?"

Still no reply. His face expressionless. He merely stared straight ahead.

"Quite a fire we made back there," I said. "It's going to turn the whole building into a pile of ash."

He suddenly stopped walking; then, as if remembering something unpleasant, he said, "Hive."

"Hive?" I looked at him. "What do you mean by hive?"

"Can't you hear me?" His face flushed an angry red. "I've told you . . . *hive!*"

"I'm sorry, I don't know what you—"

But I was talking to thin air. He'd gone. Once more he'd run like Satan himself was after his ass.

Only this time I saw that he ran toward a group of people who stood at the junction of the street. They weren't moving, but they were taking a close interest in me. I noticed, as well, that they were armed.

The kid ran straight at them to stand alongside a guy who carried a pump-action shotgun. My instincts had nearly steered me wrong with the kid earlier, and maybe I was a fool to put my trust in gut instinct again, but I put my hands out at either side of me to show that I wasn't carrying a gun. Then I moved slowly forward. I figured the time had come to speak to someone.

Sixteen

"We can't give you food."

The girl with black eyes told me this as we sat by the fire that crackled away like crazy in the yard of a house. When I say she had black eyes I don't mean that she'd been in a fight. No . . . it was the color of the irises. They were this pure onyx black. A lustrous, glossy black. Believe me, I'd not seen eyes like those before. I found myself staring as she talked to me. But then, there was something pretty compelling about her. She had a thin waif face and a body to match. Her clothes were clean, considering, while her long hair was as glossy and as dark as her beautiful eyes. I put her age at around eighteen.

"We lost what was left of our food two days ago. The last place we were staying got jumped by a bunch of hornets. We were lucky to escape with our skins."

"Hornets?" I shook my head, not understanding.

"Hornets. You know?"

I shrugged.

"Bread bandits?"

"Oh, right." I nodded.

Now she shook her head. "Have you been in hibernation? No one's called the bad guys bread bandits in months." Her face there in the firelight never broke into a smile once. In fact the whole party wore grim expressions. She continued with a nod at the boy. "He got so shaken up that he ran off the moment we got here. We'd been looking for him for hours when we saw the pair of you in the street."

"Has he told you what happened?"

"He said you found a hive in an apartment. That you torched the place." Her lips gave a little twist, the closest to a smile I'd seen on her face. "Good work. The filthy bastard deserved it."

A guy of around twenty in a cowboy hat picked up on the conversation. "What we don't understand is why there weren't any hornets guarding it. They don't usually desert a hive."

I frowned. "You're losing me again. Hive? What is this hive? The kid used the word after we set fire to it."

"Sweet Jesus, you *have* been out of circulation." The girl pushed another piece of wood into the flames. "Where did you say this town was where you lived? On the moon?"

Yeah, she was joking. But still not smiling.

I shrugged. "We keep to ourselves."

"You can say that again."

"But it sounds like a nice place to be," chipped in one of the others. "You say you've got electricity? Clean water? Food?"

"We must have gotten lucky."

"I'll say."

"I'm going to get a hold of a handful of dirt from your town and keep it in my pocket." The kid gave a grim smile. "Maybe some of your luck will rub off on me."

"A decent meal would be pretty good right now."

"Pretty good? We'd be in damn heaven."

I'd got questions that could do with buddying up with some answers, but suddenly this dog-eared group of people around the fire started shooting one-liners at each other.

"Give me beefsteak with mayonnaise."

"Mayonnaise?"

"I don't know why. I just want to eat mayonnaise. I haven't tasted it in months."

"Give me the beefsteak. A couple of pounds medium rare would work some magic for me."

"With a dozen beers."

"And an order of fries."

"Golden fries."

"Give me a loaf of bread. That's all I need right now."

"Coffee and a cigarette. It's weeks since I had a cigarette."

"You don't smoke."

"I did once. Until the crap hit the fan."

"See? Every apocalypse has a silver lining. If you don't smoke you'll live to be a hundred."

"Yeah. Live to a hundred in some shack with nothing to eat but dirt and leaves, and nothing to drink but ditch water."

"Wait," I said, breaking into their fantasy food orgy. "Tell me more about these hives."

"Do you mind, man?" The guy sounded annoyed. "We were talking about food."

"Seeing as we don't have the real thing," added the black-eyed girl.

"I'm sorry," I said. "But there's something been happening in the outside world. Something important that I don't know anything about. Listen, I find a room full of pink goo that has body parts floating in it that are still alive like . . . like fish in a damn fish tank! In my book, that's important!"

"And so is mayonnaise." The guy in the cowboy hat growled, angry now. "Or do you think we're all going to get fat dining on fucking fresh air?"

"No, I'm sorry, but—"

"Sorry my ass, you—"

Another broke in, "We take you off the street, give you protection, give you a place by the fire *we* made, and you get ticked off when *we* talk about something *we* want to talk about."

The boy spat on the ground. "Yeah, we never have enough to eat. You don't know what it's like to be so hungry you feel as if your brains are on fire."

I spoke as patiently as I could. "All I want to know is, what are these hives you're talking about? Should I be warning the people in the town where I live?" Some might have said *I should warn my people.* But Sullivan wasn't *my people.* I didn't like nine tenths of them. I bore it no allegiance. Yet I knew young children still lived in the town. And then were was Ben and a few others who were decent, including Lynne's husband and daughters. As for the rest, well, damn them. I didn't give so much as a flying fuck.

"You really want to know about the hives?" The girl looked at me with those eyes that were like black jewels.

"Of course I do. Are they dangerous? Are there lots of them? Should we be searching for them and burning them to crap? I mean, if we're—"

"Wait." She held up her hand to stop me. "You want answers from us?"

"If these things are dangerous, we need to—"

"Just one moment there." Again she interrupted. "You know the old saying, you don't get anythin' for nothin'?"

I nodded.

"Then," she said, standing, "get us food and we'll tell you what we know."

I looked at those thin, half-starved faces. "OK," I

agreed after a moment. "It's going to take a little time."

"We don't have planes to catch, buddy," growled the guy in the cowboy hat. "Take your time."

"But bring some mayonnaise," chipped in his buddy. "Big, big jar."

"And beer."

"And bring steak. We can barbecue it right here." The cowboy stamped his boot into the fire, pushing in a chunk of unburned wood. Sparks gushed into the night sky.

"I'll do my best."

"Your best my ass. No food, no hive talk. You follow?"

"It'll be a couple of hours."

"We'll be here."

"You can't go alone," the girl told me. "By rights there should be hornets crawling all over the place." She picked up the pump-action shotgun.

"I'll be just fine," I told her. "Just lend me a gun."

The cowboy laughed. "Lend my ass."

The girl shook her head. "If you knew how many of us we lost getting hold of these babies you'd realize why we don't go handing them out to strangers." She nodded at a break in the fence. "Come on, make it quick. We're hungry."

We walked through the downtown area of Lewis, heading to where I'd moored the boat at the ferry terminal. The first rays of the rising sun cast a blood-red light on rusted cars and scattered masonry.

After ten minutes of walking in silence she suddenly said, "You hate our guts, don't you?"

"Hardly. I don't even know you people."

"We must look like a rough bunch. But we didn't start out that way. Tony comes from a family of well-to-do tennis pros on Long Island, while Zak—he was the guy in the black Stetson—was studying at a Hebrew school in Manhattan when the world rolled over and died. Originally he was from Vancouver in Canada. He had those curly black side locks, you know?" She made a twirling motion with her fingers just below her ears. "But he lost all his hair in a fire when we camped in a kindergarten—some idiot kicked over a stove in his sleep. His hair never grew back. Not even his eyebrows or on his arms. He wasn't badly burned, but I figure it must be the shock . . . wait." She stopped, then looked up at me. "We've done this all wrong, haven't we?"

"Done what all wrong?"

"We're becoming so brutalized we're even forgetting the social basics." She held out her hand. "How do you do? I'm Michaela Ford."

I shook her hand. "I'm Greg Valdiva."

"Pleased to meet you, Greg."

"Likewise, Michaela."

That was rich. Standing there in a burned-out city full of skulls, shaking hands like we were meeting for the first time at a dinner party.

She continued walking. Now she looked a little more relaxed.

"So where do you come from, Michaela?" I asked.

"Me? New York. My mother was in magazine publishing. We'd just moved into an apartment in Greenwich Village. I loved it there, especially the street markets on Sundays. I even wound up helping out on a stall there that sold African jewelry."

"Sounds swanky."

"Swanky?" She smiled. "What kind of old-time colloquial is that?"

"It was a word my mother used. Swanky clothes, swanky cars, swanky houses."

"She's dead?"

"She's dead." I nodded.

"Mine, too. I was staying with my father up at his place in the Catskills when the hornets went on the rampage. Like everyone else we thought it would be short-lived, but it just went on and on. They torched schools, houses, then whole towns and cities. My mother and father had been separated more than five years, but he was still anxious about her being in New York, especially after we heard that all those people had been killed in the streets on the first day."

As we walked along the street, where naked skulls seemed to grow out of the dirt like weird white mushrooms, she talked. It seemed as if she and her father had dove into the car, then simply blazed south toward New York. Already the countryside had gone to shit. Bread bandits, or hornets, as she called them, had trashed everything. They drove past houses and churches in flames. She couldn't believe her eyes the first time she started seeing corpses lying in the road. She even told her father she was hallucinating when she saw a dozen men hanging by their necks from a bridge running over the road. Then he'd had to drive the car under the hanging bodies. The feet of the dead men had scraped along the car roof. It's still a sound she had nightmares about. Of course, the closer to New York they got the worse the roads became. Soon they were clogged with refugees flooding from the city. And every hour or so the bread bandits would attack like packs of marauding wolves. There was no one to protect the refugees. Hardly anyone had a gun. Michaela's eyes went faraway as she described how maybe a hundred or so bread bandits would run along a gridlocked road tearing people out of their cars, dashing babies against the blacktop, torching vehicles, tearing eyes out with their bare hands.

Nevertheless, Michaela's father still forced a way through the jammed highways, horn blaring, lights flashing. They were still a good twenty miles from New York when she got the call on her mobile. It came from a friend of her mother's. She was screaming into the telephone that her mother's apartment had been ransacked and that her mother lay in the bathtub. "They drowned her in her own bathroom, can you believe that? Can you believe they'd do such a terrible thing? Michaela, your mother helped these people. She worked in the canteens at the park. She did everything she could. Now they've broken in and drowned her in her own bathtub."

There was nothing to do but turn back. Now they joined the flow of cars away from New York into the countryside. It took three hours to cover four miles. Then the driver's door was torn open. Hands and arms burst into the car. Her father struggled with the attackers for maybe less than a minute before he'd gone. The mob carried him away, still struggling.

Michaela waited there for them to come back for her. She'd accepted they would carry her away. But no one came. The other refugees did nothing to help her. They'd seen it happen time and time before. They merely sounded their horns before inching past her. After an hour of this she knew there was nothing she could do for her father.

She slid across into the driver's seat, started the engine, joined the exodus.

Within a week she'd joined up with a bunch of other refugees who were camping out at an abandoned farmhouse. For months they'd drifted from place to place, looking for food and a place of safety. Usually the hornets found them and drove them out. Sometimes they stayed put and made a fight of it, but there were too many hornets. Some of Michaela's group died, so they'd eventually cut and run anyway. Now all that remained was the ten-strong group that sat 'round the campfire waiting for food.

Poor bastards.

Come to think of it, I'd had it pretty easy in Sullivan. The people sucked. But I had a home and plenty of food.

STRANGER

We'd nearly reached the ferry terminal when she asked what had happened to me that first day of June.

"The first I knew was the smell of burning. When I woke up the houses across the street were on fire . . . my mother called them swanky houses . . . you're right, she was envious. We lived in . . ." I grimaced. "Humble accommodations. Anyway, we saw that the bread bandits, or the hornets, as you call them, were lining our neighbors up in the road. And . . . you know, there was something in those refugees' faces that didn't seem human anymore. After the hornets lined up our neighbors they just walked along from man to man, woman to woman . . . they had hammers, and they just . . . well, you don't need me to paint a picture, do you?" I shrugged. "What could we do? We locked the door and watched all that shit happening on TV, how the cities were burning, the refugees flooding the streets. We even watched CNN when the bastards broke into the studios and beat the anchorman to death live on air. By that time we knew we had to find somewhere well away from the action, so to speak. We couldn't just sit tight in the house and hope that we'd be left alone, so we started to pack groceries into bags, because we knew food would be scarce. But as we cleared out the cupboards a guy just walked into the kitchen. We didn't even hear the goddam door open. He just stood there with this expression on his face. It was just so weird. Like he wasn't looking at the surface of our faces but somewhere at the back of our skulls. My mom grabbed Chelle to pull her away from him. That's when he attacked. He just flailed at her with his fists. My mom sort of hugged Chelle into her stomach, then she bent over her to take the guy's punches in her back so Chelle was protected."

I looked at Michaela. She gazed at me steadily. She must have heard this kind of story dozens of times before from survivors. But she listened with a serious expression. I even felt she was encouraging me to get it off my chest.

"Well, I launched myself at the guy who was trying to kill my mom. . . ." My voice died away.

"And?" she prompted gently.

"And I lost my mind . . . at least for a while. When I came to I was lying in this mass of broken pottery. I thought the guy had knocked me unconscious, but it turned out I'd had some kind of blackout. But I had fought the guy. He'd opened a gash on my forehead and bloodied my nose. I don't remember anything about it, but my mother told me I'd struggled with the guy, then grabbed him by the throat and smashed his head against the kitchen wall so hard it had cracked all the wall tiles. . . ." I shook my head. "My mother called those tiles her swanky tiles. She loved them."

"You saved their lives."

"Yeah, for what good it did."

"What then?"

"The guy was out cold or dead, I don't know. We picked up what groceries we could carry, then drove away. It was just luck, I suppose, but we found a house way up on a hillside, like it had been dug into a hole there. And that's where we sat it out for month after month."

"The hornets didn't find you?"

"No. Not that I remember much about it. I'd drunk water from a stream that must have been contaminated by a dead animal or something. I was sick for weeks. Most of the time I was in such a high fever and delirious, I didn't know day from night. I was out of it. I can't remember a thing."

"Your mother and sister were able to care for you alone?"

"Somehow they scavenged food from abandoned houses and stores. But like I said I didn't know anything about it."

We reached the steps that lead to the boat.

"Then for some reason we hit the road again," I told her. "I don't remember much. We wound up in a little town in the hills . . . or the remains of one. I still couldn't eat and was still pretty much out of it. I don't even know properly how it happened, but my sister and mother became sick. I was looking for help when a hunting party from Sullivan found me—Sullivan's the place across the lake, there. They got us to a doctor, but my mother and Chelle died within hours of each other. The doctor said it was some kind of blood poisoning. But I'm not sure if he really knew what it was. What are you doing?"

"Getting into the boat."

"No, you have to wait here. I'll bring the food back across to you."

"How do I know that? You might change your mind and stay across there on paradise island and forget all about us."

"I'll bring food," I told her as she slipped the shotgun off her shoulder. "Or are you going to blow a hole in me if I don't do what you tell me?"

"And where'd that get me? You being dead won't bring us the food." She lay the gun on one of the bench seats.

"Look, Michaela, I'm not allowed to bring strangers onto the island. Hell, I'm not even supposed to leave the island myself."

"I'm coming with you."

"No. If I'm found with you, they'll kill us both. Believe me."

Her voice stayed firm. "Greg, I'm coming."

Seventeen

Short of punching her unconscious and dumping her back on the harbor wall, what could I do? As I tied the boat to the jetty nearest my cabin, I whispered to her, "People tend not to wander down here in the early hours, so we shouldn't meet anyone, but keep as quiet as you can. OK?"

Shouldering the gun, she nodded. There was more than enough light to reveal us to anyone who happened to be taking a dawn stroll, so instead of using the track for the three-minute walk to my place I took a slightly longer route through the woods, where we'd be concealed by trees. I just thanked my lucky stars there'd been enough mist on the lake to conceal our crossing from Lewis to Sullivan.

This was no ideal situation for sure, but I remember Michaela's hungry friends. They deserved a chance, too. Besides, those nice, smiling bastards of Sullivan could spare some food. With luck I could run the supplies across to Lewis in the battery-powered launch and still be back before the dawn mist melted away.

When we reached the cabin Michaela was amazed. In awe, she stared at the cans and jars I'd dumped on the table and worktops and never gotten 'round to putting into the cupboards.

I'd already pulled the blinds down so I said, "You can relax now."

Still overawed, she just nodded. She didn't look any more relaxed.

"Michaela, you can talk normally as well. We're a quarter of a mile from the nearest house."

"OK," she said in a tiny whisper.

"Sit down. I'll fix you something to eat."

"I'm all right. Let's get the food to the boat."

"You don't look all right." Maybe it was the sight of all that food after living on raw potatoes for a couple of days that did it, but she'd started to sway; her dark eyes suddenly unfocused.

"It'll take me a few minutes to get the stuff together. Sit down at the table. Here." I put bowls in front of her. There were tomatoes, grown locally in greenhouses. Heaped in a basket were plums and mushrooms. A real dog's dinner of a mixture, but she began to eat. I'd still got a good-sized chunk of bread that wasn't overly dry and a can of corned beef. She watched me open that like I was producing diamonds from the can, not a block of boiled beef that was close to its "best by" date. Even though she must have been hungry as hell she didn't eat like a hog. She sliced the corned beef with a knife, then slipped it between her lips. Then it hit me that I hadn't eaten for more than twenty-four hours either. I filled a jug from the faucet and grabbed a couple of glasses.

"You've water mains, too?" She sipped it like fine wine. "I wasn't wrong: This is paradise."

"Water's pumped from a well nearby. More?"

"Please."

I refilled her glass, then ate, too.

"I can't believe you've got all this food. Haven't hornets hassled you at all?"

"No. Well . . . there've been a few, but they came in just ones or twos. They didn't even attack. They just turned up asking for food and shelter."

"They were still in the early stages of it, then. What happened to them?"

"I killed them." I spoke matter-of-factly, but she shot me a startled look.

"You killed them before they went full-blown and started attacking people?"

"Yes. . . . Try these pickles. They're good." I aimed to change the line of talk, but she was having none of it.

"You mean you kill every stranger that walks into this town?"

"No. I think I've got some cheese somewhere if you want to try—"

"Greg, I don't understand. You mean to say you've got some way of running medical screening? That you can tell if people are infected with Jumpy?"

"No . . . nothing like that."

"What then?"

"You tell me about these hives, then. That thing I found in the apartment was weird, you know?"

"They are weird as hell, Greg. But I'm not saying anything about the hive until my people get the food you promised them."

I looked at her. She recognized something so serious in my expression that she stopped eating.

"Michaela, I won't make a game of it," I told her. "The truth is I might kill you."

A tremor ran through her face. Her dark eyes widened in shock.

"Listen." I clasped my hands together tightly in front of me, just in case they flew at her to crush her throat. "I don't know what happened to me last year, or if it's something I've always had . . . I know I'm not explaining this well. But if someone has got that thing in their blood I know. It's instinctive. They might not have any symptoms. They might be sitting like you're sitting there now, but I get this twitching in my stomach, the muscles in my back writhe like a whole heap of snakes, then before I know it I've killed them—man or woman. It's like lightning inside my head. Pow, bang, then by the time I've got my control . . . my self-control back I'm standing over a body that's hacked to pieces." I took a breath, sickened by the memories that started to flood me. "It's like a bomb hitting me. It's that sudden."

"You don't feel this . . . this twitching with me now?"

"No."

"Did you feel it when you were back with my people?"

"No. I thought I felt it when I followed the boy into the apartment. I know now it was because I was so close to that thing you call a hive. But there's no guarantee it won't happen." Then I told her about the local guy who'd arrived in town a few days ago, that I knew he'd got Jumpy running in his veins and how I'd killed him in the street. "So this epidemic *has* changed," I told her. "We thought it could only affect people from South America. Now it looks as if no one's immune."

She nodded. "That's our experience. It looks as if that funky old Jumpy bug just took a little longer to get into the Yankee bloodstream." She tried to talk in a lighthearted way, but I could see from her face that she was deadly serious. "The question we've been asking ourselves is, why haven't we been infected yet?"

"Maybe some natural resistance."

"Maybe. Or maybe we just managed to keep out of infected areas by chance. Just as you've put yourself in quarantine on this island."

"Then we're living on borrowed time? It's going to come here whatever we do?"

She sipped her water. "Which is a depressing thought, you have to admit."

"You know, I have a friend who can't stop asking questions. For months he wondered why the whole country fell apart so quickly. How millions of people with the best armed forces and the best medical care in the world could just go." I snapped my fingers. "Implode in a matter of days. Not even weeks."

"You reckon the question he'd be asking right now would be: Were Americans in the early phase of the disease when the hornets launched this—what did the press call it?—Tet offensive and rioted all over the damn place?"

"Makes you wonder, doesn't it, Michaela?"

"It does make you wonder, Greg. It makes you wonder what's gonna happen next. And that question terrifies me. Oh, God."

"What's wrong?"

"Nothing . . ." She shrugged, tired-looking. "I feel like hell, that's all." She shot me a faint smile. "Those days on the road are catching up with me. I don't think we've slept more than two hours straight in the last week."

"Wait there, I'll run you a bath."

"A what?"

"I'll go fill the tub. While you have a soak in some hot water I'll load food into the boat."

Again that incredulous look. "You mean to say you've got hot water as well?"

"Sure. There's an electric immersion heater. The electricity will have been cut at midnight, but it stays hot in the tank for hours."

"Jeez. You're the kind of guy who girls like me want to marry." She suddenly blushed. "Take that as a figure of speech . . . but I wouldn't say no to a bath."

I stood up, ready to go run the water for her, but she waved her hand. "No, just point me at your bathroom and I'll do the rest. You best get those supplies loaded."

"It's at the top of the stairs. First door on the right."

"Thank you, Greg. I mean it . . . but just don't go killing me before I've had at least ten minutes up to my chin in hot water, will you?" Wearily, she shook her head. "Sorry. Bad-taste joke. I'm terrible for that. I always joke about inappropriate subjects. But then, didn't Freud write a paper about that?" She smiled again. "Sorry, Greg. I'm so tired I'm rambling."

Within moments of her going upstairs I heard the water running into the tub. I grabbed a pair of heavy-duty holdalls and packed as much canned and dried food as I could carry. After three trips down to the boat I'd emptied the kitchen of every last bag of rice, pasta and bottle of beer. For a moment I considered taking the truck up to Ben's to collect more food. I knew he'd got access to a cold store that was fed by electricity all the time. There'd be cheeses and sides of beef there, but to do that I might as well drive with the horn blaring and a sign on the truck roof that read JUST GETTING FOOD FOR STRANGERS, YOU MORONS.

Then what?

The townspeople would either lynch us there and then, or maybe they'd do it nice and slow, like they did with Lynne, and pile rocks on our chests until we suffocated. Those nice smiling bastards of Sullivan really knew how to squeeze the revenge juice out of a victim.

It took me less than an hour to make those trips to get all the food onto the boat. It wasn't a great supply, as you can imagine. But it should keep Michaela's group fed for a few days at least. With luck they might be able to find a house tucked away in the woods that hadn't been picked clean.

I returned to the cabin to find the lamp had burned out and the place in near darkness, with all the blinds shut. Closing the screen door behind me, I listened. It had that special kind of silence, the tomb silence that seems more than there being no sound. There was a sense of the building holding its breath. Secret, secret, secret . . . there's something hiding here you shouldn't see, Valdiva.

Immediately the thought came to me that Michaela had been discovered. That maybe Crowther and his buddies were waiting in a darkened room with rifles cocked.

Shit. Where was Michaela? Why was the place so damned quiet? I'd only been down at the jetty less than ten minutes. Surely I'd have heard if some guys had pounced on her. Not risking relighting the lamp, I allowed my eyes to adjust to the thin wash of daylight filtering through the blinds. Then, walking as quietly as I could, I went upstairs. A candle still burned in the bathroom. The tub had been emptied. Trying to move like I was nothing more solid than a wisp of smoke, I crossed the landing to my bedroom.

In the gloom I saw a figure lying on my bed. Slowly, slowly, slowly, I eased myself into the bedroom. Michaela lay on the bed. She must have decided to lie down for a moment (while no doubt promising herself, *No, I won't let myself fall asleep*), but there she lay, dead to the world, wearing nothing but my big bath towel, her long hair spread out against the white sheet in gleaming dark strands. Her breathing was slow, rhythmic. The poor kid couldn't have slept in a clean bed for weeks, if not months.

At that moment, as I looked down at her, my stomach muscles twitched.

She'd turned over in her sleep, the movement making the towel come adrift where she'd fastened it high on her chest. The twitch came again. Following that came a tingle in my fingertips.

This was another kind of twitch. Not that fatal twitch

that signaled I would attack. No, no, my man, this was very different.

For the first time I saw how beautiful she was. The dark arches of her eyebrows. The relaxed face that was a near perfect heart shape. She possessed a waiflike beauty that made her look so vulnerable asleep there on my bed. The towel had slipped down, exposing a smooth mound of breast. She breathed deeply in her sleep, raising her chest, making the towel slip down farther to expose skin almost as far as her nipple.

I moved quickly, closing the door behind me before going downstairs. Seconds later I'd lit the spare lamp in the kitchen and got busy making a jug of hot coffee on the camping stove. *Let her sleep,* I told myself. *We can spare another hour here.*

Boy, was I wrong. Was I wrong by a wide, country mile.

Eighteen

"Oh, hell's bells." I used the phrase Mom would use when Chelle spilled her milk on the couch or the crotchety old car wouldn't start.

"What's wrong?" Michaela whispered from behind me in the boat.

"Damn battery's dead." I let out an annoyed hiss between my teeth as I checked the battery meter. Yup, the needle was in the red. Deep, deep in the red. "Damn thing . . . it runs off truck batteries, but from the look of them they're older than my grandmother. They're just not up to holding a charge for long."

Michaela glanced anxiously at the thinning mist out on the water. "We'll be in clear view soon. Can you find a replacement?"

"Not here."

"How about recharging them?"

"I can only do that tonight when the juice starts flowing," I said, nodding at the power cable that ran along the jetty. "But it will take around five hours to get enough charge in the batteries for a round trip across the lake."

"Then we're stuck."

"At least until dark."

"Shit. My friends need that food."

"Will they wait for you?"

She shrugged. "They will unless some hornets find them. Then they'll have to run for it."

"Damn." I slammed the boat's steering wheel with my fist. "I should have checked that those batteries weren't goddam antiques before I took the boat. Look at the crust on them."

"Don't blame yourself. After all, you weren't planning this kind of operation when you took the trip across there, were you?"

"No. The truth was, I'd just downed a bottle of whiskey and needed to get out of Paradiseville here for a change of air."

She tilted her head as if to ask why.

"Long story. I'll tell you another time, but we need to get these supplies covered up. Can you give me a hand with the tarp?"

"What now?" she asked as she helped me pull the sheet over the bags of canned food and packets that I'd dumped into the bottom of the boat.

"You need to keep out of sight until dark. Then I'll run you across the water." I stepped off the boat onto the jetty and held out my hand.

She shook her head. "I'll lay low here."

"You can't stay in the boat all day."

"But from what you've said, Greg, if the townspeople find out that you're helping me you'll be in big trouble."

"Don't worry, they won't find you. All you need to do is sit tight in the spare bedroom in the cabin. Then we'll leave after dark."

"OK . . . if you're sure?"

"Sure I'm sure; now give me your hand."

I grasped her slender hand and helped her off the

boat. After that I pulled the cable that ran from the boat's batteries and plugged it into the jetty power point. OK, the batteries weren't tip-top. But with a full charge they'd make the return trip easily enough tonight.

With the mist now melting fast we walked quickly back to the cabin. There, I showed Michaela the spare bedroom. At least she'd have the day to rest up.

"Don't raise the blinds," I told her. "Or use the electric light when the power comes on this evening. I don't get many people down here, but there's always a chance one or two will drop by."

Yeah, it's sods law, as the saying goes. No. *One or two* didn't drop by; there was a steady flow. As if the whole freaking island had sniffed my little secret on the breeze and wanted to come and see the stranger for themselves.

First by was Ben. He stood there on the porch with his hands shaking worse than ever. He said he'd been down the day before, couldn't raise me and guessed I was sleeping. Clearly he was concerned that I had done something stupid after Lynne had been murdered by the townspeople (no, he didn't use those words exactly). But I told him my eyes had hurt like hell after getting a face full of Mace, and that I'd stayed in bed for the day with a companion by the name of Jack Daniel's.

"I don't blame you," he said, his fingers fluttering like butterflies. Poor kid really *was* worried about me. "I just didn't want you to—to go and do anything stupid."

"I stayed home," I repeated the lie (repeat a lie three times and it starts to sound like the truth—even to the person who mouthed the lie) but of course I did do something stupid. I took a nighttime cruise across to the ghost town. I got mixed up with something weird called a hive and a bunch of people late of New York City. Now there was an eighteen-year-old stranger hiding up in a bedroom in my cabin. But I couldn't tell Ben that. He wouldn't snitch, I knew that much; but he might give something away with that nervous, jumpy (note: small *j* jumpy) manner of his. Besides, it wouldn't be fair to burden him with my little secrets, would it?

He wanted me to roll up to his apartment in town for breakfast and maybe burn off a few hours listening to some music. I thanked him but said I needed to saw up a mountain of logs for the firewood deliveries (although I had no intention of doing the rounds that day).

I decided it would look good to any outsiders passing by if, for me, it was business as normal. So I fired up Big Bertha the chainsaw, then started chewing up logs. Yeah, business as usual, but in my mind I walked upstairs to see Michaela lying there on the bed, no doubt listening to the buzz of the saw. Even though I tried to keep the image from my mind I recalled how she looked last night, lying on my bed naked but for the towel, her hair fanned out onto the sheet, her eyelids closed, those dark eyebrows that formed a pair of neat twin arches, the smooth rounded shape of her breasts and the way they—

Hell. The chainsaw bucked up at my face as it hit a nail in the wood. *You're going to loose your nose if you don't concentrate, Valdiva.* But then, it was hard to concentrate with Michaela lying on the bed upstairs, maybe gazing at the ceiling with her eyes that were as glossy and as black as onyx.

What's more, if I managed to shut off images of her I replaced them with images of the thing that filled the apartment room as completely as water in a fish tank. The organic smell of the thing came back to me, the heat of it when I touched it. How that face came lunging out at it me. That was weird, believe me. Weird in a dark and dangerous way.

But somehow a familiar way—that was something that made no sense at all. There should be nothing familiar about it. I'd seen nothing like it before, had I?

Maybe I'd subconsciously linked it to the head Ben found in the driftwood a few days back. That was weird and inexplicable as well. There it was, lodged in the branches. A human head with a spare set of eyes bursting out through the skin of the cheek like a pair of tumors. Shit weird, if you ask me. Maybe that block of pink gel had got—

"*Greg . . . Greg? Turn off the . . .*"

I suddenly realized that someone was shouting my name. Killing the saw's motor, I pulled up my goggles.

"Hello, Mel. What can I do for you?"

Mel was an easygoing redhead of around twenty-five who ran the fresh produce round. Milk, butter, bread, that kind of thing. She grew marijuana with her tomatoes on the other side of Sullivan. Although she wasn't one of the town bastards she'd got old family going way back. You know the sort; she might be one of *us* today, but she could as easily switch to one of *them* tomorrow. It might seem a harsh judgment, but at a Christmas party she nearly sucked my damn face off, only the following day she pretended nothing had happened.

Today she seemed her friendly self. "I tried to leave your milk and bread in the kitchen, but you've locked your door."

"Have I?" I shrugged, aiming to look casual. "I must have done it out of habit."

"So I haven't been able to put your milk in the refrigerator. I put it under the table. It's not in the sun at the moment, but it might spoil if it's left there too long."

"Thanks. I'll go move it." I laid down the chainsaw, dusted my hands on the seat of my pants and headed off to the cabin. I was surprised to see that she'd followed me.

"How are you for fruit and tomatoes? I've got loads with me if you need more."

"I've got plenty, thanks. The milk and bread will do me fine. I might go up to Ben's later. He mentioned that someone was holding a barbecue."

Shut up, Valdiva. I realized I was talking too much. I was cooking up excuses I didn't need.

Mel still didn't leave.

She's seen Michaela somehow.

The smile on my face felt more unreal by the second. "Can I get you anything, Mel?"

She glanced back at the truck. I saw a young guy there. I didn't know him, but I'd seen him and Mel hand-in-hand a week or two back. Her latest flame, I guessed. He was also a pal of Crowther junior—the man who tried to rearrange my features with a hunk of firewood. Sweat trickled between my shoulder blades.

What's more, Mel wore a sudden secret smile. "Mel?" I prompted, wondering what was coming next.

"Greg." Her voice dropped. "This is something you don't want to go spreading around . . ."

She knows about the outsider in my cabin.

"Just between us, Greg, I've grown a beautiful crop of grass. Do you want some? I've got a little of the first cut in the truck."

Jesus. I thought she knew everything about Michaela, and all she was doing was pushing some homegrown narcotic. I shook my head, smiling with relief. She probably thought I was grinning like a loon.

"No, thanks, Mel," I said.

"Go on, just take a little as a gift." She leaned toward me, her eyes glittering. "You need something to help you to relax . . . you know, after what happened to Lynne."

"I'm fine," I told her in an honest-to-goodness friendly way. "Thanks, but I'm just going to get stuck into my work. That'll help best of all."

"Are you sure?"

"I'm sure, Mel. Thanks again. I appreciate it."

At last she went back to the truck. I watched her boyfriend fire up the engine and drive her away. She sounded the soul of compassion, the embodiment of neighborliness. But I recall she was one of the first to put a brick on Lynne's chest. Funny old world, huh?

That afternoon a few more people dropped by. Old man Crowther with a request for more firewood. I'd drop it off, I said. No, he said, he'd be obliged if he could take some right then, as he'd run clean out; his brother had caught a batch of fish; they were going to eat them while they were fresh. Blah, blah, blah. So I carried bundles of wood to his shiny Lexus and put them in the trunk. Miss Bertholly called. *We regret what happened on Monday,* was the gist of what she said, *but we live in extraordinary times that call for extraordinary measures to maintain our security and our safety. So, please, Mr. Valdiva. No hard feelings. We want to embrace you into our community.* . . . Blah, blah, blah.

Then Mr. Gerletz trundled by to make sure his boats were all present and correct. I thought he'd check the lone battery cruiser tied to the jetty just down from my cabin, but he lumbered by in that old pickup of his. Almost immediately after that came my twice-weekly delivery of two-stroke for Big Bertha. Gordi Harper always wore a checkered shirt like a jacket over his regular shirt, even on the hottest of days. And this was a warm one. He rolled the drum of two-stroke into the toolshed, took out the empty, then rolled it back to his truck. He waved. I waved back.

As each visitor left I shot a look up at the bedroom

window, hoping so hard it hurt inside that I wouldn't see Michaela's face in the frame. But she had a powerful streak of survival. The blinds stayed shut. She must have lain there all day, not moving, just in case a movement of air disturbed a blind or a telltale-tit creak of a floorboard might give her away.

I cut more wood. Sweating, I glared up at the sun. *Set, damn you, set.*

Tick followed by tock followed by tick. Time dragged on. Snails moved faster than those hands of my watch. All I wanted was for it to get dark. Then I could sneak Michaela into the boat, then head for Lewis. Within the hour I'd be back home in bed. God knows I was ready to sleep twelve hours straight.

At six in the evening the juice started to flow through the wires again. Now I could fix a meal without having to light the little camping stove. Not that I had anything else but the eggs, bread and milk Mel had brought earlier in the day. I saw she'd also left a bag of fresh mushrooms. That would be enough for omelets with the bread and coffee.

I made a meal, took Michaela hers which she ate in her room. There was still a chance of callers, with it being so early in the evening.

Mine, I ate on the porch, washed down with ice cold water. I still aimed to present a picture of normality. Even though the tension compressed my stomach so much I didn't want to eat much, I forced down a couple of omelets and almost half the loaf. It might be a while before I got the chance to eat again. I'd also have to find a way of replacing around two weeks' worth of food (for me, anyway) in the kitchen without drawing attention.

At close on eight I decided to check that the batteries were charging properly on the boat. All that afternoon the thought of them nagged at me. I didn't trust them. They were old. Maybe water had got into the electrics. Perhaps that's why the juice had drained from them so quickly. And why the hell hadn't I switched the boat for another? But then, that would mean hoisting the food into the replacement boat. In daylight that would be risky.

I'd reached the cabin door when I saw Ben pull up on that old 250cc dirt bike of his. He smiled when he saw me. He was still smiling when he walked up onto the porch; then the smile turned into an angry mask as he hissed. *"Greg, you idiot. They know what you're doing. The damn Guard are on their way!"*

Nineteen

"Michaela . . . Michaela!"

Heightened survival instincts made her move like a cat. In a flicker of movement she appeared on the stairs, aiming the shotgun at Ben's chest.

"Easy," I said as I grabbed a holdall. "This's Ben. He's OK."

"They know I'm here?" she asked.

"And they'll be here in around thirty seconds flat," Ben said, his hand trembling like crazy. "I was in the editor's office and saw the alert come up on the PD screen. I tore down through those woods like a demon."

"Dammit to hell." I shook my head as I grabbed the rifle from the rack. "How did they find out so fast?"

"Mel Tourney reported to old man Crowther that she thought you were acting strange."

"Figures."

"Christ, Greg." Ben watched as I scooped boxes of ammo from a drawer. "What y'gonna do, shoot your way out?"

"Not if I can help it. We've got to run for it. Ready, Michaela?"

"When you are." She moved to the doorway. "No sign of anybody yet."

"I reckon it will take them a good ten minutes to assemble and drive down here." The only road down here was a switchback track that took vehicles away from this part of the shoreline before it doubled back on itself to run alongside the lake. We might make it. Just. But there was another problem now.

"Ben, what are your plans?"

"Plans?"

"They're going to find out that you tipped me off, buddy. That's got to be a capital offense these days."

"He can come with us," Michaela said.

Quick as the old greased lightning I stuffed my file of notes and cuttings into the bag, pulled on my leather jacket, then shouldered the rifle. "Looks as if you've no choice, Ben."

Michaela called out, "I see a cloud of dust . . . yup . . . around a dozen cars coming this way."

"That'll be the Guard; make for the boat, Ben."

Ben stood there, his fingers seeming to vibrate. He'd seized up solid. "You mean leave?"

"You can't stay here, Ben, not now."

"You fucking idiot, Valdiva! You've killed us, that's what you've done! Why couldn't you leave her wherever you found her?"

I heard the roar of approaching motors. "Ben, there isn't time for this. Run. Just fucking run, will you?"

Michaela already tore down the path to the jetty.

"Oh, man, you're an insane—" Ben started saying it, but I finished it by shoving him through the screen onto the porch. "Run!"

The sight of those cars barreling down the road did it for him. He followed Michaela, running so hard his arms became a blur. Me? I didn't give my home of ten months a backward glance. With the holdall and the rifle bouncing like wild animals on my shoulder, I pounded across the dirt.

By the time I'd reached the jetty Michaela had already pulled the plug on the power cable that had been juicing the batteries. "Ben! Get the rope at the stern. . . . No, don't untie it, pull it up over the post."

The Guard were maybe half a mile away, clearly visible in the low sun that glinted like gun flashes from their windshields. They swept by bushes so fast they ripped off leaves and raised dust devils that swirled around them. I knew there'd be guys standing in the backs of the pickups, rifles cocked and ready. Jesus, this was going to be tight.

I made it to the boat's control panel in one jump that sent the whole thing tilting madly to one side.

"Careful," Ben yelled. "You'll tip us in."

"Keep your heads down!" I roared at them. "They'll blast us with everything they've got."

Sweet Jesus, I hoped those batteries had taken the charge. With the sun shining on the gauge I couldn't see whether the needle was in the red or not. One thing in our favor—you didn't have to fire up the motor like you would a diesel or gas engine. You switched the thing on like a goddam Hoover. The downside? There's always a downside, isn't there? The thing had the horsepower to match.

With the electric motor rising to a hum the boat moved away from the jetty. Slow, too damn slow. These things were built for tourists to amble around the lake while sipping Chardonnay or lazily peeling an orange.

I looked back to see the jetty moving away, the water white from the boat's propeller. Cars, pickups, a police truck with lights flashing and siren whooping raced up to the quay. Michaela and Ben squatted on their haunches watching the Guard jumping down from the pickups, then running along the jetty.

Michaela chambered a round into the shotgun and aimed.

"Keep your heads down," I shouted at the pair. "I'll take it out of sight 'round the headland."

I swung the wheel over, opened the throttle as far as it would go. On the jetty those guys were in a rage. In their eyes I was a traitor, I guess. I'd disobeyed the Caucus. I'd bought a stranger onto the island just like the old cop, Finch. But I had reasons that were good reasons. So I believed, anyway.

Then the Guard blasted us. Man, whatever they had they let fly. Even though we were more than two hundred yards out in the lake I heard a frenzy of cracks and thumps.

I threw myself into the bottom of the boat, allowing the thing to steer itself. The plastic windshield turned white as milk as buckshot tore into it. Bullets hit the hull as if a lunatic with a hammer beat it with a mad rhythm. Flakes of paint swirled all around us like snow. Michaela knelt up with the shotgun.

"Aim over their heads," Ben yelled. "I know those people."

"So why are they trying their damnedest to kill us then?" She squeezed the trigger, sending a bunch of shot back at the jetty. I saw she had aimed high. But still low enough to make the Guard duck their heads and spoil their aim. She ducked down herself behind the gunwale. "They weren't ready for this kind of shooting," she called at me. "They're armed with shotguns and handguns. They're not going to sink us with those."

Yeah, maybe. Even so, there were enough hits to bite chunks of plastic out of the case that housed the control panel. If a bullet sliced a cable we'd wind up drifting like a leaf on the water. It wouldn't be long before the Guard grabbed a boat and came out to find us.

The firing from the jetty began to falter as they emptied their guns. Now was the time to see where we were headed. I risked a look and saw we were heading straight for the rocks of the headland. I swung the boat's nose 'round and took her 'round the reef. Seconds later the tip of the headland slipped between the Guard and us.

"You can put your heads up now. They can't see us." I glanced back to see heads raised. Flecks of white paint salted Michaela's dark hair. They both looked dazed. "Are you two all right?"

They said they hadn't been hit. But I noticed Ben running trembling hands over his limbs and chest like he couldn't believe that a slug hadn't found its way through the hull to pierce a lung or arm.

The boat had taken a mauling. Thin jets of water squirted in through the hull where bullets had punctured us below the waterline. All being well, the pumps in the bilges should cope with that for the short trip to Lewis, that godforsaken ghost town.

Come to think of it, the place was no fair exchange for Sullivan, with its bars, diners, stores and warehouses bulging with food. But I'd made my bed, as my mother would have said. Time to go lie in it.

The only sting of regret? Yeah, there was one: looking back at the headland to see the mound of milk-white stones that marked the graves of Chelle and Mom, I knew I'd never be able to visit them again.

After a while I swung the boat so its nose pointed across the lake to Lewis. Even though the sun shone I saw what a forbidding place it was. Skeletons of blackened buildings. Ghostly dark voids behind shattered windows. Streets lousy with human skulls where a peeled human face might roll by in the breeze like a tumbleweed. Boy, oh boy. It looked like the 'burbs of hell.

Twenty

Ben hated it; you could see that. He helped pass the supplies to where I stood at the bottom of the harbor steps, but he hated it. The idea of being in Lewis terrified him. Being in the company of a stranger sweated him with fear. He kept shooting looks back across at Sullivan with its tennis courts, neatly trimmed lawns, comfortable homes, supermarkets and ordered lives.

I nodded across the water. "You can't go back there, Ben, you know that?"

Again he shot a longing look at the tidy little town on the far side of the lake. I suddenly had a mental image of him taking the wheel of the boat and powering home. But he shook his head, his expression worried as hell. "I know," he said. "Here, don't forget your rifle."

"Thanks." Then I looked at Michaela. "We won't be able to carry all this food at once."

"I'll go ahead with Ben, then bring back help."

Ben nodded, that expression of uncertainty pasted all over his face. Walking through a burned-out city

ruin with a stranger for company must have been as
appealing to him as stepping out through hell with Satan on his arm. Like a man going to his execution he
walked up the steps (taking them one unhappy riser at
a time). "It's the first time I've been off the island in
more than six months," he admitted. "It feels weird."

"You'll get used to it," Michaela told him crisply.
"You got a gun?"

"No."

A gun in Ben's hands with those twitchy fingers?

"We'll have a spare you can have."

"Well, I don't use guns. I don't think I'd—"

"You've got to, buddy. If you want to last more than
a day out here."

His look of uncertainty darkened into one I'd call
depression. He appeared to me a man on a suicide
mission. Before he picked up a sack of cans he shot
me a glare that as good as said *Valdiva, you moron. How
could you do this to me?*

Michaela paid no attention. Turning to me, she
jerked her head in the direction of Sullivan. "You think
those guys will follow us across here?"

"I doubt it," Ben said with feeling.

I shook my head. "Unlikely. They're terrified of contamination. And like Ben, they've lost the knack of leaving the place."

"Yeah, I lost the knack," he muttered under his
breath. "Lost it big time when everyone started dying."

"Greg," she said, "you best sit tight here and guard
the food."

Ben looked 'round at the dead tomb of a town.
"Guard the food? You think there are actually people
here who'd try and take it."

"I don't think," she told him. *"I know."*

"Jesus."

"Stick close to me." Shouldering a holdall that

159

clanked with cans, she rested the shotgun barrel on her other shoulder. Safety off, I noticed.

"We'll be back in twenty minutes," she told me; then, with Ben following, his head turning this way and that as he anxiously scanned the wrecked buildings, they walked away.

So I sat there in the ghost town with the sun going down. Shadows crept along the street like the buildings themselves bled darkness. It oozed over sidewalks, joined with more pools of shade and crept toward me. Cool air moved in from the lake. When the shadows crawled over me at last the chill of the evening slithered over my skin. Silence oozed in with the coming gloom. Even the birds stopped their chirping. I began to notice the smell, too. That compost smell that made you think of mushrooms, damp basements and decay.

Twenty minutes became half an hour. Still no sign of Michaela or her people to collect the supplies. *They're not coming back, Valdiva. . . . Face it, you're alone.*

To close off the thought I checked that the rifle was loaded (even though I knew it was), then counted how many cartons of shells I'd stuffed into the bag. Nine cartons. That should be ample for a while.

I stared along the street, expecting to see Michaela or Ben turn the corner at any second. As I stared I suddenly had this sensation of cool air playing on the back of my neck.

Someone's behind you.

I twisted fast to see who was there. Maybe Crowther junior couldn't resist making the trip across the water to blow off my head when I wasn't looking. Instead of Crowther leering down a rifle at me I saw a rat slinking through all that crud on the ground. It must have gotten the scent of the food I'd brought. Its claws rustled shreds of paper. When I stood up it disappeared under a burnt-out truck.

Forty minutes had crawled by since Michaela and

Ben had left. Maybe she'd need to find her people if they'd relocated in the last twenty-four hours. That yard where they were camping was hardly the lap of luxury. They might have found a house somewhere that hadn't been trashed.

Darkness was coming down a storm now. Clouds ballooned over the horizon to bury the sun as it rested on the hills. Soon nothing remained but a bloody smear of red across the western quarter of the sky. It grew cooler. I zipped up my leather jacket, then shivered to the roots of my bones. Now I found I couldn't sit still. I paced the stretch of road where we'd stacked the food supplies. A police car rotted by the ferry terminal. Another rat sat in the back seat cleaning its whiskers. Across in Sullivan the town lights burned bright. Even though it wasn't much more than three miles away, now it could have been on Neptune. Ben and I wouldn't be welcomed back there with open arms for sure. In fact, it was my guess that the Caucus would issue an order that we be shot on sight if we even came within spitting distance of the place.

With the barrel of the rifle resting on my shoulder I nosed into the abandoned ticket hall of the ferry office (bread bandits had even torn the carpets up), then I crossed the street to look into what remained of a general store (nothing but empty boxes and baby bones). Next to it was a hotel that seemed pretty much intact. A canvas awning projected over the sidewalk. It looked dirty but otherwise undamaged. I began to ask myself if this would serve as a place to stay until we decided what we should do next.

I backstepped into the road, looking up at the six-storied building. Its facade could have been a tear-stained face. Rain teamed with soot from the fires that destroyed most of Lewis to create the illusion. Black bands ran down from each window. A pretty little bitch she wasn't, but she might do for we poor waifs and strays who had no roof over our heads. Hell, even the glass in the windows was intact. And get this; this was the odd thing. All the glass in the windows must have been set at a certain precise angle because as I looked up into the dark face of the building I could see my reflection in a dozen or more windows.

I gazed up, and my reflection gazed down with a wide-eyed intensity that—

Shit. Those aren't reflections, Valdiva.

There, looking down at me, with a silent, brooding intensity, were men's faces. There was something alien about the way they didn't move. Only their eyes moved to follow me as I, not taking my eyes off them, edged slowly away.

Only when I had moved out of their line of sight did I turn my back on them. Then I moved quickly—but not running, not looking scared—because if I ran, a little bird with terrible frightened eyes told me, that would provoke those guys in the hotel into chasing me.

Ahead of me a group of men blocked my way. Pulling back the rifle bolt, I raised the muzzle, aimed.

"Greg. Whoa . . . it's us. Don't shoot. *Don't shoot.*"

I wiped the perspiration from my eyes to see Ben waving his hands above his head. With him were the people I'd seen yesterday, including Michaela. The others were more interested in the food bags. They hurried forward to drop down onto their knees, where they rooted through the supplies like excited kids at Christmas rifling through their stockings.

"Corned beef . . . hey, tinned chili."

"Bread! Beautiful white bread!"

"Creamed chicken."

"Get a load of this, tinned peaches. Wow!"

Heart thumping, I ran up to Michaela. "Get your people to pick up this stuff, then get out of here."

"Greg, give them a minute or two to enjoy this, can't you? They haven't seen food like—"

"Michaela, get these people away from here!"

Instinct kicked in. She glanced 'round, her senses suddenly razor sharp. "What's wrong?"

"There's a bunch of people in a building back there."

"They look like hornets?"

Ben frowned. "What the hell are hornets?"

"Bread bandits."

"Oh, shit."

Michaela slipped the shotgun from her shoulder. "They see you?"

I nodded. "But they didn't seem to be in any rush to follow me."

"If they stayed put we should have time to get away. They're probably guarding a hive."

The memory of that thing I found in the apartment came back to me like a bad taste in my mouth. "You mean there are more of those things 'round here?"

"Hives? Yes, probably dozens in a place this size."

"Hornets? Hives?" Ben looked bewildered. "What are you guys talking about?"

I said, "Hell on Earth. That's what we're talking about, Ben. Hell on Earth."

Twenty-one

We carried the supplies through darkened streets. Zak led the way, almost smelling the air for trouble. I counted ten in Michaela's gang. They were all young and I couldn't place anyone over the age of twenty. The youngest was the kid I'd first clapped eyes on when I arrived in Sullivan after my drinking binge (and who I nearly killed). He'd have been around ten years old.

As I walked I held this whispered conversation with Michaela. Ben tried to follow what we were talking about, although his expression, one that bonded fear and bewilderment, told me he understood precious little.

"Those hornets in the hotel," I said, "they were guarding a hive?"

"I don't want to see for myself, but my guess is that they are."

"They won't follow us?"

"Some of them might."

"While the rest guard the hive?"

"That's about the size of it."

"But hornets don't as a rule carry firearms, so we should be all right."

"I'm glad you're confident."

"Meaning?"

"Meaning if twenty or thirty jump us we won't have the firepower to kill them all fast enough. Some might get through. They'll have machetes, clubs, wrenches, knives."

"You've lost people before like this?"

"Greg, when we started out our group numbered more than thirty. We're down to ten. See?"

I nodded. "But the hive I found . . . I didn't see any hornets. Why wasn't it guarded like that one back there?"

Even under the burden of bags she shrugged. "A tainted hive."

"You mean they go bad somehow? Or become corrupted?"

"Your guess is as good as mine, Greg. We've found hives with a couple of hundred hornets guarding them. They must be the really important ones. Usually the guards number between twenty and thirty. Then again . . ." She shrugged. "Sometimes there are none. It's as if the hive's gone wrong and they abandon it."

"What actually is a hive, then? What's its purpose?"

She smiled. "Questions, questions. I don't know, Greg. We don't have any professors of biology here, or even a two-bit test-tube jock. We're just a bunch of kids trying to keep on the warm side of the grave. You follow?"

"But it's just this hive. The smell of it, and how it looked . . ."

"You're right. They're weird. They're also a God almighty mystery. . . ." She looked at me with a sudden sharpness, as if she'd read something in my expression. "What else is there, Greg?"

A strange churning sensation had started in my

165

head. "I can't explain it. . . . I know it's impossible, but these hives . . . I think I've seen one before."

Back at the yard that served as the makeshift camp Michaela had a hurried conversation with Zak and Tony. Then she came across to where Ben and I sat by the fire. "We'll move on at first light," she told us. "You best get some sleep now."

Ben cast some pretty scared-looking glances out into the darkness. "What about the bread bandits, I—I mean hornets? Won't they come looking for us?"

"It's unlikely at night. But we'll be taking turns to keep watch. Yours will be between two and three. So get some sleep now."

He looked startled that he'd be expected to keep watch.

"Don't worry," she told him, "just keep your wits about you, then shout as loud as you can if you see anything. Think you can handle that?"

"Don't worry." He looked scared sick. "If I see anything you'll hear me yell, all right."

She added, "We've already loaded the bikes now so we can be away fast."

"You've got bikes?"

"A nice pack of Harley Ds. We found them in a dealer's showroom a couple of months ago." She shot me a grin. "You didn't think we walked everywhere, did you?" With that she pushed back her hair and lay down on a blanket. "By the way, Greg, take the watch after Ben's." She grinned again. "Sweet dreams."

Yeah. As if.

Twenty-two

"One thing we don't have," Michaela said the next morning (after a quiet night, thank God), "is a spare machine. You and Ben will have to ride double."

The bikes looked in good shape, despite the burden of supplies they carried either strapped over fuel tanks, or in a trailer pulled by one monster of a Harley D that Zak rode. I saw the ten-year-old hop onto the trailer like he was riding on the back of a camel.

Ben went up to sit behind Tony. Michaela tied back her hair. "You can ride with me."

I slipped the rifle across my shoulder. "Where are we headed?"

"Away from here's the main priority." She patted the bike's fuel tank. "But we're getting low on gas. We need to nose out a new supply. Luckily these things are pretty . . . shit, Greg, what are you doing?"

I did it in one movement. Slid the rifle from my shoulder, pulled the bolt, aimed, fired. Boy, the sound cracked back from the walls.

Grunting like a wild pig, the man charged from the

bushes at the side of the yard. I chambered another round—*tried* to chamber another round—but the little fuck jammed. Zak and Tony moved fast, pulling guns from holsters. Only they couldn't shoot because Michaela and I were in the firing line. The grunting guy moved faster—*helluva lot faster*—eyes blazing with pure ferocity. He bore down on where Michaela sat astride the Harley.

I cursed, jerking the rifle bolt, trying to clear the bastard so I could fire again.

With a grunt that became a full-blooded groan the guy flopped forward, smacking his face into the dirt. He didn't get up. Come to that, he didn't move; he didn't breathe.

I saw the exit wound between his shoulder blades where my bullet had tumbled out at the speed of sound.

"Nice shot," she said to me in such a matter-of-fact way she could have been complimenting me on my taste in coffee. "But don't stand there all day. We need to be moving."

There was no fuss or excitement with these guys. They'd seen it all before. For Ben and me this was something different. Bread bandit, hornet or just a poor goddam refugee with a bad case of the Jumpy—stick him with any name you want, this was the guy I'd just shot through the lungs the second he rushed from the bushes. I hoped my instincts always stayed as keen as that. Hell . . . in the back of my mind I couldn't help but wonder what I'd do if any of these people who had somehow adopted Ben and me came down with a case of the Jumpy. Especially Michaela. What would I do if I found myself looking at her down the barrel of a gun?

"See?" Michaela called back over her shoulder as we rode through the forest. "We didn't choose the bikes for their looks. Short of using a battle tank, they're the only thing that'll get you through this crap."

She wasn't wrong. The roads were totally crapped out. Every few yards there'd be a car or a truck or a bus lying rotting to hell. Many were at the roadside; others spanned the entire highway like they'd been deliberately employed as roadblocks, something that might not be far from the truth. Then there was the usual mess of broken bottles, boxes, fallen trees, human remains. What seemed odd was that skeletons could rot clean of meat and skin, but the clothes didn't decompose as fast, so you'd find endless sets of articulated human bone still dressed in pants, jackets and shoes, complete with battery-powered watches on bone wrists that had quietly ticked off the seconds all these months. Anyway there was our band weaving 'round the obstacles on the bikes, heading south through the wooded hills in a loose convoy to God alone knew where.

God alone knew where wound up being a barn on a hillside that overlooked a cluster of lakes. The barn looked untouched since the day of the Fall. At one end bales of straw nearly reached the eaves, while a red tractor stood under a coat of dust at the other end.

"I'll do the usual," Tony said before opening the throttle on the bike and tearing off across the field.

Michaela unbuckled the straps that held the supplies on the back of the trailer. "We've got this like clockwork," she told me. "Tony's checking to make sure that there are no hornets in the neighborhood. We make the camp, build a fire, cook up a meal if we've food for the pot. You can help Boy collect firewood. Make sure you take your gun. We still don't know if we've got company out here."

Everyone knew their job. Everyone worked quickly. They brought the bikes into the barn (out of sight of any hornets who might amble by). Zak got to work with a can opener, opening tins of corned beef fresh from my cabin larder, dumping the blocks of pink meat into a big cooking pot. I saw him for the first time without that cowboy hat. Even though he'd just turned eighteen there wasn't a hair on his head. He didn't even possess eyebrows. Shock does weird things to people. Like Boy, who I'd been assigned to help collect firewood (yeah, I was the firewood guy again; there must be something in the way I walked that always got me that particular chore). Boy must have gone through plenty of bad stuff after the Fall. Bad enough to make him ditch his name and kill his old identity as if that might be enough to rid him of all the bad memories, too.

The noonday sun had burned through the cloud and it was really starting to heat up. I slipped on my sunglasses. The barn was well and truly in the middle of nowhere, with nothing but grass fields all around that had grown straggly and weed infested all these months without farmer intervention. There were no houses I could see. There wasn't much in the way of trees to conceal any hornets. Even so, I checked that the rifle's magazine carried a full load of shells.

Boy walked fast, with his jaw jutted forward. He scanned the ground with what your schoolteacher would have called a "practiced eye." "Pick sticks for kindling and thicker stuff for a slow burn," he told me. Told me? Ordered me, more like. But he seemed like a good kid to me. He was just doing the job that kept him and his bunch of buddies alive. "No, don't bother with green wood," he said as I picked up a branch. "Go for dry stuff. It doesn't make as much smoke. That fence over there: Go rip out some palings; they'll burn good. You hungry?"

"Yes."

"Always eat as much as you can at meal times. You never know when your next meal's gonna be." He picked dry sticks out of the grass. "I like chocolate. But you don't find chocolate these days. When it was my eighth birthday I got a chocolate car. As big as that." He held his hands more than a foot apart. "It was a Formula One racing car. I ate chocolate every day for two weeks."

"Who gave you it? Your parents?"

"Did they, hell. Have you got any chocolate?"

"No, I had to bring the boring stuff like dried pasta, flour, rice, canned meat, salt and—"

"You didn't have chocolate in that place you lived? Michaela said you'd got food coming out ya ass."

"I guess she was right, but I didn't have time to bring any chocolate."

"But you had chocolate in that place?"

"Yes. But I guess that will run out some day, along with coffee and other stuff they can't produce locally. They'll have to make do with—"

"I'm going there."

"You want to go to Sullivan?"

"Yeah, if they've got chocolate."

"I wouldn't recommend it."

"Why not?"

"They're frightened of strangers."

"I'm just a kid. I'm ten."

"They still won't let you in."

"Yeah, the bastards. They don't want to give away the chocolate. Do they have huge shakes? I used to have a shake maker. You put milk in the top and chocolate powder, then pressed a button and chocolate shake came out through a pipe. It buzzed so loud you thought your teeth would come out. They'll have chocolate shakes in Sullivan, won't they?" In the grass lay a skeleton wearing striped pajamas. Angrily, he kicked the skull from the shoulder bones. Suddenly, in my mind's eye, I saw the farmer coming out here to check his precious cows. It's late. He's still in his pajamas. But he's heard that hornets are on the rampage nearby. His wife begs him not to do it, but he's desperate to make sure his animals are safe. In this field some hornets jump him and batter the shit out of him, leaving him to die in his blood-soaked PJs with the funky stripes.

Then ten months later an angry kid with a candy craving kicks the poor bastard's skull clean off. Funny old world, huh?

Like a darting insect Boy snatched sticks from the ground.

"Don't forget the fence," he said without looking at me. "Get as many palings as you can carry."

I kicked off the palings, then gathered them up as best I could with the rifle slipping forward off my shoulder. Sweating in the sun, we made our way back to the barn. "Remember the thing we found in the apartment?"

He didn't answer. He walked sullenly with his arms stretched 'round a huge bundle of sticks.

"It was an ugly bitch, wasn't it?" I said, trying to get him to speak.

Boy still kept clammed tight.

"You said it was a hive. Have you seen them before?"

"Yeah, lots." He spoke as if he didn't want to go into detail.

"Do you know what they are?"

"Yeah."

"What are they?"

"They're trouble. Capital *T* Trouble. You just want to stay clear of them. Once . . . once I saw them suck a girl dry. Sue and me went into this house and opened a bathroom door, just like you did in the apartment." His eyes became glistening and wet-looking. From not wanting to talk at all the words started to shoot out like he was spitting them because they tasted bad in his mouth. "We'd just gone in there because we thought there'd be food in the kitchen. We hadn't eaten for days. 'Course the bastards had cleaned out the cupboards, but we found this little piece of chocolate in the back of the refrigerator. Just one little square. Sue cut it in half and we licked it so we could make it last a long time. God, it tasted lovely. Really lovely." He licked his lips. "I can taste it now. Then we went upstairs to see if there was anything worth taking, or if someone had hidden any food. Sue was twenty. She only kept one thing from home. It was gold medal she'd won for running. She told me it was because she could run so fast that she was still alive. She could run faster than the hornets. Then she opened the bathroom door. And there was all this pink stuff like in the apartment. She wasn't afraid; she looked into it . . . you know? Really into it, like she was looking into a pool of water. She said she could see hands and arms and legs and things. But then she screamed. She was shouting that it had got hold of her face. I don't know how, but her face was stuck to it. I tried to get her away, but it held on to her; it glued her there or something. I couldn't run away. I don't know why, but I just stood there. . . . I thought it would let her go after a while. But then I saw these things come through that jelly, like they were swimming through it. They came right up to her. I was there for hours. I watched as they sucked everything out of her. She wrinkled up and just kept getting smaller, like she was a balloon that was going down bit by bit. That thing sucked her dry! That's what hives do. They'll suck me dry if they get me."

"You mean the hive sucked the blood out of her?"

He looked at me in fury. "Why did you have to go talking about it? I didn't want to remember! You dirty rotten bastard! I'm going to tell Michaela about what you've gone and done to me!"

With that he ran back to the barn. But he kept clinging to that bundle of sticks like a lost child clinging to a teddy bear.

Twenty-three

"What did you have to go upsetting the kid for?" Zak's bald head turned pink. He glared at me. And with those eyes that had no eyebrows, no eyelashes, there was a snakelike quality to his looks. To top it all off, the angry way he locked his eyes onto me made me think of a rattlesnake getting ready to strike.

"I didn't intend to upset Boy. I was only talking to him."

"About what?"

"I asked him if he knew anything about these hives."

"What did you have to cross-examine the kid about it for? Why didn't you ask me or Tony or Michaela? Why interrogate a little kid?"

We were standing arguing in the barn. Michaela stood with her arms 'round Boy while he hid his face in her chest. He might have been crying, but I couldn't tell.

"I'm sorry," I said, but my tone was angry rather than remorseful.

"You should be sorry." Michaela's expression was

pretty ferocious, too. "Dear God, Valdiva, don't you think we've all been pushed to the edge here? We're hanging on by our fingernails above an almighty crevasse. We don't need you blundering 'round pounding questions at us."

"But you said that if I got you the food, you'd tell me—"

"Tell you about the hive? Yes, I will, but when we're ready." Then she added in a way that was stiff and formal-sounding, "And thank you for the food. Just in case you think we haven't been grateful enough."

I shook my head. "I didn't know I was gonna upset the kid. Like I said, I was just talking to him."

Zak shot me a suddenly shrewd look. "Why're you so fascinated with the hive?"

I shrugged. "Just curious, I suppose. I've never seen anything like it before." The moment I spoke the words I felt those cold spider feet across my back. *I've never seen anything like it before.* Why did that sentence feel like a lie in my mouth? And why was I so curious about the hive? OK, it was bizarre. Something completely alien. But when I thought about the hive it worked its way under my skin. It became an itch I wanted to scratch. I don't know why, but I wanted to find out more. Maybe deep down I was getting obsessive about it. Unhealthily obsessive at that.

Ben stood by the tractor while this fiery scene played itself out. His hands trembled, his face the picture of unhappiness. You could tell he didn't want to be here with a gang of strangers. He didn't like their straggly hair. He detested their worn-out clothes. He despised the gaunt faces hardened by hunger and daily battles for survival. Old Ben, my buddy of nine months, hated everything; was scared of everything. All he craved right now was to be home in Sullivan.

Michaela looked at me. She seemed calmer. "We'll talk about the Hive when we've finished establishing the camp. People need to eat and rest first. You get to learn what your priorities—Greg? Where are you going?"

I was pissed. But was I pissed at them? Or at the little kid who ran back blabbing like he was going to tell his mom because I'd played rough with him? Or was I pissed at myself for maybe lacking tact? Maybe I thought that when I delivered food to this bunch they'd sit down to explain what the hive was. So was I pissed at not getting the answers I expected? Because there was something about the hive. It was more than the shock—and disgust—of seeing that repulsive thing. There was something else I just couldn't put my finger on. Like seeing a face in a crowd that you're sure you've seen before. You find yourself ransacking your memory for a name. It bugs you. You keep thinking about it. *Oh, hell, Valdiva, go do something useful.*

I walked uphill from the barn through blazing sunlight. Passed the striped pajamas that skeleton boy was wearing. Then I kicked the crap out of the fence. I was telling myself I was procuring a little more firewood. The truth? I poured my anger and frustrations into that fence through the steel toe cap of my boot. *Pow!* A paling burst into splinters. *Crash!* A post snapped in two. *Crack!* A railing busted to hell.

Anger roared through my blood. Why did the nice bastards of Sullivan murder Lynne? Why did they have to be so fucking brutal they crushed the life out of her? Why did the whole town participate? Why did they keep their smiling heads stuck in the goddam sand? Why did they pretend that they could keep their little isolated society running like it always had forever? Didn't they know that somewhere down the line, in ten or twenty years, the gasoline would run out? And sure as hell they'd run out of canned food long before then, or it would eventually spoil in the tins. They were like Adolf Hitler in his bunker way back, when he sent orders to armies that no longer existed and the Russians were overrunning Berlin. Sullivan shut out the inevitable. They were like people suffering from terminal cancer who were saving for a retirement condo they'd never live to see.

I kicked the fence so hard sparks flew from my boot where it struck a nail.

And I knew I was angry because I'd gotten Ben into this. He should be at home writing stories for the newspaper while listening to his Jimi Hendrix albums.

"Are you planning on knocking every fence down, or do you intend to stop when you reach Wyoming?"

I looked up to see Zak watching me. He wore a pistol pushed into the belt of his pants.

"Valdiva, it's not a good idea to go off by yourself without a gun."

"It's not a good idea to shove the gun into your pants like that. You might blow your dick off."

"It hasn't happened yet."

"*Yet.*"

He watched me, his hairless head looking as shiny as a pool ball in the sun. "You must be angrier at us than we thought."

"I'm not angry. I'm collecting more firewood."

"What are you going to do? Roast a cow?"

"Might as well get a good supply."

"Rule number one: prioritize. Don't do work that isn't absolutely necessary."

"Don't worry, I'm learning fast."

His unwavering stare fixed on me. "Valdiva, you've got plenty to learn. This world out here's completely different from that island. This world is never safe. There's never enough food. There are no certainties." He shrugged. "With the exception of hunger and death. If we see one hornet there's sure to be more of them. So we move on."

"It looks quiet enough 'round here."

"Take my word for it, they'll come. It's like they can smell us."

I began gathering the wood into a neat pile I could carry. "You should find yourself an island. There are plenty in the lakes 'round here."

"But they don't have big stores of food. We've got to keep moving from place to place to find supplies."

"Nomads, eh?"

"We're not nomads for fun, you know? We're dog-tired, but we've got to keep moving. Finding food. Finding fuel. Looking for fresh water. Running from the crazy guys." He smiled. "So there's no wonder we're grouchy. It must feel like you're walking on eggshells when you're with us."

I didn't answer but collected the wood, then used the skeleton's stripy PJ pants to tie the wood into a bundle. Zak watched me for a while, then said, "We might look like a bunch of misfits, but we're close. Probably closer than most families get in a whole life-time. So if one of us is hurt we all feel hurt. Boy's endured tough stuff. We get protective over him. We really care about each other, but that might seem dopey to you. But to risk repeating myself, I'm closer to these people than my own family. And as a family we Samuels were pretty close. Even if I did give my mother and father a hard time. My father ran a health insurance business in Canada, so we lived in Toronto most of the year. Thing is, my parents wanted me so much to become a rabbi, so they sent me to Hebrew school in New York. From the age of eleven I was flying back and forth on my own. I did well academically, but I wanted to be a stand-up comic. That's what I loved doing. I loved to make people laugh. When I was six-teen I'd sneak off to a little comedy bar just off Broad-way where you could put your name down for a five-minute spot on stage. They called it the Kamikaze because you had to be suicidal to stand there in front of a bunch of New Yorkers and try to make them laugh. Boy, they could give you heat if you sucked. So what I'd do is this." He bunched his fist, then put it into his pocket. "I'd say, 'Ladies and gentlemen, I have very funny jokes for you tonight. You must laugh because I have a cute little puppy in my coat pocket. If you don't laugh I will squeeze its throat with my hand. Right, this is joke number one. Yesterday, I went to see my doctor. I told him I keep thinking I'm a moth. The doctor said, So why did you come to see me, then? I replied, I couldn't help myself. I saw your light in the window.' Then I'd glare at the audience with a real look of irritation. 'I don't hear you laughing,' I'd say. 'Listen, I warned you, didn't I?' Then I'd pretend to squeeze the imaginary puppy in my pocket and make these crying puppy sounds, you know like a ventriloquist? Without moving my lips? Well, the puppy in the pocket routine worked like a charm. I got loads of laughs and bookings, but then it all went bad. Some construction workers came in for a beer but left their sense of humor back home. They got really angry and started yelling that I shouldn't be hurting the puppy in my pocket. That's when I got cute and told them that if they didn't stop heckling me I'd squeeze the goddam puppy until its eyes popped."

I found myself smiling. "What then?"

"They ran up on the stage to free the puppy . . . my beautiful, fluffy, *imaginary* puppy. 'It's not real, it's not real,' I screamed at them. *Really* screamed, because they were big guys, with stronger muscles in their eyelids than I'd got in my entire body. And they're yelling, 'You've got a puppy in your coat because we hear it yelping in pain.' I decided it was a good time to leave. As they grabbed me by the coat I slipped out of it and ran as hard as I could. It was a month before I went back. I never used the puppy routine again." He grinned. "No, sir. I used an imaginary kitten instead."

I found myself laughing. Zak joined in with the kind of chuckle that makes you want to laugh even more.

Then, wiping his eyes, he said, "Let me give you a hand with that firewood. The food should be ready anyway and I'm starving. So, Greg? Are you going to come quietly?" He bunched his fist in his pocket. "Or do I have to torture this cute little puppy?" *Without* moving his lips he made pained, whiney sounds in the back of his throat.

I couldn't keep the grin from my face. "OK, OK, I'm coming."

Chatting easily now, we carried the firewood down to the barn. Things had lightened up down there. Tony had lit a fire. The sun shone in a perfect sky. Michaela and Boy threw a Frisbee to one another, and I saw Michaela call to Ben to join in. He caught the Frisbee and spun it back to Boy. When Boy easily plucked it out of the air his laughter carried across the field.

Michaela must have worked her magic to cheer up the kid. That image of a few carefree moments stayed with me. It wasn't always going to be like that. You know as well as I do, when life starts to look nice and easy that's the time you really should start to worry.

Twenty-four

"Watch and learn, Valdiva . . . I'm going to show you how to make bread. Our kind of bread, that is, so it won't come in a fancy wrapper." Tony called across to Ben, "You best watch, too. You'll be on bread duty in a day or so."

Ben joined us at the fire that burned just outside the doorway of the barn. Sitting in the fire was an oven that looked to be made out of a steel toolbox. Soot encrusted the thing to hell and back—pretty it wasn't. I'd seen Tony unloading the contraption from the bike trailer earlier. The others in the group were busy with their own chores: checking bikes, pumping tires, cleaning spark plugs, oiling firearms. Some sat in the shade fixing worn or torn clothes with needle and thread. A fifteen-year-old with bleached dreadlocks hammered tiny nails into the heel of his boot where it flapped loose. Only Zak took it easy. He'd climbed up onto the bales of hay where he'd fallen into a corpselike sleep with the black Stetson over his face. We could hear his snores from here.

STRANGER

Tony used a box lid to fan the flames until the embers burned white beneath the makeshift oven. "Stand the oven on stones or bricks or whatever's at hand so there's a gap between the bottom of it and the ground. The heat needs to be drawn through there to get it good and hot. You see? OK. Now you scoop a jug full of this flour from the red tub into the mixing bowl. Then replace the tub lid straightaway, because someone always winds up putting their foot in it and knocking it over. And flour is like gold dust these days." He picked up a tin mug. "Now use this to add two mugs of water. Add a good pinch of salt. Mix the flour, water and salt together. When it's the consistency of mud start kneading it with your hands."

Ben frowned. "When do you add the yeast?"

"We've got no yeast. We've never had yeast."

"What makes it rise, then?"

"It doesn't. This is the kind of bread they'd make in the old, old days. You know, Bible days? Ancient Egypt days? That's right, guys, we're living in the past. OK, it's flat as your grandma's pancakes, it tastes bland as toilet paper, but it fills that hole in your stomach."

Ben caught my eye. I knew what he was thinking. That to survive we were going to endure some Stone Age living conditions.

Tony continued. "When you've kneaded the dough, break it up into small patties about the size and shape of a hamburger—economy-size hamburger, that is. After that, put them on this tray and into the oven for thirty minutes. There," he said like a TV cook, sliding the tray with its cargo of dough lumps into the oven. "Nothing to it, is there?" He shot us a grin. "Of course the first half dozen or so times you do this you'll make a king-sized mess of it. You'll burn the bread one day. The next it'll come out raw. You'll drop the dough into the dirt and everyone will get mad at you." Smiling, he

183

shook his head. "I should know, it happened to me plenty, but you'll get used to it."

"I don't think I want to get used to it," Ben said.

"It's that or go hungry."

These people had got a little industry running like a finely tuned motor. Of course, what that industry produced was survival—survival one day at a time. Here they all were, busily keeping their bikes running, their clothes mended, making enough food to fill their bellies. It was an industry hanging by a thread. Call me pessimistic, but I wondered what happened when they ran out of gas for the bikes or flour for the bread.

Tony left me in charge of watching over the bread in the oven (it needed careful feeding with thin sticks of firewood, then fanning with the speed of a lunatic to keep the heat up). He took Ben across to the bikes, where he showed him how to ride the big Harley. A few of the others gathered 'round, amused when it appeared that Ben would fall off. Little did they know he was an expert on that old dirt bike of his, and he soon mastered the machine.

I broke sticks, eased them into the embers. I blew on the fire to get it blazing, then fanned it with my hand, which was pretty hopeless really. Soon my fingers felt as if they'd fly off from the knuckles, I was fanning that frantically.

"What are you doing, Valdiva? You look as if you're spanking the invisible man."

"I might as well be, for all the good I'm doing." I squinted up into the sun to see Michaela standing there, watching me with obvious amusement.

"Here, this might be better." She offered me a piece of stiff card.

"Thanks."

"Are you getting the hang of it?"

"Making bread?" I shrugged. "So far so good. How's Boy?"

"He's fine now. But as you see it doesn't take much to upset him. His nerves are still raw after what happened to his sister."

"The girl was his sister? I didn't know."

Michaela sat on the ground beside me. She nibbled a shoot of grass, the tip of her tongue every now and again touching the stem as she tasted sweet sap. "He'd been living rough with his sister for a while. We don't know how long exactly because he refuses to say anything about his past or where he was from, or even to admit what he's really called. We found him in the house where his sister had been killed by the hive."

"You mean he was living there?"

Her expression was grim. "Not living there. He'd just laid down at the top of the stairs. He'd have died if we hadn't found him when we did. In fact, he was so dehydrated we thought we were going to lose him anyway."

"Poor kid."

"It was the shock, I guess. Seeing what that thing did to his own flesh and blood."

"What did it do to her?"

She fixed me with those eyes that were so dark I'd swear they were black as coal. "You'll keep asking me about the hive, won't you? You're never going to give up."

"You said you'd tell me everything."

"In exchange for the food."

"Things have moved on since then. The way I look at it now, Ben and I are going to be dependent on you for survival, aren't we?"

"More wood?"

"Huh?"

She nodded at the fire. "You've got to keep feeding the fire with sticks, otherwise the bread won't bake properly."

I broke more sticks and pushed them into the embers while she fanned the flame with the card. "I will tell you about the hive, but I've got something to confess."

"Oh?"

"I know precious little. I knew you were keen . . . well, almost lusting after information about the hive would be more accurate. I'm afraid I exploited your curiosity to get food." She gave an apologetic smile. "I figured you might not deliver the food if I didn't have some lever on you."

"But you know something?"

"A little. Not much." She gave me a sideways look. "At least not enough to satisfy your curiosity."

"OK, cough up what you do know."

"You've got a charming turn of phrase, Valdiva. You know that?"

I shrugged at the same moment that I heard cheers and applause. Ben rode 'round the barn, his face blazing with the sheer joy of mastering the monster bike. When he returned to the others they slapped him on the back and rubbed his hair. He grinned back at the mass of grinning faces as he killed the motor.

I turned back to Michaela and smiled. "OK. The hive. What is it?"

"We're going to wind up calling you Mr. Persistence." Despite affecting a weary sigh, she nodded. "OK. About three months after the Fall, our group picked up a warning on a CB radio. Someone—we don't know who—warned everyone who'd listen to him to beware of something he called a hive. When he described a hive—that it looked like a mass of goo filled with human body parts hanging suspended like pieces of fruit in strawberry Jell-O—we pretty much wrote him off as drunk or crazy." She gazed into the fire as she fanned the flames, but I could see she was seeing something terrible in her mind's eye. "The first time we saw a hive was when we found Boy. We were searching houses for food. Of course they were all abandoned by that time. And the hornets had started their destructive rampage. You see, after they killed everyone that didn't have Jumpy they went back and destroyed all their possessions. You might have missed it if you were holed up on that island. The hornets would go into a house, take all the food for themselves and then they'd just smash everything, tear clothes to pieces, or they'd just torch the place. I think military people call it 'scorched earth policy.' You destroy anything and everything that might be of use to your enemy." She took a breath. "So we went into the house where we found Boy. That's when we saw the hive and what it had done to his sister."

"What had it done?"

"Sucked her dry, Greg. If you ask me those things are like vampires. They batten onto people, only I don't know how they do it. Maybe with some kind of teeth in the gel or disgusting tubes that burrow into the people it catches. Then it draws the blood right out of them. We've seen it again since. Victims look like pieces of dried fruit. Their faces become wrinkled and ridged like raisins, which sounds like a funny description, funny ha ha, but it's not. If you saw for yourself you know how sickening it is. You want to puke when you look into those dried-up faces. Even their eyes shrivel."

"What is a hive?"

"I don't know," she said, fanning the flames faster, as if trying to waft those mental images away. "Some disgusting parasite, maybe."

"But you said that bread bandits—I mean hornets—guard them."

"Mostly . . . not always." Despite the heat I saw goosebumps pucker the skin of her arms. "We decided we had to destroy them. The one that killed Boy's sister we burned with gasoline. Where they were guarded by hornets we picked off the guards with our rifles, then torched the hive."

"What stopped you killing more?"

"Because there were so many of them. We only had limited amounts of ammo. If there were twenty hornets guarding them it would still take more than twenty cartridges to kill them, even if our shooting was pretty good."

"You've no idea at all what they might be?"

She sighed. "I think they're connected with the Jumpy somehow. Zak believes Jumpy isn't so much a disease but a metamorphosis. The early symptoms, the overwhelming panic, then this mindless urge for them to kill people that aren't infected, were the first stages of that metamorphosis."

"You mean that people infected with Jumpy will end up becoming hives?"

"That's what we've figured out. If there's a team of scientists still alive out there they might tell us it's all crap. Until then, that's our theory. What do you think?"

I nodded. "It seems as good as any to me."

"There's some other stuff as well." She spoke as if the subject sickened her; she wanted to get off it fast. "So far we've only found hives in buildings, and they're always either in a bathroom or a kitchen. Zak figures they need to be near a water supply. They also tend to be guarded, as I've said. And it seems as if they need food."

"That's why they pull the vampire trick?"

"That seems to be the case. They trap unwary people like Sue."

"And the one back in Lewis nearly got me the same way." I remembered the head lunging through the gel with the wide-open mouth.

"Or"—she stood up—"or the hornets who guard them procure victims for the hive to feed on. Any more than that I don't know."

A thought occurred to me. I stood up and reached out to catch her arm to stop her walking away. "But if this is some kind of metamorphosis, this hive must be the larval stage. So there must be a final stage."

She looked up at me, then shrugged in a way that suggested she agreed. "You may be right, Greg. For all we know there may be something like a big, beautiful butterfly waiting to hatch out." Her eyes hardened. "But until then we do know some facts. And the main fact is that if you get too close to one of those things you die." She held eye contact with me for a while. Then she glanced down at the fire. "Greg, you've burned your bread."

I looked down to see wisps of blue smoke coming from the top of the oven.

Crouching down, I opened the oven door, used the pliers to pull out the oven tray and saw a dozen bun-shaped cinders.

"Damn."

"See," she said. "Making our daily bread is tougher than you think."

"Back to square one." I set out the mixing bowl and tub of flour.

She smiled. This time there was warmth in it. "I'll give you a hand," she said. "Don't worry, there's no rush. This is for the meal tonight and breakfast tomorrow."

The thing is that bread was going to burn, too. Because twenty minutes later Zak came running out of the barn with straw still stuck to his clothes from his makeshift bed. Panting, he shouted, "There are bad guys coming down through the valley." He pulled the pistol from his belt. "There are hundreds of the bastards."

Twenty-five

Zak sounded cool . . . in control. But he wasn't dragging his feet. "There are hundreds of hornets down in the valley," he called as he loped toward us.

Michaela shielded her eyes as she looked down toward the lakes. "Are they coming this way?"

"They don't seem to be, but you can never tell with those sly bastards. They might be doing that on purpose; then they could double back over the hill to encircle us."

Ben jogged up, scared-looking. "I guess this is where we leave pronto."

"Not yet," Michaela said. "There's no point in running until we know their intentions."

Zak nodded. "This is a good place to stay for a few days. They might just pass straight by."

Tony appeared with a pair of binoculars. He climbed a fence to stand astride the rail. For a good thirty seconds or so he studied the men and women flowing by in the valley bottom. From what I could see against the sun's glare they moved in groups of twenty or so. They were walking purposefully enough away from us, but as Zak had said, it might be a trick. After passing out of sight they might return when we least expected it.

With the binoculars to his eyes, Tony spoke. "Oh, crap . . ."

"Have they seen us?"

"No. They're on a hunt."

Ben's hands shook. "That's bad, right?"

"Right." Tony lowered the binoculars. "They're hunting people like us. There's a group of around twenty down there, carrying backpacks. They're still well ahead of the hornets, but do you see what I see?"

He handed Michaela the binoculars.

"There's a second group moving parallel to them higher up the hill," she said. "As far as I can tell a river joins the lake right in front of them." She handed the binoculars to me. "They're heading into a trap. Only the poor devils don't know it."

Raising the binoculars to my eyes, I viewed the figures in sudden brutal close-up. "You've seen this before?"

"Oh, yes. Lots." She sounded grim. "Remember what we were just talking about?"

"They're hunting those people for a hive?"

"I can't swear to it, but let's say I'm ninety percent sure."

"What are we waiting for, then?"

"Greg, what do you mean 'What are we waiting for'?"

"Those people need our help."

"Ben, there are twelve of us. There are hundreds of bad guys."

"But we—"

"We can do nothing but watch and make sure they don't attack us." She stared at me. "It sounds uncaring, but what can we do? You'd need a couple of helicopter gunships to take out those: They're a whole army." She tossed her head back to where a clutch of rifles leaned against the barn wall. "We've got a few peashooters."

I studied the group of survivors. They were all burdened by bundles of blankets, backpacks; most carried sacks that I guessed were stuffed with food. They were a desperate bunch. They knew they were being pursued, but they weren't going to ditch their precious foodstuff just yet. Maybe they thought they could outrun the hornets. Only they didn't know they were being driven into a narrow point of land that would be bound by a lake at one side and a fast-flowing river at the other. I panned to the right. A half mile behind were the hornets, moving in groups of around twenty. I couldn't count them all, but I saw the murdering bastards numbered in their hundreds. The binoculars were powerful enough to show individual faces. The men all had thick tangled beards, with a thick tangle of hair. The women had tumbling manes of curls. Most wore rags. Some were naked. It was their eyes that really punched you in the gut. They were so goddam vicious. They blazed from those wild clocks of hair like fucking laser beams. And each pair of eyes had locked onto the men, women and children in front who were trying to outrun them.

Zak shielded his eyes with the cowboy hat as we watched. "We need to send a couple of people down to keep an eye on them."

"I'll go," I said.

"I don't think that's a good idea, do you?" Michaela said.

Tony shook his head. "We get the feeling you might do something heroic." He nodded down at the hornets swarming along the valley. "The kind of heroic that will get all of us killed."

Zak said, "Michaela, Tony, take the bikes down the track across there. That'll bring you close enough, but you'll still be uphill from them. . . . Keep behind that line of trees. They won't see you there."

"What about the sound of the bikes?"

"Don't start the motors," I said. "Freewheel down. Only fire them up if you're seen."

Zak gave a grim smile. "He's starting to think like one of us."

Ben looked uneasy. "But if they see you we'll all have to run for it, won't we?"

"We will," Zak agreed. "But we'll have a head start and we'll be on bikes. They'll be on foot."

Michaela began to walk back to the bikes. "Zak, you best be ready to move out fast just in case. OK?"

He nodded. "Don't worry, we'll be ready."

Within moments, Michaela and Tony were coasting down the hill, using gravity alone, not the big Harley motors, to power their descent. Even from just a few yards away I could hear nothing but the whisper of tires on soft dirt that had accumulated on the track. Seconds later I heard nothing at all as I watched them leave.

Zak immediately got the others to gather up their belongings just in case we had to quit this place like greased lightning. That left me at the fence watching through the binoculars. The bunch of survivors were still well ahead of the hornets. They looked confident they were going to make it. Most had rifles ready in case they were attacked, but they still weren't going to ditch their belongings so they could move faster. Those pitiful supplies were all that kept them from starvation.

I checked the groups of hornets, who didn't move in a great hurry either. But then, the cunning monsters knew that the people just ahead would run out of dry ground within the next ten minutes. At the foot of the hill Michaela and Tony had coasted down to the line of trees that hid them from the bad guys. OK. So far, so good.

But wait . . . all those hornets in the valley moving in plain view across the meadows were eye-catching. You couldn't miss seeing them for sure. I felt a twitch, just a flicker of a twitch in my stomach. That instinct was reaching out of the depths of my bones. It wasn't quite the Twitch I'd experienced before. But it was something like.

I scanned the line of trees farther to the right that followed the line of the track. I damn well knew it . . . *I damn well knew it.* The hornets were still a good quarter of a mile away from Michaela and Tony, now at a standstill on their bikes as they watched the bad guys pass by farther down the valley, but sure as hell and high water there were a group of around twenty of the monsters moving along the *same* track. But that shouldn't be too much to worry about, should it? They were a good distance away. And they weren't walking fast.

No. There had to be something else.

Again I used the binoculars to sweep the line of trees. This time I made the pan much slower. Seeing each bush in turn. There had to be something else that—whoa. Got it.

Maybe a hundred yards from Michaela and Tony, just around a curve in the track, I saw a group of five, maybe six people huddled against a tree. They weren't hornets, I was positive of that. They seemed to be in a tight clump, with one guy carrying a shotgun moving backward and forward across the track. Even from this distance I could tell he was nervous as hell. He knew the hornets were following them. What he didn't know was how far away the monsters were. I swept the binoculars back to the knot of people. A young woman sat on the ground. Her legs were somehow awkward under her, as if she wanted to stand only her legs were too weak. Others clustered 'round, trying to help. A girl of around thirteen wrapped an object in a large towel or piece of sheet.

She handled the object gingerly, like it was incredibly fragile. All I could tell was that it was red. Not at all big.

Hell . . . a goddam baby. That's what it was. A newborn baby! The woman must have just given birth. I stared so fiercely through those lenses it felt as if my eyes would dry out. But I saw clearly enough now. The girl was wrapping a newborn baby still smeared with blood in a towel. The other people were trying to help the mother to her feet. Christ, she gave birth running from those monsters, now she had to get up and run again before they caught her and tore her face off.

Once more I scanned the line of track. I saw another figure. This one had gray hair. He was—he was . . . damn. I forced my eyes to focus. That's it. An old man. He was standing guard between the group with the newborn baby and the hornets bearing down on them.

I watched a full five minutes as the old guy waited. A brave old guy at that. There must have been twenty bad guys and they were young and homicidally crazy. At least he appeared to carry a gun of some sort. It was too short and stubby for a rifle. A submachine gun, maybe. The guy would need formidable firepower against an enemy like that.

It ended faster than I expected. The hornets came 'round the corner of the track. Not running, but moving quickly. They saw the old guy, made straight for him. Then this stupid thing happened. It was like watching an old comedy movie . . . only there was nothing funny about it . . . not one fucking bit funny . . . but it was fucking stupid. He aimed the submachine gun. I waited for the crackle of exploding cartridges and the jet of smoke from the muzzle.

Nothing. Fucking nothing.

The old guy looked at the gun. He jerked at the bolt, then the trigger. I saw him shake his gray head in disbelief.

And then . . .

Over.

That was it. Finished.

One of the hornets pushed him, sending him dropping down onto his behind. He turned 'round on the ground, trying to stand. Only his old bones didn't work as fast as they used to.

Then the hornets were on him. I thought they'd pounce like mad dogs, but they just flowed 'round the old guy as he sat there on his backside in the dirt looking up at them as they walked by, ignoring him.

Only the last one in the pack didn't. He carried a heavy steel bar that must have been the length of his arm. He raised it above his head in a way that seemed almost casual. The old guy sat there in the dirt. He supported his top half with one hand against the track while with the other he tried to block the blow.

The hornet swung the bar easily, missing the guy's arm. The end of the iron bar whipped down, hitting into the old guy's skull square in the top. The old boy looked as if he'd suddenly gotten way too tired. Slowly he lowered himself facedown into the dirt and lay still. The hornet struck him once more in the head with the bar. Then moved on without looking back.

I found myself staring at the old guy lying there with his open mouth pressed against the road, willing him to get up, grab the gun and blow those bastards to shit. But he didn't move and his gray hair turned the color of cranberry juice.

While this happened I'd been locked into my own world, staring through the binoculars. I turned and ran back to where Zak readied the people near the bikes.

I grabbed one by the handlebars and rocked it forward from the stand.

"Hey!" Zak shouted. "What do you think you're doing?"

"There are hornets down there we didn't see before. They're going to find Michaela and Tony."

I was ready to punch my way through Zak if he argued. Instead: "OK. Catch." He threw me a rifle. "It's loaded with ten rounds. And it's a semiauto. Just point and squeeze."

He swung a pump-action shotgun over his shoulder, then made as if to start the bike's engine.

"Zak. Freewheel down there."

I didn't want to signal those hornets with the sound of motors that their blood enemies were on the way. And I hadn't told Zak everything, of course. I hadn't mentioned the woman who'd just given birth on the road. Or the old man's murder. Or that right now I planned to give those murdering sons of bitches a little taste of something they'd never forget.

Twenty-six

Dammit if the track didn't have enough bumps to nearly throw us clean off the saddles. What's more, it was steep enough to bring us close up to forty without having to fire up the Harley engines. Gripping the handlebars tight, the grass banks rising high and over-grown at either side of us soon made it look as if we were whistling through a green tunnel that blurred as we moved faster and faster.

I glanced at Zak. He concentrated on the track ahead, avoiding ruts and holes in the ground. The thing is, it was so quiet. All I could hear were the whisper of air by my ears and the hiss of tires on dirt.

At the bottom of the track Zak braked to bring him-self to a stop where Michaela and Tony now shot us surprised looks. Only I didn't stop. No way was I going to even touch the brake. I passed them in a blur, keep-ing the momentum going.

Now the track had leveled out. Bit by bit the bike began to slow, but I was still doing thirty when I passed the bunch of men and women with the newborn baby.

STRANGER

The guy with the shotgun looked as if he was making up his mind whether to shoot me or not when I called out, "Keep moving! You're being followed!"

Temptation started to bite now. I wanted to fire up the motorcycle and power up to that bunch of killers that must still be heading along the track. But I fought it down. When I arrived I wanted surprise on my side.

The bike slowed as the track began to run uphill.

Twenty miles an hour . . . fifteen.

I saw a curve ahead.

Ten.

I put my feet down, my soles brushing the soil.

Five miles an hour.

I stopped. Then, with my feet balancing me I slipped the rifle off my shoulder and aimed along the track.

For a while I sat there. The sun shone down. I heard birds in the trees. Butterflies flitted among yellow flowers in the meadow. Honeybees buzzed through the long grass. Sweat trickled down my face; my heart pounded with a dark funereal rhythm.

The track ahead lay deserted. Maybe they'd gone back? Or cut through the trees into the field?

But then I got it. The Twitch. Not for the first time I wondered if bread bandits, hornets or whatever you called them carried some smell so faint I didn't consciously sense it. But the old dinosaur brain locked deep inside the folds of primate brain still sniffed it bright and clear on the hot summer air. My stomach muscles twitched. In my neck and back more muscles snapped tight. So tight the contracting neck muscles pulled my head back and forced my chin up.

The bastards were here. They were right around the . . .

Then they walked 'round the bend. I pulled back the bolt. I'd only have to do that once because this little beauty had a self-cocking mechanism. *OK, Valdiva. All*

you need do is aim . . . squeeze the trigger . . . aim and
squeeze . . . aim and squeeze. . . .

Muscles twitched like they danced in my gut. Blood sparkled through my veins. My whole being squeezed into that cubic inch behind my right eye. The one that looked through the sight and along that gleaming barrel. I concentrated on nothing else now.

There they were. A group of guys in their twenties and thirties, I figured. They moved purposefully toward me. Not running. Their eyes locked on me.

But they wouldn't spook me.

I waited until they were maybe fifty yards away before squeezing the trigger.

The first shot punched clean through the chest of the one in the lead. The bullet tumbled out through his back to smash into the mouth of the guy behind him. His teeth vanished in a cloud of red glory and enamel splinters.

Both dropped down into the dirt. Two with one bullet! There was an angel on my shoulder today.

Forty-five yards away I dropped the next guy with a chest shot, too. He went down kicking his legs, vomiting blood. That bastard was dead meat.

I'd expected them to charge. There were still seventeen of them. I had eight rounds left in the clip. Do the math; I'd have to cut and run in the next ten seconds.

Forty yards and closing.

Bang . . . dropped the next with a head shot. A bald guy. The top of his scabby dome lifted off in one piece like you'd slice the top off a boiled egg. His comrades didn't flinch when the guy's brains spattered their faces.

Thirty yards. Bang, bang. I dropped two more with head shots through their eyes. One round exited the back of the sick fuck's skull to slice off the guy's ear behind him. The one who lost the ear bled like a pig but it didn't stop him. I had to drop him with a shot through his lungs. He sat down on God's earth to cough blood into his cupped hands.

Four rounds left. Thirteen mad fucks remaining.

They were twenty yards away. If they ran now they'd reach me in maybe ten seconds.

I fired again. *Lousy shot, Valdiva.* The bullet gouged out the hornet's eye, but it exited through the side of his forehead, just below the temple. Most would have gone down with the sheer trauma of an injury like that. But his expression hardly flinched. His good eye still burned at me. And even though blood turned the righthand side of his face into a red mask he kept moving.

Where have you gone, sweet angel of mine? Now I had to use another precious bullet on Señor Solo Eye. It caught him in the throat. He went down gurgling to claw at the ground like it was the earth itself that hurt him.

Fifteen yards.

Then the goddam sly bastards went and did it. They cut and ran.

The twelve that remained burst through the bushes at the side of the road to disappear into the trees. They left the tail-end guy, though. The one who'd killed the old man back along the track. He still had that steel bar, too. He ran straight at me with the bar raised above his head. Old man brains still stuck on the end. Christ, he was so close I could see the moles on his face that bristled with black hairs.

I aimed at the center of his chest.

But I didn't fire the gun. Not then. What got into me, I don't know. Maybe the angel on my shoulder moved over for a devil to settle there to whisper in my ear.

Instead of blowing a hole in the killer's chest I dropped the muzzle. When I fired the metal-jacketed slug smashed his balls. It might have chewed off his dick, too, I don't know.

With that high-pitched squeal you only hear when you accidentally stand on a dog's paw, he dropped down into the soil at my feet. There he rolled from side to side, both hands clutching the blood-soaked mess between his legs.

I didn't have time to put a second slug in his head.

I knew what remained of the hornet gang would be running as hard as they could to reach the people with the newborn baby. Now was the time . . . I started the Harley's motor, revved it until it howled like a phantom war cry, then blasted down the track, the back wheel throwing up a geyser of dirt as high as the treetops and coating the fallen man in filth as he writhed in agony.

It took seconds to reach the group. They hurried along the track. Some helped the mother, whose thighs were still slick with blood. A girl of around thirteen carried the baby. And there, cutting them off from going farther, hornets ran out of the wood. The young guy dropped a couple of them with the shotgun. Then he started fumbling with the thing, trying to reload.

Slowing the bike, I fired my last shot. The hornet went down with a hole in the back of his head you could have shoved your fist through.

There were still more than half a dozen left. I had to slow the bike, but I cut past the little band of survivors. I had nothing but air in the ammo clip now. Instead I accelerated toward the surviving bunch of killers. They were still intent on claiming their original prey and sidestepped me. One wasn't fast enough. I caught him across the forehead with the rifle butt. He went down onto his back. Down but not out, he started to sit up. Whipping the bike 'round, wheels throwing out dirt like a smoke screen, I rode toward him. The front wheel bounced up over his chest, pinning him down to the ground. Slowly, hardly touching the throttle, I eased the bike forward until the rear tire pressed down deep into his belly. Frantically, he beat at my legs. His eyes bulged wide; spit bubbled through his lips in fast, glistening gobs. *Bye, bye, freak boy.* I opened up the throttle until the engine screamed; the back wheel blurred, spun and ripped out his intestine as efficiently as a chainsaw.

That left me with the other hornets who closed in on the group. The guy still fumbled shells into the shotgun breech, dropping them on the ground in the process, picking them up, dropping them again, picking them up again, panic distorting his face into a mask from which jutted two terror-stricken eyes

But then it was over.

In a blur motorcycles buzzed past me. Zak, Michaela and Tony rode alongside the surviving hornets. Balancing their shotguns in the crooks of their elbows, they fired. And, man, you knew they'd done this before. In less than ten seconds the half-dozen-strong bunch of bad guys lay dead in a growing pool of their own blood.

Down in the valley the other hornets would have heard the bikes and the shooting. They'd come looking for us now. It was time to get that tired bunch of people with the newborn baby up the hill, then the hell out of there.

Twenty-seven

On the road again. There was ample saddle space for the group we'd rescued. The mother (who couldn't have been more than sixteen herself) was another matter. No way could she ride double after giving birth just hours before. There was the newborn baby, too. Despite Zak's joke, you couldn't let it ride in the pannier. Finally Michaela and Ben worked out a way to seat her on the two-wheeled trailer that Tony pulled behind his Harley. They created a kind of armchair from boxes of food, spare gas cans and blankets. She sat looking backward with the baby in her arms. The girl seemed dazed by it all and didn't comment on the strange traveling arrangements. She just sat with the baby wrapped in towels, staring into its face. Incredibly, there was an aura of calm about her. I don't think she even realized a battle had been fought down on the dirt track.

There were six of them, if you counted the baby. There was the mother, the thirteen-year-old girl (the most self-assured of the group), twin Malaysian women in their twenties who'd been vacationing in New York when the Fall happened along and smashed civilization to crud and Ronald, a guy of around thirty, with a goatee that looked more like brown froth than hair. Constantly, he looked 'round with these scared blue eyes that you'd swear were close to bursting clean out of his skull. All the time, as we loaded the bikes at the barn, he'd repeat over and over, "We've got to get away. Those things down there are killers. We've got to get away."

The hornets had heard the gunshots and the roar of the engines. Around forty of them began prowling their way up the hill like a pack of dogs looking for a rabbit. But they were on foot; we had the bikes. We got away with time to spare. By late afternoon we were miles from the valley with its lakes. We didn't see what happened to the group of ordinary Joes the hornets were pursuing. Only it took no genius to surmise what did happen to them when they found their way blocked by the river merging with the lake. A few shots fired, then hundreds of hornets would overwhelm the little band of survivors. End of story.

We figured the best route would be simply to head away from the valley where the hornets had clustered. By late evening we reached a garage. One of those backwoods outfits with a couple of gas pumps, a tiny store that sold everything from toothpaste to ammo and fish bait. It had been picked clean, of course. Although Ben did find a single pack of gum behind the trashed counter. Alongside the store was a repair shop. Here a few cars sat gathering dust in varying stages of repair. A big old Chevy in strawberry red with a cream stripe down its side and whitewall tires stood on blocks. Someone had been lovingly restoring the old girl when civilization rolled over and died. The vast back seat made an ideal bed. Michaela guided the new mother to it and settled her and the baby down there. As Michaela got busy arranging blankets, fixing her a hot drink, finding clean towels for the baby to keep it warm, I found myself watching. Hell, I admired Michaela. She was so together. She always moved in a purposeful way, as if even the smallest chore was an important link in the survival chain. Which I guess it was. She cared for people, you could see that. A warm sensation flushed through me as I watched her slip a pillow she'd found in one of the cars beneath the new mom's head. Despite Michaela's external toughness she had a tender heart.

She caught me staring at her. She said nothing. Her let's-get-down-to-business expression didn't falter, but I found myself blushing when she made eye contact with me. So I did what I was good at: I found firewood.

By this time the sun had all but set. Zak arrived back from his search of the neighborhood. "Quiet as a grave," he told me as he climbed off the bike. "No sign of hornets or any ordinary Joes like us. But the houses nearby have either been picked clean or torched." He slapped the dust from his pants with the cowboy hat. "With luck there might still be some gas in those cars, or in the underground tanks."

Then it was business as usual. Tony rigged up the bread oven where the fire would be. The others did chores—making supper or mending clothes. Ben dug out the tub of flour ready to make more of the pancake bread.

With plenty of trees nearby firewood was easy to find. Soon I had it piled in the yard (well away from the gas pumps, just in case). Once it was lit people gravitated toward it as darkness crept like a hungry ghost through the forest. Ben baked bread as Zak fanned the flames with his Stetson. The new arrivals got to know their rescuers. People made a fuss over the mom and her baby. Michaela made use of the rearview mirror in another car; she sat brushing her hair. I found myself staring again. But then, there was something compelling about the slow, rhythmic way she ran the brush through her long dark hair.

"Supper's ready," Ben sang out while he set the flat loaves to cool. Before, mine had come out black; his were pale gold. They smelled good, too.

Zak crouched down to look at them. "What have you done to these?"

Ben looked anxious. "Is there something wrong with them?"

"No, they smell great . . . hmmm. How you do that with bread and water?"

Ben's face switched to a boyish grin. "I found some garlic growing wild in the hedge bottom."

"Garlic! Hey this guy's a genius. Garlic! Sweet Jesus! Oh, boy, did you hear that?" He laughed as he clutched his stomach. "My belly's rumbling." He called out to the others. "Come on, let's eat."

I'd packed enough beer for a stubby apiece. Michaela said it was a good time to pass these out and celebrate the birth of the child and the expansion of our group by six—if the new people wanted to join, that is?

Yes. They were all keen to hook up with us. Rowan, the thirteen-year-old, said that the hornets had been following them for more than six hours before the showdown in the lane. They'd run short of supplies. Most of the guns had been lost in a boat accident. The old guy had been a Marine and despite crippling arthritis had dived into the lake to retrieve what he could. One of the guns he found underwater in the mud had been the machine gun. That pretty much explained why it hadn't fired as the hornets bore down on him. Added to those troubles Kira had gone into labor. Most of the others in the group had been for dumping her, as she slowed them down. But the old guy and these few had refused to leave her to die at the hands of the hornets and had done their best to help her.

Like all survivors these days, this was a resilient bunch. Despite the trauma of what had happened earlier they soon relaxed (helped by the beer, I reckon) into the sense of security the fire offered. And the fact that we sat there cradling guns on our laps.

As we sat 'round the crackling fire I took the opportunity to oil a pump-action shotgun Zak had told me was getting sticky. The cocking mechanism had become stiff, but I spent ten minutes or so dry firing it until the action became smooth. All the time the people 'round the fire swapped stories about what had happened to them over the last twelve months. Despite the fact that the nation had been laid to waste, it was surprising the funny stories people had to tell. Zak even made a joke of how his hair had fallen out after he'd been burned in the fire. "I went to sleep one night only to wake up in the morning to find all this hair covering the ground. I couldn't believe what had happened. I looked in a mirror and saw my head was as smooth as a pool ball. The thing was, when I went back to my sleeping bag I found birds were taking my hair up into the trees to make nests. I remember running after them to try to get my hair back." Zak rubbed his nude scalp. "As if it would have done me any good if I could." He grinned. "It would take some pretty strong glue to hold all that in place."

The newcomers laughed. I could see that one of the Malaysian girls especially was warming up to him. I loaded the shotgun, then finished my bread ration. Ben had worked miracles. Flavoring the bread with crushed wild garlic had to be a stroke of genius. I hadn't tasted anything as good in a long while.

The thirteen-year-old girl darted to the repair shop and came back with news that baby and mother were fast asleep in the back of the Chevy. Boy showed off a card trick that impressed everyone. The new guy with the goatee beard sat opposite me on the far side of the fire. Smiling, he said he could make a stick turn to rubber. He did the old trick you'd do with a pencil, only this time he held the end of a piece of firewood in his fingertips and flicked it up and down so it gave the illusion of becoming rubbery. God, yes, a cheesy old trick, older than Noah's goddamn Ark. But it raised a laugh from everyone. Boy grinned so hard I'd swear you could see every single tooth in his head.

Ben nudged me. "Don't tell me that I've gone and poisoned you."

I looked at him, puzzled. "What do you mean?"

"You've just eaten the bread." He smiled. "Now you're rubbing your stomach like it's given you a bellyache."

"And here's another neat trick," Ronald said, stroking his goatee.

That's when I fired the shotgun blast that tore his head from the roots of his neck.

Twenty-eight

"Whoa, keep your hands up against the wall, Greg. Both hands . . . feet apart. I said feet apart!"

Like the old-time cops, they had me spread-eagled against the repair shop wall.

"Jesus, Greg," Tony said as he jammed the rifle muzzle into the side of my neck, "what did you have to blow off the guy's head for? What'd he ever do to you?"

"I had to. He was—"

"Keep facing the wall or I'll blow a hole in you."

"You don't understand, I—"

"You bastard. You murdering bastard!" This came as a shriek from the mother, who advanced toward me with the baby in her arms. Her shoulders had hunched up to her ears. She looked like a wild cat ready to jump and claw my eyes out of my head. "You bastard! Why did you kill my husband? Ronald hadn't done anything to you. He didn't even have a gun and you fucking murdered him." She crackled with hysteria. It sounds crazy, but purple lights seemed to detonate in that wild shrieking sound she made. "Wha' ya plan to do with us? Ya going to kill all of us? It that it? Ya going to kill my baby? You going to kill her?" She looked 'round in terror at the others in Michaela's gang. She thought they were going to leap on her and mutilate her. Michaela spoke soothingly to her. With the help of the Malaysian girls she got her back to the Chevy, where she sat in the front seat rocking backward and forward, eyes staring like light bulbs, the baby grunting in her arms.

"See what you've fucking done, Valdiva?" You could hear the horror juicing through Tony's voice. He couldn't believe what'd just happened out by the campfire.

I said, "Listen to me. I had to kill him; he—"

"What's wrong? Didn't like the shape of his face?"

"No, it's not that. I had to kill him. Listen to me, I couldn't stop myself."

"Listen to that," Zak said, behind me. "The guy's psycho."

Tony added, "Lucky we found out before he killed any more of us." I heard a gun cock, and another muzzle pressed into the back of my neck. They were going to kill me there and then. In twenty seconds there'd be a splash of my blood right up that cinder block wall in front of me. The muzzle bit so deep into my neck it pushed my open mouth against the wall, grating my teeth against the blocks.

Then Michaela's voice came close by. Disbelief turned it to a whisper. "What on Earth possessed you, Greg? Are you crazy? Is that why those people kept you out of town in the cabin?"

"No . . ."

"The poor guy was innocent. You just—"

"No," I snarled into the cinder block. "Listen to me. I killed him because he was infected."

Zak spat. "Valdiva's out of his mind."

"No, he's not." It took a second to place the softly spoken words.

"Ben, you better tell them." I panted as the muzzles pressed harder against my skin. I could almost hear fingers tightening 'round triggers.

"Greg's right when he says he couldn't stop himself." Ben spoke in a calm voice. "He's been like that ever since I met him last year."

Zak's voice: "What do you mean?"

"Greg can tell when someone's infected with Jumpy. I don't know how he does it, but he knows before they start to display even the earliest symptoms."

"That guy looked like an ordinary Joe to me," Zak snapped.

"Didn't he look edgy to you?" I said. "And isn't irrational panic one of the first signs?"

"Shit. You'd be panicking if you were in his shoes today, with a bunch of hornets making for you."

"It was more than that. He was panicked. He was losing control."

"So he was scared."

"Believe me," I said, "I can tell when someone has Jumpy. It doesn't always happen straightaway, but when I sat in front of him by the fire it hit me. I knew it. He was riddled with Jumpy. In a few days he would have tried to kill us." They were quiet now, so I rammed home the point. "You know how it works. You've seen it before."

"But we've only got your word for it," Michaela said. "Ben might be providing an alibi."

"You could always take a trip across the water to Sullivan and ask the people there," I told her. "Only I don't recommend it. They're likely to shoot any stranger the moment they clap eyes on him these days."

Zak pressed the muzzle of the gun into my jaw. "We only have your word for it."

"He's telling the truth." This time it was Rowan, the

thirteen-year-old, who'd had the presence of mind to wrap the baby in a towel when it was born.

Tony said, "What makes you so sure?"

"It was how Ronald acted. He'd been brave in the past. Once he'd climbed right into the top of a tree when I hid from some men who were trying to catch me. He got me out and he was always calm. But in the last few days he started getting frightened . . . like he was frightened of his own shadow. I didn't think anything about it right up until now, but I'd never seen him getting panicky like that before, even when the hornets nearly caught us a few weeks ago and they killed Lana and Dean."

"There's your proof," Ben told them. "Let Greg go. He's more likely to save your necks than harm you."

"Whoa. No, wait a moment here." Zak didn't remove the gun from my neck. "This is how I see it, tell me if I'm wrong, OK?"

"OK."

"Greg Valdiva here has got some natural, in-built early warning system. He knows . . . or divines, somehow, when a person has Jumpy. And he knows before anyone else recognizes the symptoms, right?"

"That's right," Ben said.

"Then some kind of red mist comes down inside his head. Before he knows what's happened he's killed the infected person."

"Yes, it's as involuntary as . . ." I pictured Ben shrugging as he searched for a suitable illustration. ". . . as involuntary as hitting your knee and triggering the classic knee-jerk reaction. It's instinctive."

"Yes, yes, that sounds great. Greg here will screen any strangers we meet. If his instinct tells him that they're infected then he executes them. If not, then we're free to team up with them if that's what everyone wants."

"So," Michaela said, "what's the problem with that, Zak?"

"The problem is, what if that little alarm bell inside his skull starts ringing when he sits down next to one of us one day? What if he starts killing us one by one?"

Sighing, I shook my head. "I don't feel it when I'm with you. With any of you, and that includes the people we found today with the exception of Ronald. He's the only one infected."

"For now." Zak sounded like a lawyer nailing his man in court. "But what if you sniff those symptoms on us? Or what if you have a foul-up day and *think* one of us is lousy with Jumpy?"

"Zak, it doesn't—"

"Do you blow my head off? Then say, 'Oops, sorry, my mistake, Zak.' Yeah, right, that will make me feel pretty damn joyful when you leave a personal note of apology on my grave."

Ben said, "It doesn't work like that."

"Says you. But don't you see?" Zak was like the lawyer addressing the judge and jury again. "If we allow Greg to stay with us, won't it to be like sitting on a ticking bomb? OK, we might be fine this week and next week, and next month, but there might come a day when Greg gets the feeling on him. . . . Do you know what I'm saying? We're not going to know when we sit down to eat breakfast with him whether he's going to say, 'Pass the salt, please' or, 'Meet your maker. *Boom.*' Can we handle that kind of uncertainty?"

Michaela said, "Ben's got a point, too. Greg here could be the best weapon we have. If he can detect Jumpy in people before they can harm us, that gives us another hatful of chances to survive."

Zak's voice turned cool. "Until he sees Jumpy in you, Michaela, or you, Tony, or you, Ben."

Michaela stayed firm. "My vote is that Greg Valdiva stays."

"I say he goes," Zak said. "Tony?"

"Couldn't we just disarm him?" Tony answered. "If he doesn't have a gun he can't hurt us."

I sighed. "If this thing comes down on me the way it does, I'd kill you with my bare hands."

"Shit."

"I can't help it, Tony. It's something inside me. It just won't stop."

"OK," Michaela said. "Greg's unarmed now. Let go of him."

The mood of the people in the repair shop did seem calmer. Tony and Zak took the guns out of my neck and stood back. I turned 'round to look at those faces in the lamplight. Their eyes were as intense as light-bulbs. They stared back at me. I'd seen that expression in faces back in Sullivan. These people were frightened of that *thing* I had inside me that had the power to look into people and *see* the infection. They were fearful I'd see it in them. Now this bunch of accidental nomads had to decide what they did with me. Or *to* me.

They thought it best that I wait outside while they put it to a vote. Whether I stayed. Or went. Or whatever . . .

Michaela and Tony looked apologetic when I returned to the campfire to pile on more wood. Zak had been shrewd, thinking through the implications of what I'd got inside me. I believe he really was reluctant to take the hard line he had. But part of me agreed he was right: I was dangerous. If I detected any sign of Jumpy in man or woman I'd kill. Hell, come to that, I couldn't *stop* myself killing. I'd be like a dog after a rat.

A guard had been posted outside to watch out for any hornets happening by. But I did ask myself if they weren't also keeping an eye on me while they continued their discussions behind the closed doors of the repair shop.

I prodded the fire with a stick that sent a gush of

sparks into the night sky, where they lost themselves among the stars. The air was warm; moths darted in toward the firelight. Some set their wings alight and spiraled, fluttering, to the ground. They were governed by instincts, too, something so deeply embedded in their insect bodies that they couldn't stop flying toward a light. If it resulted in their being damaged or dying, that mattered absolute zero to them. Most creatures were governed by instinct. Birds migrated. Bears hibernated. At given times of the year different species mated. I was no better and no worse than they were. Instinct ruled me.

A couple of hours later, close on midnight, the repair shop door swung open. Backlit by the lamps inside, I saw Michaela in silhouette. She stood, looking out at me, with a rifle in her hand. I guessed the band had reached a decision.

Twenty-nine

Valdiva, kneel before the ditch. **Bang** . . . *rifle bullet chews my brain. Zak pushes me into the ditch with the toe of his boot . . . Now you're rat meat. . . .*

That scenario played out bright and clear, I can tell you, the moment Michaela stepped out of the repair shop. The others came, too, to form a line behind her. Wood in the fire snapped like pistol shots. Sparks climbed into the night sky. And it seemed all the stars in creation gazed down to see what would happen next.

"What's it to be then?" I asked her. "You going to give me to the count of ten before you start shooting?"

"Greg . . ." She sounded pained. "No, nothing like that."

"Oh?"

"But we do have to decide what's best for the survival of our group."

"I've been sitting out here thinking through your options." I spoke to the group as much as to Michaela. "I figure you've got three ways to go with this. One: Let me continue staying with you. But I don't consider

217

that viable. Two: Kick me out. Three: Put a bullet in my head."

"Greg—"

"After all, if you do exile me I might come back looking for you."

"Now just you wait one minute, Greg." Michaela's eyes flared with anger in the firelight. "This hasn't been easy for us. But we've got to decide what's right. We've had strangers who've joined us in the past who have been infected. We've woken up in the night with them trying to hack out our brains. See!"

I didn't anticipate what she'd do next. She lunged forward, grabbed my fingers and pushed them into her hair on top of her head. "Feel that ridge of skin? That's scar tissue where a sweet little fourteen-year-old girl tried to open up my skull with a wrench. Of course, first of all she was chatty, friendly and perfectly normal-looking, so we had to sit down and talk it through among ourselves. Yes, she was a stranger. Yes, she might be infected. But, no, there were no symptoms. And we weren't so brutal, Greg, that we decided to turn her away to die of starvation out there. We took her in, fed her, but a week later she went crazy and attacked. Tony, here, had to put three bullets through her back to get her off me. She was like a wildcat." Michaela spoke fast, angry and hurt all at the same time. A huge glittering tear swelled in her eye before rolling down her cheek. "So, you see, Greg, we didn't make this decision lightly."

I took a breath to speak, but Ben held up his hand. "Listen to what they have to say, Greg."

I nodded. "OK. What's the verdict?"

Tony said, "We like you as a person—"

"Oh, please . . ." Sarcasm ran deep in my voice.

Again Ben spoke up. "Greg, hear them out."

"But if you continue living here among us it's going to tear our group apart. Some of us won't be able to accept the uncertainty. That one day you're going to be our pal—"

"The next our executioner." This came from Zak. "But we realize that you'd be an asset to us. You'd be able to screen strangers for Jumpy."

"That's why we don't want you to leave." Michaela looked at me. Her eyes, compassionate and yet . . .

"You mean," I said, "I'm like the old-time nuclear deterrent. Can't live with me, can't live without me. Well, that fills me with a warm, rosy glow, I can tell you. Many thanks. I feel like a leper . . . a leper with a sack full of marijuana at a dope fiends reunion party." OK, so that comparison didn't make a hat full of sense, but I was too angry to speak with any clarity, or logic, come to that.

"So what we've decided is," Michaela pressed on despite my scornful remark, "is that we're going to stay here for a while. We've food to last a week, there's a fresh water well in the back yard, we've got a roof over our heads and there aren't any hornets close by."

"Sounds sweet. Go on."

She continued, "You might not go along with what I'm going to suggest next. You might tell us to go to hell, but we think it's as fair as it possibly can be under the circumstances."

"Well?"

"There's a house about five miles down the road. It's been burned out, but the garage is still in once piece."

"You want me to move in there?"

"If you agree . . . then we can still be of use to each other, but you'd be far enough away to remove this sense of danger that some of us feel when you're with us." She paused. "What's your answer, Greg?"

I looked at the dozen or so faces watching me expectantly in the firelight.

"It stinks," I told them. "It stinks like a mountain of

crap." Then, sighing, I shook my head. "But until we can figure out something better I'll go along with it. For now."

Home is a garage with one window, a lawn mower and an open-topped Jeep so old that the dirt crusting the bottom could be pure Danang delta mud. Zak, Ben and Michaela delivered me to the place the morning after I blew off the stranger's head. They left me with supplies, my rifle, plenty of ammo and instructions that they would call on me—not the other way 'round, you'll note.

Zak shook my hand. "Sorry it has to be this way, Greg. But you have to be a walking time bomb." He smiled in a good-natured way. "We'll see you soon."

"Yeah," I said. "Don't be a stranger." I meant it, too.

In the back of my mind I still harbored a suspicion they'd quietly leave without telling old Greg Valdiva, the guy with the Twitch that might just turn out fatal—*for you.*

Ben's hands shook. I half wondered if he'd offer to camp out here with me, but this was the wrong side of paradise. The house, which had been burned to its foundations, lay at the edge of dark forest that looked sinister enough to be the lair of any number of murderous demons. In a dried-out swimming pool human bones lay in tangled heaps. A place of breathtaking beauty it wasn't.

After they'd carried my gear into the garage, said some complimentary things about my new home (in the way I suspect parents spoke when depositing their kids in new rooms at college) they climbed onto the bikes and fired them up.

Michaela called me closer to speak to me. She rested her hand on my forearm as she spoke in a low voice so the others wouldn't hear above the sounds of the Harley motors. "Greg, they're frightened of you. And this is all new to them. Give them some time to come 'round to the idea of what's inside you." She squeezed my arm. "Listen to me; they're going to realize soon that you're special, and that they're going to need you."

I gave that you-might-be-right-you-might-be-wrong kind of shrug. "Drive carefully, Michaela." Then I called out to the others, "See you soon, boys."

Ben saluted and Zak waved his cowboy hat.

As they rode away into the misty morning light I found myself wondering if I'd ever see them again.

221

Thirty

"Twat!"

The ancient profanity erupted from my mouth as the wrench I was using to slacken the nuts on the Jeep slipped and my knuckles slammed into the wheel arch. "You sonnafabitch. You twat!"

After three days of waiting for hornets to find me (not one showed) I'd finally gotten bored enough to start work on the Jeep. I figured if I could get the machine roadworthy it might come in useful. Also, it gave me something to do. Those summer evenings alone had started to stretch out to something little short of infinity.

So, welcome to the Valdiva home. The garage was clean, dry and rat and bug free. I rigged up a bed in the corner. Rummaging through boxes at the back, I uncovered a barbecue and charcoal that served as a stove. I also found a hammock that I strung between a couple of trees not far from the bone-rich swimming pool. A box full of paperbacks provided light entertainment. They were mainly old thrillers, but what the hell?

STRANGER

When I became too restless to work on the Jeep or lie reading in the hammock I walked miles through the woods. There were no sign of any hornets, or anyone else come to that. In fact there was something eerie about the forest. I guessed it was ancient woodland where there'd been no tree felling to speak of. They just seemed to go on forever. Densely packed trees, thick canopies of branches overhead that roofed you in so completely you wouldn't even catch a glimpse of sky. I walked deeper and deeper into them. It was almost dark beneath that ocean of leaves. Silent, too. A silence so strong you half believed you could reach out and sink your fingers into it.

Every so often the breeze would catch the leaves. Then there'd be hissing sounds. A thousand snakes sliding out of the earth all around you. At least that's the image the *hissss* put into my mind.

The strange thing is, there was something compelling about the forest. It hypnotized you. Pulled you in. You longed to walk deeper and deeper and lose yourself there. Never come back. Never see the outside world. But keep walking among those trees, with that whispery *hissss* all around you . . . everything still . . . peaceful. I recalled that some Native Americans said the Wendigo haunted forests. That was the spirit of the forest. The Wendigo had the power to creep into your brain. Slowly it possessed you. Once it had control you suddenly ran away into the wilderness. Never to be seen again.

That forest did it to me. Maybe there was something in the old Wendigo legend after all.

Anyway, after taking a strip of skin from my knuckles as I tried to loosen the wheel nut rusted to damnation, I decided to take a lungful of fresh air. The late afternoon sun slanted down across the wood. Again it was silent except for the call of a lone bird in a tree. Despite the demon wheel nut, I'd put some good work into the Jeep. I'd cleaned the plugs, filters, topped up the oil from a sealed can I'd found in the garage. Once I'd replaced one badly worn tire with the spare all I'd need would be the gasoline. Then I saw myself roaring along those country roads in the rugged little Jeep, the breeze blasting through my hair. Sounded good.

After shouting "*Twat*" at the corroded nut a good half dozen times I was ready for a break anyway. There'd be little chance of Michaela, Ben or any of the others turning up now. They'd called by early morning to say that they were out on a gas search that would take all day. Of course, I offered to go along and help. They thanked me but passed on my offer. Some in the group were still uneasy about me. But then, witnessing the goatee guy having his head exploded by buckshot must still be as fresh in their minds as his mess of brains sticking to the fence.

I circled the barn two or three times like a restless dog. In my mind's eye I found myself picturing Michaela's face. She hadn't spoken about relationships, but had she formed an attachment to . . . attachment? No, this was a visceral world now. Had she mated with Zak or Tony? Yeah, *mated;* that's the word. I counted skulls in the swimming pool. Got bored by the time I reached eighteen . . . and I'd seen the telltale holes in the tops of the skulls where fractures radiated in a sunburst affect—that was a sure sign that hornets had rounded up everyone in the neighborhood, then killed them with a blow to the head. I guess a pathologist would describe the injury that killed those poor bastards as a "grievous insult to the brain." In other words the hammer blow would crunch right through the skull to rip the victim's brain like wet toilet tissue. Then they'd been dropped into the swimming pool to rot.

So, to stop picturing those scenes of mass murder . . . complete with the screaming, the shitting of pants, the begging, the tears, the blood (see what I mean? It's insidious, isn't it?). To stop those mind movies I collected my rifle before heading off into the forest. And, perhaps, I even needed to get Michaela with those beautiful dark eyes out of my mind, too, for a while. Because right then I didn't want her mated to anyone. The truth was, old Greg Valdiva experienced a tingling stir of interest.

For God's sake stick to the path, Valdiva, I told myself. *If you wander off it you'll never find your way back. You'll be lost our here until hell gets ice.*

The moment I stepped into the shade of the trees it was like stepping into a cathedral. One of those big old Gothic ones, where even on a summer's afternoon it's cool inside. And here, too, the fat columns of tree trunks rose up into a gloom-filled roof.

The path in front of me might have been made by ramblers. Then again, it might have been a million years old and formed by long-extinct animals with evil pig eyes and tusks that could rip you right through to the backbone. I walked deeper into the wood, the rhythm of my footsteps somehow matching the rhythm of my heart. Joining that was the rhythmic shush . . . shush . . . shush sound as a breath of wind whispered through the leaves.

Underfoot, there wasn't much grass to speak off. Long fallen leaves, dead branches and moss formed a velvet shroud the same color as that dark, moist green that creeps over the faces of corpses within a month of burial. Grave moss. That's what it looked like. Cool green grave moss.

That sensation took over again. *Walk deeper, Valdiva. Keep walking. Lose yourself in this place. Lose yourself forever. . . .*

Leaves whispered all around me. . . .

Those snakes are slipping out of the grave moss, buddy. They're following you. They're licking your heels with forked tongues. I moved steadily on. Crazy as it sounds a promise of oblivion haunted this place. I wanted that cool, moist air of the forest to embrace me. To pull me in deeper. I smelled damp moss, decaying leaves, the rich scents of a million years of dead timber that formed the earth beneath my feet.

This is good, Valdiva. You can dissolve in here. You can forget about your mother and your sister lying beneath the stone tomb. You can forget that the world has toppled and broken into a million pieces. You can forget that thing in your blood that makes you kill infected men and women. You can forget, you can forget, you can forget . . .

The rhythm of words padding through my head merged with my footstep; they merged with the beat of my dark and bloody heart, my respiration and the *hiss-hissss* of leaves. In a trance I walked. The columns of trees appeared as a dense wall in front of me. I began to feel like a microbe passing through the skin of a beast into its muscles and nerves.

I lost track of time as I walked. It might have been blistering sunlight above the tree canopy; then again, it might have been dusk. I couldn't tell down in that cool, unchanging gloom. Here, the air was still, with the odor of mushroom stirred richly into it. A dead bird that had been picked by ants down to bones and feathers lay on the path in front of me. I stepped over it, moved on, walking deeper into the forest.

Once, the path took me by a woodland pond. Round and deep, it looked like a bomb crater filled with water. That water was green as moss, too.

As I passed through the filter of trees my mind roved ahead, instinctively searching for any danger hiding out there. A gang of hornets maybe. Lurking behind trees, watching Greg Valdiva walk by. Easy meat, they'd think to themselves. We can crack his head like an egg, then watch him as he lies on the ground kicking and puking as his brains run out through the hole in his skull.

STRANGER

A sound came from my right. A sort of crunching sound like a foot pressing down on a long-dead branch with the heartwood rotted right out of it. The leaves hissed their warnings. *Bad things in this place, Valdiva. Only no one knows what they are. No one ever sees them. Until it's too late.*

Wolves might still roam out here. There'd be bears as well. Grizzlies with bristling fur, savage eyes. With a jaw full of teeth that can bite you clean through. There'll be snakes bloated with venom. Maybe there are other things, too. A million years ago beasts without names hunted here. Things that were part pig, part bear, maybe even part demon. They had cloven hooves, thick haunches, pelts of shaggy, rust-colored hair. Heads that were as big as a bull's with teeth like knives.

Who's to say that they're extinct? That snuffling sound now coming way off to your left might be one. Its wet snout might be picking up the smell of your skin.

This time I did pause to slide the rifle from my shoulder. With the faintest of clicks I eased the bolt back. When I walked again I kept the rifle ready in my two hands. I scanned the forest, searching for a pair of eyes burning at me from the gloom. I didn't get the Twitch now, but I sensed something out there watching me.

When I looked down at my feet a jolt like an electric shock ran from my balls to my throat. Goddammit. I'd left the path and never even noticed. I looked back into the wood, searching for that dark band of earth that feet, or paws, or cloven hooves had pressed into a hard track over the last million years or so. But nothing. Nothing but grave moss in a dull green blanket.

Shit, that's your wake up call, Valdiva. You've gone and done it now. You're lost. You've gone and lost yourself in the fucking dark wood.

I took a deep breath. OK, keep moving. You'll pick up the path again. Hell, you might walk another ten minutes and find the end of the forest with a highway and a town complete with fast-food joints and super-markets. But then again, another voice whispered, dark and low in the back of my brain: *You might find that the forest never ends; that it gets darker and denser and more tangled, and you end your life crawling on your belly, dying of hunger.*

Gripping the rifle, I walked forward, determined to find a path. Only as I walked I found the trees in front of me were disappearing into shadow. The moss on the ground looked black as a lake at midnight. "It's getting dark, you idiot," I hissed. "You've been walking so long you haven't realized how late it is. Now the sun's gone. It's dark. And you've lost yourself in a goddam forest."

Keep moving, keep moving . . . I repeated this as I walked. But, hell, it got so it was like walking through a cave deep underground. I could barely see individual trees now. A mist filtered through the wood to glide around me. Maybe these were the old ghosts of the forest coming to claim me. Darkness oozed up out of the ground. In a few minutes I'd be as good as blind. Then all I could do was lie down on the ground to wait until morning.

But hell . . . to spend a night here curled up on cold earth. Not being able to see what might be an arm's length from me. That reptile hiss started as the leaves moved in the night air. How long would I lay there in the grave moss before I felt something reach out to touch me in the dark? A snake slipping up over my stomach? A wet mouth closing over my face? A cold hand clasping mine? The point of a knife penetrating my eye?

Those mental images of being touched in the dark-ness kept me walking fast. Although now I had to walk with one hand in front of me. In the gloom tree trunks appeared as suddenly as phantoms bursting out of the shadows.

Five minutes, ten minutes, I hurried through the wood with the weight of all that darkness and gravelike silence pressing into the back of my neck like a corpse's hand.

Then the forest ended. As simple as that.

Once there were trees encircling me like a cage; now there were no trees. I stood blinking, looking into a clearing. Above me, I saw sky. Still blue, yet tinged with red; I realized the sun had just begun to set. Straight-away the air felt warmer. Flying insects moved in that slow, rotating dance of theirs.

In front of me stood a large house with a smaller building alongside it. The roofs were covered with dark shingles and the walls had been clad with boards that had been painted white. A road ran neatly up to the front door. The lawn was tidy. It gave the appearance of a rich person's house that had been left untouched by the madness that had erupted in the outside world.

Only there was something unusual about the place.

I looked at the lawn again.

Then I said to myself: "Who's been cutting the grass?"

My eyes returned to the house for a second, closer look. This time I saw what it really was. And I remember whispering to myself with a whole lungful of air, *Jesus Christ.*

Thirty-one

"Quick," Michaela shouted as she stopped the bike outside the garage door. "Grab your things and jump on; we're moving out."

"Whoa, just a minute," I said holding up my hand. "There's something in the woods across there that's worth taking a look at first."

"We're short of time, Greg. Zak saw some hornets three miles from our place. They're heading our way."

"Trust me, Michaela. This is worth seeing."

"Maybe. But we don't have time. Just grab your stuff and climb on."

"Hell, no," I said. "You've got to see this. This might be the most important find of the year."

Michaela sat astride the Harley revving the motor so it surged in throaty barks. She seemed in no mood to wait for me to tell her about my walk in the woods, or what I'd found. Or that I finally got back to Maison Valdiva at two in the morning by moonlight. Christ, I was bursting to tell her about my amazing find. I'd pictured her look of amazement, even admiration, as I told her. But no. She was shaking her head, talking about getting out of the area as fast as we could. Something like a dirt devil came roaring up the road. It turned out to be Ben on a dirt bike and Zak on the big Harley. His hat swirled behind him by the strap in the slipstream.

"What's the holdup?" Zak called. His bald head gleamed like a steel ball in the morning sunlight. "There's around a thousand hornets back there."

Michaela looked back. "I'm trying to get Greg moving, but he doesn't want to leave."

"Christ, Greg." Ben sounded shocked. "You should see the bad guys in the valley. There's a whole army of them."

I began, "Ben, you're not going to believe what—"

"Hurry up, man. They're going to tear us apart if we don't move out now."

Zak said, "I don't want to do it, Greg, but we'll leave you here if you don't come now."

"Wait!" I felt anger flush through me. "Wait thirty seconds while I tell you this."

"And that thirty seconds could cost us our lives." Ben looked scared. "Come on, Greg, don't piss us off."

"Jesus. I'm trying to tell you about something that might save our necks." I glared at them. "Look . . . how far away from here is the place you're staying? Five miles? Six miles?"

"About that."

"Then bring everyone here," I told them. "If the hornets move this way it will take hours for them to get here."

Michaela suddenly appeared to take what I'd said seriously. "Just what have you found in there?" She nodded at the forest.

"To be honest I'm not exactly sure. But I've got a feeling it might be—"

"Oh, you schmuck, Valdiva." Zak slapped his forehead. "Why're you wasting our time with this?"

Michaela flashed Zak a shut-up look. "Give him a chance to explain, Zak."

"We don't have time for explanations."

"OK," I said, "It'll be quicker to show you." I slung the rifle over my shoulder. "Michaela, slip back onto the pillion."

"Greg." She sounded reluctant. "We really don't have time."

Zak folded his arms. "And I'm not going on wild-goose chases."

"Neither am I." Ben could hardly keep his hands still. They fluttered like edgy doves on the handlebars of the dirt bike. "We don't stand a chance if the hornets catch us."

"Then don't let them catch you." My patience had all but burned dry. "Listen. You've got to bring everyone along this road anyway, otherwise you'll run slap into the arms of the hornets, right?"

Michaela nodded.

"So go back to the gas station and bring them up here." I shrugged. "One, you don't lose any time moving people out. Two, Michaela and I will be back by then."

"OK, OK." Michaela gave in. "If Greg says it's so important it's worth checking out."

Zak grumbled, "Sounds like a waste of time to me, but what the hell do I know?" He took a deep breath. "OK. I'll go back and bring the others here. We can do it in one trip anyway; we found a truck yesterday that's still in running order." Opening the throttle, he swung the rear wheel around in a blur of dust. "We'll be here in under an hour." He shot Michaela a significant look. "I'll wait here. But if those hornets arrive we move on without you. OK?"

"OK." As Michaela nodded she slid back onto the pillion, allowing me to climb onto the seat. I felt her hand slide 'round my waist to hold on. The palm of her hand felt warm through my shirt.

Ben's expression had changed now that I seemed to have resolved the immediate problem. "Greg," he called over the clatter of Zak's Harley as the man roared away, "just what have you found in the woods that's so interesting?"

"Why don't you come along and see for yourself?"

"You're on." He shot me a grin. "But only because you've made such a damn mystery of it."

What had taken a couple of hours on foot in the dark took just minutes on the bikes in broad daylight. The night before, after grabbing a closer look at the house and that neatly trimmed lawn that just couldn't . . . or shouldn't exist . . . in this ruined country of ours, I'd followed a road as it wove through the wood away from the house. Hell, it got dark. A darkness that you could carve with a knife. But I stuck to the blacktop. Eventually the road connected with a highway that I'd recognized from a walk earlier that day. Well, I recognized the burned-out school bus at the junction anyway, with a skull embedded in the melted windshield. After that it was a straightforward enough walk back to the garage I called home.

Now I rode down the center of the road with Michaela holding on to me, her long hair blowing out, all fluttering black like raven's feathers. Ben rode just a little behind, shooting anxious glances into the forest. Maybe he sensed something sinister in there, too.

Barely ten minutes after leaving the garage I pulled up at the entry to what I'd first taken to be a house.

Ben stopped alongside me. He shook his head at the trimmed lawn. "My God, will you look at that," he said. "Who the hell's cutting the grass out here?"

"Wow," Michaela said in something close to awe.

"Now that's what I call gold medal standard gardening."

"Take a closer look. It's not what it seems." I nodded at the brilliant green lawn. "It's synthetic. Probably astro turf."

Michaela looked at the neat collection of white painted buildings. "So that's no ordinary house?"

"Got it in one. Hold on." I opened the throttle to take the bike skimming through the gates onto the driveway. Seconds later I stopped outside the front door. "See?" I said. "It's all as phony as the grass. The windows aren't real. They're painted onto the walls. Even the door's painted."

"Jeez!" Ben looked incredulous. "It looks like a movie set."

Michaela spoke. "Not a movie set. Look . . . solid concrete."

"You got the Cold War to thank for that little beauty," I told them, switching off the motor. "That and a multibillion-dollar defense budget."

Michaela slipped off the bike to stand there gazing up at the imposing face of the fake house. "It's a nuclear bunker, isn't it?"

"A grade-A pedigree one at that," Ben said. He climbed off the bike to walk quickly to it, where he ran his hands fluttering over the painted door. "Heck. They've even painted the handle in gold paint." With a sudden playful grin he rapped on the make-believe door. "Knock, knock, anybody home?"

For a second we paused. Maybe even waiting for an answer to come from within that blast-proof building. But there was only silence. And if silence can be amplified, that silence was great enough to make your eardrums tingle.

"Well, gentlemen." Michaela touched the wall. "I guess there's no one home."

"There must be some other way in." Ben began walking along the path that run around the building, his eyes scanning the walls for some hidden entrance.

"These people certainly went to a lot of trouble to make this place look like a house. There's even a swimming pool. Or what *looks* like a swimming pool, but it's just a layer of blue tiles with sheets of glass over the top of it for water."

Michaela ran her fingers over the window with its painted blue drapes. "From a spy satellite, or if you saw this from a distance, it's good enough to fool anyone. Look, they've even painted a cat in the upstairs window."

"Now you know why I wanted to show you this. If we can find an entrance . . ."

"There should be supplies inside. Food, gasoline."

"There's probably enough canned and dried food in there to keep us alive and well for—*ufff* . . ."

"Greg." She looked at me in alarm. "What's the matter?"

I rubbed my stomach. "Get back on the bike, Michaela."

"You're getting that thing again, aren't you?"

"Yeah." I shot her a grim look. "My God-almighty Twitch. I think the boys are back in the neighborhood."

As Michaela eased the pump-action shotgun from its holster strapped to the side of the bike, I slipped the rifle from my shoulder and looked 'round. The Twitch came again. Like a pair of tiny fists gripping chords of stomach muscle, then twisting.

"Ben?" I didn't shout his name; I spoke it softly. "Ben. You there, buddy?"

At that moment he rounded the corner. "Hey, Greg. I couldn't find an entrance, but I think—" He stopped when he saw me with the rifle. The look that flashed across his face told me he thought I'd got the Twitch when I saw him. "Greg . . . Greg, I'm all right. Believe me, I'm clean."

"Ben, I know. Just get back on the bike."

"But you've got the Twitch."

"Got it sharp, too. Hornets must be close by."

"Dear God . . ."

"Don't start the engine yet."

"Shit, Greg. We need to get outta here."

"Believe me, old buddy, we're going. Like greased lightning." I slipped onto the seat of the Harley while Ben climbed astride the dirt bike with its big front wheel and tires as knobby as an alligator's back. "Start the engine on the count of three. OK?" Michaela tightened her grip 'round my waist.

"OK."

"One—"

"Here they come," Michaela whispered. "See them?"

"Yup." I glanced at Ben. "They're still in the woods but right behind you."

Color fled Ben's face. It bleached white as milk.

"Ben. Concentrate, buddy. One, two, three. Now!"

I thumbed the START button. First time; the Harley's engine purred like a big cat. Ben put his foot on the kick start, then bore down on it. I heard nothing, but the expression on Ben's face said it all.

No go.

Thirty-two

Ben stamped hard on the kick start. Still nothing. I drew the bolt on the rifle.

Shit. There was no point in popping at the hornets. There were maybe thirty of them. I had five rounds in the rifle. If they charged we'd be mauled. Michaela, still sitting tight behind me, chambered a round into the shotgun.

"Hold your fire," I breathed. "They're not in a hurry yet."

Hornets filtered through the trees at nothing more than a stroll. So, OK, their eyes locked onto us with a burning intensity that made you shudder to the roots of your bones. But they were taking it slow. They were cunning creatures. While those had let themselves be seen there might be more working their way 'round the other side of that fake house.

They grew nearer. Now I could see the features of our would-be killers. Their hair fell in straggling locks, looking more like a head full of snakes than real hair. Probably crawling with lice, too. One guy had been in a fight with a wild dog or even a bear. His face looked like a ripped backside. A gash had opened up the side of his face, exposing both rows of teeth almost as far as his ear. One eye had gone, too. The empty socket looked like a bullet hole. But it hadn't bothered him. The wound gave his face a distorted grin. The single eye glared at me so ferociously I recalled the phrase Mom was so fond of using: *If looks could kill . . .*

I glanced back at Ben, who still worked the kick start. His face had a shiny glaze of perspiration on the skin now. "Have you flooded it, Ben?"

"No! I . . . I don't know."

"If it's flooded you can't start it like that."

"Hell, Greg! What do you suggest?" Panic bit into his voice.

"Wait . . . give it a few seconds."

"You've gotta be kidding me!"

"No. Leave it alone. Let the gas evaporate."

"Greg." Michaela's voice came calm but forceful. "Greg. We've got to get away from here."

"I know; just give it a few seconds."

"Well, I reckon we've got around twenty seconds before they reach us."

She lifted the shotgun, aiming it at the one-eyed guy as he slowly emerged as Mr. Nightmare Man himself from the forest. Then in a flat voice she said, "Fifteen seconds, fourteen, thirteen . . ."

I looked at Ben; he'd put his foot onto the kick-start pedal. He was going for it again.

"Not yet, Ben. Wait."

"Jesus, it's easy for you to say." He jerked his head 'round to stare in horror at the evil-looking bunch oozing from the forest. I aimed the rifle, too.

And, yeah, if it was you or me seeing someone point a gun at your heart, it would either stop you dead or send you running in the opposite direction. Not these damn guys. They didn't even see the guns. At least it seemed that way. You could fire bullets so near their heads it shaved hair from their skulls but it didn't faze them. They'd keep on coming toward you. You needed to put a shell in their head or their gut before they'd take notice.

And if they came that bit closer that's what we'd need to do.

"Ben," Michaela said, "if the bike doesn't fire next time, jump up here behind me. This thing can carry three."

White-faced, he nodded. I saw sweat drip from the end of his chin.

Michaela counted down as the hornets approached. "Ten second, nine seconds. They're getting close, Greg."

I saw most of them gripped iron bars or hunks of tree branch in their fists. They raised them.

"Eight seconds."

"OK, Ben. Now!"

He lifted himself up, then bore down with his foot on the kick start.

Glory days!

The motor uttered a mushy-sounding cough. Unburned gas sprayed from the muffler to wet the path.

But thank Christ and all His shining angels, there was goddam blue smoke, too. Ben throttled up, and the mushy cough morphed into a crackling roar. He rocked the bike off the stand to blast away across the astroturf and onto the drive. A shower of fake grass settled on my arms. Hell, even the devil couldn't catch up with Ben now. There was nothing but blue haze on the driveway where he'd been.

Michaela's arm encircled my waist, holding tight. In the rearview mirror I saw she was looking back, aiming the shotgun one-handed. Hell, she must have had some toned muscle in that left arm of hers.

"Greg, they're here!"

I heard her shouting the words over the roar of the engine as I opened up. In the rearview I saw the one-eyed man begin to run toward us. His ripped face filled the mirror. At any second I thought he'd grab Michaela and tear her from the back of the bike. G-force dragged at my body as the bike accelerated. I followed the concrete path, not trusting a shortcut across what might be slippery plastic grass. Then I swung onto the driveway. The bike leapt like a wild animal under me, carrying us away from the bunker and into the forest. I glanced left and right, expecting hornets to lunge at us from the trees. I even cradled the rifle across the gas tank, expecting to have to shoot our way out.

But all I could see in the forest were those tree trunks that lost themselves in dark swirling shadow. I sensed the bad guys were there, though. They were watching us pass for sure.

"Any sign of Ben?" Michaela called.

I shook my head. "The speed he was hitting, he's probably in Manhattan by now."

It was a damn poor joke. Even poorer when I saw Ben next.

The forest hemmed the road in until it seemed as if I rode the bike through a deep gully. Above me burned a strip of blue sky. And all the time the cold shadow beneath trees oozed out onto the road, as if threatening to engulf us. I sensed eyes watching as we passed. I eased off the gas, allowing the bike to slow to around forty-five. Crows glided from the trees, nearly keeping pace with me.

I heard Michaela's voice close to me. "See those damn things?" She must have been referring to the crows. "They seem to know when there'll be fresh carrion."

Yeah. I looked at them, calling to their brothers and sisters. They could have been singing out, *Supper's up*.

STRANGER

Go for the girl with the dark eyes. Those will be sweetest. . . .

If I didn't get us out of here then we really would be crow meat.

She suddenly shouted, "Greg, look out! There's Ben . . . oh, dear God in heaven."

I braked just in time. There in the center of the road was Ben. Grouped in a tight bunch perhaps fifty yards beyond him were hornets. Anything from eighty to a hundred would be my guess. They stood glaring. Cunning bastards. They'd laid an ambush for us all along. Those guys back at the phony house were only the beaters to flush out the prey.

I eased the bike alongside Ben. He stood astride the dirt bike, the motor knocking out balls of blue smoke from the muffler. He'd been staring at the hornets blocking his way with such intensity, he never even noticed me draw alongside him.

After a pause I said, "They've got us penned, haven't they?"

Startled, he turned his head to me. "Hell, Greg. I was beginning to think the pair of you hadn't made it."

Michaela shifted on the pillion behind me to get a better look. "We could try shooting our way through."

"You think we could drop enough of them?"

"There's a chance."

I shook my head. "We'll run at them. See if we can make them scatter."

"You think they will?" Ben asked.

"We've got to try. You ready, Ben?"

He nodded, his facial muscles so tight they formed a mask. A death mask at that.

Sticking side by side, we opened up the throttles, sending the two bikes screaming toward the men and women standing in the road. They fixed their eyes on us, the stare so cold, so fucking brutal it was like trying to break through a force field. But hell . . .

241

I signaled to Ben to stop. "They're not going to move," I shouted. "We'd need a truck to break through there."

Shoot our way through? Bust our way through? *What now, Valdiva?* Damn, those options were running out fast. I glanced to my right. In the wood more hornets on the move. They were going to try to get behind us. Then we'd be trapped between two walls of human flesh. Then the walls would roll in on us.

Michaela called to Ben, "Leave the road. We'll cut back through the forest."

"Hell." He looked like someone had told him to jump out of a plane without a parachute. "In there?" Uneasily, he looked into the pool of creeping shadow.

"There's no other way. Don't worry. You've got the dirt bike; you'll make it."

Ben could really ride a dirt bike. He'd gotten plenty of practice on Sullivan. The big Harley wasn't in the same category. A great road bike, but off-road?

Ben didn't wait. He swung the front wheel of the bike 'round, opened up the throttle and coasted into the woods. The rubber teeth of the tread coped easily with the woodland floor. I followed. Then it all went to shit.

The second I touched the throttle the rear wheel fishtailed on that neverending rug of moss. I slowed a little, then accelerated as gently as I could. Damn . . . the rear end of the heavyweight bike flicked left and right so savagely I had to lower both feet to steady her. Then *bad* got *worse.*

To prevent the bike from skidding out from beneath us I had to stop. The second I did so the heavy bike, bearing the weight of two people, sank through the moss into the mantle of mush and rotting leaves beneath. Michaela slid off the seat; together we pulled the bike clear. Without us riding the machine we could push it forward. However, the second we climbed on it would sink again.

Ben rode back, the rear tire shredding moss into a psychedelic green fountain behind.

"No good," I called to him. "We'll never make it on the bike."

"You have to." He nodded behind us.

Michaela groaned. "Oh, God, Greg. They're here."

Hornets moved like wolves through the woods toward us. Ben drew a pistol, steadied the shaking hand by gripping his wrist with the other, then let fly a couple of rounds. One guy clutched his face and stumbled sideways to lean against a tree. He didn't fall, but I figured he wasn't coming any closer either. Blood streamed through his fingers down into the rags he wore. Michaela let fly with the shotgun, dropping a woman carrying an ax.

"There are too many." I pushed the bike forward. "We can't shoot our way out."

"Drop the bike, Greg." Ben's voice rose to something close to a screech. "It's no good to you."

"We can't outrun them on foot, buddy."

"Greg—"

"Ben, get back to the others. Tell them what happened."

"I can't leave you here."

"Do it, Ben! I'm going to find another way out!"

Ben looked torn. Not wanting to leave, but not wanting to stay to confront the hornets closing in. At last he shouted, "OK. I'll meet you back at the garage." Then he was gone, the bike's rear wheel spinning like a circular saw, hurling up leaf mold and shit into the faces of the people now closing in.

With Michaela guarding my back I shoved the bike back through the woods to the roadway. I'd hoped the hornets that had blocked the way would have followed us, giving me a free run out of there. But they were smart enough to leave around fifty or so blocking the road.

What now?

Come on, Valdiva, think. Think!

But there was no time for thinking through any rational or even any *sane* plan. All Michaela and I could do was scramble on that bike, then ride the hell away from immediate danger. But what's that saying, out of the frying pan, into the fire? There was only one way open now. Back to the phony house, where we'd no doubt encounter the one-eyed man and his clan.

So, that's what I did. With Michaela hanging on tight, I roared the bike along the road, leaving the bunch of hornets behind. I didn't feel it, but I tried to sound optimistic as I called back over my shoulder, "There's got to be a second access to the defense site . . . The military wouldn't restrict themselves to one road in and out."

Oh boy, oh boy, but they had. Maybe they'd spent so many IRS dollars on building the thing with its painted windows, make-believe swimming pool and cut-to-measure astroturf that they couldn't afford the second vehicle access.

Twice, three times, I roared along the path that skirted the house.

Michaela's arm gripped so tight around my waist that it felt like a steel band. The girl was frightened. She'd seen for herself there was no way out. She'd also seen that one-eyed Joe and his buddies were back. They walked across the plastic lawn, their eyes burning with all the fury of hellfire at us. They wanted our blood. They wanted it now.

No way out, Valdiva. No way out.

I stopped the bike outside the painted door of the bunker, then killed the motor. Silence rolled in on us in a wave. Hornets moved silently across the lawn. They didn't shout. They made no fuss. They didn't have to.

STRANGER

We were going to be easy meat for them. Sure, we'd kill some before they got us. But there were dozens of them now. Michaela climbed off the bike. As I slid off the seat I felt her hand close over mine.

"Don't shoot," she said in a calm voice.

"It's the only way, Michaela."

"No. Look at me, Greg. Don't shoot them. Shoot me."

I looked her in the face. Shoot her? But I knew it would be better to die cleanly than fall into their hands.

"No," I told her. "Not yet. We're going to take some of them out first."

I aimed the rifle.

"Save one of those bullets for me, Greg. Please." Her dark eyes seemed huge in her head. "They don't always kill. We might be intended for a hive. I don't want that. Not after what I've seen. . . . Please, Greg?"

I turned back to the hornets. One-eye had just walked by the swimming pool, his bare toes whispering through the fake grass. That single eye of his fixed on Michaela. And, boy, was there a hungry light burning there.

I aimed the rifle at the center of his forehead.

I never even touched the trigger, but the explosion felt like a punch in the ear. One-eye disappeared in a gush of smoke.

I stared dumbly, not understanding what the hell was happening. One-eye Joe now lay on the astroturf. A neat circular hole had appeared where he'd once stood. It didn't look much larger than a soup bowl and it was still smoking. Michaela pressed herself close to me. She was stiff with fright, but she watched, too, as One-eye stood up and began to walk. Only he wasn't as tall as before and he walked weirdly, with a kind of hop-and-limp stride. Then I saw why. His feet had been blown clean off above the ankles. He walked on two stumps that squirted blood and trailed strings of meat and tendon and dripping goo.

This didn't stop the others. They closed in toward us. But a second later another explosion shattered the still air. A tall, thin guy tumbled upward before falling flat to the ground. This one didn't get up. The force of the explosion had torn his legs apart like a wishbone right up to the collarbone.

What was it? Hand grenades? I looked 'round in a daze, expecting to see Zak or Tony lobbing grenades at the hornets. But all I could see were trees, the clearing and the two concrete buildings.

To my right another hornet stepped forward. This time I saw the rush of smoke and flame shoot from the ground. The man fell, with one leg torn clean off at the hip. Like a flipped crab he struggled to roll off his back. But only for a moment. A severed artery shot his lifeblood ten feet into the air. Moments later he flopped back, lifeless as a rock.

But still the relentless advance on us. Those explosions wouldn't stop all of them. Aiming, I blasted the face off a hornet who walked along the path toward us. Michaela dropped another on the driveway.

Then came a voice. Male? Female? Young? Old? I couldn't tell. My ears rang from the explosions. I was still dazed by images of exploding people rollercoasting through my head.

"Move to your right," the voice ordered. "Move to your right to the small building."

One-eye had now reached the path. Still he walked, balancing on those bloody, shredded stumps. He reached out toward me, hate burning in his eyes. I fired from the hip, the bullet popping his heart. With a grunt he fell forward. I heard his face slap the concrete path.

"Move to your right. To the small building. . . . Follow the path. Do not step onto the lawn. I repeat, do not step on the lawn."

Michaela got her head into gear first. "Come on." She grabbed my arm.

I ran with her, not knowing where we were going or where the phantom voice came from. Spilling out of the woods, I saw more hornets. They moved faster now. This time we didn't waste time shooting any more of the bastards. For one, there were too many of them. And, two, Michaela pointed at the smaller building that could have been taken for a stable block. "Look, a door!"

There in the gable end of the building lay an opening. In fact it looked more like a slit rather than a genuine door. But with hornets running at us from left and right there wasn't a whole lot of time to chew over what we might be getting into.

Michaela ran inside first. I followed, turning sideways to slip through the gap into an interior that had all the velvet darkness of a tomb.

Turning, I looked back out onto the sunlit lawn. Hornets moved at a full-blooded run toward the entrance. A guy built like a wrestler had all but reached the opening when I heard a hiss. The sound of air brakes on a truck, and then the thick slab of a door crashed shut. The boom of its closing went echoing deep into the earth to God knows where. The sound of a tomb closing.

Thirty-three

With the door closing there was darkness. I mean absolute, total, incontrovertible

BLACK.

No light came around the seals of the door. No artificial light in the room. Only blackness that pressed against your face like a pillow. I heard Michaela give a shuddering whisper that might have been, "Oh, my God." Then louder: "It's so cold in here . . . freezing. Feel the walls. They're like ice."

I reached out in the dark. My fingers met soft flesh. *Hornets! They're in here with us.*

That spat into my head. Somehow the mob had gotten in, too. A second later I felt Michaela's hand grip mine and she said, "Sheesh, we're like two kids lost in the dark, aren't we?"

Good God, I'd reached out and touched her, not a hornet.

"Can you feel the wall?" I asked.

"My other hand's touching it now."

"See if you can follow it. There must be another door or a light switch."

For a second all I could hear was our breathing echoing back from the walls. Then, faintly, as if coming from far, far away, another sound: like fingernails tapping lightly on glass. An image came to me of hornets battering the other side of that slab of a door. The thing was so thick—thick enough to withstand a nuclear blast—that only a ghost of the sound of their enraged battering made it through.

"Don't move."

That voice again. I sensed a confidence and professionalism there, but darn it, I still couldn't tell whether it was male or female, young or old.

"Please stay where you are."

Michaela's voice rose in the darkness. "We can't see. Can you . . . Christ, what's happening?"

It began without a sound. I flinched, as if a cold hand had reached out and clutched at my face. Darkness disorientated me so much I wasn't sure what was happening at first, but as the noise rose to a roar I understood. A cold blast of air appeared from nowhere to blast us backward on our heels. The power of it could have been nothing less than gale force.

"Stand where you are. Don't be alarmed." That calm voice again.

"What are you doing?" Michaela called out.

I felt her stagger against me before the pressure of the winds tearing through the room.

"Standard decontamination procedure. There's no cause for concern. The air is being drawn out to be replaced with sterile atmosphere."

The wind tugged at my hair. "We're going to be able to breathe, right?"

"Perfectly. Please do not move about the unit."

I heard Michaela hiss, "How can I stop moving? I'm damn well being blown away."

The *away* sounded abruptly loud as the flow of air stopped equally suddenly. There we were again, standing staring into the darkness, just wondering what goddam surprise was coming next. I sniffed the air; it had an artificial air-conditioned scent to it . . . sort of electrical, with just a suggestion of disinfectant.

With a buzz a line of fluorescent lights flickered on. We looked at each other, blinking in the sudden brilliance. I saw we stood in a passageway with featureless walls of stainless steel. The white-tiled floor made me think of hospital emergency treatment rooms . . . so much easier to hose away the blood . . .

Michaela's eyes were wide as she looked at me as if to ask, *What now?* I shrugged. Hell, yes, we were safe from hornets. But did the owner of the professional voice expect us to stand there for the rest of the day?

For a while we did stand there. A voice in the back of my head warned me not to antagonize The Voice needlessly. Our lives were in his or her hands.

Then: "Remove your clothes, please."

"Pardon me?" Michaela looked 'round for the source of the voice. There were no visible speakers.

"Remove your clothes. You'll find a metal flap to your right. Press that. Inside there is a plastic sack dispenser. Put your clothes into the sack. If you wish to retain your clothes for—"

"Hey, wait a minute." Michaela sounded annoyed. "I'm not getting naked for you, buddy."

"Yeah," I said. "Just what is this?"

"Remove your clothes and bag them. It is standard decontamination procedure."

"It might be your standard decontamination procedure, but it's not ours."

There was a pause, as if The Voice considered Michaela's refusal but then continued as calmly as before.

"Those are the *fucking* house rules. If you don't comply I will open the outer door and let you go." The Voice added softly, "Remove your clothes now. All of them."

"Let us go?" I whispered to Michaela. "What they really mean is that they're gonna open the door and let the hornets rip us to pieces."

Michaela looked at me, then said in a no-nonsense way, "Greg, turn your back." Then she slipped off the jacket and began to unbutton her shirt. "It looks as if we've got no choice."

I turned my back and began to undress. I hadn't expected her to be so coy. But then, deep down, what did I expect from her? As I undressed I heard the rustle as she peeled off her clothes. When I heard the zipper go down on her jeans I saw her in my mind's eye. Her slender body toned by months of fighting to survive until it was graceful, catlike, and God yes, I found myself staring at her blurred reflection in the steel wall. I could make out the sweep of her dark hair on her bare shoulders as she peeled off her clothes with her back to me. I made out the narrow waist and the swelling curve of hip.

Maybe it wasn't the right time . . . but I thought to myself, *Turn 'round, Michaela, turn 'round.* Blood tingled in my veins; my heart beat harder—

"The metal flap is at waist height." The Voice again. "Press the edge. That's it."

I'd found it. The metal flap popped like a cupboard door. Inside a roll of heavy-duty sacks in a drab army green sat on a spindle. I pulled off two.

The Voice continued: "Either put the sack full of clothes in the disposal chute you can now see under the sack dispenser or leave them by the door for when you leave. Your choice. Leave your weapons and ammunition by the door, too. Unauthorized firearms are not permitted inside the residential units."

Now naked, we did as The Voice asked. It was a

clumsy operation, as Michaela insisted we remain back-to-back. Our butts brushed one another as we bent over to stuff the clothes into the sack. Michaela said more than once, "I'm not a cheap peep show, Valdiva. Keep your eyes away from me." She didn't sound hostile at all, just matter-of-fact.

But it was hard to avoid catching a tantalizing glimpse of bare skin as I stowed the sacks and guns by the door.

"Now move forward along the hallway," The Voice told us.

"You go in front," Michaela said, facing the wall, so she wouldn't reveal her body to me. Good God, she *was* shy. Funny how social niceties remain embedded even when civilization's gone out the fucking window.

Anyway, I did as she asked. Then I heard a loud hiss. Instantly a fine aerosol spray hit us. I felt cold droplets hitting me from head to toe.

"Cover your eyes. Hold your breath. This is the decontamination procedure."

Good warning, only five seconds too late. My eyes burned like fury the moment the spray hit.

"Shit, what is this stuff?" Michaela hissed. "It burns like poison ivy. Hell, it's all over my body . . . shit, I'm stinging. Hey, why did—"

Her voice cut short as a blast of water struck us. From showerheads embedded in the walls, ceiling and floor jets of cold water hit every square inch of my body. I heard Michaela gasp and figured that those cold fingers of water had thrust themselves deep into even the most intimate quarters of her body.

I was gasping, too. The water was nothing short of liquid ice. What's more, the force and sheer number of water jets made it hard to breathe. I turned away from a stinging torrent to take a breath. The moment I opened my mouth more water exploded against my face. Blindly, Michaela blundered into me, then staggered away, losing her balance. I reached out, grabbing her in my arms to steady her.

That's when the torrents stopped. She pushed me away. Her head hung down over her chest as if she was embarrassed. Water ran from her hair to course down her body in rivulets.

"Ahead of you at the end of the hallway you'll find another metal flap. Open it. Inside there is a paper towel dispenser. Taking as much care as possible to cover all your body, wipe your skin firmly, then dispose of the used paper towels in the chute."

My patience snapped. "Hey! Listen, I know this is house rules and all, but did you have to subject us to that? Jesus Christ, do you know how degrading and unpleasant this is?"

"Please listen. You are about to enter a sterile quarantine unit. You must enter that clean of any possible contamination from the outside world. What you have done is pass through a government-approved decontamination procedure."

"And we're supposed to walk 'round naked?"

"Under the circumstances, I think you might have thanked me for saving your lives. All I am doing is asking you to respect the house rules in order to prevent contamination of the other occupants."

Behind me, Michaela shivered. From the corner of my eye I saw her wet mat of hair. She looked miserable and cold.

"OK, OK." I sighed. "Thank you. It's been a tough day. I apologize for getting—"

"Just get to work with the towels, sir."

The towels were about as pleasant as using newspaper to dry yourself; they scraped you dry rather than absorbed water. After I'd used one towel I dropped it into the chute, where a hiss of air sucked it away to the incinerator . . . wherever that was. Michaela didn't say anything. She merely worked to dry herself with the scratchy oblongs of paper. I guess her being naked made her feel vulnerable. She didn't speak during the entire process.

"Here," I said as gently as I could. "Women can never dry their backs properly. They always miss between their shoulder blades."

She gave me a small smile as she turned her back and lifted her still dripping hair. I dabbed her back with a fresh piece of towel. "Sorry if it feels rough," I said. "It looks like the kind of stuff you'd use to take rust off metal."

"Don't worry, Greg. I'm tougher than I look."

"This might not be luxurious, but at least we're safe from the—uh."

The Voice cut in over me. "The procedure is complete. Proceed through the open doorway."

I hadn't even noticed it open. I guess some pneumatic system had done the trick, but a steel panel had swung inward. I stepped through, followed by Michaela. As brightly lit as the hallway shower room lay another room with a tiled floor.

. . . easier to hose away the blood, Valdiva . . .

On a smaller scale I saw we'd entered what could have been a gym's locker room. Benches ran along one wall. Clothes hooks were screwed to walls. Shelves contained shoes. There were metal lockers, wall-mounted hair driers, mirrors.

The Voice followed us in here, too. "In the lockers you'll find everything you need. Choose a pair of sandals from the shelf. Once you have everything, pass through the red door into the residential area. Have something to eat; make yourselves comfortable."

Michaela still stood there, her hair dripping, her bare skin red from the pummeling of the high-pressure shower. She looked up. "Listen, thanks for letting us in here."

"Don't mention it. Some of us haven't abandoned all traits of civilized society."

"Will you be in the residential area?"

"No. You'll be alone for now."

"We'd like to be able to thank you in person. This intercom stuff's a bit impersonal, you know?"

"We'll be able to talk later. But it can't be face-to-face yet, unfortunately. You are being housed in the quarantine annex. For obvious reasons, as the name implies. You understand?"

"Yes. Of course." She rubbed her hands. I noticed her fingertips were blue with cold. "Thank you. It's really good of you."

"I must go." The Voice quickened, as if in a hurry. "Good-bye."

"Greg." She shot me a warning look. "I told you, I'm not a goddam peep show."

"OK, you first." I turned my face to the wall. Soon I heard locker doors opening as she hunted through them. Meanwhile I noticed that the door to the decontamination unit had closed. There was no door handle. I didn't try it, but I'd guess it would be locked tight.

"OK, you can turn 'round now."

I turned to see her standing facing the open lockers. She'd wrapped a large white bath towel 'round herself that reached from above her breasts to her knees. She'd found a smaller towel that she now fastened turban-style 'round her head.

"By the way, Valdiva, on your butt you've got a bruise the size of Idaho. You might have to eat standing up."

For the next ten minutes we finished drying ourselves with soft cotton towels. In the lockers were hard, mysterious objects encased in plastic. I looked at them for a moment before exclaiming, "Hey, shrink-wrapped clothes." Using my thumb, I tore a hole in the plastic. With a hiss the packaging softened, expanded, like a shiny lung inhaling. Inside were a sweatshirt and pants in a cool shade of green. Neatly folded there were also a white T-shirt and two pairs of underpants. "Hey, they think of everything."

"Check the label first," Michaela said. "You've opened a child's size. See? Small, regular, large, extra large."

Soon we were dressed in matching green outfits. For our feet there were something like rubber beach sandals in hospital white. Another locker had been stacked high with individual toiletry sets marked either *Male* or *Female*. When I opened a *Male* I found disposable razors, shaving foam, a toothbrush, toothpaste, soap, talcum powder and a comb. I grinned, feeling, absurd to say, like a kid at Christmas. "Look. Just what every nuclear calamity survivor needs."

Michaela didn't share my absurd sense of fun. She sighed. "I'm hungry." Then she picked up a *Female* toilet pack before heading for the red door that The Voice had indicated.

Thirty-four

Maybe I should have been asking questions about our immediate future in that place, but to step through the red door was to step into a different world.

Whereas the first two rooms we'd passed through had been utilitarian and colder than a zombie's goodnight kiss, this suite of rooms was warm, comfortable, even luxurious. Like a pair of vacationers in a new hotel room we explored. On the first level was a kitchen painted in warm oranges with a modern stove, refrigerator, sink and countertops in stainless steel. Bolted to one wall were a whole bank of microwave ovens.

"Looking at these"—Michaela opened a microwave door—"you can guess what will be on the menu."

She guessed right. A walk-in pantry had been stacked floor-to-ceiling with every microwave-ready meal you could think of. While the refrigerator had been packed with what I first thought were racks of toothpaste. Only a closer look revealed that these were labeled NASA PATENT PENDING. I saw they were marked either *cheese, mayonnaise, cream* or *butter*. "Butter from a tube?"

"Good God." Michaela's eyes widened in sheer wonder. "They have butter? I've forgotten what butter tastes like."

I picked up more tubes. "But which one of these contains the bread?"

"Idiot." She smiled. And it was such a breathtakingly beautiful smile that I found myself grinning back at her. She broke away to open a cupboard full of knobby vacuum packs. "There's the bread." Taking out the tennis ball–sized lump, she read the label. " 'Remove all packaging. Place on oven tray and bake for twenty minutes' . . . partly baked bread. We're certainly not going to starve here. I wonder if they've got any coffee."

"It's in the drum by the kettle."

She turned on the faucets. "Hot and cold. It looks pure."

"It'll be pumped from a sealed well, I guess." I looked up at the lights. "They must have a good set of generators, too, and a heck of a lot of fuel. They're not worried about rationing."

Stroking a clean countertop, she gave a sigh of pleasure. "We might as well enjoy it while it lasts. It's unlikely the government'll keep us here as guests for long."

"I guess not."

A living room came next, with comfortable sofas, deep armchairs, fluffy rugs, a wall-mounted TV screen that was bigger than your bedroom door. Again the place was pleasantly warm and decorated in luscious orange with a pale yellow ceiling. "Some nuke shelter," I said, running my hand over a lush velvet drape beside a false window that showed a painted view of a stag drinking from a stream.

"I read somewhere that these bunkers were all decorated in bright colors and furnished like this after psychologists said that people who spent long periods of time in them would go crazy or start killing themselves."

"You're hardly likely to suffer cabin fever here," I said. "Look at those potted plants. They're real. They've even got their own automatic watering system."

"If you're going to keep people in a concrete box for months you've got to look after their creature comforts." She picked up a remote from a coffee table. When she pressed a button soft music padded into the room from concealed speakers. "Ambient music."

"No doubt chosen by psychologists, too. There are probably subliminal messages of hope and optimism buried down in the mix."

"Don't knock it, Greg. I think we've just stumbled into heaven on earth."

"Let's hope so."

She smiled. "Cynic. Come on, let's explore."

Carpeted stairs led down below ground level to a hallway, again painted bright yellow, with a frieze of dolphins and palms. One door led to a corridor lined with yet more doors. These were the bedrooms (although they resembled ship's cabins). These were a little plainer but had comfortable beds, closet space, tables, mirrors, washbasins: the usual stuff. There were also a couple of bathrooms, too, for shared use.

Back at the other side of the stairs, a wide door opened up into a plain white painted corridor. There weren't as many doors—and these were all hard steel—and locked. Beside each door was a keypad where the bunker people would tap in their open sesame code. The doors bore stenciled notices that said things like *Back-up Ops* or *Sick Bay* or *Service Center* or *Q.A. Boardroom.* In the middle of one wall were a set of large twin doors (but no keypad, I noted). Those doors were labeled *Comm-Route,* whatever that was.

"That looks to be the extent of it," she said. "Come on, let's make the most of paradise."

The Voice didn't visit until that evening around ten hours later. I say evening because I only had my watch to go on. Of course, there were no windows in what was, when all's said and done, a grande deluxe bomb shelter. Part novelty and part hunger, we both ate half a dozen microwave meals apiece. Mexican, Chinese, Italian, French cuisine. They tasted wonderful considering they came out of vacuum packs. And when we'd baked the fresh bread (again from a little bag) it smelled so mouthwatering we tore off lumps and squirted NASA butter all over it in a gooey, golden stream.

After pigging out, I checked the TV in the living room area. Three of the channels showed the equivalent of ambient music. Channel One carried a single view of the ocean washing over rocks. Two showed a view of trees in the fall; flocks of birds came and went but not much else. Three played a static shot of a farm with cows grazing in green pastures. More psychologist-inspired programming, I guessed. Other channels were more promising. A comedy channel showing old TV sitcoms. Music channels for every possible taste. Sports, replaying classic football games. The last channel appeared devoted to lightweight action movies.

By midnight I slouched low in an armchair watching an old cop movie. By that time I was too drowsy to follow the plot. While sitting with her bare feet up on the sofa, Michaela flicked through a magazine that must have been the last one to roll off the press before society turned over and coughed out its heart.

Then came the return of The Voice. "My apologies for taking so long to come back to you. We've had a busy time down here today. You wouldn't believe the paperwork government departments still need. Good evening to you both." I looked at Michaela, who smiled. She felt the same; talking to a disembodied voice was weird. Nevertheless, we chorused, "Good evening," back at the walls.

"Did you both find everything you needed?"

"Yes, thank you."

"When you shower run the hot water for a while. It takes time to warm up. But, believe me, it gets there in the end."

Michaela said, "My name is Michaela and I'm here with Greg."

"Of course, how ill mannered of me." The Voice sounded as softly spoken as ever. "I never introduced myself."

"Things were hectic," I said. "At the time we were just glad to get inside here in one piece."

"Of course. We're happy to help. Well, to begin at the beginning, my name is Phoenix . . ."

Phoenix? That didn't help. I still couldn't tell whether Phoenix was a he or a she. Then again, there was something she-male about the voice.

". . . my role here is the emergency services coordinator." Her (His?) voice padded from the speaker. "The center's commander is Rachel Peake, but if you need anything just press one of the green buttons that you'll find set in the wall. That *pings* me." Phoenix paused before saying *pings*, as if it had some double meaning for her (or him). "Help yourself to food, drinks, entertainment. It sounds stuffy of me to have to say this, but I need to mention house rules. Please remember, switch off lights when you're not in a room so we can conserve fuel; please keep the place tidy and dispose of all refuse in the chutes. Doors that are locked are secure areas for authorized personnel only; please respect that and don't try to force them open . . ." As the Voice continued the do's and don't's I rolled my eyes at Michaela. She stifled a laugh behind her hands, then wagged her finger with a pretend stern look on her face. She mouthed: "Don't make me laugh. Please!"

". . . no windows, for obvious reasons. External doors are hermetically sealed. The atmosphere is recycled. To all intents and purposes you can imagine we're living in a submarine at the bottom of the sea. We are completely self-contained. Food and fuel stores are amply sufficient. Any questions, Michaela? Greg?"

"Again, we can't thank you enough for saving our lives," I said to the four walls. "But what now? After all, we can't remain here forever, can we?"

"That's absolutely correct. In the past visitors like yourselves have stayed here for anything up to three days before moving on."

"Then we could leave now?" I didn't particularly want to leave at night, but I wanted to test the water.

"Not advisable, Greg. Look at the TV screen."

We looked at the screen, which showed a police car bouncing up and down the hills of San Francisco. With a flash the scene changed.

"I think you recognize the location. There's no color because it's dark outside—the camera is in infrared mode."

Hell, yes, I recognized it. The TV revealed a view of the astroturf area where we'd been trapped earlier. I saw the Harley, or what was left of the machine. The hornets must have hacked it to pieces in their frustration after we escaped into the bunker. Out on the lawn lay the bodies mangled by the explosions. As we watched a brown bear ambled out of the forest with a pair of cubs. Mama Bear began tearing at one of the corpses with its jaws, ripping out glistening strings of gut. The cubs joined the feast.

I said, "Phoenix? They were landmines that blew the bad guys sky high, right?"

"That's correct."

"Then why doesn't the bear detonate them?"

"Good question." I sensed Phoenix smiled as he/she spoke. "Antipersonnel mines are embedded in the lawn. For safety reasons I can arm them electronically from a keyboard here. In theory you could have a football team stomping up and down there without tripping one . . . but personally I wouldn't put it to the test. So when you do leave here stick to the pathways and the drive."

"Don't worry, we will."

Michaela looked closely at the screen. "But it's clear of hornets now."

"Hornets?"

"Yes. Bees? Bread bandits?"

"Oh, the refugees? It appears clear here, but let me hit Cam Two. Just wait a second while I . . . there. Not so friendly out there, is it?"

The screen flashed, replacing the scene with another shot at a lower angle. This must have been the view from our bunker. There, standing unmoving in the darkness, their faces expressionless, was a group of hornets. I counted ten of them. But there could have been more off camera.

"It looks as if we need to stay put a little longer," I said.

"You're more than welcome." Phoenix's voice whispered around the room. "We know life is hard out there now. Treat this as a rest break."

Michaela turned away from the impassive, somehow alien faces of the hornets and said to me, "Don't you feel them, Greg?"

I rubbed my stomach. The Twitch had stayed away. Even seeing the monsters on screen hadn't done anything to provoke my gut muscle.

"Nothing," I said.

"But I thought you felt this Twitch when you were close to them." She nodded at the people on screen, waiting for us as patiently as vultures beside a dying calf. "You don't even have to see them, do you?"

"No. But as Phoenix pointed out, this building is air-tight."

"So you don't think this is some kind of sixth sense? That you know when someone's a hornet by telepathy?"

"Telepathy? No." Irritation spilled into my voice. This Twitch made me a freak. I never enjoyed talking about it. I didn't want to discuss it now. "I smell them, that's all. Cows can smell water in a desert twenty miles away. It's like that. Unconsciously or subconsciously, or whatever the crap it is I can smell their pheromones, or hormones, or even their fucking hornet shit. I don't know how the hell it works, Michaela."

Her eyes widened. She looked hurt by the anger in my voice. "I'm sorry, Greg. I thought this might be an interesting—"

"Experiment?"

"But you—"

"OK, OK." I softened my voice. "Let's just leave it, shall we?"

After a heavy silence Phoenix spoke. "I'm sorry; if this is a bad time, I can speak to you later, only I guessed you might have some questions for me." Another pause. "Greg? You don't feel well? A stomachache?"

"No," I said, keeping my voice under control. "I'm fine, I really am."

Pause—leaving that kind of silence you feel obligated to fill.

"It's, well . . . when I'm close to a hornet or someone who's infected and incubating the condition I can tell."

"But how, Greg? Our medical teams are still working on developing a blood test, but nothing shows in blood or tissue samples."

Boy, oh, boy, Phoenix is fishing for information. That

made me uneasy. "It's instinct. My stomach muscles get twitchy. That's all I know."

Again a silence. I sensed Phoenix—wherever he was, snugged away in the bunker complex—was digesting the information. Yeah, that made me goddam uneasy. Now I didn't feel like a refugee from the madness of the outside world. I felt like a lab rat just about to be sliced and diced before going under the scope.

Just as I'd decided to be evasive when Phoenix asked the next question the whispery voice said, "I won't be able to cover everything in detail, but I guess you're curious about this place. And about its staff." Brisk now, Phoenix spoke like the guide on a tour bus. "You know there are bunkers like this all over the States, not to mention all the missile silos. They were built in the Cold War in case of attack with nuclear weapons, nerve gas or biological agents, hence the elaborate decontamination procedures you experienced. The bunkers' purpose was to provide a refuge for medical and administrative staff and a store of food, fuel, hospital supplies and so on in the event towns and cities were destroyed by nuclear weapons. It sounds like a tall order, but our job is to safeguard the civilian and military command structure . . . and to try and pick up the pieces after the radioactive shit hits the fan."

Michaela said, "I thought these places were built entirely underground."

"Not all. If we're disguised as we are and as long as we're not at ground zero—that's why these places are situated in wilderness areas—then these can take nuclear blasts without excessive damage."

"Phoenix, let me get this straight," I said. "When those guys went crazy last year and started ripping people and whole cities apart your bunker team came out here and locked yourself in?"

"That's about it. We're supposed to have a complement of thirty-four. When all hell let loose, twenty made it through. Some of us were brought in by police helicopter. Man, those roads were clogged with cars. I can still smell the smoke of towns burning as we flew over them. Right then, I remember thinking, 'My God. This is hell. Pure hell.'"

Michaela shook her head. "So your people are going to sit here until hell freezes back over?"

"No." I imagined Phoenix shaking his/her head. "No, we're in touch with the government at all levels. Plans are being devised to bring this under control. It won't happen overnight, but when it does this facility will coordinate the restoration of law and order in this district. Then comes the long job of rebuilding our towns."

"They are that confident?" I heard skepticism in Michaela's voice. "You know, it's a mess out there. Apart from the hornets that pretty much control the state, maybe even the whole country or even the world for all I know, all I've come across are small groups of people who are scavenging an existence from the wreckage."

"Michaela, I didn't intend to paint a rosy picture, but things will be back under governmental control soon."

"So you're in regular contact with these other bunkers?"

"Yes, there are several hundred of them. We all—"

"And the hornets have overrun the entire United States?"

"A temporary state of affairs."

Michaela stood up to talk to that phantom voice. Suddenly she looked cold, as if she'd begun to see the whole picture—devastation, death, dissolution. "Phoenix, what about the rest of the world? Is it like this in Europe, Asia and Africa?"

"Greg, Michaela, I won't lie to you. At present, yes, it's bad. This infection has been like an influenza epidemic that's gone global."

"Jesus."

"After all, we lived in a world of international travel. You could step on a plane and be anywhere on the planet in twenty-four hours. Imagine a typical day at JFK. All those tens of thousands of people flooding through Customs into the country. They're coming from China, Japan, India, Argentina, Mexico, Kenya, Germany, Russia, you name it. Customs can screen them for cocaine and guns but can't screen them for what they carry in their blood. . . ."

There was a pause. I could hear the sound of Phoenix breathing. It whispered from the speakers. It could have been the sound ghosts make, soft but sort of shimmering and unreal in the air. I shivered.

"We will beat this." Phoenix's voice was hushed. "We will do it. Believe in us." When the voice came again it was louder, more direct. "Now, I don't want to keep you up all night. You've been through hell today. But first I want to show you something. Although you'll understand that this is a top-secret establishment, my boss has given me clearance to show you our recreation area. She and I thought you might find it reassuring that although this might appear an unusual place to you, life goes on normally enough. See for yourselves. This is some of our crew at play."

The TV screen flashed. A banner appeared at the bottom of the screen stating CAM 6:RECREATION. We saw a brightly lit room with potted ferns and a big wall TV screen something like the one we now watched. Some middle-aged guys were watching an old Buster Keaton movie while sipping beers. At the far end of the room a couple of young women played pool. Like this room, there were comfortable armchairs and sofas. Men and women lounged about talking, reading books; an older guy sat at a table writing. As we watched a man in a military uniform walked in with a clipboard under his arm. He shared a joke with the pool girls. They laughed.

Phoenix spoke. "That's about half the team. The others are at their workstations or sleeping. The white-haired gentleman at the table is Dr. Roestller. Before you go he'll want to inoculate you."

"Oh, what against?" Michaela spoke casually, almost as if making conversation, but when I looked at her she made eye contact with me. She seemed suspicious of something.

Equally casual Phoenix said, "We have a multiple vaccine shot. It was developed as a cover-all after a nuclear strike, when sanitation and normal healthcare would be disrupted. Some joker called it the Morning After Armageddon Pill. A single injection protects you against cholera, hepatitis, meningitis, influenza, septicemia, typhoid, malaria, intestinal parasites . . . all the visitors who've passed through here have had the shot. You might be drowsy and run a low fever for a couple of days, but that's the extent of the side effects." Phoenix didn't wait for any answer or further questions. Instead: "Well, I've reached the end of my shift. I'm allocated six hours' sleep now, so I best make the most of it."

Michaela yawned. "OK, Phoenix, good night."

"And thank you for taking the time to talk to us."

"Don't mention it, Greg. My pleasure. Good night, you two."

"Good night."

Silence settled on the room again. Michaela shrugged. "Well, I guess I'm going to turn in." She gave a tired smile. "It's going to be novel sleeping in a bed again. I hope I remember how."

Thirty-five

It was one in the morning when I closed the door of my room. For the next five minutes I got the bed ready. There wasn't much to do. A sleeping bag in that shrink wrap sat on a bare plastic mattress. I tore open the packing and something like a concrete block in hardness and size expanded and softened as the air rushed in. I unrolled the sleeping bag onto the mattress, then kicked off my sandals. Bolted on the wall next to the bed was a radio that couldn't have been much larger than a pack of cigarettes. The controls consisted of a single push button. I pushed it. All I got was more of that ambient elevator music. I switched off.

"Greg?"

"Come in, Michaela. It's not locked."

She opened the door and looked in. Her hair fell loosely 'round her shoulders. It was damp from a recent shower. She wore a T-shirt for a nightdress. Shyly, she smoothed it 'round her hips to keep the hem down over her thighs.

"This might sound silly to you . . ." She smiled, looking awkward. "But do you mind if you leave your door open a little? I'm leaving mine open." She blushed. "I've got so used to sleeping 'round a campfire with a crowd of people that it's going to be strange sleeping alone in my own room."

I smiled back, trying to be reassuring. "Of course. And relax—we're safe in here. This place is built like a fortress."

"That's going to take getting used to as well. I'm used to sleeping with someone standing watch."

"I could sit with you until you go to sleep if you like."

"I'm sure I'll manage." She yawned. "I can't wait to lay down on a soft mattress. It's going to seem like heaven. Thanks anyway."

"Make the most of it. Sleep late tomorrow. I'll fix breakfast."

She grinned. "Now you're spoiling me."

"You deserve it."

"Good night."

"Good night, Michaela. Just shout if you need anything."

When she'd gone I sat on the bed. Through the thin partition wall I could here her moving 'round for a moment or so, then came the click of the light switch. After that there was only silence. I guessed she'd fallen asleep straightaway.

Switching off the light, I slipped into the sleeping bag and lay there on my back with my fingers knitted behind my head. Despite the time being well south of midnight I didn't feel ready to sleep yet. A lot of what Phoenix had told us was rattling through my head like a neverending train. I suddenly thought of dozens of questions I wanted to ask. But that's always the way, isn't it? You only think of the smart questions long after the opportunity has passed you by. What was life really like in these bunkers for the twenty or so men and women who crewed the place? Did they suffer from cabin fever? Did it get so you wanted to rip off the guy's head who snores in his sleep? These partition walls between the bedrooms were little more than boards skinned with plaster. Were romantic entanglements banned? Or were there red-hot orgies every night? Did these people ever leave the bunker to take the air and see real daylight? But I guessed not. These people were so afraid of contamination they wouldn't risk poking their head outdoors in case they inhaled an airborne Jumpy bug. Like nuclear subs that remained submerged under the Arctic ice cap for six months at a time, these people stayed sealed away in their concrete lair.

I lay in the sleeping bag with those questions going 'round my head. Johnny Christ. How come your thoughts seem loud enough to keep you awake at night? It's nighttime when all those anxieties and fears that you keep locked down all through the day come stomping out. They keep you lying there wide awake looking at the ceiling. You've as much chance of sleeping as levitating yourself off the bed and flying 'round the room. Even as I managed to stop thinking about what Phoenix had told us I immediately found myself wondering if Ben had made it. He was good on that dirt bike. He'd be able to leave the hornets chewing on nothing but moss thrown up by the back tire as he powered away. In my heart I knew he was safe. All I had to concern myself with now was sleeping. But that wasn't easy.

Count sheep?

Yeah, I tried that.

But all the sheep turned into hornets. Then my imagination had them creeping through a back door of the bunker. I listened. With no TV or conversations with Michaela to distract me I could hear clicks and whirring sounds behind the walls. They were just the bunker plumbing and air-conditioning units. Of course my imagination turned those sounds into some bare-footed, murdering bastard shuffling down the corridor outside. Jesus, I wish I'd kept my rifle. I wish I'd . . . crap to this. I switched on the light.

Come on, Valdiva, settle down. It's only your imagination winding you up. Relax. You're safe. Michaela's safe. No hornets can get through those walls. Yeah, as if your imagination ever listens to you when it turns itself into a tormenting devil. It just quacks on and on, leaving you more wide awake than ever. I climbed out of bed, went to the bathroom, drank some water, then returned to my room. Of course the corridor was deserted. No murdering hornets. Nothing could enter here from the outside. Hell, not even a mosquito.

I paused outside Michaela's room. Through the door I could hear the regular sound of her breathing. *Take her lead, Valdiva, old buddy, sleep.*

When I was back in my room I pushed the door three quarters shut. For the first time I noticed a plastic envelope pinned to the back of the door. It must have been there all along, but this was the first time I'd noticed it. Not that there was much to notice. Through the plastic I could see the words. CIVIL DEFENSE AUXILIARY INSTALLATION. EMERGENCY PROCEDURES. PLEASE DO NOT REMOVE FROM ROOM.

Great, a little bedtime reading.

Memorize these alarm sounds.
1. *Continuous siren: Incoming missile alert.*
2. *Alarm in pulse mode: Nuclear detonation in Bunker vicinity.*
3. *Alarm in horn mode: Internal fire.*

And so on. I'd have given the notice no further attention if it hadn't been for a penciled addition to the list that ran: *In case of direct nuclear strike kiss your fanny good-bye.*

STRANGER

Someone with a sense of humor had stayed here. On the paper I could make out impressions that made me think that whoever had slept in that bed before me had written some witty comments on the other side of the doom-'n-gloom notice. The plastic envelope was open-ended, so it was simple enough to slip out the sheets. I took them across to the bed and sat down.

Valdiva, I scolded: *sitting on your bed at 2 AM reading someone else's bored-out-of-their-skull doodles is the act of a desperate man.* A desperately bored one, that is. I turned over the sheets of paper to the blank side. Sure enough there were pencil doodles including a man entering a woman from behind with the caption: *Dr. Roestller's preferred injection procedure.* A speech balloon came out of his mouth: *"This won't hurt, my dear. You'll just feel a little prick."* The scribbler's humor reserve seemed to run dry after that. Everything else jotted down there seemed to relate to meal times, work rotations and the warning to run the shower on hot until warm water made it through the pipes from the main bunker. Yeah, we'd had that warning from Phoenix, too. In my mind's eye I saw one of the civil defense bunker team who was new to the job sitting here and jotting down these notes to remind himself or herself what time supper was and when they were expected to start a shift. In the bottom righthand corner of the sheet were also columns of numbers.

6731
4411
8730
9010

They were too short for telephone numbers. And some had a couple of letters tagged on: *7608—SB, 4799—Q* and so on. At the bottom of the page in shouting capitals was the word MEMORIZE! An arrow pointed to heavily underscored words that didn't make a bunch of sense: *maple-eagle-green*.

I checked the other sheets. Apart from the printed emergency procedures and do's and don'ts—*No smoking in bathroom. Dispose of sanitary products in chute provided NOT in the toilet*—there weren't any more handwritten notes. With the notice's entertainment value well and truly exhausted I turned out the light to try to sleep.

Five minutes later I sat up in bed. A minor revelation had just crackled across my brain. Suddenly some of those inexplicable handwritten notes made sense. Also gut instinct told me to be on my guard. Faking restlessness, I walked through every room in the bunker from the locker room, with its shrink-wrapped clothes, back to the kitchen to drink some orange juice, then into the lounge to flick through the TV channels, then back to the corridor with the sealed steel doors, then back to bed.

When, at last, I turned out the light I knew I had something to tell Michaela in the morning.

Thirty-six

"Hey, Michaela, come and take a look at what I've found."

Stifling a yawn, she walked into the kitchen, her eyes still sleepy. "Some fine vintage wines, I hope . . . pardon me." She yawned again. "Thanks for breakfast, by the way. Breakfast in bed has to be a first since God knows how long." She pushed back her hair. "What have you got there, Greg?"

"Popcorn."

"Popcorn? Thought of everything, didn't they?"

"See? It's the kind you cook in a pan." I put the pan on the stove and began to tear open the foil wrapper to expose a block of golden corn fused together by butter. "Great stuff, this. When I was ten I nearly lost an eye making it. A piece of corn shot from the pan and hit me. Red-hot it was, too. I had to sit for an hour with a wet sponge pressed to my eye."

Michaela laughed, bemused. "But popcorn at this time of the morning, Greg?"

"We're on vacation, aren't we? C'mon, break some

rules. Let's make popcorn and watch a movie."

"Are you sure you aren't crazy?"

I grinned and yattered away in a lighthearted way. But there was method to my madness. "Look at this, Michaela." I showed her that the pan had a glass lid. "Now we can see the corn popping before our very eyes."

She grinned. "You are mad, Valdiva. Now I'm going back to bed."

"You can't miss this. Marvel at how these little seeds become puffs of snowy white corn. Be amazed at how a block the size of a cigarette carton grows miraculously to fill the pan."

"You're nuts. I'm going back to sleep."

"You'll miss the popcorn!"

"Well, my loss."

"Wonderful popcorn."

"I don't even like popcorn."

"Of course you do. Everyone loves popcorn."

"There are always pieces of corn that don't get popped and you wind up cracking a tooth on it."

"Michaela, my love—"

"You been drinking, Greg?"

"You lay on the couch, my darling. I'll pop one piece through your red-rose lips one delicious morsel at a time."

Her grin faded. "Greg, you're starting to make me nervous."

"Help me make popcorn, my love."

"No, really . . . stop this, Greg."

"I'll stop on one condition?"

"What's that?" She looked uneasy.

"Help me make the popcorn."

"Greg—"

She looked ready to storm out of the kitchen. Could I blame her? I was acting weird.

"Michaela, listen, it used to be a big thing at home.

STRANGER

Saturday evenings Mom would put up her feet after working all day. Chelle—that's my sister—and I would wash up the supper things, then make popcorn together. It was a . . . a ritual, I guess you'd call it. We made the popcorn year in, year out. I must have made hundreds of pansful. . . . Of course, I was always so curious to see the corn popping I'd take a little peak into the pan and *bang!* Hot corn would come flying out like machine-gun bullets."

"Your mom must have loved popcorn."

"As a matter of fact she didn't. She always complained that there'd be an unpopped piece of corn that would chip a tooth." I smiled. "But it was our ritual."

"So making the stuff was the best part of it."

"Absolutely."

She gave a good-natured sigh. "OK, then. Let's make popcorn." She dug me in the ribs with her finger. "But no more weird stuff, right?"

"Right."

"OK, start cooking."

"Come close . . . closer, right up close to me."

"Greg, I warned you."

"You want to see the corn pop, don't you?"

"No funny stuff, OK?"

I turned up the heat, then dropped the block of buttered corn into the pan.

"Don't forget the lid, Greg. I've got two eyes and I want to keep it that way."

She did stand close to me, but she kept shooting me looks that said loud and clear that she was suspicious of me. Maybe wondering what I'd do next. "See, the butter's starting to melt."

"Thrilling."

"It's bubbling now."

"Exciting."

"Are you humoring me, Michaela Ford?"

"I am, Valdiva. I could be in bed sleeping instead of watching—"

"Whoa, I think we have lift off. No . . . false alarm."

"You have been drinking."

"Hear it, hissing? Should be any second now that we . . . No. It needs to be hotter. I'll give it more gas." The first piece of corn popped. Through the glass I saw fluffy white erupt from the shell of the corn. "Don't miss any of this, Michaela."

"Greg?"

I put my arm around her waist and pulled her close to me so she could look into the pan through the glass lid.

"Greg, maybe we should talk about personal boundaries. I don't think—"

"Whoa, here it comes. Sounds like firecrackers, doesn't it?"

"You are nuts. And you're making me nervous, so—"

"Wow, here it comes." As the clatter of popping corn swelled I still kept the fascinated look on my face as I gazed through the lid, but I whispered low enough to keep my voice beneath the sound of frying corn, "Michaela, humor me. Do you get the feeling Phoenix is listening to every word we say?"

To her credit she didn't react. She fixed her eyes on the popcorn pan. "You thought it, too?"

"And watches us."

"I don't see any cameras."

"Neither do I," I whispered, still standing with my arm 'round her while grinning like a loon at the popping corn. "But think back to the decontamination procedure. The way he told us to move from one part of the room to the other suggested he could see us. Hey, there go a whole bunch of corn. How do they expand like that?"

"Search me."

The popping of corn came in sporadic bursts like

machine gun fire. We had to synch our conversation to the clatter of exploding corn to make sure Phoenix didn't hear us over microphones that must be concealed nearby.

As the bang of corn grew louder again I said, "When we went through decontamination Phoenix was watching us."

"And probably juicing himself watching our reactions as we stood there, scared half to death."

"He didn't warn us about the disinfectant spray or the cold water shower. . . . There should be some more corn in there to pop."

"There always is. Remember what I said about our teeth?" Once more the clatter of exploding kernels filled the kitchen. "Something isn't right here, is it?"

"I feel like a peep show."

"Those guys have been isolated in here for months. We might be their favorite TV show."

"Possibly . . . You want salt on the popcorn . . . or they want something else from us."

"Like what?"

"Who knows, but I'll tell you something . . ." The popping paused for a second before restarting. "We're unarmed; we depend on these bunker people for food and protection. I'm starting to feel we're at their mercy."

"So what do you propose?"

"Last night I found something written on a sheet of paper that could be useful."

"Useful? How?"

The popping paused. Without the loud popping to mask my voice I reverted to chitchat. "Do you want coffee with this? Or there's soda in the refrigerator." I gave the pan a shake. The corn must be all but used up. Popcorn had reached the lid. "Hey, here we go again." The bangs and pops started up, nice and loud. I whispered, "There were sets of numbers on some paper. Code numbers for the locked doors. What do you say to some late-night exploring?"

"Michaela, Greg. Good morning." The voice of Phoenix broke in quickly. "Did you both sleep well?"

We broke the clinch and turned to reply to that disembodied voice.

"Fine, thanks," Michaela said pleasantly. "We helped ourselves to breakfast."

"Of course, be our guests." Phoenix's velvet voice padded from the speaker. "After all, your tax dollars paid for it. Be sure to make yourself at home and enjoy the rest of your day."

"Thanks, we will," I said.

"Any plans?"

"We thought we'd stay home today."

Phoenix laughed. "You might as well. It's raining out."

"Any sign of hornets?"

"Oh, the infected people? Yes, they're still waiting outside the door. They won't quit for a day or so yet."

"Do you know what became of your previous guests, Phoenix? People like us you invited in to stay for a while?"

"They moved on. Of course we—the bunker crew, that is—don't know where they went. Naturally we pray they found some safe haven. What's that sound?"

"A sound?" Michaela asked the question innocently.

"Yes. It sounded like gunshots."

"Oh." She smiled. "It's just popcorn."

"Popcorn? It sounded so loud." Phoenix paused.

I said, "The pan must be close to a mike."

"Maybe," Phoenix agreed. "Now don't go burning yourselves, will you, guys?"

"We won't." Michaela laughed. "Why don't you come across and join us?"

"I wish I could, Michaela. Only the rules don't allow it."

"Rules are made to be broken."

"An intriguing thought. Now, if you'll excuse me, I have to go. We've got a little incident happening at one our sister installations."

"An incident, Phoenix? What kind of incident?"

But there was no reply. We stood looking at the kitchen walls for a moment, waiting for the voice of Phoenix to return.

"I guess the man's busy," I said. "Let's watch some TV."

"What are you doing, Michaela?"

"Nothing."

"You're sketching."

"Uh-huh."

"Are you sketching me?"

"Nothing else to sketch."

"I'm flattered."

"Don't be."

"Are you ticklish?"

"Do you bleed?"

"I bleed, but I'm going to tickle you."

We were in the lounge area. I'd sat eating popcorn while watching a batch of sitcoms. I only just noticed that Michaela had curled herself into a big, plump armchair, where she worked with a pencil on some scraps of paper.

I hooked my hands like claws, then shambled across to her; my knees bowed like a gorilla's. "Gonna get pretty lady. Gonna tickle her good and hard."

"You do and I'll bust your lip." She laughed and threw a cushion at me.

"That's don't hurt Mungo," I grunted. "Mungo tickle pretty lady."

"Here, let me draw Mungo. Hold still while I sketch that big bulbous forehead of yours."

"Like this." I struck a pose with my arms reaching out over her monster-style.

"Yeah, like that."

"Mungo like pretty lady?"

"Mungo very pretty." Smiling, she worked the pencil. "I'm drawing Mungo's big round nostrils, the big wart on his nose. His staring eyes, shaggy eyebrows; his bug-ugly yellow teeth."

"Mungo see now."

"Mungo can wait."

"Mungo impatient." I grunted like a gorilla, but oh, Jesus, keeping up this playacting was making me crazy. I wanted—hell, no—I craved to have a proper conversation about Phoenix and my suspicions, but by this time I'd convinced myself that not only were there microphones dotted about the bunker but hidden cameras, too. Those things were probably implanted in the walls, and of course the lenses would be little bigger than pinheads. To all intents and purposes they were invisible.

"Right, show me the picture or I tickle good and hard," I told her.

"Oh, all right. Here. Sit down beside me." She patted the cushion. I sat beside her. Then she pointed at the drawing. "I think I've got the lips just perfect, don't you?" She pointed at what I took to be a drawing of a face with a long smiling mouth. Instead of lips I realized she'd run words together: *Good-Idea. The-Popcorn-Scam-Worked.* Then she pointed to the chin, which was formed by the words: *Didn't-Hear-Us-Did-He?*

"What do you think?" she asked, fixing me with her eye.

"My God, Michaela, you've really caught my chin, but where are my eyebrows?"

"It's a work in progress."

"Here, give me the pencil." Above the eyes I wrote:

Careful, he'll be watching. "There; eat your heart out, da Vinci."

We sat 'round some more. All the time I felt conscious of camera lenses burning into the pair of us. I guessed that Michaela felt the same way. She continued to sketch, but she looked a little on edge. Try as I might, it was hard to concentrate on the TV. My eyes kept sliding off screen to try to find those hidden camera lenses.

"Say, people, good news!" Phoenix spoke so abruptly that Michaela started. "Listen, I've been given security clearance from the highest level to show you something."

Michaela and I looked at each other. Phoenix sounded excited.

"So, Greg, Michaela, if you could move into the lounge so you can see the TV screen . . ."

I said, "We're already in the lounge, Phoenix." But then, he knew that, I'd wager. He'd been sitting in his lair watching us all along.

Michaela put down the sketches. "What you got to show us, Phoenix?"

"I hope you guys are going to be as thrilled as I am about this. We're implementing something called Reach Out. At last we're allowed to start doing what we've been put here to do."

"How does that work, Phoenix?"

"As the program title states we're going to Reach Out to bands of survivors like yourselves to provide you with food, ammunition and medicines."

"You mean you're going to help us?" Michaela's eyes were wide.

"That's right."

"That's going to be a tough one, Phoenix," I said. "You haven't seen the mess the cities are in, or how few there are of us who survived in the outside world."

"Oh, but there are." The velvet voice gushed now.

"There are more than you think, Greg. Of course, this epidemic hit the country hard, but there are hundreds and hundreds of facilities like this. Most are far bigger, housing a hundred or more people."

"You make it sound like Noah's ark."

"Think of it as hundreds of arks. Each with stores of food, seeds for planting new crops, fuel. There are agricultural experts as well as engineers, mechanics and scientists, ready to help rebuild." The enthusiasm made his voice soar. "This is a new beginning. You, Michaela and Greg, can be part of it."

"How do we fit in?" Nice and easy does it, said the cautious voice in the back of my head. Something's brewing here. Someone's been making plans.

Phoenix gushed, "We need people on the outside to bring survivors like yourself to the bunkers."

"Why?"

"We can provide food, clothing, everything you need. You can make a start by bringing your own people here. Like yourselves, they can rest, enjoy some of our hospitality while we help you get organized into a secure society. You will be able—"

"Whoa, Phoenix. Hold on." Michaela stood up. "You know we're still outnumbered out there by thousands to one. The hornets are everywhere. We've tried to settle in one place, but they keep driving us on."

"We can help you." Phoenix paused. The excitement exerted him. I could hear his breathing rasp from the speakers. "We will be dispatching military units in armored vehicles. There'll be helicopter gunships. They will use all the firepower at their disposal—and believe me, it is formidable firepower—to create safe homelands for our people."

I shook my head. "You mean you're going to clear cities of hornets. Then what? Build a big wall around Chicago or Atlanta?"

"I understand you might be skeptical after what

you've encountered in the outside world. But there are areas of America that are largely free of affected people, the hornets as you call them."

"Excuse my skepticism," I said. "Really, I want this to work as much as anyone, but it's going to be a tall order."

Michaela nodded. "It's a wasteland out there. You're lucky to find a single house that hasn't been smashed to pieces or burned."

"We can build new houses. We can repair those that aren't badly damaged."

"You're asking us to put our faith in you?"

"Yeah." Michaela sounded angry. "Where were all you people when our nation was being torn apart and citizens being killed by the thousand? You were hiding here in your bunkers watching *Friends* or snacking on microwave weeners."

"Michaela." Phoenix's voice oozed with calm sincerity. "Michaela. We were taken by surprise. We've needed months to regroup and reorder ourselves. Many of our armed forces were destroyed along with civilians. Besides, we couldn't bomb our own towns and cities, could we?"

"OK," she said, not backing down. "Tell me what you and your bunker buddies are going to do to help the likes of us."

"I don't have to tell you, I can show you. Please watch the TV screen."

Thirty-seven

Somewhere in the bunker Phoenix operated the big TV on the wall. One second a sitcom I didn't even know the name of had been playing, the next the canned laughter vanished, to be replaced by a view of a desert with a dust road and hundreds of Joshua trees. The morning sun blazed down from a cloudless sky.

"This," Phoenix said, "is the scene from a big military bunker complex in Texas. Exactly where I can't say for security reasons. You're seeing this live as it happens. Any moment now you'll see why I'm so optimistic about things working out. Right-o. We're going to switch to another camera. Here we go." At the bottom of the screen ran a code that didn't make much sense at first: *TX 03/23. EXT. CAM 3.*

When Phoenix said, "Here we go," the scene shifted. Now we looked from a camera mounted on some high point perhaps thirty feet above the ground and showing the edge of a large concrete structure that had been painted a dappling of browns and dull yellows to camouflage it against the desert. Now part of the code changed. The first part remained the same, *TX 03*. I figured that was the location, *Texas* followed by some identification number. The next code had changed to *EXT. CAM 5*. That was easy enough to figure: *Exterior camera number five.*

Phoenix's voice was breathy with excitement. "Do you see what's happening now? We're moving out. We're taking back what's rightfully ours."

I looked out across the desert scene. Among the Joshua trees were hundreds of figures. From their ragged clothes and wild hair you could tell they were hornets easily enough.

"There they go!" Phoenix's voice rose to a shout as from an opening in the bunker rolled tanks, APCs and maybe another dozen armored vehicles. They immediately plunged into the desert, crushing the Joshua trees to pulp. Seconds later they'd reached the hornets, too. Men and women by the dozen went under the caterpillar tracks or fell victim to guns of many different calibers. Tracers spat fiery sparks across the terrain to drop the hornets into the dust by the dozen. Then came the bigger guns, lobbing high explosive shells into clumps of hornets. They vanished in a flash of flame.

"That's right," Phoenix panted. "We're fighting back. It's like this all over the country."

We watched the screen as lines of troops appeared to walk toward the surviving hornets. Of course hornets never run. You can't even make them flinch. They stood there with their God almighty hammers and clubs at the ready, but the GIs simply picked them off one by one with their automatic rifles. At last the bad guys had met their match. We were fighting back. We were winning.

We sat there for maybe an hour, watching the one-sided battle. When the troops had finished with the hornets armored bulldozers moved out to scrape the desert clean of all that butchered flesh. After the corpses were piled into heaps they were soaked in gasoline and burned. By lunchtime funeral pyres shot smoke into clear blue skies.

We watched as if we'd been welded to the seats. This was nothing less than a miracle. We were seeing the rebirth of a nation. Our nation.

"I've clearance to show you some more scenes," Phoenix told us. "Sit tight."

The banner at the bottom of the screen contained the text: *WYMG* (Wyoming?) *04/18. EXT. CAM 2.* This time helicopter gunships passed overhead to pour down bone-shattering rocket fire on a cluster of hornets running toward the camera. The same pattern followed. Armored bulldozers shoved the corpses into mounds. Then came the gasoline. Burn, baby, burn. I felt the blood roaring through my veins. Yes! We were doing it! We were wiping out the goddam monsters!

"Next scene," Phoenix said. He sounded pleased. "You might find this a little different. Again I'm not permitted to give you a specific location other than that it's an island in Hawaii."

I saw a tract of grass dotted with palm trees, ending with rocks, then sea. In the distance surf rolled in creamy waves across the beach. The midday sun shone down, making the place look like paradise.

"This can't be live," Michaela said. "It'll still be night in Hawaii."

"You're right; this was recorded yesterday. And I think this might be the best news yet."

Not a lot happened in this scene. Half a dozen guys were lazily playing baseball on the grass. Strolling into the picture came a couple of young women in army fatigues.

"What are you showing us, Phoenix?"

"What do you see?"

"People enjoying the sunshine."

"Exactly. What you don't see are any hornets. The crew have left the bunker."

"You're saying there aren't any hornets on the island?"

"There aren't anymore. We destroyed the last one a week ago. Those people are safe to stroll 'round the place unarmed, take in the sun, go for a swim. Looks great, doesn't it?"

"It does look great," I agreed with feeling. "What time does the next flight leave?"

Phoenix gave a soft, breathy laugh. "I'm afraid you're going to have to be patient, Greg. But one day . . . who knows?"

I looked at the text at the bottom of the screen. Along with the camera number were the letters: *MKI*. That had to be the Hawaiian island of Molokai.

Phoenix spoke: "So you can bring your people here to the bunker. See for yourself; we've begun the battle to liberate America."

I looked at Michaela. There was such a look of enchantment on her face as she watched those happy people in the island sunshine. They were in paradise.

That night everything changed again.

Thirty-eight

Michaela sat up in bed when I switched on the light. She looked uneasy. "They're going to be sore if we start snooping 'round those bunker rooms."

"You really think they're going to throw us out to the hornets?"

"I wouldn't like to chance it."

"They'll never know. They'll all be asleep at this time of night."

"OK. Just give me a minute to get dressed."

I backed out through the doorway of her bedroom and waited in the corridor as she slipped on the green sweatshirt and pants. The time was creeping up to two in the morning. I'd waited until I guessed the bunker crews in the main part of the installation were asleep, and I was wagering that the sealed rooms in our annex weren't wired to an alarm. I know there really wasn't a good, logical reason to poke 'round in places that were off limits. But I still had a sneaking suspicion something wasn't right. I remembered how Phoenix had put us through the degrading decontamination procedure while no doubt ogling himself rigid (and, yeah, I had a gut feeling that Phoenix was a HE, not a SHE). We knew, also, that he spied on us and eavesdropped on our conversations.

"You got the numbers?" Michaela asked as she stepped into the corridor.

"Right here." I touched my pocket.

"You know, if sirens start screaming because we've tripped some alarm we're going to be in the crap waist deep."

"Don't worry."

"These military types don't like people disobeying orders."

"Phoenix said he was on the civilian side of things."

"But there are army personnel here."

"I'll tell them I was sleepwalking."

"Yeah, right, and you just happened to dream access code numbers to locked doors."

"There's probably nothing behind them anyway."

"Then why bother risking our necks to poke in some storerooms full of pails and brooms?"

"Phoenix isn't telling us everything."

"And what makes you think he's not listening to us right now? There could be bugs hidden in the walls."

"There might," I agreed. "But the guy's got to sleep sometime."

She sighed. "Let's get this over with then."

We walked along the corridor, past the stairway that led up to the living room level, through the double doors and into the bleak-looking concrete passageway beyond with the sealed doors that had a brooding quality about them. It was colder here, too. Michaela shivered, gooseflesh raising her arms into bumps. She folded her arms.

"No, Greg. Whichever way you look at this I don't like it." Her shoulders gave another shiver. "These doors are locked for a reason."

Simon Clark

I pulled the sheet of paper that contained the porn doodle of Dr. Roestller and the columns of numbers from my pocket. "See this?" I said, and read out the four-digit number. "Seven-six-o-eight. The letters by this one are SB." I nodded at the door labeled SICK BAY. "I guess this one matches with that number."

Michaela's unease grew. "You're not looking in there, are you? All you'll find are Band-Aids and bedpans."

Glancing down at the list of numbers, I matched doors to code numbers. Beside each steel door was an illuminated keypad, inviting me to tap a number and—open sesame!—I'm in. "One of the doors doesn't have a keypad." I nodded toward a set of twin steel doors. I read the word stenciled there. "Comm-Route. What do you think that means?"

"I don't know, Greg. Come to that, I don't really care. Listen." She touched my arm. "I don't think we should be doing this."

"You think I'm being goddam nosy?"

"Yes. Phoenix has invited us to bring the rest of our people here. Don't louse it up for Zak and the others."

"But there's something he's not telling us."

"Such as?"

"Didn't you think that sudden invitation to Phoenix's house party seemed convenient?"

"You saw what I did on TV. The military have launched an offensive against the hornets."

"I know. I'm as pleased as the next man."

"But?"

"I don't know, Michaela. I just don't know. . . ." I murmured the words as I ran my hands over the twin doors marked COMM-ROUTE. These were more solid than the doors to the sick bay and boardroom. What's more, a lip of steel ran 'round the doorway to seal them tight. They made me think of bulkhead doors in a submarine. I ran my fingers 'round the edge of the doorway. "Rubber seals," I said. "It's meant to be airtight. But look at this at the bottom." I crumbled a piece of rubber between my finger and thumb. "It's rotted."

Meanwhile Michaela looked 'round, as if she expected a voice to boom out, ordering us to return to our rooms.

"Hell," I said, "this stuff is coming away by the yard." A length of rubber looking like black spaghetti came away in my hand.

"Greg, leave it, please. They'll go ape if they think you're wrecking the place."

"It's rotted to crud."

"Greg, I'm going back to my room. You do the same . . . *please.*"

"Michaela—"

"I don't know what you're expecting to find, apart from a whole heap of trouble. But we've got a chance to bring our people into a place of safety. Don't you understand what that means? They can eat and sleep and take it easy just like we have. Listen, Greg, Phoenix is giving us a chance to live normal lives again. We can't just . . . *Greg, what's wrong?*"

I squatted by the door. Another strip of rubber seal came away. Wet and cold. Condensation had been working on the rubber for years. The rubber lay limp as a dead snake in my hand. The moment it fell from between the door and the steel frame I felt a jet of air play against my lips and nose. Cold as ice, it carried the smell of damp, confined spaces. When you lever back the slab of a tomb it must feel and smell like this. Faint toadstool odors. Moss. Damp. Decay. Chilled air that sends a shiver down your spine and fills your head with images of shriveled eyes and long-dead bones.

"Greg? You don't look well." She sounded anxious. "What's wrong?"

The jet of air struck my face . . . something liquid

about it . . . a sense of poisons floating there . . .

"Greg, are you—Greg, don't!"

I slammed against the door. My fist punched at the steel. I punched again. My skin ripped across the knuckle, sending blood streaming across gray paintwork, smearing COMM-ROUTE.

I snarled through gritted teeth, "They're in there . . . *they're in there!*"

"Hornets?"

I nodded, my muscles snapping so tight in my stomach and back that I wanted to roar with pain. "Comm-Route . . . it means Communicating Route, doesn't it?" I pushed myself back from the door to stop myself trying to tear it down with my bare hands. "That's the tunnel link between this annex and the main bunker."

"Easy, Greg . . ."

I clenched my fists as my stomach muscles spasmed like they were trying to rip out through my skin. "They're in there. They're inside . . ."

"That can't be right. We've talked to Phoenix. We've seen the bunker crew. This place is secure; it's like a fortress; hornets can't be—"

I backed away from the door, shaking my head, perspiration running down my face, my heart pounding. "They're here . . ." My voice came in a rasp. "They're here . . . I don't know how . . . but they're here . . ."

Her eyes were frightened, huge-looking. "Greg, come away from the doors . . . no, right away." She pulled me back. "Let me see your hand; you've cut it."

"No. I'm going to find out what's happening here."

I yanked the sheet of paper from my pocket. Scanning it, I compared the words on the doors to the numbers I'd copied down. "Sick Bay. Boardroom . . . they don't seem important. What's this one?" I looked at a steel door. "Quartermaster store. There should be firearms in there."

"I'll feel more confident with a gun in my hand."

Michaela suddenly became businesslike. "Tell me the code."

"Four-seven-nine-nine."

"Got it." She tapped the number into the keypad. The electronic lock buzzed, then clicked. Michaela pushed the door. It opened easily. A light flickered on inside. "Oh, hell."

"What's wrong?"

"Empty. Someone cleaned it out."

I glanced into the storeroom. Bare shelves. Empty racks that must have once held rifles. "There were guns here," I said. "But Phoenix's people didn't want guests helping themselves. Try the next one." To do this I had to pass the big double doors with my blood smeared across COMM-ROUTE. Instantly the Twitch came back to me. God, yes, those sons of bitches were in there. But how did you get through those twin doors? No keypad, so no electronic lock. No handles. It must be locked from the other side.

"Greg . . . Greg? Are you sure you want to do this?"

I looked at Michaela, my stomach muscles jumping.

"Greg, you don't look well."

You look crazy. That's what she wanted to say. I knew my nostrils were flared. I was panting. My eyes would be blazing like the fires of hell. But then, this was a bad one. I could believe there were a thousand hornets lined up there, waiting to burst in and pound us to bloody hamburger meat.

I took a deep breath to try to steady my racing heart, but, hell, nothing would stop the muscles in my stomach writhing like a bunch of snakes. "There's nothing written against the next numbers," I said. Jesus, I felt surprised at how calm I sounded. "Try all of them."

"OK. First one."

"Six-seven-three-one."

She tapped the number into the keypad beside the

door marked BACKUP OPS. She waited for a moment. No buzz. No click.

"Next," she said.

"Four-four-one-one."

She punched in the code. Nothing.

"OK. Next."

"Eight-seven-three-o."

Buzz. Click.

"Bull's-eye, we're in." She pushed open the door. Inside, the room had the feel of a dark cavern.

"Take it easy," I said. "I don't know if we've got company in here." I leaned in, feeling the inside wall for a light switch. My fingers located a plastic pad. I pushed it. Instantly, fluorescence came with a fluttering brilliance. "Looks as if we've struck the jackpot."

Michaela stepped in, her eyes wide with awe. "Just look at this place. Look at all the equipment! It's like a TV newsroom."

Good description. The room was maybe thirty-by-forty feet. In two rows, one behind the other, were workstations complete with keyboards and monitors, while filling just about the entire end wall was a vast booster screen. At the side of it were a bank of electronic clocks.

I glanced at my watch. "They're showing the time coast to coast."

"This must be the backup command center in case the one in the main bunker gets knocked out."

"If this is a duplicate of what's in the main building, then we could do all the stuff that Phoenix does, accessing other bunkers."

"I guess." Now thoughtful, she ran her fingers along the desktop, drawing furrows in the dust. "If we knew how to work it."

"Try."

"Greg? I don't know where to begin."

"You had a computer at home, didn't you? You used one at college?"

"Sure, but—"

"Then the principle must be the same." I pressed a button on one of the computer terminals. Nothing happened. "Huh. Maybe there's some central control you need to switch on first. A circuit breaker or—"

"Greg." I felt her hand on my arm. "Look at the big screen. Something's happening."

The booster screen that filled the wall had developed a snowstorm. A second later that flickered out, to be replaced by a color bar test pattern with the words HIT ANY KEY through the center. Michaela reached forward, her slender finger running beneath the computer monitor. She rotated a control beneath it and the screen brightened, to reveal a screen identical to the one plastered across the wall.

"Hit any key," I said. "Here goes." I tapped a key at random on the keyboard.

"Better make it fast," Michaela said. "Somewhere I'm sure the alarm bells are ringing."

"OK, five minutes, then we're out of here. What now?"

"Wait, it looks to be booting up."

"Here." I pulled up a swivel chair. "You're going to be better at this than me."

She shot me a grim smile. "Thanks for your confidence . . . uh, that doesn't look good."

I read the words on the screen. " 'Enter password.' "

"Any ideas?"

"Is there a way to bypass it?"

"Sure there is, only I haven't a clue how to begin." She looked at the now bloodstained paper in my hand where my wound had leaked onto it. "Anything on there?"

I scanned the note. Straightaway my eyes went to the meaningless phrase that had been heavily underscored beside the word: *MEMORIZE!* I murmured, "Thank the Lord for our forgetful friend. Type in *maple eagle green*."

She did so, slender fingers racing across the keys. God, she was good.

But: " 'Incorrect password.' Try again?" She sighed. "It looks like a dead end. We should get out of here before—"

"No . . . it's me. I'm a blockhead. I didn't give it to you properly. In lower case type *maple dash eagle dash green*."

"OK. Enter." She pressed the key. We both stared at the screen, as if waiting for marvelous things. What came next might not have been marvelous, but it was something. The huge booster screen suddenly filled with lists of words.

"We've got menus," she said. "What they mean, God knows."

I scanned them, reading at random. "Inventory. Fuel stock. Quartermaster regime. Comms mail. Comms voice. Comms vid. Archive. Personnel Register. Personnel Directory." I shook my head. "It's not looking very helpful, is it?"

"Not a great deal. The computer's inviting us to choose whether we want to e-mail people or communicate by voice or, I guess, by video conferencing system. Yup, look up on the wall."

I followed her line of vision. Bolted to the wall was a closed circuit TV camera.

"Let's hope they're not watching us now." I searched the menu list on the screen again. "Try this." I pointed at a box. "The one marked Installation Directory."

Using the arrow keys she brought the cursor down to the box then hit ENTER.

"We might have something," I said as the screen changed. "See this column of letters ALA, ARK and so on right down to WYNG?"

"Abbreviations of state names?"

"They appeared at the bottom of the screen when Phoenix was showing us what was going down at those other bunkers."

"You want to see more?"

"It couldn't hurt."

"Which one?"

"Try TXS. Phoenix showed us the Texas bunker launching an attack on the hornets."

"OK." She selected TXS. "You've got a choice of around fifteen."

"Each TXS letter code is followed by a number code. It must represent different bunkers in Texas. I can't remember the number code."

"I'm pretty sure it was TX-o-three."

"OK, go for it."

"Computers." She hissed the word in frustration. "It's giving me a whole list of camera locations. Interior and exterior."

I rubbed the back of my neck. "We can't have much time left. Take pot luck."

She brought the cursor down at random before clicking on one marked *11. INT.* The screen had an appetite for frustration. It flashed up another menu of options. *Select: Night Scope. Daylight. Sound On/Off.* She didn't select any; she merely rapped ENTER with her thumb.

I looked up at the booster screen. The identification popped up in white print along the bottom, but otherwise the screen was dark.

"It's bust," I snapped.

"It's also dark. We might be seeing the canteen or some warehouse in darkness."

"Or a bedroom. Hear that?"

"I hear something. It sounds odd."

"Someone breathing?"

"Could be."

"I'll try another."

"Go for another interior camera. It'll still be night-time in Texas."

She returned to the camera menu and plucked out *01. INT.* "Might as well go for numero uno," she said. She grunted. "Oh, no . . . that doesn't look right."

The image was black and white. "It's in nightscope mode," I said. "But I don't understand what we're seeing. Have we got the same bunker as we saw yesterday?"

"According to the reference it's the same. But look at that . . . oh, crap . . . oh fucking, fucking crap . . ."

She sighed. I heard disappointment as much as anything in the sound. Thing is, when I looked up at that massive screen I felt it, too. There, from wall to wall, was an image that could have been subtitled *Abandon Hope.* We were looking at what could have been some garage in the bunker. The nightscope showed everything either in inky blacks or blazing fluorescent whites. In the center of the bay sat a tank; beyond that were two massive steel doors. They lay part open. Spilling in through the opening came desert sand. It had flowed across the garage floor to bury the tank's tracks. Tumbleweeds had rolled in. Bleakest of all were the number of bodies—or what were left of bodies. Skeletons, some with dried husks of faces attached to skulls, lay all over the place. Some were partially covered by sand. A corpse mummified by the dry air sat in the tank's turret.

"Wait, do you see that?" Her voice was a hiss. "Something's moving."

Through the doorway glided twin points of light, like two little stars that moved together across the garage floor. For a second I stared at the two lights, trying to figure out what I was seeing. Then it moved away from the camera.

"A rat," she said. We'd been seeing the meager light reflected from its eyes, which had been amplified into twin burning points by the nightscope lens.

"I have a feeling I know what we're going to see, but try the other cameras, Michaela."

"Yeah, what you see might be of a disturbing nature . . . to use the old TV phrase. So, ladies and gentlemen, look away now if you're of a nervous disposition." Quickly she worked through the camera menu. This time she knew what to do and activated the nightscope lens on each camera. The first camera we tried when we heard the rasping sound revealed a coyote asleep in the corner of a room that could have been a clone of this one, complete with TV screens. Other cameras revealed rooms that had been trashed out of all recognition. Mummified corpses lay in army uniforms all over the damn place.

Michaela spoke with a flat voice. "Something went wrong during the attack. The hornets overran them in the end."

I shook my head. "This makes no sense. Phoenix showed us live images of the attack yesterday. This bunker was overrun weeks, if not months ago."

"He lied to us. He showed us archive footage. See the archive icon there?" She tapped the screen. "If we were to access that I'd wager we'd find what Phoenix claimed happened yesterday."

"But why? Why go to all that trouble to deceive us?"

"Maybe he wanted to give us hope. That everything wasn't as bleak as it seemed."

"Jesus, I think he's just made everything seem a good deal worse. Try the other bunker installations. The one in Wyoming."

"Do you remember the identification code for the bunker?"

I shook my head, sighing. "I don't think it matters now, do you?"

Face grim, she worked through the bunker codes. Within ten minutes we must have looked at a good dozen or so. All showed the same thing. Every bunker had been overrun at some point. Bunker teams lay dead in kitchens, in bathrooms, in lounges, at workstations. Total devastation. Absolute annihilation. Even the one on the Hawaiian island lay with its doors gaping open; skeletons picked clean by seagulls gleamed in the sun.

"So there you go," I whispered. "Not one left intact. So much for Phoenix telling us that the government was still in control." I nodded at the screen, which carried the words BUNKER COMMAND ONE with a room that duplicated the Oval Office in the White House. Smoke stained the walls. Rats gnawed at a figure wearing a business suit that sat in a slumping position beneath a portrait of George Washington. "I doubt if you'll find as much as a single senator or army general still alive."

Michaela shook her head. "But we're able to access the cameras by remote control, so who's maintaining the bunkers?"

"My guess is they have automatic self-maintenance systems. Computers will run what's left of them for months before the generators' fuel runs out."

Michaela's eyes glistened as she stared at the screen. "So it really is over. All of it."

I put my arm 'round her shoulders. "We're still hanging in there, buddy. There's Zak and Tony and the rest. There's bound to be more like us out there."

"But for how long . . . those hornets . . . they're like a disease we can't cure. They're going to kill us all one day. Every last one."

"No, they won't, Michaela. We're going to make it, just you wait and see."

"For what purpose?" Tears bulged over the rim of skin beneath her eyes, then trickled in glistening balls down her cheek. "For what purpose, Greg? Answer me that. To live in rags, drinking ditch water. Slowly starving to death. Getting so old and so tired that you can't run from the monsters anymore. So you sit down in the dirt and wait to die."

"Listen, you're going to live. And you're going to do it in style."

"What the hell for?"

I crouched down beside her and stroked her face lightly with my fingertips. "Who else is going to have my babies?"

The sound that came out like a hiccup from her lips was a cross between a sob and a laugh. "Idiot, Greg. Babies? If I thought you could spirit us away to a tropical island I might take you up on it."

Then she did start to sob. She put her arms 'round my neck and drew herself in tight against me. The sobs shuddered through her thin shoulders. I felt her tears wet my throat. It was like a dam had given way, releasing months of pent-up grief in a tidal wave of weeping that paralyzed her. I felt her body sag against mine as the convulsions of emotion ran through it. I stroked her hair and whispered over and over that I'd do everything I could to make it right for her. That I wouldn't let her come to any harm. Just when I thought she'd never stop weeping, she did stop. That iron will of hers that had carried her through the madness and murder reasserted itself. She caught the sobs in mid-flow and stopped it just like you or I would switch off a TV.

"I'm sorry, Greg. I shouldn't have let myself go like that."

"You had every reason to. You can't carry that kind of grief; it'll eat into you like—"

"No. I'm OK now." She loosened herself from my arms to turn back to the keyboard.

"Michaela, leave it now. We've seen everything we need to."

She spoke crisply. "No, we haven't. There's one bunker installation we haven't looked inside." The cursor sped down the screen. *"This one."*

Thirty-nine

Surviving isn't just avoiding being swamped by events. It's about avoiding being swamped by your own emotions to the extent that you can't function. I watched Michaela snap her runaway emotions into line and return to work at the computer keyboard as if nothing had happened.

"Let's see what's really happening in the main bunker."

"How do you know which one it is out of all those?" I nodded at the bunker directory that listed three hundred facilities like the one we now stood in, either as guests or as prisoners.

"Easy. The bunker reference is printed on everything. It's even stenciled on the chairs, in case any go missing at stock taking."

"Thank God for government bureaucracy."

She tapped in the code, her fingers blurring with speed. "I'm in."

"Stick to the interior cameras."

"Here goes." She picked one at random from the

computer screen. Immediately the big booster screen showed the image of a gloomy concrete corridor that could have been anywhere.

"Next," she said, hitting a key.

"Ah, the torture chamber," I said as the screen showed the room where we underwent decontamination.

"And just as we thought. Phoenix watched us as we stood there in the dark."

"Then got his perverse cookies seeing us undress and getting sprayed with disinfectant. I'm really starting to have my doubts about that guy."

"Me, too." She accessed the next camera. It showed the kitchen where we'd cooked popcorn. One of the faucets dripped into the sink.

"Can you up the sound?"

"I'll try . . . yes. Oh . . . there's a volume control, too." She pointed to a slider switch that popped up on screen.

"Turn it up full." I watched the dripping faucet in the kitchen as a glistening pearl of water fell into the sink. Using the cursor, Michaela increased the volume. Instantly the drip of water on stainless steel filled the room. It sounded like ball bearings dropping into a metal pail. "So old Phoenix boy could watch and listen to us whenever he wanted. It makes you wonder if he even watched us taking a shower."

"I guess that's the least of our problems now. Take a look at that."

Michaela had accessed another camera. This showed a room that was a duplicate of this one. "That must be the command center across in the main bunker. See the red lights flashing on the screen?"

"An alarm?"

"I guess so." She shook her head. "The bunker computer's trying to tell people across there that someone's trespassing in their backup center in the annex."

"But where is everyone?"

"I'll keep trying the cameras. . . . Wait . . . that looks like their kitchen. Jeez, what a mess."

The kitchen in the main bunker, just fifty yards or so away from the annex we now stood in, shared the same layout as ours, only it was around twice the size. Used microwave cartons had been carelessly stacked on worktops, chili sauce and dried rice smeared the plastic containers. Around twenty dirty cups littered the table.

Michaela wrinkled her nose. "Ugh. They're not house proud across there, are they?"

"Maybe you don't notice after you've been sealed away here for months . . . but wait . . . can you zoom into the table . . . those things in the middle? I thought they were plastic spoons. Can you make out what they are?"

"Wait a minute. I have to go back to the main camera menu. Ah, got it. I'll enlarge the image a hundred percent. Wow."

I looked at what littered the table. "Those people aren't relying on caffeine for a high. How many hypodermics do you see?"

"Hell, around a dozen or so. You can even see blood on the needles. I hope those guys haven't been falling into bad habits and started sharing."

"So, it *has* sent them kooky in there. They must have raided the sick bay for the happy potions. Check out all those empty Demerol cartons."

"Well, I haven't seen anyone yet."

"They're probably sleeping off their narcotics party."

"And that might explain why no one across there has picked up the intruder alarm."

"Vigilant bunch, aren't they?"

Michaela ran through shots from the closed-circuit cameras. Image after image burst on the booster screen. I saw storerooms, bathrooms, corridors, a sickbay (with some naked-looking drug cabinets).

STRANGER

"Say cheese." Michaela nodded up at the big screen.

There were the two of us, looking at images of ourselves on screen. The next image revealed the recreation room Phoenix had shown us soon after we arrived.
Then there had been people playing pool or sitting
reading or watching TV. I expected to see at least a
couple of dope heads sleeping on couches.

"Hell . . . they've let the place go in the last twenty-
four hours." I looked up at the screen that showed the
big room in a generally crappy state. Spent microwave
cartons all over the floor. Empty wine bottles strewn
across the pool table. There were more hypodermics,
along with empty phials on the coffee table. It looked
as if someone had thrown a handful of shit at the walls,
then smeared it into big looping circles.

I shook my head. "Phoenix has been fooling us
again. That place never got into such a state over the
last few hours."

"He must have showed us archive shots from months
ago."

"So what's his game? Why is he deluding us?"

"Maybe there is no reason. Other than what's in
those phials he's been injecting into his veins."

"You mean he's delusional?"

"Maybe even downright insane." She shook her
head. "Greg, I'm starting to get the feeling that there
is no specialized bunker team here."

"So the guy's here alone."

"And probably has been for months. No wonder he
has to sweeten his life with all those chemicals. He
probably hasn't talked to another human being since
society took a flip. Come to that, he probably hasn't
seen daylight since last year."

"Jesus." I felt a prickle of unease. "I think our priority
should be to get out of here. If he's one sick kiddo
then he might try playing some of his pervert tricks on
us."

307

"Get out? How?" She looked 'round. "We're in a building with walls three feet thick and steel doors without handles."

"There must be some other way of—"

"Shit."

"What's wrong?"

"I think those alarms have got through to someone."

It was hard to see where the figure came from. Maybe it had been sleeping in an armchair turned away from a camera, but suddenly it came lumbering into view.

"Christ almighty." The figure—a man, I guess—had a huge mane of black curling hair; its face was painted white and the eyes had been lined with thick black kohl. The whole effect was of some Gothic Egyptian pharaoh who had suddenly quivered back to life. Its eyes were glazed but puzzled-looking, as if that *someone* had been woken from a deep sleep by an unfamiliar noise.

Michaela nodded at the screen. "If that's Phoenix he's going to know where we are soon enough."

As the figure passed out of sight I said, "Try to get back to the camera in the main operations room. That's where he'll be headed."

"What now?"

"We try to talk to him."

"From the look of him I don't think he's going to be in a sweet mood."

"We might be able to reason with him."

"*Might* is the key word. He looks pissed to me . . . got it." She hit a key. Once more the image of the room that was a duplicate of this one flooded the screen. There were the banks of TV monitors, computers. A vast booster screen filled the end wall.

Michaela let out a breath of air. "Here he comes."

We watched as the burly bear of a man with the Goth pharaoh face and tumbling black locks lumbered into the room. For a second he stood watching a dozen computer screens all flashing the same red disk. Michaela turned up the volume, and a repetitive pinging sound filled the room. The man ran his hands through his hair in a way that suggested what he was thinking right now was *So what the hell's happening?*

He shook his head, no doubt trying to shift a drug-induced purple haze from his head. Then he froze.

"I think that's the moment of realization," Michaela murmured.

Suddenly the man turned to look up at where the camera must be fixed to the wall. That white face appeared as a vast skull floating there, with its kohled Egyptian eyes surrounded by a mane of Goth hair. The drowsy expression flashed to one of fury. Clenching his fist, he slammed it down onto a computer monitor. The man's animal snarl rumbled from the speakers.

The next moment his fingers stabbed keys at one of the computers. That was when the screen behind him flashed into life. It showed Michaela and myself there in the center of the room.

When the man shouted I knew it was Phoenix. Only the softspoken burr had gone now; rage blasted the voice at us. "You were told not to enter rooms that were off limits! You have trespassed on restricted areas!" He glared up at the camera, his huge eyes blazing out at us from the booster screen. "You know what the penalty is for willful destruction of government property? This is a state of national emergency!"

"Phoenix—"

"If you do not return to your rooms immediately I will order in the guard. You will be shot, do you hear that? You will be executed by firing squad for—"

"Phoenix!" Michaela's clear voice cut across his rant. "Phoenix. There is no guard. You're alone in there, aren't you?"

"The bunker personnel are asleep in their quarters.

If you don't leave that room immediately I will wake up the guards. Man, will they be pissed. They're gonna bayonet you two in the guts. I tell you guys, you are fucking dead. Fucking dead, fucking buried, fucking history, fucking . . ." His voice rose to a scream.

"Phoenix!" I shouted. "There's no one else in the bunker with you. You are alone. There are no marines, there are no engineers, no doctors."

"How do you know that? Hey, how do YOU know!" He paused, suddenly looking edgy, as if a thought had occurred to him. A thought he didn't like one little bit.

"Hey. Have you two hacked into the computer?"

"We found a code. We've been able to access the closed-circuit TV cameras at the other bunkers."

"Shit!"

"We know that you've been feeding us old footage. We know that hornets have overrun the bunkers somehow."

"Bastards . . . you interfering bastards . . ."

"Phoenix, we know that all the personnel in those bunkers are dead. That there is no government any more, or even any kind of emergency military command. It's all been smashed."

For a moment he paused, staring up at the camera. A look of horror distorted that weird-looking face. He seemed to be thinking through what I'd just told him.

"Admit it, Phoenix," I said. "You're alone in the bunker, aren't you?"

He chewed his thick red lip, considering. Then: "OK, OK . . . I wanted to make things look good for you . . . hell, guys, I just wanted to be *nice*, OK? This is a shit world now. I just wanted . . . hell . . . it makes me feel good to see people enjoying themselves again."

"What now?"

"Now?" He shrugged. "Stay longer if you want, guys. Enjoy the facilities. Eat as much food as you want. Hey, you can even walk around naked, I don't mind."

"I bet he doesn't," Michaela muttered under her breath.

"And what I said still goes. Bring your friends into the bunker. We can party, huh? Your tax dollars bought nice things here. You can forget all that crap outside those walls. In here it's safe, you can relax—"

"Get high on stuff from the drug cupboard?"

He looked stung. "Hey, you've been across here? How did you get in?" He looked 'round, as if to see if anything had been disturbed.

I played it cagey. "We've seen enough, Phoenix."

"What have you seen? Did you access the cameras?"

I shrugged, and saw my image shrug on the booster screen behind Phoenix.

"Phew . . ." He playacted a big OK-so-you've-found-me-out shrug. "So what's your reaction?"

"We're hardly going to sit here in judgment," I said. "What you do across there is your own business."

"Yeah, got to pass these long hours somehow, haven't I?" He smiled now, relaxing. "So just leave those rooms alone. That's my only condition. Then bring your people here and we can really . . ." He made a show of flicking his hair back with those white, spidery hands of his. "We can really let our hair down— right, guys?"

Michaela nudged me with her elbow. Then hissed so he wouldn't hear. "It's not the drugs he was worried about. He's hiding something else." Then, in a louder voice, she spoke to Phoenix. "Things must have been tough on your own."

"Oh, I spent a lot of time alone as a kid."

"Oh?"

"I stayed in my room and listened to music. Other kids always thought I looked weird. . . ." He flicked back his hair again and jutted out his face so it filled the screen. "I can't imagine why, can you?" He laughed at his own sense of humor. "I mean, what's wrong with

311

a guy wanting to look different from the rest of the herd?"

"Nothing, Phoenix."

"You've heard that old Kinks song with the lyric that goes: 'I'm not like everybody else.' "

"I've heard it, Phoenix. Neat song."

"That's my anthem . . . the soundtrack to my life, if you will."

"Individuality is fine." Michaela smiled, then talked to him in a friendly, chatty way. "What kind of party have you planned when we bring our friends here?"

"Hey, whatever you want. I've got some stuff in here that makes you feel as if you're vacationing in the Milky Way. If you want to get horny I've got pills that get you as horny as a timber wolf in the rutting season. You get me?"

"Sure."

"All I require from you guys is to keep out of that room. There's sensitive equipment in there. It's easily damaged."

"Why worry about that, Phoenix? From what we saw, it's redundant now. There's no government to sue us for trespass."

"I know, guys, but . . . well, you know how it is? I kind of feel responsible after all this time."

She hissed again. "He is hiding something . . . watch him, watch him," she warned in that low whisper so he wouldn't hear. "He's trying something."

I looked up at the screen. Phoenix had backed toward a desk, where he sat down beside a computer. Almost idly, as if toying with the keyboard, he slowly tapped the keys with one finger.

Michaela sang out: *"He's shutting us down!"*

"Phoenix," I shouted, "what are you doing?"

"Oh, nothing really, guys. But running two communications centers really shoots away the juice. I'm just conserving fuel. Don't worry, it's cool. Go back to the lounge and we'll chat there. Help yourselves to some—"

"Oh, no, you don't." Michaela punched keys. "What are you hiding across there?"

"Shit, nothing. Now get out of that room!" Panicky, he turned 'round to begin hitting the computer keys, his face locked onto the screen, watching the cursor fly through the menus.

Michaela's fingers sped faster across the keyboard, hitting camera code after camera code. Once more images flew across the booster screen.

"It's only going to take him a few seconds," she said. "He'll be able to shut down this backup system from across there."

"Can we do the same to him first?"

"If I knew how, maybe."

"What are you doing?"

"Trying to access as many of the closed-circuit cameras as I can before he switches us off . . ." Her eyes flicked across the images now racing across the booster screen. "Didn't you sense it? When he realized we were talking about his drug habit he was relieved. There's something else across there that he doesn't want us— *there!* I'm into a new batch of cameras. Keep your eyes on the booster screen."

Images tumbled one after another. I saw shots of corridors, stairwells, doorways, locker rooms, laundry rooms, bedrooms, a boardroom, the sick bay again, with the empty drug cartons, a shot of Phoenix hitting computer keys with all the force of a maniac. He roared, "Get outta there! Get out! Get out!"

Another image flooded the screen. This showed a corridor lit with weak ceiling lights. Michaela struck another key. Now the booster screen showed a room that seemed to be underwater. Through the murk I could make out the line of a closed door, then a bathtub.

"This doesn't make sense," I said at last. "You must have two camera shots overlapping each other."

"No, that's not possible."

I stared at the bathroom, wondering if it had filled with mist or smoke. The whole thing had a pinkish tint. And were those objects hanging there, as if suspended by invisible wires from the ceiling?

"I'll zoom in." Michaela hit a key.

The lens homed in on one of the hanging objects. Something dark and roughly round in shape filled the booster screen. It could have been a sick-looking planet hanging in space with frayed material floating from it disgustingly, while the surface had been deformed by lumps and swellings.

Then the object rotated upward.

"Oh, my God!"

Michaela's scream jabbed my ear. I started back, too, my throat muscles contracting because there, filling the screen seven feet high, hung a vast misshapen face. Rattails of hair swirled in the liquid that supported the head.

Then the eyes opened. Two colossal circular eyes that were disks of sticky whiteness. From them two pupils stared out fiercely. The mouth yawned open with all the ferocity of a shark's. And from the mouth came a sound that was part moan, part roar, part warning.

This was the secret Phoenix had been hiding.

"My God, it's in the bunker." I backed away from the screen as if tumors erupted from it. "It's a hive."

Forty

It's a hive . . .

The words rolled 'round that concrete room then back at me with the ferocity of a punch. **It's a hive.**

"It's in the main bunker." Michaela's seemed to shrink before that monstrous stare.

"Jesus, he's living with that thing. *Why?*"

Shaking her head with disgust, she returned to the keyboard. "I'm trying something different." She worked the keys hard, perspiration glazing her face. "I'm going to try to see what he's doing before he pulls the plug on us. . . . Keep watching the screen, Greg."

The booster screen still contained the image of that great, bloated head floating in pink gel, the eyes burning with hatred fixed on the CCTV lens . . . but my God, they seemed to be looking right at us. As if it *knew* we were there. Now Michaela opened up more camera shots, but instead of replacing the image of the head they flashed up around the edge of the screen to form a border.

"I'm trying to keep as many views of the bunker on

screen as possible," she explained. "We need to have a complete view of what's going on across there."

"If Phoenix will let us." I glanced back at the door. "You never know—he might walk in here any minute with a gun."

She shook her head. "He's frightened of contamination . . . genuinely frightened. We went through decontamination, remember?"

"Yeah, but if he's living with a hive in the main bunker . . . he's already run the risk of infection."

"Not him. *It*. He's protecting it."

"You've got the main communications center back." I nodded at one of the smaller images on the edge of the booster screen. It revealed Phoenix, working like a madman at the computer. Either the program's complexity slowed him down or maybe he knew as much about the operating system as we did.

Phoenix's voice bellowed over the speaker. "You're gonna regret this . . . you guys are dust . . . fucking dust!"

Then Michaela accessed a camera that showed something entirely different.

"Take a look, Greg. Now we know." Her eyes narrowed. She wiped her mouth with the back of her hand, as if something repulsively slimy had just wormed its way in through her lips and over her tongue.

"Hell, the bastard . . . the filthy, murdering bastard . . ."

The inset screen seemed to hang beside that floating head with its venomous, staring eyes. Rattails of human hair coiled in the fluid. A black tongue worked with a hungry kind of gloating across blistered lips. But for once it was the smaller image revealed by another camera that had my attention nailed. It showed a pair of double doors that stood wide open. Beyond those a pink wall of gel pulsated. The membrane was just like the one I'd found back in the apartment in Sullivan.

Objects were stuck to the wall . . . no, it's cruel to say *objects*. People. That was what they were. Or what had been people once. But now the damn thing called a hive had taken them, then turned them into objects of ruin. I saw shriveled bodies that had been sucked dry. They were nothing but bones with a covering of skin that looked like dry paper.

"That's why Phoenix was so hospitable," Michaela whispered.

I swallowed. "He fed his visitors to it."

Some of the shriveled corpses still wore clothes. I recognized the green sweatshirts and pants. The corpse of a young child with holes in its face where the eyes had been still wore those absurd white rubber sandals. Those goddam rubber joke sandals that would have people laughing at you in the street.

There was something pathetic and cruel about those dead people all at the same time. Phoenix had lured them across there. I saw it in my mind's eye. How he'd sprayed them with disinfectant, then drugged his victims, then forced them face forward to that pulsating, membranous sac. And then what? Maybe it had grown wormlike tubes that had reached out of the pink Jell-O and pierced the victim's' skin. The monster had drained them of their blood like some filthy vampire.

"I warned you," Phoenix shouted. "But you wanted this . . . you were greedy to know things that were secrets . . . *my secrets* . . ." His voice trembled with anger. "This is payback time, guys . . . I don't get mad, I get even!"

"You're a monster, Phoenix!" I yelled back. "In fact *you* are the fucking monster. Not that thing! You fed children to it. You're a—"

Phoenix turned and gave a little wave with his fingers. "Bye-bye, losers."

I watched the screen as he made an exaggerated show of lifting his hand above his head, showing his middle finger with a fuck-you flip. Then with the same finger he pressed a computer key. Instantly the giant booster screen blanked. I looked down at the computer. Its screen crashed to black, too.

"That's it." Michaela sat back, her hands lifted up in resignation. "He shut us down."

"It's time we got out of here. We don't know what stunt he'll pull next."

"I won't argue with that."

As she stood up I heard a loud echoing click from the speakers. Then, with a crashing roar, thunder tore through the room.

An explosion, I told myself. The mad fuck had detonated a bomb. I saw Michaela reel back with her hands over her ears. Only this was no explosion. This was the voice of Phoenix amplified to a head-splitting decibel.

Out . . . out! Michaela couldn't hear me above the thunder of that amplified voice. I mouthed the words. Her dark eyes fixed on mine. She nodded. I followed her out the door, slamming it behind me. But the voice of Phoenix smashed through the air from speakers in the corridor.

He ranted at us like a demon. "MORONS. THAT'S IT, RUN. RUN! RUN AS MUCH AS YOU WANT. BUT THERE'S NOWHERE TO RUN. AND NOWHERE TO HIDE! YOU'RE LOCKED IN A CONCRETE BOX WITH NO WINDOWS. LISTEN TO ME, GUYS. I OWN YOU NOW. I FED YOU UP NICE AND PLUMP." The voice became gloating. "YOUR VEINS ARE FULL OF SWEET RED BLOOD . . . FULL OF VITAMIN GOODNESS, OOZING WITH YUMMY NUTRITION." He laughed. "HEY, YOU KNOW SOMETHING, GUYS? I SEE YOU RUNNING. THAT'S IT, UP THE STAIRS INTO THE LIVING ROOM. YOU CAN'T SEE ME, **BUT YOU STILL HEAR ME, DON'T YOU?"**

I thought Phoenix already had the volume cranked

high. But he turned it higher still. We ran with the palms of our hands crushed to our ears, but that sound seemed to take a shortcut right through our skulls.

Where we were running I don't know. Right at that moment I knew I had a burning need to escape the thundering voice. It felt like a crazy man hammered hot nails through my eardrums. I glanced at Michaela. The sound hurt her so much her eyes bled tears.

"YOU ARE IGNORANT FOOLS, AREN'T YOU?" Phoenix spoke, pitying us now. As if we were stupid kids who'd burnt our fingers in a campfire. "DON'T YOU KNOW WHAT I AM DOING HERE? I AM NURTURING THIS ORGANISM YOU CALL A HIVE. THAT'S INSULTING. IT'S NOT A HIVE. THIS IS HUMAN EVOLUTION. THIS IS NEW LIFE IN A LARVAL STATE. SHE WILL GROW INTO SOMETHING BEAUTIFUL. THE FINAL STAGE OF A METAMORPHOSIS IS THE IMAGO. BUT YOU DON'T KNOW THE MEANING OF THE WORD, DO YOU? IMAGO? A BUTTERFLY IS THE IMAGO OF THE UGLY LITTLE GRUB THAT EATS LEAVES."

We ran from room to room. Now I was looking for a way out. It didn't take a genius to figure out that Phoenix had plans for us. And those plans centered on feeding us to that monster in the bathroom.

"THIS IS THE END OF THE HUMAN RACE AS WE KNOW IT. AND DON'T YOU FEEL FINE? MEN AND WOMEN WERE THE MONSTERS. YEAH, YOU HAD ALL THOSE WARS AND MAN'S INHUMANITY TO MAN. YARDY-YARDY-YA . . . BUT WHERE DOES IT START? I'LL TELL YOU, PEOPLE. IT STARTS IN THE SCHOOLYARD, WHEN KIDS WITH CRAP FOR BRAINS PICK ON DECENT KIDS. WHEN YOU'RE BULLIED FOR BEING DIFFERENT. WHEN YOU GET PUSHED 'ROUND THE LOCKER ROOM BECAUSE THEY SAY YOU TALK DIFFERENT. OR YOU SHOW AN INTEREST IN THINGS OUTSIDE THEIR

CRUDDY LITTLE WORLD. RING ANY BELLS, GUYS? WERE YOU DIFFERENT TO THE OTHER KIDS? DID THEY TRIP YOU UP IN THE LUNCH ROOM SO YOU SPILLED YOUR LUNCH TRAY ALL OVER THE DAMN FLOOR? DID THEY TWIST YOUR ARM OR SPIT IN YOUR EYE AND LAUGH IN YOUR FACE? DID THEY, GUYS, HEY, DID THEY?"

I ran through into the kitchen. Still the voice followed. It shook the plates in the rack and when Phoenix boomed: **"LISTEN!"** a glass on the table shattered.

Grabbing Michaela by the shoulders, I swung her 'round so my body was between her and shards of flying glass. A burning sting flared in my cheek. When I touched my face I saw blood.

"We've got to get out of here!" I shouted. "He's going to do something."

The voice roared: "LISTEN. THIS IS THE END FOR YOU BARBARIANS. THERE'S A NEW MAN COMING. ONE YOU WOULDN'T BE FIT TO LICK THE CRAP FROM HIS FEET . . . THAT'S IT! RUN! RUN! BUT YOU ARE GOING NOWHERE!"

I kicked open the door to the locker room. There was a way through the decontamination chamber to the outside. But those doors were pneumatic. There were no handles. Nothing even to grip on to to try to rip it open. Phoenix controlled those doors from his command center.

"OK, GUYS. YOU'VE HAD YOUR FUN. NOW PHOENIX IS TAKING CHARGE."

I stopped dead in the room. Michaela grabbed my arm, a scared look on her face. The guy was going to start playing his Mr. Sadist tricks. The sound of his respiration came over the speaker. It sounded like storm winds . . . in . . . out . . . in . . . There was excitement there now that carried into his breathing. Hell, the amplification was so loud I could even here the deep bass sound of his heartbeat. The mushy beat pounded through the tiled room, and all the time it was overlaid by the sound of him sucking air through his wet mouth.

My ears still rang from the sheer volume of his voice. But I sensed the sounds in the bunker were different now.

Michaela got there first. "I can't hear the air-conditioning."

I held out my hand to one of the ventilation grills. Nothing. "He's switched it off. . . . This place is air-tight. He's trying to suffocate us."

"There's enough air in here for days. What's the point in—"

"I'M A PATIENT MAN, GREG. I CAN SIT HERE FOR A MONTH AND WATCH YOU AND YOUR BITCH SLOWLY RUN OUT OF AIR. I CAN WATCH YOU PANT AND SEE HOW YOUR EYES BULGE AS YOU SLOWLY . . . SLOWWWW . . . LEEEE SUFFO-CATE."

"Aw, go fuck yourself, you jerk."

Michaela added, "Yeah, that's what he probably does anyway."

"GO ON, MOCK . . . MOCK! BELIEVE ME, I GREW UP WITH THAT. I'M USED TO IT. I'M ARMOR-PLATED NOW. NOTHING CAN HURT ME . . . BUT I'M GOING TO HURT YOU. I'M GOING TO HAVE YOU CRAWLING ON YOUR HANDS AND KNEES BEGGING ME FOR YOUR LIVES." He laughed. "BUT STICK AROUND, KIDDIES. I'VE GOT SOME SUR-PRISES FOR YOU. **AND THEY'RE COMING REAL SOON.**"

Forty-one

"LISTEN . . . GREG? MICHAELA? LISTEN TO ME.
WE CAN HAVE SOME FUN HERE. YOU TRY TO
GUESS WHAT I'LL DO NEXT. I'VE GOT ALL THESE
OPTIONS UP ON THE SCREEN IN FRONT OF ME.
COME ON, GUYS, TAKE PART. . . . GUESS WHICH
BUTTON I'M GOING TO PRESS. HEY, TALK TO
ME."

As the voice pounded my ears I looked 'round the
locker room. No way was I going to surrender to Phoenix. Something told me he'd mess with our minds before he fed us to the hive. That guy craved some nice
juicy kicks. If he had his way, we were going to be his
toys. No way, crazy man. No way.

But what the hell could I do? I couldn't open the
door to the decontam chamber. It was fucking steel.
And if I got through that there was another steel door
as thick as your mattress to the outside world. Michaela
and I were about as safe as two bugs caught in some
loopy kid's glass jar. How long before he decided to
pull off our wings? Michaela looked 'round, too. But

what the hell was there? It was a locker room. So there were tiled walls—no windows. There were wooden benches. There were lockers. There were shelves piled with vacuum-packed clothes and rubber sandals. The ceiling was nothing more than a huge concrete slab fitted with strip lighting.

"AW . . . PLAY WITH ME, GUYS."

Michaela shouted, "Go play with yourself!"

Phoenix's voice came back. He was panting. The guy was getting all hot and excited. I could picture him there, sitting at the computer terminal, rocking backward and forward, his face red, his hands getting all sticky. And there on the booster screen would be us in the locker room. Searching for some way out. Hell, we really were just like bugs caught in that glass jar. Scurrying to one end of the room. Feeling the walls for a hidden exit, looking under the bench, looking into the air-conditioning duct for a passageway to freedom. But we were stuck. We were caught in this madman's odious paws.

"YOU KNOW I COULD DO SOMETHING TO YOU THAT'S REALLY COOL!" He snickered. I could hear the saliva squelching in his mouth. "YEAH, SOMETHING REALLY COOL. DO YOU KNOW WHAT IT IS?"

Michaela yelled back. "Go take a flying fuck, OK?"

"I MIGHT TAKE A FLYING FUCK AT YOU, YOU HORNY LITTLE BITCH. DO YOU KNOW SOMETHING? I'VE SEEN YOU NAKED IN THE SHOWER. WE'VE GOT CAMERAS EVERYWHERE. YOU'VE GOT A NICE CHERRY BUTT. I COULD PUT SOME WORK INTO THAT. GET YOU ALL HOT AND SQUIRMY . . . MAYBE MAKE YOU SCREAM A LITTLE . . . YOU'D LIKE THAT, WOULDN'T YOU, GIRL?"

"OK," I said. "Phoenix? What's this cool idea of yours? What y' going to do?"

"OH? SO YOU WANT TO PLAY THE GAME AT LAST?"

I stood in the middle of the locker room and nodded. "Surprise us."

"WELL, I WAS JUST SITTING AND LOOKING AT THE TEMPERATURE CONTROLS. YOU KNOW THIS THERMOSTAT CONTROL GOES ALL THE WAY DOWN TO BELOW FREEZING? I COULD TURN YOUR ROOMS ACROSS THERE INTO AN ICEBOX. THE JOHN WOULD FREEZE OVER. ICE WOULD FORM ON THE WALLS. I COULD SIT HERE AND WATCH YOUR FACES TURN BLUE. COOL, HUH?" He laughed at his own joke.

"You wouldn't do that, Phoenix, would you?" Michaela looked up at the walls as she spoke. "We've done nothing to hurt you."

"YEAH, *RIGHT!*" He paused, the sound of his respiration rasping around the room. "MICHAELA. YOU KNOW, I MIGHT WARM TO YOU IF YOU DO SOMETHING FOR ME."

"Yeah?"

"ONE BY ONE AND NICE AND SLOW . . . TAKE OFF YOUR CLOTHES. START WITH THE SWEATSHIRT. YOU KNOW, MAKE IT FUN. TEASE ME A LITTLE. IF YOU'RE GOOD I'LL LEAVE THAT OLD THERMOSTAT ALONE. MMM? WHAT DO YOU SAY?"

Yeah, but when you get bored with that, what next? I didn't trust Phoenix one little bit. I looked 'round the room again. And this time look, I told myself. *Really look!* There's got to be something here.

"THAT'S IT, MICHAELA . . . LIFT IT UP OVER YOUR WAIST NICE AND SLOW . . . SLOWER . . . THAT'S IT, YEAH . . ."

The breathing rasped louder. Michaela had got hold of the bottom of the sweatshirt and lifted it in one slow movement, exposing her flat stomach. I knew she was playing for time, but this wouldn't give us long.

I looked at the lockers again. They stood against the wall from floor to ceiling. They were in three sections, each containing a dozen individual lockers with combination locks, standing side by side along the wall. Then I glanced down at the floor. A line marked the floor, leaving chipped and scratched tiles. Someone had dragged an object—a heavy and hard one at that—across the floor. My eyes returned to the lockers. The curving line scored into the floor ended at the bottom of the farthest cabinet. It was just the kind of mark you'd make dragging a heavy piece of furniture by yourself across the floor. Now I barely heard Phoenix's breathy noises of approval as Michaela lifted the sweatshirt up over her breasts. My eyes traced the scratches in the floor to the locker cabinets. The one at the end stood maybe an inch forward of the other two. Someone had been single-handedly shifting that heavy piece of steelwork around. Someone maybe like Phoenix . . . now why should he go to all that trouble?

"TAKE IT OFF . . . TAKE IT OFF NOW!"

As Michaela slipped the sweatshirt up over her shoulders I told her, "Move back to the wall."

Surprised, she stepped back, pulling the sweatshirt back down over her chest.

"HEY, MICHAELA, DON'T GET SHY ON ME NOW. TAKE IT OFF!"

"Stay right back," I shouted to her, then I reached up, grabbed the locker cabinet and toppled it forward. It fell with a tremendous crash. Tiles cracked, splintered. Michaela looked at me, stunned, as if I'd lost my mind.

"HEY! STOP IT! GET OUT OF THERE!"

"Too late, Phoenix. I've found what you've been hiding." I nodded toward a heavy-duty door that had been concealed by the lockers. I whispered to Michaela, "Pray that this is an exit."

325

"Hell, it might lead to Phoenix."

"If it does, I'm going to rip his big ugly head off." The door didn't have a handle but rather a steel wheel in its center. I spun it. Behind the door I heard some mechanism turning with a clicking sound.

"LEAVE IT ALONE. YOU CAN'T GET OUT OF HERE!"

I shut out the voice. Instead I threw everything into turning that wheel. Just when I thought I'd have to turn the thing forever a click sounded, followed by a hiss of air. "Stay close, Michaela." I pushed. The door swung open, revealing something no bigger than a closet.

Hell. It couldn't be a dead end. There had to be something that—

Yes. The closet-sized room had no ceiling. I hit a switch and the void filled with light. There, running above my head, was something like a large chimney flue. In one wall metal ladder rungs ran up fifteen feet to a hatch.

I felt Michaela's hand on my arm. I pointed upward and mouthed: *Follow me.*

By this time Phoenix thundered like some old god of the barbarians. His rage-filled voice blasted the room.

"YOU BASTARDS! I TOLD YOU I'D GET YOU. . . . I PROMISED YOU REVENGE. I PROMISED I'D HURT YOU. . . . NOW . . . YOU DIDN'T EXPECT THIS, DID YOU?"

I braced myself for an explosion or flood of poison gas.

Instead the lights went out. As simple as that. And without windows the darkness was total. I mean it was just like being sealed into a coffin ten feet underground.

Behind me, Michaela whispered, "Oh, Christ . . . I can't see a thing. Greg?"

"Hold out your hand. There . . . got it."

"He's switched off the power."

"Never mind that now. Just follow me. Walk forward. That's it. Feel those?"

"Yes."

"Those are the rungs of a ladder."

"Jesus Christ . . . what's he going to do next?"

"He can't do a thing. He's over there in his hidey-hole."

"But—"

"But what we're going to do, Michaela, is climb. I'll go first, you follow."

"But what if the hatch is locked?"

"There's a steel wheel like the door we came through. It must be a manual lock. Phoenix can't do anything to that." I began to climb. "That's why he hid the doorway in the first place, to stop others he trapped here from escaping. Are you behind me?"

"Yes."

"Go slowly. Don't rush."

Hell, the mental image of falling and breaking a leg came only too sharply. If we did that we might as well be dead and buried. So . . . nice and slow . . . one rung at a time. I climbed the ladder up the shaft in total darkness. God, what a darkness. It coiled 'round you like black smoke. You opened your eyes so wide they hurt, just to see a glimmer of light. But there was no light. And your eyes played tricks on you until purple death's heads blossomed out of thin air right in front of you.

Now Phoenix had stopped ranting like a mad old god of yore. He was pissed, I knew that much. But he kept quiet. Maybe there weren't any of those night vision cameras in this shaft. Maybe he was listening hard through those concealed microphones, trying to hear our hands and feet whispering on the rungs. Or maybe for a sudden yell if one of us slipped back down into the black void to smash our bones on the concrete floor below.

"Nearly there," I whispered. Yeah, nearly there. How the hell could I know that, but I wanted to encourage Michaela. She was somewhere below me. Sometimes I felt her hands brush my ankles in the dark as she felt for the next rung. Once I put my foot down on her fingers, but she didn't cry out.

I guessed also that every second that went by she expected a hand to close 'round her own ankle to yank her downward. My heart beat louder and louder. The silence made me edgy now. Phoenix had something else planned. Maybe he could lock that hatchway above my head. Then we would be stuck here, waiting to suffocate or freeze at his leisure. But that didn't add up. No, he wanted us full of blood and healthy for his big pink vampire across the way. Maybe he could flood the place with some kind of narcotic gas that would knock us out. The next time we woke we could be kissing that pink gel, feeling tubes burrowing into our skin as a prelude to it sucking us goddam dry. *Jesus, would this ladder ever end?*

I kept climbing. One rung at a time. Nice and easy does it. One rung at a time. Don't hurry. Don't rush. One slip and you'll break your bones at the bottom. You'll bring Michaela down, too.

Then the voice came roaring back up the shaft like an erupting volcano. "HEY, GET THIS: THERE'S A TV SCREEN NEAR THE BATHROOM DOOR. LATELY I'VE BEEN SHOWING WHAT YOU CALL THE HIVE FOOTAGE OF YOU, AND GUESS WHAT?" Phoenix's voice rose with excitement.

I didn't reply. Just concentrated on climbing that ladder through the darkness.

"THE MOMENT SHE SAW YOU, VALDIVA, YOU SHOULD HAVE SEEN HER REACTION."

My head bumped against the hatch. "Don't move, Michaela. We're at the top."

"DON'T YOU WANT TO KNOW HOW SHE RE-ACTED, THAT BEAUTIFUL BABY OF MINE?"

"OK, Phoenix." I braced myself, feet against the rung, shoulder pressed up hard against the hatch so I could turn the steel wheel with both hands. "Tell me what you saw."

"I'VE NEVER SEEN HER DO THAT BEFORE. YOU SHOULD HAVE SEEN THE EXPRESSION ON HER FACE. SHE WAS PLEASED—REALLY PLEASED, YOU KNOW?"

Turn, baby, turn. The steel wheel screeched. "Why was she pleased, Phoenix?"

"BECAUSE YOU'VE BEEN KEEPING A LITTLE SE-CRET ALL YOUR OWN, HAVEN'T YOU, VALDIVA?"

"What little secret's that?"

"SHE RECOGNIZED HER OWN KIND. YOU'RE THE PRODUCT OF THIS THING YOU CALL A HIVE, VALDIVA."

"Well, I'll be, Phoenix."

"YOU'RE NOT EVEN HUMAN, ARE YOU?"

"You don't say?" I humored the madman as I gave the wheel an extra quarter turn. There was a click. "So what do you expect me to do about it?"

"COME OVER HERE AND SAY HELLO TO YOUR SISTER."

"I've got other places to go, Phoenix."

"VALDIVA, YOU MUST STAY. DON'T YOU REAL-IZE? SOMETHING WONDERFUL HAS HAPPENED TO YOU."

"Yeah, right, Phoenix." I pushed up against the hatch. Like you open a can of soda, it hissed. Air swirled up 'round us as the pressure between inside the bunker and the outside equalized. "As if we'd be-lieve anything you say."

"LISTEN TO ME, VALDIVA, YOU ARE THE FIRST OF A NEW BREED."

"Good-bye, Phoenix."

"DON'T TAKE MY WORD FOR IT. REMEMBER? IT'S YOU WHO CAN SENSE WHO IS UNDERGOING THE TRANSFORMATION."

I pushed upward, opening the hatch until it swung back to crash back against the concrete roof. Moonlight flooded the shaft. Fresh, cool night air swirled 'round my face, chilling the perspiration on my forehead. In triumph I hissed down to Michaela, "We're out!" I scrambled onto the roof.

"YOU ARE HIVE, VALDIVA. YOU ARE HIVE!" Phoenix's voice rose to a roar. "AND THE HIVE SHALL INHERIT THE EARTH!"

"Give me your hand." I reached out to Michaela. In the moonlight I could see her shrink back, clinging so tightly to the rungs that her knuckles turned white. "Michaela, hurry."

"Greg. What if he's right? What if you *are* one of those things?"

"Listen to him, he's crazy."

"WHAT ARE YOU GOING TO DO WITH *YOUR* KINGDOM, VALDIVA? WHAT ARE YOU GOING TO DO WITH MICHAELA? SHE'S ONE OF THE OLD SPECIES, YOU KNOW? THE ONE THAT'S DIVING DOWN TOWARD EXTINCTION."

"He's lying," I panted. "He's trying to trick us into staying. Come on, take my hand."

"VALDIVA, YOU KNOW AS WELL AS I DO YOU'LL KILL MICHAELA ONE DAY."

She looked at me for a moment, her eyes gleaming like black diamonds. Doubt twinned with fear flitted across her face. She couldn't go back into the bunker. But did she want to leave with me?

At last she made up her mind. She reached up. I caught her hand in mine and helped her up.

"YOU'LL BE BACK, VALDIVA. YOU'VE GOT FAM-
ILY HERE NOW. YOU'LL NEED TO SEE YOUR
BLOOD RELATIVE HERE, WON'T YOU? YOU
SHOULD SEE HER. SHE'S OPENING HER MOUTH.
SHE'S CALLING YOU. CAN YOU HEAR HER?"

Distorted by the concrete shaft. Echoing. Muffled. I
heard it. A long, wordless cry, like a child pleading not
to be left alone. The eerie sound raised the hair on my
scalp. As I stood there on the bunker roof listening, a
shiver started in the root of my spine to creep up over
my back like a million insects had burst out of my back
from a—

HIVE.

The word snuck into my head before I could stop it.
Hive. I looked at my hands. Man hands? Or monster
hands?

My body began to shake in a series of tremors as I
heard that mournful, pleading cry come swirling in a
rush from the shaft.

"Greg." Michaela took my hand. In a suddenly gentle
voice she said, "Come on. We're getting out of here."

I crossed the flat concrete roof to the edge. The
drop to the ground was perhaps fifteen feet. In the
moonlight the area 'round the bunker looked peaceful. Astroturf gleamed an unnatural green. The place
looked deserted. There were no hornets. Even the remains of hornet dead had been cleared by bears and
wild dogs.

After a moment's search I saw a way down. The
branches of a tree had grown close to the bunker. They
seemed sturdy enough. I glanced at Michaela. She shot
me a smile, her white teeth catching the moonlight.

"Don't worry," she said. "I can do it." With that she
launched herself from the top of the bunker to land
on the branch with the agility of a cat. In seconds she'd
reached the trunk and climbed down to the ground. I
followed. The branch creaked under my weight but

331

held. Soon I dropped down to stand beside Michaela.

'Round us the forest stretched away into the moonlight. A vast and silent place. Not even a breath of wind disturbed the trees. We didn't have to speak. Michaela inclined her head toward the forest. I nodded.

Side by side we ran.

Forty-two

Moonlight speared the branches, shooting down thin beams of silver to the ground. All 'round us tree trunks formed eerie, Gothic columns. Beside me, Michaela ran, the white rubber sandals flicking soundlessly across the moss. We ran fast. And for some reason we didn't become breathless. The exhilaration of leaving that concrete tomb where dwelt the madman and the monster gave us wings. For half an hour we raced through the forest, picking up the path, then following it to the road. A little later we found the garage where the Jeep that I'd cursed over all those days before stood there as if waiting for us.

"Crazy." Smiling, Michaela shook her head. "Crazy. Did I dream all that? Were we really trapped in the bunker?"

"We were." I took a deep breath. "And my God, it's good to breathe fresh air again."

She leaned back against the hood of the Jeep, fanning her face. "Hell, this sweatshirt's hot. . . ." She lifted a sleeve to her nose. "It smells of that damn place, too."

In one smooth movement she pulled the sweatshirt up over her head and hurled it to the corner of the garage. Then she stood there looking at me. Moonlight caressed her bare shoulders. She flicked back her hair and I saw her bare breasts. The tips darkened as cool air stroked them.

Her eyes locked on mine. "Greg. Prove to me you're human." She reached out to gently touch my jaw. "Can you do that?"

I pulled off my sweatshirt. "There's my heart. That's a human heart." I took her hand and pressed the palm to my chest. "Feel the rhythm?"

"Prove you're human."

I slid my hands over her shoulders until they met behind her back. That's when I pulled her in against my chest. Her cool breasts pressed against my skin, which burned like hot metal. I pressed my mouth against hers. Her lips came back at mine doubling the pressure, her tongue working against my tongue.

The whole world, the whole universe imploded into that kiss. She caressed the muscles of my back while I crushed her tight against my body. The air from her lungs rushed into my ear. "Greg, Greg," she whispered, breathless. "Prove it. Go on, prove it to me."

My fingers slid down her back to reach her pants. My thumbs hooked the waistband and drew them down. Panting, she pulled down mine. Then went down, kissing my chest and stomach.

It came roaring down at me, spitting flame, hurling out sparks. A great volcanic eruption of passion that was a burning fire inside me. It was some cousin of the instinct that drove me to kill. Now that instinct exploded inside me, driving me to do what I did next. And I could no more have stopped myself than stop myself busting skulls with the ax.

I lifted her bodily from the floor; her cool hair tumbling down over my naked arms. She gave a surprised gasp as I swung her 'round so her feet were clear of the floor. Then I sat her on the hood of the Jeep. In the moonlight I saw the crazy veil of hair across her face. I saw the hungry glint of her eyes. The flash of teeth as her mouth opened with a sudden spasm. Her naked legs lifted until her feet hooked behind me into the small of my back. Her arms wrapped tightly 'round me, as if she braced herself for some sudden stab of pain. Even her eyes closed tightly as she anticipated what would happen next.

Pushing my hips forward, I slid into her. Her gasp came in a rush in my ear. Her body enfolded me tightly. She whispered words breathlessly. Not that I understood them. Not that I needed to. Instinctively I knew what she wanted. Gripping her waist as she sat there on the car's hood I buried myself deep into her.

"*Oh!*" Her sudden gasping cry echoed back from the walls. "Don't stop now, please don't stop now," she panted.

I couldn't if I wanted to. As my body moved in rhythm with hers I found myself watching her mouth. Her lips pressed together hard with the effort of pushing her hips forward. Then the lips slid back revealing those beautiful white teeth as she smiled. Then they as quickly pursed together to kiss me. There was something fascinating about watching her mouth up close. It moved constantly. The lips reddened and grew enlarged as her breathing came harder. Her tongue ran across them. Then as I pounded into her, shuddering the car from axle to axle, her lips fluttered as a cry started in her throat, growing louder and louder. Her teeth bit her lip as if she couldn't stand that tidal wave of sensation anymore.

"Harder . . . please harder . . . *yes!*"

That's when the wave of sensation overwhelmed her, submerged her; she thrashed her head from side to side, her dark hair whipping the hood of the car then whipping back across my shoulder. Her cries filled my ears. Her body arched up to mine, pushing my whole body upright as I bore down hard against her. That's when even the atoms in my bones seemed to explode all at once.

The next thing I remember we were holding each other so tightly I thought we'd fuse into a single being. And that's how we stayed for a long time, holding each other, not moving but listening to the sound of each other's breathing gradually slowing. Allowing the world to slip back into focus once more.

Forty-three

Birds called in the forest. Their cries ran through the trees to die out there in the wilderness. Still tingling from making love to Michaela, I sat on the fence to gaze dreamily into the morning mist. Images of her beautiful body seemed to overlay the view of the surrounding trees and the meadow that ran down from the garage.

My bag had still been where I'd left it in the garage. I'd dressed using the spare clothes I'd brought with me from Sullivan, only they didn't amount to more than a pair of jeans and a shirt. My boots and leather jacket remained beyond reach in Phoenix's bunker. Michaela still lay dead to the world in the sleeping bag. And for the first time I began to wonder about the future. Had the lovemaking been a spur of the moment thing after our escape? Or would something longer lasting come from it?

I hoped so. Believe me, I didn't want to face the future alone.

Sunlight burned through the mist. Soon I felt its

heat on my hands and face, and, boy, was it good to see real daylight after being locked away in Phoenix's concrete fun house. No sooner had I felt sheer relief at being in the open air again then I remembered what Phoenix had said. He claimed I was the product of a hive. That the monstrosity he was harboring had somehow recognized me.

No way, Phoenix, you insane son of a bitch. You invented that to keep us in the bunker. Your only motive was to feed us to the hive. If we'd stayed, we'd have wound up as sacks of dry skin and bone, sucked dry of blood, then left to hang there like clothes on a line.

You're a murdering fuck, too, Phoenix. Anger burned under my skin. He'd lured people in there, given them food and shelter, then fed them to the monster. If I could find enough dynamite I'd stack it against the building and blow it all to hell.

"I guess we're going to have to find our own breakfast this morning."

I looked back to see Michaela standing by the garage door. Without any spare clothes she'd chosen one of my T-shirts. The hem reached the top of her thighs like a miniskirt. Arms folded, her dark hair tumbling down over her shoulders, she walked up to me.

Suddenly we both seemed lost for words. I found myself thinking: *Is this where we pretend nothing happened last night? Yeah, we're just good friends, a kiss on the cheek, a slap on the back . . . that's as far as it goes, OK?*

But I didn't want that. I realized we were good for one another. We connected. Not just physically either.

"Greg . . ." she began, as if to say something significant. Then she glanced down at my bare feet. "No shoes?"

"No. But I'm not wearing those rubber sandals again."

"Me neither. I wouldn't be seen dead in them." She

gave a tight smile. "Bad choice of words. We saw people who were."

"Last night . . ." I began.

"Yes?"

"Well, I liked what happened. It seemed as if it was . . ." I struggled for the right word, then chose the wrong one. "Natural."

She shook her head, smiling. "It was natural, Greg. Very natural."

"Sorry, I'm not good at this, but . . . hell . . . run away screaming if you want . . . but, dammit, I liked what— no, not liked: loved. I *loved* what we did, and I don't want it to be just a one-off . . . a one-night stand, I think—"

She lightly touched my lips. "Shh. I *loved* it, too." She smiled, her eyes glinting. "I've been waiting to find someone special for a long time."

I began to speak.

She touched my lips again. "You run away screaming if you want, but I think I've found him."

Sliding her hands deliciously 'round my neck, she pulled me down to kiss her lips. Her breath tickled my ear as she spoke. "Come back inside. Prove to me last night wasn't a fluke."

After we made love we fell asleep. I woke to see the shadows of two figures thrown against the wall. I scrambled up from the sleeping bag, shielding my eyes against the sunlight streaming through the open door. Two men stood in the entrance, and one held what seemed to be a club.

"Jesus, I beg your pardon, Greg. I'm sorry. I didn't realize you were—well, you know?"

"Ben? Zak? Didn't anyone teach you guys to knock before you walk in?" Despite their sudden appearance I found myself grinning so much my cheeks ached.

Ben's hands fluttered as he raised his hands in apology. "Jeez. We didn't expect to find anyone here. And we thought—huh, Michaela? Oh, man, sorry, I didn't realize you two were—"

"Ben," Zak broke in. "I think we should give them some privacy, don't you?"

Laughing, I shook my head. "Give me a minute to get on some clothes."

They backed out through the door, Zak resting the shotgun I'd mistaken for a club over his shoulder. Once the door closed, Michaela reached across to stroke my leg. "Well, if we intended to keep this relationship a secret I guess we've gone and blown it."

I smiled. "I'm pretty relaxed about that."

"Me, too." She kissed me. "Don't keep the guys waiting. I guess they want to hear what happened to us." She looked down at my feet. "Looks as if you're going to wind up wearing those pretty white sandals again."

"Aw, crap."

After Zak and Ben had heard about our experiences in the bunker, and after telling us that they were convinced we were raccoon meat (even though they had regularly checked the garage for our return), they carried us on the pillons of their bikes to the ruins of a strip mall. Then they set about fixing us up with replacement clothes from the stockpile they had tucked away in an old water tank (now dry as a bone.) Michaela kept my T-shirt but dumped the bunker green sweat pants in favor of shorts and sneakers. She found a denim jacket, but the temperature had climbed high enough for her to tie it 'round her waist. After going through a packing case full of shoes, boots and sneakers I hauled out a pair of brown work boots that fit perfectly. Zak went through plastic sacks crammed tight with coats, jackets and parkas.

"Here," he said, throwing a bundle to me. "It smells a bit ripe, but it should fit a big guy like you."

STRANGER

The leather jacket must have belonged to some biker who, I'd wager, had gone to the big Harley roundup in the sky by now. It smelled of gasoline and had become musty as hell from sitting in the bag for months on end, but it appeared in good shape, apart from some pale scuffs at the elbow where the long-gone biker had enjoyed a rumble or two in the past, or maybe just taken a roll on his bike. Painted on the back, surrounded by a starburst of studs, a Norse dragon's head breathed fire.

"It's OK," Zak told me. "I didn't peel it off a fat-bellied corpse. Boy found it hanging on a peg in a chapel around six months ago. If you throw it over a fence for a couple of hours it'll soon freshen up."

For an hour or so the time was taken up preparing a meal from a few cans Zak carried in the pannier of the big Harley. Ben took the usual run on the dirt bike 'round the neighborhood to check to see whether any hornets were nearby. He came back to report the all-clear, then we set about eating.

They told us that Tony had moved the clan to a cluster of vacation cabins they'd found out in the hills. The place looked untouched by hornets. With luck they could spend the summer there before moving south for the winter. Once more the dark reality of life out here away from Sullivan struck me. Supplies were scarce. Hornets kept them moving from place to place. How many years could you keep living the life of a rootless refugee? What happened when the fuel ran out? What did they do when they couldn't find spark plugs and tires for the bikes? There was only a limited amount of canned food to be picked out of the ruined buildings. When that went, what then?

As I sat there watching them spoon food into their mouths my mind flew forward five or six years. I saw how it would be. There we were, half-walking, half-crawling through the snow. We were clad in rags. We were so starved our cheekbones cut their way out from inside our faces. One by one we were dropping into snow drifts. Our fingers were blackened from frostbite. Toes snapped off inside boots. One by one we were dying. And I saw this as clearly as I saw Zak scratch his bald head with the end of his spoon. As clearly as I watched Ben unlace his boots with those jittery fingers. I saw Michaela glance across at me and smile. And I saw her in five years' time; she was staggering through that blizzard with a baby in her arms that was too cold and too hungry to even cry. I saw all that like it was a goddam vision from the Bible. That wasn't imagination. *That is what will happen.* OK, OK, I wasn't claiming supernatural second sight. Nothing like that. But if those people didn't die in a snowstorm it would be something else. They'd be so worn down by exhaustion they'd die of infections. Or they'd drink contaminated water. Or they'd be caught by the bad guys. One way or another, the people sitting here with me had the clock ticking against them. Counting down the seconds until bad luck tore the life force out of them.

I had to slam the plate of food down because suddenly it was choking me. A surge of blistering fury climbed up through my throat. I stood up, began pacing 'round the clearing, grinding my fist into my palm.

Michaela looked up at me. "Greg, what's wrong?"

I looked at Zak and Ben. "These cabins you've taken everyone to: There's clean water there?"

"Sure." Zak looked puzzled, wondering what had gotten into me.

"There's a deep well," Ben said. "A big old one with a crank and bucket. It's not going to dry up for years."

"Did you check whether it was clean?"

"Clean?" Zak's puzzled expression grew more perplexed.

"What are you getting at, Greg?" Michaela looked puzzled, too.

I looked into my cup. "Where did this water come from?"

"A bottle we brought with us." Zak nodded at empty plastic bottles lined up by a wall. "I was going to fill them here."

"But there's no water main close by."

"No, but the last time we were here we found a well."

Michaela explained, "Most homes out here drew water from their own wells; that's why we stayed. After all, the water mains in towns and cities failed months ago. And one thing we do need if we're going to survive is a good supply of clean drinking water, otherwise— Greg? What's wrong?"

"Zak, show me the well."

"Now?"

"Sure now; come on."

"OK, OK, but I don't see the hurry."

"You will in a minute. Ben, you got a flashlight?"

"Yeah, sure."

"Bring it to the well."

Zak led the way to the backyard of a trashed motel, then along a path downhill. We'd only been walking a few seconds when he pointed to a steel hatch set beside the path. "Before the Fall the motel drew their water supply from there. There's an electric pump under the hatch. Of course, that's no good now."

"What do you use to get the water?"

Zak shrugged, as if I was asking a bunch of stupid questions for the goddam stupid fun of it. "A bucket and a line. Lower it down—splash—haul it up with the water."

"When did you use this well last?"

Michaela frowned. "What are you driving at, Greg?"

"Got that flashlight, Ben?"

"Here you go." He handed it to me. "Zak, can you open the well cover?"

Again he gave a mystified shrug. "Sure." He reached

down to the steel ring and easily hauled open the metal cover that was perhaps the size of a house door. "There, knock yourself out." He grinned at the others, as if I'd got myself wrapped up in some idiotic obsession about well water.

I flicked on the flashlight and shone it down the well shaft. About twenty feet down the water glinted in the light. I clicked my tongue. "See what I see?"

They all looked. Ben recoiled, like something had burned his face. Michaela stepped back, swallowing. Zak looked a little longer, then sighed. "God . . . what a mess."

I looked down again. A man floated in the water. Decomposition gases had bloated arms and legs and face into a cartoonish figure with little piggy eyes and a black, puckered mouth. I checked for the characteristic death blow to the head. Yup; I could just see the head wound through molting corpse hair.

"He's been knocked on the head and thrown down the well," I said, looking down at the corpse that bled its poisons into the water.

"The murdering bastards."

"Yeah . . . but they murdered one of their own kind."

"Hell, why on earth did they do that?"

"Think about it. How do they get rid of our kind?" I snapped off the flashlight and nodded to Zak to drop the metal cover back down. "They can hunt us down and kill us. But that takes time, energy and manpower. Or they can starve us by taking all the food they can find. What they can't carry they destroy. But . . ." I nodded down at the well. "The subtle way is to poison the water supply."

Michaela nodded. "They wrecked the main supply months ago. So now they're poisoning the wells."

"Damn right." Ben looked as if he'd just bitten into something rotten. "The quick way is to kill one of their own kind and drop him into the water."

"So they either finish us with cholera or typhoid . . . or they get lucky and infect us with the bug that's swimming 'round in their own blood and we all turn Jumpy." I shook my head. "They're pushing us closer to extinction, guys."

"So we check the wells first," Zak said. "They can't find every well and spring, can they?"

"Maybe not," I agreed. "But they'll find most in a year or so." I tapped the metal hatch with the toe of my boot. "And I guess one adult corpse will crap out the drinking water for a good five years or more."

"We could boil it."

" 'Course you could. But you'd have to boil every drop of water you used for drinking, cooking and washing."

"We'd manage." Zak sounded defiant.

"And you'd really want to drink something with chunks of rotting face and genitals floating in it?" I shrugged. "Be my guest."

Michaela folded her arms, her face tense. "So that's why you asked about the well at the cabins?"

"If our people drink water with one of those rot boys down the hole then they're going to wind up sick, if not dead."

Michaela started to walk back to the bikes. "How far away to the cabins?"

"About an hour's ride."

I threw the flashlight back to Ben. "Ride up there and warn them about the well."

"There's a chance it might still be all right. The place hadn't been touched by hornets."

"It might be sweet as a nut," I agreed. "But the hornets could be getting cute. They might be content with dropping a corpse down the well and leaving it to do their dirty work."

They started to walk back to the bikes but paused when they saw I'd squatted down by the fire.

Ben looked back. "Greg? You're coming, too?"

"I'll wait for you here."

"Why? We'll be staying at the cabins."

I shook my head. "You can't guarantee the water will be fresh. You've hardly any food. You're low on ammunition."

Ben looked bemused. "Yeah, I know . . . but what do you suggest?"

I shot him a smile that he must have read as crazed. "Well, old buddy, I've decided it's high time we went back home to Sullivan."

Forty-four

They were back within three hours. And when they saw I'd found one of their precious stores of gasoline—a niggardly thirty gallons stored in cans beneath a mound of motel debris—they were pissed—really pissed.

Tony roared up first on the Harley in a cloud of swirling dust. He glared at the remains of the fuel cans lined up against the remains of the motel wall. There was no, *"Hey great to see you, buddy . . . glad you made it back alive."* Instead: "What the fuck are you doing, man? Michaela told me you're going back to Sullivan."

"That's right?"

"So, you're running out on us, huh? Going back to a nice soft bed . . . man, you are a pile of shit, you know that?"

"I need to go back."

"Yeah . . . *need.* You need to save your yellow neck." Climbing off the bike, he rocked it back onto the stand. "And how the hell did you find that gas? That's ours."

"I followed my nose. Look." I pointed at one of the Jerry cans. "It's leaking. I could smell it twenty paces away."

"What do you need all that gas for? There's thirty gallons there."

"Twenty-five now. You stored it in cans that leaked."

"Hey, but we need that."

"But I need it more."

Tony's hand went to the butt of his pistol. "There's no way on earth we're going to let you take what's left of our gas so you can go running back to your soft, pussycat town."

I looked at him. "'What's left of our gas'?" I repeated his exact words. "You mean this is all you've got?"

Tony looked uneasy, as if he'd let some secret slip. "Sure, we've got more gas. We've got a store up at the cabins." He slapped the tank of the bike. "What do you think we run these on—morning mist?"

"How much gas? Ten gallons? Fifteen?"

"Enough, Valdiva."

By this time the others had killed their motors and had climbed off the bikes. Ben looked puzzled. Michaela and Zak were angry. They immediately replayed the conversation I'd just had with Tony. Why did I need the gas? It wasn't my gas. It was theirs. Why was I scuttling back to Sullivan like a whipped puppy?

Ben chipped in. "You're crazy, Greg. You know what happened last time. They'll lynch you if you go back there."

Michaela shook her head. "You rat. After last night . . . I mean, I thought we had something together. Now you're leaving?"

Tony spat. "He's got a yellow streak up his back . . . this wide." He held his hands apart.

Disgusted, Zak swept his hat from his head to strike it against his thigh. "Go back to Sullivan, homeboy. But don't expect a lift from us. And don't think you can take that gas, because we—"

"'Because we need it,'" I mimicked. "I know."

"So what are—"

"Just listen to me for one minute, OK?"

Grudgingly they looked at each other, then Zak nodded. Michaela still glowered.

"First answer some questions."

Zak sounded suspicious. "What kind of questions?"

"How much gasoline do you have?"

Michaela shrugged. "With what you've found around fifty gallons."

Tony added defiantly, "But we'll find more."

"OK. Where?"

"We're good at finding supplies."

"Yeah." Zak nodded. "See for yourself. We've done all right so far."

"How much ammo have you got left?"

They shrugged.

"OK, don't give me an audit down to the last shotgun shell," I said. "Give me an approximate figure."

"OK, OK." Michaela held up her hands. "We have around a hundred shotgun shells. Maybe three hundred rifle rounds and a few dozen rounds for handguns."

"That's not much, is it? Not if you're going to keep twenty people alive over the next few months."

"Like I said"—Tony rested his hand on the pistol butt where he'd pushed it into his belt—"we can find more."

"But where? The towns are picked clean."

"We'll do it."

I moved in close to meet him eye to eye. "Tell me: When was the last time you found some gas? Some ammunition?"

Tony glared back. "Two weeks ago. A stack of rifle shells."

Michaela sighed. There was a defeated look in her eye. "Greg, it was three weeks ago, and we found three rifle shells in the trunk of a wrecked car."

"Three shells won't win a war, will they?"

"*Michaela.*" Tony glared at her as if telling her to keep her mouth shut.

"What have we got to hide, Tony? It's looking like crap. We haven't found any gas in a month. In a couple of weeks we'll have to dump the bikes and go on foot."

"We can manage, Michaela. We got by in the past."

" 'We got by in the past'?" I echoed. Boy, oh boy, this time I let them have it. Words came out like machine-gun bullets. "What good is that? Don't you see? You can't live like this, grubbing for cans of beans in ruins and running from place to place. Listen to me; it's time to stop living like hobos. It's time to start living like Vikings!"

"Like Vikings?" Tony gave a dismissive laugh. "Yeah. What do you suggest, Valdiva?"

I took a deep breath. "Do you have any dynamite?"

"Dynamite! Hell no."

"What do we need explosives for, Greg?" Michaela asked, astonished. "We carry what's essential. Food. Ammunition."

"I didn't think so."

"And what's this talk of Vikings?" Ben asked, bemused. "What do Vikings have to do with anything?"

"Because, Ben, we're going to start *taking* what we need to survive."

Zak scratched his bald head. "Well, Valdiva, you talk the talk, I'll grant you that. But how we going to *take* what we need?"

I looked 'round at the faces that were either puzzled or downright hostile. Only Michaela's had softened. I sensed she trusted me to offer some kind of hope. Jesus, I prayed I could. "Listen: This is the plan. There's a Jeep back at the garage I've been staying in. All it needs is gas. Once I have a full tank I drive to Sullivan. There, I'm going to pick up explosives. I'm sure they've got dynamite and detonators, haven't they, Ben?"

"Sure, there's a place that supplied the quarries, but—"

"Once I've got the dynamite we open up that nuclear bunker. There's a crazy guy there who's sitting on enough gasoline to float a ship. There'll be military hardware. Mortars. Rocket launchers. Grenades. Machine guns. And probably a million rounds of ammunition. See? We're going to start living like Vikings. We're transforming ourselves from losers to winners. We're taking control of our lives again."

Michaela's face lit up. Zak nodded, a grin breaking across his face. Even Tony's expression changed to one of excitement.

Only Ben looked worried. "Greg, that's a great idea. But everyone in Sullivan will hate our guts. How do you propose to get them to hand over dynamite? All you're gonna get is a bullet between the eyes."

I shot him the devil of a grin. "Trust me, Ben. We're Vikings now. We can do anything."

Forty-five

When people—or the goddam world in general—push you around it makes you unhappy. When you lose control of your own life you feel powerless. You feel dead from the neck up. Believe me, that's one thing guaranteed to saturate your life in complete and utter misery.

Live like Vikings! So far that was all I'd been able to tell them, but as they funneled gas into the Jeep back at the garage their faces shone; they laughed, cracked jokes. They were happier . . . they were taking control of their lives again. Suddenly they were optimistic about the future.

After the confrontation over those paltry gallons of gas, they'd really locked themselves into the dream I'd sold them. By now it was evening. Zak had already ridden back to the cabins with the news: We were going to crack open the Aladdin's cave stocked with more food than we could ever eat. Those half-starved devils had cheered him. With an almighty grin pasted across his face he'd returned with more guns and ammo. For a while we worked on the Jeep, pumping air into the tires. I greased up the cable linkages in the engine. Michaela and Ben checked the guns.

Tony still tended to question everything I suggested. But it seemed now more from habit than any real desire to wreck my scheme. "Why don't we use the bikes? They're more maneuverable than the Jeep. They'll use less fuel as well."

I slapped the hood of the Jeep. "Because I'm going to need dynamite—lots and lots of dynamite. More than the bikes can carry."

"How're you going to blast a way into the bunker, Greg?" Michaela's dark eyes looked searchingly into my face. "The walls are thick enough to withstand nukes."

"There's a way, trust me."

The question bug catching, Ben looked up from where he loaded a rifle. "And I still don't see how you're going to just turn up in Sullivan and ask for dynamite. Those people aren't going to hand over their stuff because they'll be too busy ripping your head off."

I smiled. "You're thinking like a nice middle-class boy, Ben. You've got to think like a warrior who drinks his enemy's blood from his shattered skull."

"Yeah." Ben grinned. "Silly me, I never thought of that."

Michaela chipped in. "So who is the enemy, Greg?"

"That's easy. *Everyone.*" I wiped my hands on a cloth. "Everyone who stands between us and survival. . . . Now, let's see if this little beauty's going to deliver." With the battery long dead I slotted the starting handle into the engine socket that exited through the radiator grill.

"You think it's really going to start?" Ben asked.

"It's going to have to," Zak said, looking through the open door. "Here come the bad guys."

*　　*　　*

Got to make this work, Greg, I told myself. We're using the last of our precious supplies on this venture. At best we go hungry if it fails. At worst . . . well, fill in the blanks.

There they were. Hornets. Lots of fucking ugly hornets. Big, bad and monstrous, just like they'd come lurching out of your worst nightmare.

"Jesus," Ben breathed. "There are hundreds."

Zak looked at me, then at the Jeep. "Is that old junk pile ready to run?"

"It'll work. These babies were built for battlefields."

"Let's hope you're right."

"Don't worry about me. You get the bikes." I ran to the front of the Jeep. Glancing out through the doors, I saw the road that ran up through the forest. It was thick with hornets. They shuffled forward in the evening sun. If the wind had been in the right direction you could probably have smelled their greasy hair alone. In a little while the Twitch would set my stomach muscles jumping. Ben, Zak and Tony fired up the bikes and eased them through the doorway onto the driveway that led to the road. Michaela hopped into the open-topped Jeep in the driver's seat.

"Make it quick," Tony shouted. "They've seen us!"

I glanced back through the doorway. They were still two hundred yards away, but all those feet were raising a dust cloud nearly as high as the trees. They'd spotted us, all right. They were coming this way. And as the saying goes, they were walking like they meant it.

I swung the starting handle. It made a puttering sound.

"Lightly press the gas pedal," I called. "The carb's dry."

I tried again. This time it made a sharp coughing sound. Only it didn't fire properly. Instead, the misfire yanked the starting handle from my hand and whipped it backward so the iron handle cracked against my forearm. Pain blistered white hot through the bone. Shit. I whispered a little prayer to my guardian angel that the blow hadn't snapped a bone.

"Are you OK?"

I glanced up to see Michaela anxiously looking through the windshield. I shook my hand. My fingers tingled like crazy.

"Fine. She misfired, that's all."

I wish.

Once again I took a grip of the starting handle. My arm didn't hurt any more intensely. Come to that, it didn't hurt any less, either, so I figured I hadn't broken a bone.

"I reckon you've got fifteen seconds to get moving," Zak called. He cocked the shotgun.

"Fifteen seconds is plenty, buddy." Gritting my teeth against the pain, I swung the handle again. This time the engine roared. With a thumbs-up to Zak, who sat astride the Harley, I jumped into the passenger seat. Michaela hit the gas and the little 'Nam vet Jeep bulleted out the doorway like it was rocket-powered. The three bikes kept just a little ahead as we swung onto the main road, then powered away. I glanced back to see a dozen or so hornets break away from the pack to run after us. The rear wheels of the Jeep flung dirt into their faces and we were gone.

As soon as we were well clear of the hornets we settled down to around forty. Now I had a chance to sit in the open-topped vehicle and enjoy the breeze shooting through my hair, and to feel a good meaty slice of satisfaction. I'd done good work on that old engine. OK, so it ran with a throaty roar, but everything functioned a hundred percent. Every so often Zak or Tony or Ben would glance back to give a thumbs-up sign. The roads were clear. What debris the Jeep couldn't ride over it nimbly sidestepped. Beside me, Michaela's dark eyes locked onto the road. She had the concen-

tration of a hawk. There wasn't a stone or a bottle on
the road she missed. I found myself gazing at the waves
of dark hair rippling in the slipstream. In fact it was so
wonderful it was hard for me to look away. And here's
the craziest thing: I felt this big, goofy smile on my face.
Michaela was something else.

When she realized she was being watched she turned
and shot me a warm smile. Once she even reached out
to rest her hand on my knee.

For a while I allowed myself my reward: to ride in an
open-topped Jeep through a forest wilderness. Beside
me, a beautiful woman with raven feather hair and eyes
black as onyx. Now that's a good enough reward for
any man. I took that hour's ride as the sun set and cut
it free of a lousy past and a dangerous future. I just
wanted to live in that moment.

But here's the brutal part: I couldn't for long. Because I knew I'd lured these people into something
called hope. At the best of times hope is as fragile as a
butterfly's wings. Sure, I knew we were headed to Sullivan to collect the dynamite. Sure, I knew I planned
to bust my way into Phoenix's concrete fairy castle, with
its treasure house of food stocks that would keep our
bellies full for years. But by doing that I'd forced this
little bunch of hunted teenagers to gamble what little
resources they had. They'd use up their gas and their
ammo on this scheme of mine. If it failed, at best
they'd go hungry. At worst . . . well, you'll recall what I
said about filling in those blanks . . .

We camped out on a hill overlooking Sullivan. The
town was probably no more than ten minutes' ride
away. There were no hornets in the neighborhood to
give us a sleepless night. And no way would we get any
surprise callers from Sullivan. That little community
was locked down tight. No one went in, no one came
out; those were the rules. They were broken on pain

of death. After we'd made camp beneath the trees I noticed Ben standing on the edge of a bluff, looking down over the lake toward the town. With the time before midnight, Sullivan's lights still burned out of that vast sea of darkness. Hell, that darkness had encompassed the whole country. Because make no bones about it, every other town and city that had ever existed had been shattered to their foundations. Only Sullivan had streetlights that lit the roads. Across the black lake water there'd still be some kids in the diner. Or maybe some held a party by a pool, complete with a barbecue and a tubful of cold beers. Maybe a little of Mel's weed was being smoked, too. Just for a moment I thought I heard music. Any night could be party night in Sullivan. Hypnotized, we stood there in the warm night air and watched

At last I saw Ben shiver like something cold had just crept over his grave. "You wish you were still back there, Ben?"

"Of course I do. I wish I was sipping a beer and listening to Hendrix. That would be enough right now."

"Sounds like paradise!"

"You can say that again."

"But you know the place was going rotten, Ben."

"Maybe it would have held together."

I shook my head. "The people are so paranoid they'll wind up burning each other in the streets. Remember what happened to Lynne?"

"They were just scared, Greg."

"Yeah, so scared they were prepared to murder their own neighbors."

He still stared out across at the town's lights.

"You can't go back there. You know that, don't you?"

His Adam's apple bobbed in his throat. "I can dream, buddy. I can dream."

Lightly, I slapped him on the back. "Come on, buddy. Time to turn in. We've got a big day tomorrow."

Forty-six

"You're out of your mind, Valdiva! You're getting nothing!"

"I need two hundred pounds of dynamite. Detonators. Fuse wire."

"Valdiva, if you don't get the hell out of here all you will get is shot. OK?"

"Mike, we need that dynamite. Believe me, we need it to keep people alive out here."

"Get away from here, Greg. You're not welcome in Sullivan. Neither are your friends."

Ben squatted beside me in the ditch that ran within a hundred yards of the high fence that separated Sullivan from the outside world. "See? I told you they wouldn't give you any dynamite." His hands shook as he clasped the rifle to his chest. "Did you really think they'd say 'Oh, welcome back, boys. Here's what you need'?"

"No, but they'll give it to us in the end."

"For crying out loud, how, Greg?"

We squatted low in the ditch with the dirt wall ending just above our heads. Sullivan must have had hornet trouble, because around a dozen hornet corpses with bullet holes in their chests rotted down here with us. The stink felt strong enough to peel the top off your skull.

"Jesus, Greg, I'm gonna throw up if I stay here any longer."

"Come on, Ben, I need you, buddy. We'll get the stuff."

"Some time, never. Aw, Jesus, I've been kneeling on a head . . . what a smell! Christ, it's full of maggots."

I let Ben alone as he complained. He had some cause to. This wasn't going to be easy. OK, so the first part had been simple enough. At sunrise Ben and I had come down here on foot. No way was I going to give any trigger-happy guard on the gate an easy target, so we'd crept as close to the gate as we could along the drainage ditch. I didn't count on rotting dead men for company, though. I'd recognized the guard on the gate as Mike Richmond. I didn't figure he'd shoot if he saw us: we were his old beer buddies, after all. But he was vicious enough when he saw our faces. And when I'd asked for the dynamite he turned us down flat. What's more, he must have called out the Guard. Coming up the road rolled a fleet of trucks and police cars, sirens whooping.

Ben looked over the top of the ditch. "Oh, fuck, Greg, he's invited a shooting party."

"Perfect. It gives us chance to talk to the boss."

"They won't talk, they'll fire. . . . Jesus, this stinks. I can't breathe."

When the dust raised by the tires had blown aside I eased my head up above the ditch top. The townspeople weren't tossing caution to the wind either. I saw a line of heads just above the vehicles. In the morning sun I could see the glint of gun metal, too.

"I want to speak to someone in charge!" My voice echoed back at me.

A bullhorn crackled. "I'm in charge, Valdiva. Speak to me."

"Recognize the voice, Ben?"

He gulped. "Crowther junior. You know he hates your guts. You'll get nothing from him."

"Crowther," I shouted. "We need two hundred pounds of dynamite, fuse wire and detonators."

There was a pause. Then in a friendly voice, Crowther said, "Come right up to the gates, Greg. We'll see what we can do."

That was enough to make me duck my head back down into the ditch, out of sight. "Crowther! I'm not falling for that one! Your people will blast me to kingdom come the second they get a clear shot."

The bullhorn boomed back. "Suit yourself. Either get away from here right now or we'll come out there and blow you to shit."

"You won't do that, Crowther. One: You're too chicken shit scared of infection. Two: We've got guns. You won't get through the gate in one piece."

"OK, Valdiva. Stalemate. But you're not getting what you want."

I risked a glance over the ditch. Damn ... the dust kicked up by the wheels had reached us. I got an eyeful of dust and ducked back down again. And Christ, that smell of rotting meat was worse than ever. My stomach heaved.

"Greg," Ben hissed, "let's get out of here."

He'd seen this stink was working its black magic on my guts, too. I waved him away. Then, without lifting my head, I yelled, "I'm here with Ben!"

"That geek? You're welcome to him."

I wiped the grit out of my eyes, but more blew across as I heard vehicles pull up on the far side of the fence. Sullivan was mustering an army. They came in such numbers, I could even smell aftershave on the Guard.

With a deep breath I shouted, "Here's the deal,

Crowther. We leave you alone in return for the dynamite."

"You've got to be kidding, Valdiva. You can sit out there in the ditch until Thanksgiving for all we care."

"Crowther, there are ten of us out here. We're armed with military sniper rifles. If you don't give us the dynamite we will sit out here until Thanksgiving. And whenever any of you or your neighbors walk out into the open we're going to blow their heads clean off their shoulders. We'll keep doing that until you give us the stuff. OK?"

"You're bluffing, Valdiva."

"Try me."

Beside me, Ben, edged away from a corpse with a hole in its head you could have waggled your fist in. He kept swallowing, his eyes watering. I rubbed my stomach as it gave a queasy squirm.

I'd expected some response from Crowther, but it became quiet. I guess the guys were in conference all of a sudden. Time to make my contribution to the debate. Carefully I eased my head up above the ditch. More dust carried downwind, creating a golden mist. With luck the guardsmen who were keeping watch might not see me through that swirling filth.

My stomach muscles bucked. Christ, that smell of rot had gotten itself deep down into the pit of my belly. I held out my hand. "Ben, pass the rifle."

Wiping the back of his mouth, he handed it to me. I chambered a round. Raised it to my shoulder. Looked through the telescopic sight. Sullivan had grown soft and careless. Magnification bloated the heads like beach balls. Sitting in the center of the crosshairs I saw Mike Richmond looking up over the top of a car. There were others I recognized, too. Finch, the old cop whose daughter Lynne had been murdered by the townsfolk. There was Mel, who grew the marijuana, toting an Uzi. Every so often she lifted her head above the back of a truck, an easy target. A tempting target as well, bearing in mind that she'd snitched on me that I was hiding a stranger in my cabin. But life's short anyway. I allowed the crosshairs of the telescopic sight to slide over one target after another. I counted six heads I could get a clear shot at. And even though I'd lied about the number of marksmen we had I knew we could leave a couple of our people here who'd turn this side of town into sniper's alley. Lifting the rifle a little, I could even get a clear shot of the main street. I could pick off townsfolk as they went to the mall or the courthouse.

I lowered the rifle. The veil of dust was thinning. Gold specks settled on my bare arms. *Make this quick, Valdiva,* I told myself. *They're going to see you any moment now.*

Once more I traced the line of vehicles. When I reached a truck I stopped. Although I couldn't see him I saw the bullhorn protruding from behind the front fender. Crowther had shielded himself. Even so, the bullhorn poked out like a bird's tail from behind a bush. I panned the rifle until the crosshairs sat squarely on the bullhorn; then I gently squeezed the trigger.

The sound of the bullet striking the bullhorn was amplified by the thing's mike into a shriek of feedback. The bullhorn flew out of Crowther's hand to the ground.

This time a hail of lead came back in our direction, but we were well hidden by the time it did. Once the dirt stopped erupting from the lip of the ditch there was silence again.

When Crowther spoke next it was without the aid of the bullhorn. But to be honest I didn't recognize the voice. Fear squeezed it into a high squeal.

"Valdiva! OK! You've got what you want! But you've got to promise that you won't come back here." The voice rose even higher. "Do you hear that, Valdiva?"

I smiled at Ben. I could picture Crowther all sweaty and scared and still rubbing his tingling fingers from when the rifle bullet had smashed the bullhorn from his hand.

"Valdiva! Did you hear me!"

"Yes, I heard. Remember, I want three hundred pounds of dynamite. Detonators. Fuse wire."

"Valdiva, you asked for two hundred."

"The price just went up."

"OK, you bastard, you've got it."

"Leave it outside the gate. Two people in an army Jeep will collect it. Don't harm them . . . otherwise I'll sit out here and pick you all off one by one. Right?"

"OK! OK! Give us half an hour."

Ben smiled and held out his hand. "You're the miracle man."

Smiling, I slapped his palm. "It was easier than I thought."

"That's because you scared them good and hard, old buddy."

My smile turned grim. "I had help from other quarters."

"Oh?"

I rubbed my stomach as it spasmed. "Ben, they're scared because they're in the early stages of infection."

His eyes went wide.

"That's right, old buddy; Sullivan's lousy with Jumpy. They just don't know it yet."

With Ben staring at me like I'd just punched him, I began to make my way back along the ditch to where Michaela waited with the others.

Forty-seven

"How long do you give them?" Michaela asked from the passenger seat as we drove away from Sullivan.

"A few days before the symptoms become obvious." I shifted the gearshift. "Then they'll cull the ones they know are infected. Only the ones doing the killing will be infected themselves."

She pushed her hair back from her eyes. "So why aren't we infected?"

I shrugged. "Natural immunity."

"I wish you could be so sure."

"You've been exposed to the bug enough, and you haven't been infected yet. Those people back in Sullivan managed by sheer chance to avoid contamination for so long because they were isolated from the rest of the world."

"Do you think I introduced the bug to them?" she asked. "I may not be infected, but I might be a carrier."

"I'm sure you didn't. In fact, I'm certain they infected themselves."

"How?"

"One thing the people of Sullivan ate plenty of were fresh fish. For months fish had been feeding on bodies that had been washed into the lake." I looked at her. "It adds up, doesn't it?"

"Agreed. But not everyone will be infected with Jumpy."

"No, a few will survive. They'll wander from place to place, scavenging food. But the town's as good as dead now."

"Greg?"

"Michaela?" I smiled.

"Slow down, boyfriend. Remember what we've got in the back."

I glanced at the cases of dynamite stacked in the back of the Jeep. I eased off the gas. On this rutted road the boxes were hopping about in a way that was too lively for us to be comfortable with.

"So," she said, "how do you use dynamite?"

"Search me, I haven't a clue." I shot her a smile. "We'll figure out how one way or another."

Her face broke into a slow grin. "Yeah, we're Vikings now. We can do anything, right?"

"Right."

We drove back the way we came, along roads that cut deep gullies through the forests. In the distance we caught glimpses of rivers and lakes. The afternoon sun had been buried behind a big, dark funeral mound of cloud. A flock of white birds glided along the valley to our right, over shattered houses and villages that lay bitched and broken with their living hearts torn out. *Yeah, Valdiva. We're Vikings now. Warriors of the wasteland. Lords of Chaos.* We'd inherited a ruined planet.

Ahead of us by a few yards rode Tony, Ben and Zak, in a line of three, the bikes eating up mile after mile of road. I guessed they were taken by surprise by how easily we'd gotten hold of the dynamite in the end.

Within thirty minutes of me shooting the bullhorn from Crowther's hand the townspeople piled the cases of explosives outside the gate. Tony and Ben rode up in the Jeep and loaded it; then we were away in a swirl of dust with the Jumpy-raddled people of Sullivan watching us go. Only when I was five miles from the place did the muscle spasms ease in my stomach.

When I thought about it later, it all added up. I'd been downwind of them in the ditch. I'd smelled their aftershave. I'd smelled the infection, too.

Zak rode with the cowboy hat on his head, the brim flapping in the breeze. He grinned back at us. We'd be back at the cabins within the hour.

What happened next must have been fast. Only it seemed to roll in at me in slow motion. One minute there was open road, the banks of trees on either side of us. Then figures swarmed onto the road. Braking, I swerved to avoid them. I saw one aim a swing at me with a baseball bat. It smacked against the windshield. A white star appeared in the glass. Michaela shouted a warning. I swerved again, this time not to avoid the hornet but to use the car to smash his legs to crud.

I looked to my right to see Ben's dirt bike in the grass at the side of the road, the wheels still spinning like fury. I braked hard. Zak and Tony wheeled the Harleys 'round and raced back toward the hornets. There were maybe twenty of them. Not a huge pack, but there might be more nearby. What's more, they'd managed to topple Ben off the bike.

Zak and Tony, like old-time knights on horseback, charged the mob, the pair of them firing their sawed-off shotguns from the hip. The scattering buckshot dropped three or more of the bastards with every shell. I saw them go down kicking on the blacktop. Blood spurted from wounds in their faces.

I reversed hard. Smashing the legs of any that got in

the way. One old girl went down with a screech beneath the back wheels.

"Greg, the dynamite!" Michaela shouted.

I looked 'round. More hornets piled into the road from the forest. With sticks and iron bars they struck at the car. Some beat at the boxes of dynamite, sending a flurry of splinters into the air. I lurched the car forward. A stick caught me on the shoulder, but I kept powering away from the mob. I looked back again. Zak and Tony rode in a circle 'round Ben, back tires ripping up the sod into a green blizzard that filled the air. They were keeping the hornets at bay as Ben hoisted the bike upright. Thank God the engine still fired. I could see the exhaust hazing the air behind the muffler. Hornets tried to rush him, but the ever-circling Zak and Tony kept them back with a few well-aimed shotgun blasts. A moment later Ben climbed back on the dirt bike. With a twist of the throttle he wheelied right out of there, Zak and Tony following. Zak fired back as the hornets ran after them, turning one guy's face into a mess the color of crushed strawberries.

"Damn, that was a close one," I said to Michaela as I accelerated away. Then I glanced at her. Her head rolled to the rhythm of the wheels. Her eyes were shut. Streaming from the gash in the top of her head came what seemed to be a whole river of blood. Not a trickle, but a gush of blood that ran into the soft hollows of her eyes, down her cheeks like crimson tears, then down her throat to soak her T-shirt.

"Michaela?" I shook her shoulder as I drove. "*Michaela, can you hear me? Michaela!*"

A rush of air tore the words from my mouth. "Michaela?" I kept calling her name. But as the red stained her chest my voice slowly died.

Forty-eight

"Is she dead? Zak . . . is she dead?"

"Just clear back there; let me see."

On the drive back to the cabins on the mountainside Michaela had shown no sign of life. Where her skin showed through smears of blood it had been the color of milk . . . a deathly gleaming white that chilled me to the bone. I'd carried her into a cabin to lay her on a bed. Immediately the others had gathered 'round, their eyes huge with shock when they'd seen the wound on top of her head. Boy sat on the floor with his back to the wall, his knees hugged to his chest, watching people rushing 'round with bowls of water, towels, surgical dressings. I crouched beside the bed as Zak carefully moved Michaela's long hair aside so he could inspect the wound.

I repeated the question. "Zak? Is she dead?"

"Ben, pass me that mirror."

Ben handed Zak the small mirror from the dresser. Zak held it beneath Michaela's nose. It seemed to take forever before I saw the glass mist.

"Thank God for that." Zak sighed with relief. "She's breathing. . . . It's shallow, but it's there."

"What now?" I asked.

"We've no medical training. All we can do is patch up her wound, then wait and see."

"Jesus."

Zak gently parted her hair. "But look at the size of the scalp wound. It's a big one . . . there's a lot of blood, too."

He must have seen my sickened expression.

"Greg, that's a good sign, believe me."

"Good? You call that good? The bastard nearly tore off her entire scalp."

"It shows it was a glancing blow. Instead of coming down hard into her skull, the club struck at a shallow angle, tearing her scalp." Zak peered down at the head wound. It was a three-cornered tear like when you rip clothing on a nail. Through the pool of blood there gleamed the pink curve of the skull. Zak knelt with his hands open, fingers splayed. They barely trembled, yet I noticed they were smeared red from fingertip to knuckle.

"OK, OK. I know I can do this. I can. I can." He clenched his jaw. He was psyching himself up to do something. "Tony, find me that first aid kit. Not the domestic one. The big one we found in the ambulance."

"What are you going to do?"

"This is a bad tear in her scalp . . . really bad. I'm going to have to sew it back together."

I looked at him. "You've done this before?"

"No, but trust me." His eyes were fixed on the bleeding wound. "I know I can do it. One thing, though." He looked 'round. "Clear the room. I need to be able to concentrate."

*　　*　　*

With Zak working on Michaela in the cabin I had to keep myself busy. Dark clouds overlaid the sky like a purple bruise. With Tony's help I shifted the dynamite to a spare cabin some distance from the others. This stuff should be stable, but I wasn't going to take any damn-fool chances. For a while we worked without talking. Only when I moved the Jeep to a garage alongside one of the cabins did Tony break the silence.

Wrapping a rag around his hand, he reached into the back of the Jeep to pull out a hunk of what looked like steel rod. As thick as my thumb, it was maybe two feet in length.

I stared at it for a moment.

"The hornet's weapon of choice," Tony said at last. "Evil-looking thing, isn't it?"

I nodded. "Do you think that's what hit her?"

"Could be. But there's no blood." He shook his head, sickened. "Maybe one threw it as you passed, or he lost his grip on it when they attacked." He looked more closely at it. "The problem is, they smear these things with their own shit. Whether it's a crazy ritual or whether it's to spread infection I don't know."

I found myself glancing back at the cabin where Michaela lay. "What are you saying, Tony?"

"Michaela should really have a shot of antibiotics and a tetanus inoculation."

"You mean if she recovers from the head wound she still might go down with blood poisoning?"

"It's happened to us in the past. We've lost people."

"But you've got first aid kits and medicines, right?"

"But we haven't any antibiotics or inoculation shots. They're long gone."

"Hell." I rubbed my jaw. "But I know where there are some."

"The bunker?"

"First thing tomorrow we're going back there." I shot

him a grim look. "We're going to take whatever we need from that place."

"But you said it was built like a fortress."

"It is . . . so this is where we start making the impossible possible. It's a habit we're going to have to learn; otherwise we won't survive."

"Greg . . . Greg!"

I turned to see Boy come running across the grass. His eyes were big as boiled eggs; the whites flashed in a way that sent shivers prickling across my back.

Boy shouted, "Greg . . . Tony! Zak says to come back to the cabin!"

The bedroom where Michaela lay was in near darkness. Zak had drawn the blinds and turned down the kerosene lamp until only a smudge of light burned in the glass tube.

She lay flat on her back, her black hair fanned out across the pillow. Zak nodded for me to go closer. As I crouched beside the bed her eyes opened. For a second they gazed up at the ceiling, as if puzzled by her surroundings; then she turned her head slightly to look at me.

"Michaela," I whispered, "it's Greg. You're going to be all right."

Her lips moved noiselessly for a second, then she breathed out the words: "Sorry, Greg . . . I messed up . . . should have been sharper . . . a whole lot sharper . . . uh." She grimaced.

"Don't apologize." I moved closer and squeezed her hand.

"Let my guard down . . . that was stupid of me . . ."

"Take it easy. You didn't do anything wrong."

"I did, Greg. . . . I should have kept my wits . . . these days you get lazy you're gonna die . . . oh . . ."

"Sshh . . . Easy, Michaela."

Swallowing, as if she had something stuck in her

throat, she lifted both fists to her temples. She began to press her head so hard her knuckles turned white.

"Michaela, what's wrong?"

She sighed. "It hurts . . . ssa' bitch . . . uh."

Zak ran his hands across his head, angry with himself that he couldn't do more for her. "I don't think she's suffered any brain damage. I did a good job stitching her scalp, but it's going to be sore for a while."

"Isn't there anything we can give her?"

"All we've got now is Excedrin."

"They're not even going to take the edge off pain like that."

"I know, Greg. Good God, I wish I could do more for her. She doesn't deserve this. . . . She pulled us outta more crap than I don't know what. She kept us together, like . . ." He shrugged as words failed him. "Hell, she doesn't deserve this, Greg," was all he could repeat.

She didn't deserve it. I gritted my own teeth as I watched her shudder as waves of pain ran through her. Her knuckles whitened again as she pushed her hands against the side of her head.

What's that old saying? *Life's a bitch and then you die . . .*

It came ringing back at me as I crouched there holding her hand. It came like a huge tolling bell that thundered the words 'round my head. *Be a Viking,* I said. *Work miracles,* I said. *Do the impossible,* I said. And, Jesus Christ, all I could do was watch the face of the woman I loved spasm as the agony tore through her like a goddam razor.

Forty-nine

I watched Boy through the binoculars. Disguised in rags, carrying a backpack on his shoulders that reached all the way down to the back of his knees, he limped 'round the fake house that comprised the bunker. I could see that he wore one shoe. His head hung down, exhausted.

"The kid's acting the part well," I said.

"He loves Michaela like a sister." Tony crouched beside me. "He'd give his life to help her."

Zak crawled through the leaf mold, keeping below the bushes. "Anything happening yet?"

"Nothing."

"Boy's been hanging 'round there for two hours now. Are you sure this bunker guy can see him?"

"He can see him, all right," I whispered. "He can hear, too. My guess is, he's sitting there watching Boy to make sure this isn't some kind of stunt. So keep your voices down." I glanced at Zak. "Is Ben ready?"

"He's about a mile down the road with the Jeep."

"Any sign of hornets?"

"None that we've found, but that's a big forest out there. You could hide a whole army; no one'd ever know."

We crouched there beneath the bushes just inside the forest fringe. I watched Boy sit at the main entrance to the bunker. He'd done as I'd instructed. He'd made an act of finding what you'd suppose was simply a big country house in the forest. He'd examined the fake doors painted on concrete walls, looked at the astroturf grass. Then he'd sat down, his head hanging down as if he was too tired to take another step. Every now and again a squall of rain came from dark skies. Trees groaned and hissed before the coming storm like restless animals. It was as if they sensed something big was breaking.

I kept my eyes fixed to the binoculars, seeing Boy's dirt-smeared face. In my mind's eye I was seeing Michaela, too. When I left the cabin that morning her face had a white, unnatural look, as if it were made from the same waxy stuff as candles. She breathed steadily, but she still hadn't fully regained consciousness from the attack the day before. In fact, she seemed to sleep more deeply now. I found myself asking myself how you know when someone has slipped from natural sleep into a lethal coma. It scared me more than I dared to admit. Zak had done a good job of the suturing, however. After cutting a little of her hair away from the scalp he'd neatly stitched the flap of torn skin back. That had stopped the bleeding. The rest now, as they say, was in the lap of the gods.

Minutes crawled to midday. I began to wonder again about the steel trap door on the annex roof through which Michaela and I had escaped. That would be the easiest way into the bunker, but I was certain Phoenix would have gone across to manually close it. What's more, it was locked from the inside. If I did risk climbing up onto the annex roof that would alert Phoenix that we were up to something. And that trap door was a substantial piece of metal; I'd never be able to open the thing.

Tony pushed aside a backpack to make himself more comfortable.

Zak fanned himself with the Stetson. "Treat the bag with some respect, bud. We don't know how stable that stuff is."

Like he was moving a sack of eggs, Tony gently shifted it farther from him. "Greg, you sure you know how to use it?"

I didn't take my eyes from the binoculars. "I've bundled half a dozen sticks together with a detonator and ten feet of fuse. When I tested it earlier the fuse burned at two seconds per foot."

"That'll be enough?"

"Once you light it you've got twenty seconds to get clear."

"Give or take a few seconds," Tony added. "So make sure you move fast once it's burning."

Zak gave a grim smile. "Don't worry, I'll move fast enough. They don't call me Mr. Greased Lightning for nothing, you know."

Tony chuckled. "When did they ever call you that? We have to hold lighted cigarettes to your toes to get you out of bed in the morning."

"Oh, yeah?"

"Yeah."

I knew they were letting off steam to ease the tension. The truth was, all this hung on Boy getting it right the first time. If he fluffed it we got no second chances. And I knew we didn't have enough dynamite to blow a hole through those three-foot concrete walls.

"Man, you're so slow you've got moss growing on the soles of your boots."

"You've got moss on your dick. The only time you use it is to prick the pastry."

Both crumbled into snorting laughter. Tension was eating them. They were letting it out the only way they knew how.

Tony flicked Zak's bald head with his finger. "Yeah, remind me to buy you a brush and comb set for Christmas."

Zak grinned. "You won't do that twice."

"Oh, yeah?"

"Yeah . . . I've got a cute little kitten in my coat pocket. Try that again and I'll squeeze its throat until its eyes go *pop.*"

"That so?"

"Yeah, and what—"

"Guys," I breathed. "It's happening."

Suddenly they were alert again, staring forward through the bushes. Boy had climbed to his feet. He tilted his head to one side as he hoisted the backpack onto his back.

Zak whispered, "I hope those weld joints hold, Tony."

"They will."

I watched Boy. He seemed to be listening to a voice. I angled my head, too, but couldn't catch anything. Then I saw Boy nod.

"He's heading toward the annex," I whispered. "That's what Phoenix told us to do last time."

"So it's working?"

"Pray that it is." I stared through the binoculars at the annex building that was disguised as a large garage. "There's a door operated by pneumatics, I guess. Boy will have around twenty seconds to do his thing."

Boy made a good act of plodding exhaustedly toward the annex. The backpack looked like a dead weight on his back. I guessed he wasn't playacting that part of it. The bag contained nothing but a welded steel frame that fitted tightly into it like a hand in a glove. Tony had spent half the night making the thing. Now, pray God it was strong enough.

"There it goes," I whispered. "See the bunker door opening?"

"Hell, it must be a foot thick," Zak breathed.

"As soon as he wedges the bag in the doorway, move. And for God's sake keep off the lawn. There are landmines under the grass." I glanced at Zak. "You happy carrying the dynamite?"

"I'll do it. Don't worry about me."

I nodded. "Once we're in, Phoenix will do whatever he can to make life hard for us. There'll be no light, so use the flashlights. He'll probably hit us with water. Even a lot of noise."

"If those are his only weapons we're laughing."

"Just say a little prayer he's got nothing else. Wait; Boy's almost there. Get ready. But keep down until we know the door's jammed. OK?"

Without rising from the cover of the bushes I pulled the strap of the rifle over my shoulder and checked that the .45 automatic was still strapped to my hip. At either side of me Zak and Tony checked their weapons. Tony sported a submachine gun with spare ammo clips taped together, while Zak carried a pair of sawed-off shotguns. He also hoisted the backpack containing the bundles of dynamite over his shoulders.

Hell, there was so much to check. Flashlights, ammo. I patted my pockets, feeling a rising panic. I'd forgotten the goddam cigarette lighter to ignite the fuses. *Shit, you idiot, Valdiva, you fucking class A idiot, you should*—Thank Christ. I felt hard tube shapes in my shirt pocket. I'd placed a pair of lighters there earlier. But pulling this off was like the plate-spinning trick you see at the circus. You have to make every little element of the plan work. Anything forgotten, anything mistimed, it all went crap.

"Any second now," Zak whispered.

Still playing the weary refugee, Boy made it to the bunker. I saw him stop to listen again to a voice we couldn't hear. No doubt Phoenix was giving the same instructions Michaela and I'd received in the same soft, whispering voice. Boy nodded again, then limped to the open doorway. As he entered he slipped the heavy bag from his shoulders. This time lightning-quick he spun 'round and jammed the bag lengthways into the entranceway. A second later the big armored door slid forward, as if to seal the aperture. It made it a third of the way, then stopped. It slid back. Shut again. But it couldn't slide more than a third of the way across. An alarm began to sound from the bunker.

"He's done it." I scrambled to my feet and repeated the earlier warning: "For God's sake keep off the grass. Touch that and you'll go fucking sky high."

The two followed me along the path to the bunker entrance.

Fifty

This was it. Adrenaline blasted me into overdrive. The world blurred as I ran hard at the bunker.

Boy danced outside the bunker door. "I did it, I did it!"

"Great work. Now get behind the bunker. And keep off the goddam grass." I looked down at the doorway. The metal frame inside the bag still held against the pressure of the door. Even so, it had closed now maybe halfway, leaving a two-foot opening. I heard pneumatics hiss. The steel frame groaned; there was the sound of metal on metal grinding somewhere inside.

"It's holding," I shouted. "But it might not hold for long."

Then Phoenix's voice rolled from the speakers. "Valdiva! Get out of here! You're a dead man! I'll crush you!"

"Yeah, you and whose army?"

"You are dead, Valdiva. Get away from here! Get away!"

The voice thundered across the plastic lawns away into the forest.

"You've got bunker boy all riled," Tony said as he switched on his flashlight.

"I'll go first," I said. "He's going to turn this place into a fun house the moment we go in there."

Phoenix boomed like the voice of God: "YOU'RE DEAD MEN WALKING. D'YA HEAR? GET AWAY FROM HERE. . . . *LEAVE AND YOU'LL LIVE!*"

"Sounds as if you've spooked him, too."

Zak lumbered up with the heavy pack of dynamite on his pack. He turned 'round so I could pull open the zipper on the backpack. I reached in, tugged out a bundle of dynamite, then started to unreel the fuse that I'd carefully wound 'round it.

"Tony, hold the end of the fuse. Zak, stick close to the bunker wall . . . no—farther back from the doorway." Suddenly this seemed crazy; to be standing there with five sticks of dynamite in my hand. Hell, I'd never used the stuff before. OK, I'd shoved the gleaming steel-shelled detonator into the center. But is that where it went? Jesus, sweet Jesus . . . "All right." I took a deep breath. "Stay back. The trick is to use just enough to blow the doors . . . not bring the whole house down."

Maybe Zak saw me hesitating, as if I doubted I could pull this off. "He's got a lot of goodies in there, Greg. Do it."

"Keep a grip on that fuse, Tony. If I yell *'Light it!'* just light it anyway, OK?"

He nodded, his face grim.

The door was still trying to crush the steel frame. I heard metal groaning as I stepped over it. The outer door wasn't my target. It would take a whole truckload of explosive to even dent that. My only hope was that it didn't manage to force itself shut. If I was trapped in there . . . hell, I didn't want to paint any mind pictures about that one. . . .

As I suspected, Phoenix didn't help me by switching

on the lights. Instead I moved along that same decontamination chamber I had entered before, this time a flashlight in my hand. The light danced on the tiled floor; the fuse trailed behind me. I repeatedly looked back to see if it had snagged against the door that slid backward and forward as Phoenix tried to batter the obstruction to crud.

At that moment spray hit me in the face. Hell, he was using the decontamination procedure as a weapon. The disinfectant caught me squarely, shooting into my mouth and eyes. The stuff burned like fire.

Half blinded, I stumbled forward, still holding the dynamite in one hand, the flashlight in the other, and trying to steady my balance with my elbow. Then he hit me with the cold water spray.

"Getting desperate, are we, bunker boy?" I murmured. I had anticipated his suddenly appearing in the doorway with a machine gun to blast us. He must have hundreds of weapons at his disposal. But something told me now he wouldn't have the guts to venture out of his safe house to face us.

"We're coming in, Phoenix!" I yelled over the hiss of water. "We'll find you."

"You bastards. You won't get close to me. You're dead men . . . *dead men!*"

I reached the door to the locker room. Although hardly flimsy, it was only a fraction as thick as the outer door. Carefully, I set the dynamite down so it was touching the door.

Too much explosive? Too little? Dammit, I just didn't know. Behind me metal shrieked as if in pain. I glanced back to see the outer door had all but crushed its way shut.

Taking a deep breath, I bellowed: *"Tony! Light the fuse!"*

The outer door had become a great champing mouth. It slid back, then rumbled forward to crush the steel frame. The fuse snaked across the mangled back-pack.

"You've made yourself a tomb!" Phoenix ranted. "D' ya hear me, Valdiva? I'm going to sit here. I'm going to enjoy watching you rot!"

Come on, Tony, do it . . . light it . . . if the door slides all the way shut it's gonna kill the fuse. I looked 'round for something else to wedge in the door, but this passage-way consisted of nothing but naked walls. I ran back to the outer door, tried to hold it back with my bare hands. Shit. I might as well have tried to stop the sun rising with nothing but my own two arms. With a hiss it rolled along the groove again to slam against the mangled frame, nearly pulping me in the process.

I glanced down as the flame ate the fuse, spitting sparks and fizzing. Then it ran through the doorway back toward the dynamite. Even the deluge of water from the showerheads didn't slow it. Jesus, the fuse burned faster than I had anticipated.

Tony and Zak appeared to help me with the door.

"No, it's too late," I shouted. "Get back. The dyna-mite's going to blow."

They moved back sharply, waving Boy to get down. Inquisitive as kids are, he'd leaned out from behind the bunker to get a closer look.

My eyes hunted across the ground. There, in the plastic grass, I saw it: a crowbar a hornet had used to break heads. But the ground was mined beneath the lawn. I looked at it, searching for any telltale marks in the grass. Dammit. Nothing to tell where the bombs were. Hell, what else could I do? I stepped onto the astroturf, hoping I didn't trigger a mine.

Thank you, Lord. I reached the iron bar, grabbed it, then ran back to the bunker door that had now closed the gap to around six inches. It slid back before re-turning to batter the obstruction. Cut into the floor was an inch-deep groove fitted with a steel slot where the door wheels ran. I slammed the iron bar into the groove just as the door came hissing back. It glided over the iron bar like it wasn't there. But just as I was thinking, *Shit, it didn't work,* the wheel that supported the half-ton door must have run into the iron bar. With a jolt the door stopped dead.

Zak yelled at me: "Greg! Get back! It's going to blow!"

Jesus, I'd forgotten about the fuse. I slammed myself against the bunker wall. The thunderous bang shortcut my ears. I felt a tremendous concussion in the center of my head. Instantly the bunker wall jumped at me, knocking me square in the face and flinging me back to the ground.

I pulled myself to my feet, my ears ringing, blood dripping from my nose.

"You all right?" The voice seemed to be part of the ringing. I looked 'round to see Zak and Tony helping me to stand.

"I'm fine," I lied. "Go see if we're in."

With flashlights blazing they squeezed past the crippled door and entered the hallway. I followed, shaking the dizzy sensation from my head. In the glow of the flashlights I saw water oozing from a fractured pipe. The explosion had blackened the walls, and every tile had shattered. I checked out the door inside the chamber. Fantastically, it still held tight in one piece, but it was the wall beside it that had staved in. I followed Zak and Tony through crumpled metal panels into the locker room. The explosion had picked up the vacuum packs of clothes, then scattered them 'round the place. Those white rubber sandals covered the floor as if a blizzard had hit it, covering it with blobs of snow.

So . . . I'd made it back again. I was back in the bunker, only it was different this time. No longer the prisoner but the invader.

When I reached Phoenix, and met him face to face, I wondered what he would say. Come to that, I wondered what he would do.

Fifty-one

We went through the place like a hurricane. Zak and Tony followed me, gun muzzles pointing outward like spines on a porcupine, ready to blast anything that moved. They shone the flashlights left, right and center, scanning the rooms for danger. Once we were through the pneumatic doors that Phoenix could operate remotely, the other lightweight internal doors weren't a problem. I kicked through one after another.

After screaming at us Phoenix fell silent. But he was watching; I knew that. From those concealed cameras he'd been seeing everything we did. He'd have seen us pass through the kitchen where I'd made popcorn with Michaela, through the living room, down the stairs to the operations rooms with their keypads that glowed like yellow eyes in the darkness. But I wasn't interested in those anymore.

"OK, Zak," I said. He turned 'round. I unzipped the backpack to pull out another bundle of dynamite, then I began unraveling the fuse. "There are bedrooms back through the double doors and along the corridor. Get in one of those with the door shut behind you." I checked that the detonator was in place. "Ten sticks in this one. It's going to kick like the devil. Ready?"

They nodded, their eyes on those white sticks. Now they'd seen what the stuff could do close up, they regarded it with infinite respect.

Phoenix's voice came rushing back. "I'm warning you, get out now. You don't know what you're getting into. Run, Valdiva, run!"

Get this: Phoenix didn't sound so much threatening as terrified. Something frightened him. He didn't even seem scared of us. . . . I felt that flicker of instinct in my gut . . . the little red warning light began to flash behind my eyes. The man genuinely warned us of some danger . . . only it wasn't him. He wasn't the threat. Something else lurked there . . . he was trying to save us . . .

I shook the thought from my head, but still a sense of unease wormed its way along my nervous system. *Something isn't right, Valdiva.*

"You OK, Greg?"

I nodded. "Rarin' to go, Tony." I laid the dynamite at the foot of the twin doors that were labeled COMM ROUTE. If my hunch served me right, these two meaty iron doors blocked the way to a tunnel that connected with the main bunker. There, Phoenix waited. Along with whatever surprises lay in store.

I played out the fuse behind me, checking that it didn't snag. "OK." I flipped the cigarette lighter, touched the flame to the fuse end. Sparks flew. "Take cover—here she goes!"

OK, so maybe I did use too much. The explosion knocked in bedroom doors, filling the whole complex with smoke. Even the beds we crouched on jumped halfway to the ceiling. Closets flew open, sleeping bags, pillowcases, towels flapped 'round like crazy birds. For a second we lay there on the floor, trying to retrieve the air that had had been slammed from our lungs.

"Jeez," Zak breathed. "Valdiva, you never do anything by halves, do you, man?"

I picked up the rifle from where the concussion had flung it across the room. "Come on, let's finish this now."

The corridor to the other rooms had been mutilated; you could use no other word for it. Mutilated to hell and back. Walls had been gouged by the explosion. Part of the concrete ceiling had broken away to come crashing to the floor. Every single door had been blasted inward. For the first time I saw the sick bay and the boardroom. There, tables and chairs had been upended. Exposed wiring in the walls sent out cascades of sparks. A punctured fire extinguisher sprayed a blizzard of foam.

I nodded at the twin doors that led to the connecting tunnel. "We've done it. We're in." The massive doors had been crumpled the way you can scrunch up a sheet of paper in your hand. Smoke billowed, thick as fog. It reflected the beams of the flashlights right back at us.

I approached the smashed doors. The tunnel entrance yawned like a hungry mouth, eager to swallow us into its concrete gut.

"Greg! Get back!"

Tony pushed me aside to fire the machine gun into the fog of smoke. A figure blundered out through the mutilated doors, then fell to the floor and lay still.

I looked through the smoke, expecting to see Phoenix lying there. Instead I saw a witch head of wild gray hair. A bloody mass bubbled where the face should have been.

Zak nodded down at the figure. "We got bunker boy?"

"That's not him." My stomach muscles clenched. "That's a hornet...." I moved closer to the tunnel's raw mouth. "Jesus, he must have let them in to guard the hive."

Swarming through the gloom of the tunnel, like they were a plague of hungry rats I saw them. Dozens of them. Men, women. Young, old. Their faces blazed hatred.

"Hornets!" I yelled. "They're coming this way."

Tony stepped into the doorway to fire the machine gun at them. Flame a yard long erupted from the muzzle. I could even see bullets roar into the gloom like balls of light to ricochet off walls, or to rip into bodies.

"Too many," I shouted. "Zak, hold still." I reached into the backpack on his back and pulled out a bundle of dynamite. "Get back into the stairwell." I pulled the lighter from my pocket.

A tall man with sores on his throat stumbled through the doorway. As if he'd suddenly decided to relax there for a while, he leaned against the wall. He looked down at his chest with a puzzled expression. A dark stain spread through the material of the torn-to-crap shirt he wore. He pulled it open to see a bullet hole above his breastbone that pumped big fat drops of crimson down his chest. Still puzzled, he fingered the wound. I found myself unable to tear my eyes away as he touched the bullet hole with his fingertip, then pressed harder. His finger slipped into the gory hole, his fingernail disappearing. With a look of astonishment, he watched his finger smoothly slip inside his chest as far as his knuckle. He began to rock his hand, and I realized what he was doing: He was trying to locate the bullet with his finger. Even as I watched he worked the finger inside the hole, rotating his hand from side to side, as if he'd found an object there that he couldn't quite— suddenly he coughed.

A stream of blood spurted from his mouth. His knees

gave way, dropping him dead to the floor.

Tony shook me. "Snap out of it, Valdiva. Come on!"

I touched the flame to the fuse. The moment it caught I lobbed the dynamite into the middle of tunnel. Hornets packed the place so tightly, they walked with their hands on the shoulders of the ones in front of them, grunting with bloodlust, their eyes locked on ours. A hungry kind of look that fairly hollered their craving to get hold of us and tear the skin from our bones. The dynamite bounced on the head of a bald man, then slapped into the face of a woman with boils clustering 'round her eyes. . . . Hell, these people were goddam monsters . . . you couldn't describe them any other way. Ugly creatures driven by an overwhelming urge to kill.

I waved Tony and Zak away from the entrance. I followed, ducking into the open doorway of the sick bay as my homemade bomb erupted with a roar.

We didn't waste any time. After the tunnel entrance sneezed out a huge ball of black smoke we ran back to the shattered doors. Through the smoke I could see that the explosion had toppled the hornets like a crowd of mannequins. They lay flat, covering every inch of the floor.

I didn't wait; I ran into the corridor. With no floor showing through the fallen bodies, some lying on top of the others, I ran across that mat of once human flesh. Most were dead, with hideous facial wounds where the blast had ripped at them. Some held up bloody stumps to stop me passing, but they weren't going to slow me down. No way!

As I ran, my boots crunched down on faces, chests, stomachs, throats. And as we raced across the torn bodies some of them began to recover consciousness. Immediately the air filled with a deep groaning. A great fat bass sound like a choir of madmen singing. The sound grew louder. Moans, groans . . . a deep, DEEP sound that made the teeth in your head vibrate.

A guy with a beard that reached his chest sat up, his hands outstretched to grab me. I snapped the muzzle of the rifle down and fired, exploding the top of his head. I ran over his still-twitching body and felt his hot blood spray against my bare arms. Tony and Zak, too, fired as they ran. Now the deep bass moan bore a mixture of rising shrieks as bullets ripped into bodies.

Then, ten seconds later, we were out of that gloom-filled tunnel. Ahead lay the main bunker. A huge door attempted to slide shut to seal us into the tunnel. But men and women had been hurled back by the blast to fall in the doorway. The heavy door made a mess of their bodies, but still it couldn't close fully. I slipped through the gap, screening out a sound like cracking eggshells as the steel door crushed hard against torsos, cracking bones, rupturing lungs and bursting stomachs.

I stood for a moment, blinking beneath the bright lights of the bunker. So this was it—Phoenix's den. My stomach muscles spasmed. This was where he nurtured the hive, feeding it with human captives.

The corridor ran away in front of me. Doors led off on either side. *Where now, Valdiva? Where now?*

Fifty-two

The main bunker looked far bigger than the little brother annex where Michaela and I had stayed. Room after room lined the corridor. Storerooms. Pump rooms. Bedrooms. Mess rooms. Rooms with air-conditioning plants. Rooms full of computer terminals. The place was the size of a battleship. Corridors ran off at tangents. Stairwells led to higher levels. Elevators plunged to unknown depths.

"Where'd we go?" Tony called as he snapped a fresh magazine into the machine gun.

"I don't know . . . We'll have to go through all the rooms one by one." I kicked open a door to reveal a sick bay. Spent hypos covered the floor. This must be one of Phoenix's little joy cabins, where he sent himself on cosmic journeys at the point of a needle. With narc habits like that it's a wonder the guy survived.

A hornet ran screeching from a corridor, waving an iron bar with such ferocity it flashed with blue sparks every time it struck the wall. I dropped him with a single rifle shot to the gut.

More hornets spilled from a side corridor. Tony's gun clattered. Men and women went tumbling to the ground.

"Greg, there are hundreds of rooms here. I don't think we're gonna have time to search them all." Zak blasted a pair of hornets with a single shotgun shell.

Tony pumped a tracer into the swarming bodies. "Hey, the bad guys are coming thick and fast."

No sooner had he said that than Phoenix's voice boomed in the confined space. "Move into the corridor to your right."

"Yeah," I yelled. "As if we should trust you!"

The voice echoed. "You can't shoot them all, Valdiva. There are hundreds down here!"

"And who's to say you're not inviting us to run into their open arms?"

"Trust me, Valdiva."

"Yeah, like hell I will."

From a doorway a heavyset man flung himself on Tony. He fell with the man straddling him. The monster put a pair of huge hands around Tony's throat and began to squeeze. I used the rifle butt to crush the guy's skull. He crumpled like an empty sack.

"Come on," I said. "We've got to get out of here. There are too many."

No understatement. Around fifty hornets surged along the corridor we'd just run through. Ahead, three corridors ran away into the distance.

"Come on, Tony. Get up." Zak pointed the twelve gauge in the direction of the surging mob. "You can't lay there all day."

Tony grimaced. "Looks as if I will. The big ape's gone and busted my leg."

I glanced down to see Tony gripping his shin. His face was tight with pain.

"Come on, buddy. You've got to stand up."

Tony shook his head. "It's broken. . . ." He pulled

the machine gun toward him. "I'll stay here and cover you."

"No fucking way . . . Zak, grab him by the collar and drag him."

"Which way?"

"I don't think it matters; just move as fast as you can. Go!"

The mob started to run. There were so many hornets, the sound of their feet came like pounding drums. I fired the rifle until the magazine was empty, dropping the leading bad guys. Some behind tripped over the fallen bodies. But I wasn't stopping them all. I glanced back to see that Zak had grabbed Tony by the collar and dragged him into a sitting position farther along the corridor. I followed. "Not that way. That's where Phoenix told us to go. If I know him it'll be a trap."

"Where, then?" A desperate note sounded in Zak's voice. "Where the hell do we go?"

The pounding grew louder as the hornets ran at us. Now they were maybe thirty yards away. I drew a handgun. In a strangely dislocated way I aimed and fired. I felt calm. I knew I'd simply aim and fire one round after another until the hornets overran us.

I aimed at a guy with a red beard. *Bang.* He went down with a hole through his cheekbone. Then I focused on a wiry-haired man with a hooked nose. *Bang.* Clutching his stomach as the bullet tore his liver, he did a kind of forward somersault roll. Immediately the mob charged over him. If the bullet doesn't kill him those crushing feet will, I told myself in a cool way that seemed as remote from this as if I was watching TV. *Bang.* A woman with black jagged teeth was next. The bullet popped her eye like a soap bubble. *Bang.* Another guy went down with blood pouring from his mouth.

Screee!

I stood and stared at what happened next without

any real understanding. I was going to die. That's all I knew. But suddenly a steel gate slid across the passageway, blocking it from floor to ceiling. A second later the mob slammed into it, hands thrusting through the bars, trying to reach me. I stood for a moment before the truth wormed its way into my head. They'd been stopped dead. For now we were safe. I glanced back to see Tony lying there, supporting himself on one elbow, and Zak standing with his mouth hanging open. It took a moment for them to realize, too, that the mob couldn't reach us.

I turned to them. "I don't know how long that's gonna last. Tony, grit your teeth."

After handing Zak the rifle I picked up Tony and hoisted him across my shoulder. I heard him gasp with pain. Now I could see the kink in his shin where the bone had snapped. "Zak, keep moving. If you see anything blast it."

"Don't worry, I will."

I walked hard with Zak covering me. Tony's weight nearly broke my goddam back, but I wasn't putting him down yet. I wouldn't leave him to those monsters. We'd walked perhaps twenty seconds when we passed through a set of swinging doors. I looked down because something funny had happened to the floor. I panted hard, trying to get the oxygen to my lungs, as I stared at the floor . . . That was it—*carpet*. We'd entered the residential area. I made my way straight toward a door marked NO. 3 LOUNGE. This was a bigger version of the one in the annex, with a dozen comfortable armchairs and couches. Sweat rolling down my face, I lowered Tony as gently as I could onto a couch. He grunted as I eased him onto soft cushions. Dazed by pain, he looked 'round at the soft furnishings. "Christ, I've died and gone to heaven."

"Not yet," Zak murmured, looking 'round in awe. "But close, old buddy—damn close."

"Zak, help me get the table against the door." As we barricaded the doorway the voice of Phoenix came padding into the room. "No need for that, guys."

"So what have you got planned for us, you freak?"

"That's not nice."

"Nice it ain't . . . but true."

"Valdiva, that's the second time I've saved your neck."

"Saved me for what? For that thing's lunch?"

"Listen, you people. You are safe from them in here. They cannot pass the gate."

"Unless you open it for them."

"You think I'd do that?" Phoenix still sounded scared for some reason.

"So we're not going to come to any harm?" I reloaded the rifle.

"I can't promise that."

I murmured, "Great, here comes the next mood swing."

The TV screen on the wall suddenly sparked into life. I found myself looking at a close-up of Phoenix.

I nodded. "Tony, Zak, meet our host."

They gazed in awe at the white-painted face and pharaoh-style eyes, surrounded by thick painted black lines, and framing the face itself flowered a mass of black hair.

Tony grimaced, still clutching his leg. "Hell, he's not a pretty sight."

Zak let out a whistle. "Would anyone, if they locked themselves down here on a diet of narcotics for months on end?"

I looked up at the screen. "What now, Phoenix?"

"I want you to see something." He looked away from the camera lens. I could hear a keyboard being tapped. "Remember this?"

The TV flickered. Instead of Phoenix we were suddenly seeing a bathroom. The walls were stained with a tarry substance. More of it slicked the floor like strawberry Jell-O. Beyond the doorway I could see the poor bastards who'd been drained of their blood. They lay there, as dry as Egyptian mummies, still wearing the fucking stupid rubber shoes.

"We've seen this before, Phoenix. We don't want to see any more of your sick camera work."

The scene cut to Phoenix in ultra close-up. His bloated face filled the TV screen, his bloodshot eyes burning out at us. "But don't you see, Valdiva?" he hissed. "The room is empty."

"You're telling me the thing has hatched out?"

"Not hatched . . . it has completed its metamorphosis. *Look!*" He stepped out of the shot to reveal a figure standing behind him. Desperately he whispered into the mike, *"Help me, Valdiva. Please help me."*

Fifty-three

Wherever Phoenix was in the bunker he worked the camera control. On TV I saw the image expand to fill the screen. I heard Zak and Tony breathe in sharply, as if taken by surprise. I found myself staring hard, feeling an electric shiver run up my backbone as my eyes took in a figure behind Phoenix. A girl of around twenty sat with her back to the wall. Dark hair with odd apple-red tints poured down over one shoulder. Her skin had an amber glistening appearance, as if she'd poured olive oil all over herself. Her eyes were lightly closed. She seemed to be dozing with her back to the wall, her knees raised upward. One open hand rested lightly on her knee, palm upward, fingers slightly curled. She was entirely naked.

Phoenix's voice came over the speakers in a breathy whisper. "The hive changed when you left. Its color deepened to crimson. It began pulsating as if it became agitated. Then a couple of days later I woke to find that the membrane had ruptured, releasing the fluid onto the floor."

"You're making it sound like a birth, Phoenix."

"That's exactly what it was. . . . Later I found her wandering 'round the corridors."

"You sure she came out of the hive? I mean, she isn't someone from the outside?"

"Sure she's from the hive. This place is locked down tight. Not even a bug could creep in here without me knowing."

I looked at the close-up of the girl's sleeping face. You could even see individual lashes resting on her cheeks, while her black eyebrows formed two slender arches above her eyes. A lock of dark hair hung down over her forehead.

"So you've got yourself company, Phoenix," I said at last. "What do you want me to do about it?"

"You've got to help me, Valdiva. She won't let me out of here."

"Come on, Phoenix; she can't weigh more than a hundred pounds."

"I—I can't explain it, but she's got into my head somehow. She makes me do things . . ."

Tony caught my eye and touched his temple. *Nuts.*

"Yeah, don't forget I see you, too, guys. I'm not insane. This is for real. She can get inside my head. It's like sleepwalking." Phoenix sounded agitated. "I black out and find I've sealed all the doors to the command center. Then I find I've opened the outer door to let those crazy bastards in. I mean, what the goddam fuck's going on? I can't stop myself . . . I feel like my head's gonna explode. And all she does is sit there for hours and hours. She doesn't move. She doesn't even look at me. Jesus Christ, I'm—"

"Phoenix! Has she said anything to you?"

"No . . ." He took a breath to steady himself. "No. Not one word. Like I said, she can reach into my skull. . . . Please, it's freaking me out, man. I want out of here."

"Phoenix—"

"She's really scaring me. I know that makes me sound yellow, but she gets inside my head, and I see what *she* sees. Then I remember what it's like to be in the hive. I see myself in all that pink shit. . . . It feels like I'm drowning . . . and—and I'm hungry all the time. I'm so fucking hungry I feel as if my guts are going to explode. Jesus, guys, it's a nightmare . . . a fucking nightmare." Phoenix's face suddenly ballooned onto the screen, the eyes huge and pleading. "You've got to do something! Please, Valdiva. I saved your neck twice. You owe me. A blood debt, you understand? You've got to stop her doing this to me."

I watched the screen as he backed away, his face shrinking back into focus. Behind him the naked woman sat on the floor. During the man's panicky rant she never moved a finger. The hand still remained there limply palm up, like someone waiting for the first drop of rain on a summer's day.

Meanwhile Phoenix whispered over and over to himself, "I gotta get out of here. I gotta. I can't take it any more. Please, man, I can't take any more . . . please, please . . ."

"Phoenix, just open the doors and walk out of there."

"I can't, I can't, she won't let me."

"Why not?"

"Don't you hear me right, Valdiva? She's screwed 'round with my head. I've tried . . . I get up to walk to the keypad. But then . . ." He clicked his fingers. "I'm sitting back here again. It's like being trapped in a dream."

Zak spoke in a cold voice. "Kill her."

"You don't think I haven't tried? Jesus H. Christ, I must have tried a thousand times. But the moment I move toward her I black out and find myself back here in this fucking chair again. Listen to me, she's inside my head. She works me like I work this damn computer."

"Why do you think she's allowing you to speak to us now?"

"I don't know. . . . I don't think she—*it!*—is fully formed. It needs to stay here until it's ready to leave."

"So why did she allow you to save us from the hornets? Surely she knows we must be a threat."

"Sure she knows all about *you*." Phoenix gave a grim laugh. "I'd wager she's hearing and seeing you right now. Either through my ears and eyes or in some way I know shit about . . . What do you say to that, guys?"

"So why save us from her bodyguard?"

"Valdiva, you still don't get it, do you, man? Are you deliberately being stupid or what?" Phoenix lurched forward to fill the shot again. His eyes blazed out from the TV screen. "Valdiva, you and she are the same. You are both the product of the hive . . . Am I getting through? *You . . . are . . . both . . . from . . . the . . . fucking . . . hive.*"

"That again, Phoenix? You are insane."

"List the facts, Valdiva. You've been in close contact with hornets, so that means you were probably infected months ago. You're the only person *we* know of that instinctively knows when a person is infected . . . your two pals there can back me up on that one, hey, guys?" He steamed on, speaking faster. "When you were on the run from the things you say you fell sick. Only you didn't remember what happened exactly because you were unconscious for weeks. Now, how can anyone survive in a coma for weeks without expert medical care?"

"My mother and sister took care of me."

"You bet they did." Phoenix glared through the TV screen, so close one eye filled it. Red veins crazed the glistening white. "You were hive, Valdiva. And Mom and sis procured men and women and children for you

400

to feed on, just like I did with this one." He jerked his head back at the girl.

"You're out of your mind."

"Am I? Look at the hair, the color of her skin. They're just the same as yours." He gave a triumphant snort. "Now that's what I call a family likeness."

I closed my eyes, trying to shut out the voice. "Phoenix, it's not true. I was sick, that's all." I glanced at Tony and Zak; they returned my gaze, but there was something uneasy about it.

Phoenix ranted on. "You were just like this thing in here, Valdiva. And when your Mom and sister outlived their usefulness you just wished them dead . . . and they died . . . That's what these monsters can do, Valdiva." He stopped, but his breathing continued loudly over the speaker. "But I don't care about that now. I don't care if you two become the new Adam and Eve and repopulate the world with a master race . . . because all I want is out." His voice broke. "I've had enough of this stinking, rotten nightmare. . . . I can't take it anymore. Really, I can't."

There was a pause. No one spoke as his breathing echoed in the lounge. I gestured to Zak to pass me the backpack. Pulling back the zipper, I saw two sticks of dynamite taped together with a length of fuse. For a moment I planned blasting through the doors into Phoenix's communications center. But the doors were too thick. This little bundle of explosive wouldn't do it.

Phoenix's voice rasped dryly, "So how you going to help me, Valdiva? Or are we going to sit here and watch each other until doomsday?"

I closed the backpack so he wouldn't see the dynamite through his spy cameras.

"Phoenix, how are we going to get in there to help you?"

"I told you, I can't open the doors. She won't let me."

"There's got to be a way in. Ventilation ducts?"

"Too small. Unless you can shrink yourself to the size of a mouse."

"Any hatches? Emergency exits?"

"None. If this burns I'd fry."

He sounded weary now. On screen I saw him shoot anxious looks at the naked girl. "You have to hurry, Valdiva. I think she's waking up."

"You've got to give me some help here, Phoenix. Think, old buddy; is there any other access to that room?"

"None at all. No . . . wait . . . there's one of those little elevators . . . what d'ya call them? Dumbwaiters; that's it. There's a dumbwaiter over there in the wall."

"What's it for?"

"What do you think? People working down here'd still have to eat even during a nuclear war. If they were too busy to leave, someone would send them down food to eat while they watched the US of A flame out on the screens."

"Where does the dumbwaiter come down from?"

"The kitchen. Right next to the room you're in . . . but wait . . . you don't think you're somehow gonna sneak down in that and come out guns blazing. The thing's that big." He held out his hands about a foot wide. "Like I said, it's big enough for a plate of hot-dogs, not for a platoon of marines. . . ." He laughed. An edge of hysteria cranked it higher. "But while we're talking about it, maybe you could send me down a steak and fries. I haven't eaten in days." He laughed again. "Fucking days. Man, I can feel my ribs through my shirt."

Calmly, I said, "OK, Phoenix. Listen carefully. I'm going to send something down to you. Something nice."

He shot me a look. "What do you mean?"

"I'm going to help you."

"Forget about sending a gun down in the elevator. She'll *know*, guys. She'll see it in my eyes. And you can bet your life she won't let me use it on her.

"Phoenix, trust me. I'm sending something down that's going to solve all your problems."

I watched him on the screen. You could see the wheels turn inside his head as he thought about it. Suddenly he looked up at the camera, his face filling the screen. That was the moment when I realized he understood what I'd been driving at.

"OK, Valdiva. Send down that steak. I like them bloody, so make it a rare one. Plenty of fries. Potato salad. And don't be niggardly with that mayonnaise— you hear?"

"I hear, Phoenix."

"I'm waiting, Valdiva."

"You just keep that mental image of a huge juicy steak. Think about golden fries. Onion rings. Do ya like apple pie?"

"Good God, yes. Send me a whole apple pie."

"Keep that image in your mind, Phoenix."

Picking up the backpack, I went quickly into the adjoining kitchen. Phoenix hadn't been house proud. Wrappers, cans, cartons covered the table, along with around a hundred spent syringes. Boy, the guy knew how to party.

Set in the wall was a small steel door. Beside it were two illuminated buttons. One was marked UP, the other DOWN. I pressed the UP button. Far away, I heard a click, then a faint humming.

I pulled a plastic tray from the crud on the table, then set a plate on it. A buzzer sounded behind me. I gripped the handle on the door and pulled it down. It slid open to reveal a small steel box little bigger than the interior of a microwave oven.

Phoenix's voice came over the speaker. "How ya doing, Greg? Don't burn that steak."

"I won't. I'm cooking the fries now."

Zak came to the doorway and looked in. He gave an expressive gesture as if to ask what the hell I was doing. I put my fingers to my lips for him to stay quiet. Quickly I pulled the last two sticks of dynamite from the bag. Then he understood. He helped me unravel the fuse.

"I'm just frying those onion rings," I called. "Do you need mustard?"

"Send down a whole jar. I'll go nuts."

"Steak's nearly ready."

"Nice and juicy, is it, Greg?"

"It's beautiful. You're going to love what's on this tray. Steak, fries, the trimmings. A whole pie. A jug of cold sweet cream. Keep that image in your mind, Phoenix."

The voice came back calm and genuinely grateful. "I knew I could rely on you to help me, Greg. Thanks, buddy. You're a good man."

"Here it comes." I nodded to Zak, who placed the tray containing the dynamite into the midget elevator. Loosely, I coiled the fuse inside.

"I think you ought to speed things up. My roommate's waking up. I think she's *gnnn* . . ."

Tony shouted from the other room. "Hey, come and look at this—quickly, guys."

"The food's coming down, Phoenix," I shouted and lit the fuse. As the sparks flew I slammed the door shut and hit the DOWN button. With a click it began to hum its way down to the sealed room below.

"Greg!" Tony's voice rose. "Hurry!"

I ran into the adjoining room. On screen Phoenix rose from his chair. One look told me that thing had him in its grip. His eyes glazed. He moved like a sleepwalker. Behind him, the girl still sat as she had before, not moving so much as a finger, as if asleep.

Tony grunted. "Looks like sleeping beauty woke."

I focused on the screen. Her eyes had opened. There was something cool and distant about them. They looked up at the camera that filmed her. . . . It seemed as if she gazed through the TV screen directly at us.

Over the speaker I heard the buzz as the dumbwaiter descended into the Communications Center. In a dreamlike way Phoenix went to it, opened the elevator door. For a second he stood there without reacting, even though he must have seen the two sticks of dynamite and the burning fuse.

In one fluid movement he scooped the dynamite from the dumbwaiter, then as if he was shielding a newborn baby from the rain, he hugged it to his chest before moving away from the girl. He walked to the farthest corner of the room; there he pressed himself to where the two walls joined.

In an unearthly way things seemed to stay like that for whole moments, Phoenix pushing himself face first to the wall, the fuse burning toward the explosive he clutched to his stomach.

The girl gazed at the camera. Her eyes were languid, even sleepy. I knew she understood what was happening. Only she didn't seem afraid. She tilted her head to one side, as if studying the expression on my face. Her dark hair spilled down over one naked breast. Her lips parted like she was just about to speak.

Then the flame reached the detonator. With a cracking thump a blossom of flame erupted in the corner of the room where Phoenix stood. A second later something wet and red struck the lens, smearing it so thickly we could no longer see the interior of the room.

For a moment no one spoke. The thick concrete floor that separated the lounge from the room beneath our feet shielded us. Even so, it knocked enough dust out of the carpet to mist the air. Electric lights flickered, then steadied again. The computer faithfully compensated for any damage; the backup systems kicked in, the air conditioner hummed steadily as before. Even with its human controller dead, the bunker's electronic brain would automatically maintain everything as before. Probably for months, if not years.

Zak looked 'round the room. "I guess all this is ours now."

Tony grimaced. "We still have to evict the bad guys, remember?"

I knocked the dust off my arms. "They can't spoil anything now. Besides, Phoenix will have made sure all the storerooms were locked up tight. First we need to get hold of those antibiotics for Michaela. And we need to fix Tony's leg." I smiled. "Then we can all come back here, clean the house and maybe enjoy à vacation."

"First, how do we find a way out of here?"

"We'll find a way."

Zak put his hand on my forearm. "There was something else, too, Greg."

"Oh?"

"What Phoenix said about you being from a hive. That you were the same as the girl."

I shook my head. "You saw the state that guy was in. It was all a delusion."

"Was it?"

"Keep believing it was." I gave a grim smile. "Because that's what I intend to do. OK, Tony, old buddy? If you can manage it, it's time to take a little walk."

Christmas

On the day I carried Tony out of the bunker on my back, trying not to knock his busted leg against the walls, it all changed. Only you never seem to know that you've reached one of those pivotal times in your life until much later, do you? Ben drove Tony back in the Jeep. The bottom of the vehicle almost dragged through the dirt, we'd piled so many supplies into the thing. All I knew then as I followed the Jeep was that I was grateful to be alive, that my buddies were alive and that the afternoon sunlight never seemed more beautiful to me than right then.

I rode alongside Zak on the Harley. For a while he'd talked about Phoenix and the girl in the bunker and asked me if she had some kind of telepathic powers. Would she have been able to reach inside our heads and control us, too? At last I smiled at him and called out over the noise of the motors, "Forget them, Zak. They're dead. We're not. That's all that matters."

So we rode on, seeing birds flying overhead. A deer ran alongside us for a while, as if wanting to join the pack, before peeling off to disappear into the heart of the forest. It still seemed then as if we'd carry on fighting for survival every single day of our lives. But that was the day we turned it all around.

Zak gave Michaela her antibiotic shots. It seemed in no time she was back to her old self, with those darkly erotic eyes and a smile so full of good humor you could almost light up a room with her. Tony's leg healed. Before long he was hobbling 'round with a stick. Now it doesn't bother him at all unless it rains; then he grumbles that it aches and he winds up growling like a bear with a sore rear end.

We know we would have starved if it weren't for the bunker. First we had to clear out what was left of the hornets . . . dead ones, too, so they wouldn't stink up the place. After that every few weeks we'd return with the Jeep (that now pulled a huge trailer); then we'd go crazy piling it high with fuel, food and ammunition before returning to the cabins on the hillside. What about Phoenix? Well, we never tried to break down the locked door that sealed Phoenix and the girl into what had become their tomb. "Let sleeping dogs lie," was Michaela's advice. Good advice, too. That episode was over. It was time to forget and start to live the rest of our lives.

And get this: The second half of the summer was a long and peaceful one. No hornets came our way. The biggest warm-blooded creature I saw was an elk that snuffled 'round the cabins one morning in the fall just as the leaves were turning red and the dawn mist bore an unmistakable chill. It was times like that I half believed I could climb on the Harley and roar all the way back home, where I'd push open the door to see Mom busy in the kitchen, and she'd smile up at me and say, "Hi, Greg. I made pizza for supper. Would you be a honey and go help Chelle with her homework?"

That was when ghosts came as stealthily as the dawn

mist. But when all's said and done ghosts are only memories. And memories are nothing more than movie clips from the past, right? They can't—or shouldn't—take control of your life. Even so every now and again old phantom memory would rise up. Once I dreamed of Phoenix. He was sitting on the end of the bed as Michaela slept beside me.

"I never thanked you for what you did, Valdiva," he said. "Thanks, buddy; you set me free. . . . You know she had me like a puppet . . . pull the string, pull the string . . ." Smiling, he pulled an invisible string.

"Phoenix?"

"Yes, old buddy?"

"I never asked you . . . why did you paint your face like an Egyptian pharaoh?"

He grinned. "Intimations of immortality . . . intimations of immortality . . ." He kept repeating this as he began to sprinkle rose petals from his fingertips. They covered the bed in red splotches. Just like the red splotches that covered the camera lens after the dynamite had exploded against his stomach. In the morning I recalled the dream. There were no red rose petals on the bed, though. Not that I expected there to be any. Phoenix, along with the thing that had squirmed from the hive, was dead.

Of course the time had to come when I dreamed about the girl. It was a day in October. One of those last warm, sunny days when you make the most of the heat. Boy and Tony had gone fishing. I walked with them by the river; then, when they chose a good place to cast their lines, I decided to walk on, following the flow of the stream. After a few minutes I found a sunlit spot on a bank protected from the cool breeze. It seemed a great place to relax for half an hour or so. I sat on the deep, soft grass at the edge of the river. Fish jumped for insects hovering above the surface. It was so peaceful my eyes closed.

"Greg Valdiva."

I opened my eyes to see a woman standing on the far bank. She had long dark hair and big almond-shaped eyes that fixed on me from across the water. It was the girl from the bunker, the one Phoenix claimed had hatched from the hive. More phantom memories.

"You took some finding," she said.

I yawned. "Well, you've found me now." My dream self was calm, cool and very collected. "What do you want?"

She studied me like an expert appraising an antique. I noticed she was no longer naked. The prude in my unconscious had slipped her into a white dress. Water splashed against the rocks; another fish jumped to snap a fly from the air.

At last she said, "You are the same as me, Greg Valdiva."

"I don't think so. You've got the wrong guy. You must be mistaking me for someone else."

"No, Greg. There's no one else to mistake you with."

"Is that a fact?"

"That's a fact, Greg. You see, we're the only ones who made it through the hive state."

"You don't say?" My dream persona was like chilled silk—cool, smooth.

"None of the other hives were viable. They became dessert for rats and snakes."

"That's a shame."

"But it leaves you and me, Greg."

"So you say."

She looked at me steadily across the rush of water, her almond-shaped eyes huge luminous lights. "You're not ready to join me yet, are you, Greg?"

"Nor will I ever be."

"You will. One day. When you truly wake up and realize what you are." She began to walk away, her bare feet pressing lightly against the sandy shore. She paused beneath the trees, a single beam of light picking her out, surrounding her in an unearthly radiance. "We'll meet again in the future, Greg."

The bushes seemed to fold 'round her and she was gone. Her feet made no sound as she glided away into the forest. After a while the eerie silence ended as the birds began to sing.

"Hey, Valdiva, are you going to sleep there all day?"

"Yeah, look at what we caught."

I opened my eyes to see Boy and Tony standing over me. I squinted up against the light as Boy held a bunch of fish that dripped all over my face. Laughing, I waved him away. "Come on; we'll make a barbecue of it." I wiped water from my chin. "The way that wind's shifting, I figure it's going to be the last cookout this year."

That should have been it. But as they roasted fish on the barbecue I went down to the river again, crossed it by the stepping stones, then followed it downstream to where I'd been sleeping on the far river bank. And there, where the girl in my dream had been standing, I saw a bare footprint in the sand. I scrubbed it out with the heel of my boot, returned to the barbecue and never mentioned it to another living soul.

There were seventeen of us in those log cabins. I shared a big room overlooking the river with Michaela. When nights dropped cooler as fall crumbled into winter we learned new tricks to keep each other warm.

Life continued its peaceful progress deep into the winter. North winds brought deep snow. Christmas came. We kept the parties going: we were a family; we were having fun. Christmas morning I crept out of the warm bed, leaving Michaela sleeping there with her hair spilling out onto the pillow. There'd been a fresh fall of snow. Now the world seemed to be made up of horizontal black and white lines. First came the white-covered lawn, then the black line of the fence. Beyond

411

that a snow-covered meadow ran smoothly down to the thick black river. Beyond that were snow-covered fields and lines of black forest, until a dark horizon yielded to white, snow laden skies. Christmas Day. Soon everything would change.

The turkey might have come from bunker tins, but it still tasted good. Boy went to bring more wood for the fire that blazed in the hearth. A second later he was back.

"Get your guns! They're coming up the hill!"

Hornets. Thousands of them. Tens of thousands. They surrounded the hill on every side. A gray tide surrounding an island. They moved like human slugs. Slowly getting closer and closer. Zak and Tony ran for their guns. Michaela reached out, grabbed my hand, held it tight. "We're not running . . . and we're not fighting, Greg," she said gently. "There are too many of them."

That was when a kind of calm crept down on us as gently as the snow falling from the sky. We stood there out on the lawn. We watched them advance slowly across the snowdrifts, turning the landscape from white to filthy gray.

Boy walked a few paces down the hill as if to meet them halfway. He was unarmed. Not that it mattered now. I knew there were too many. And for once the muscles in my stomach didn't react. My breathing was steady. My heart had the good grace to beat with a slow, steady rhythm. No one spoke. No one even moved. We just waited, knowing that everything was moving to a close. Whatever we'd planned or dreamed about, this huge cycle of events had reached its end. But we'd done the impossible. We'd formed bonds in our community that had never broken. We wouldn't be the ones to break them now.

Michaela's hand gripped mine. I watched as the

mass of gray resolved itself into thousands of individuals moving toward us through the snow. I saw the gray faces, the snowflakes speckling beards and hair. Their eyes fixed hard on us. Moments later the first ones moved away from the crowd that stretched for mile upon mile before us. The big man moved toward Boy, a hand outstretched. Boy never flinched. He stood, watching. Waiting for the final act.

In human beings the strongest instinct is to survive. In these creatures now moving across the snowdrifts toward us I realized that their overriding instinct was to kill. That is, to kill their enemy—us. They weren't going to stop to eat, to find shelter; they'd walk a hundred miles through the snow to snuff out a single member of the human race. And that, I saw, was where Mother Nature had made her big mistake.

The man was a near giant. He waded through the snow toward Boy. His eyes locked onto the child's face; he stretched out his arms as if to encircle the small neck with his huge hands. Then the man faltered. He struggled to raise his arms higher and failed. The blue lips twitched. That's when Boy himself reached out and, without any fuss, without any exertion, pushed the giant in the chest. The man crashed down on his back. He didn't even attempt to struggle to his feet. He lay there panting. I looked at his feet. Every single toe had vanished, eaten away by frostbite. Through the creature's rags I saw a chest that was barely covered by gray skin. Cheekbones protruded through the man's face. His blue lips were split and bleeding, destroyed by sheer cold. For a second his eyes locked on mine, the jaw working like he wanted to speak. But then with a sigh his head rolled back against the snow.

"He's dead." Boy gazed down at the lifeless face in awe. "He's dead, Michaela."

Michaela looked at the crowd toiling up the hill through the biting wind. Then she looked up at me, her eyes glistening. "They're all dying, aren't they?"

For a while we watched them struggle toward us. One after another fell exhausted into the snow where they died, arms outstretched toward us.

"Nature got it wrong this time," I said, hearing the hush in my voice.

I looked at the others as smiles transformed their faces. Zak slapped Tony on the back. Ben ran forward through the dying multitudes, whooping wildly and shouting, "Extinction! All right! All fucking right!"

How long can you stand there on a freezing Christmas Day and watch men and women—or things that had once been men and women—drop down dead from starvation and frostbite? An hour, two hours? But then, we carried an instinct to survive. Before the cold damaged us we returned to the cabin. There, we sat, drinking beers and talking about what we'd seen and what it meant for us. We expected that there'd be at least one knock on the door. But there wasn't. Not one.

Fourth of July

"Call me crazy," I told them. They did call me crazy. They tried to persuade me not to do it. Only I am crazy. Or at least half crazy, I guess. Only when they saw that I'd go alone if need be did they come, too. On the morning of the Fourth of July I loaded the Jeep with fireworks. I'd found them in a warehouse in the weeks after the hornets had died by the thousand outside our cabins.

Now we lived in a different place, of course. In houses by a lake. We're alone. No hornets bother us now. We all agreed that they'd simply starved or frozen to death during the winter. We didn't see any human beings either. Most of us believed we were the last people on the planet.

Me? I thought different. That was the reason I drove out that morning with fireworks piled in the open-top Jeep. Ben, Zak, Tony and Michaela came, too. Partly to see what I did, partly to stop me doing anything *too* crazy. I drove all day, heading for the highest mountain on the map possessing a road to the top. The little Jeep that was a veteran of Vietnam climbed steadily all the way to the top. From there I could see a hundred miles of forest in every direction. Michaela and the rest watched me as if maybe even more craziness was running through my blood. But it was something I had to do. If this didn't work I'd go back down the mountainside with Michaela. I'd agree that we were alone in the world. And we'd live the rest of our lives as well as we could with that understanding. But I had to give it one last shot.

First we had to wait for the sun to go down. I sat on the hood of the Jeep gazing out over a hundred miles of America. She'd gone through hell during the last eighteen months, but she still looked as beautiful as she'd always done. Beneath perfect blue July skies I allowed my eyes to roam over forests, rivers and lakes. From here I could even see Lake Coben, with Sullivan showing as a pale speck on the shoreline. Of course the town was finished now. I'd been back there to walk through the deserted streets. The courthouse lay in ashes. Even my old cabin had been burned to the ground. Everyone had gone. Or were dead. I'd seen old man Crowther and that son of his decomposing on their own driveway. Their bodies were lying with their hands 'round each other's throats. What drove them to kill each other I'll never know. Nor do I care. They deserved each other.

After that I left the ghost town to visit the white block of stones where I'd buried Mom and Chelle. Maybe I'd buried secrets with them, too. More than I dare speculate about. I picked up a football-sized piece of rock and stood it on the mound of stones. "There," I told them as they lay together in the ground. "It's finished now."

Then I drove out of the place without looking back.

*   *   *

Now I sat and I waited. No one said anything as the sun slipped out of the sky to sink into the horizon. As the stars came out I fired the first rocket. It climbed, leaving a trail of fire. A thousand feet above the mountaintop it burst, sending out red and silver balls of light.

In a near whisper Tony said, "Happy Fourth of July."

I fired another. A huge chrysanthemum of purple sparks expanded to cover half the sky. The explosion rolled down the mountainside and out across the face of a darkened America. I gazed outward, too, searching for the light of a house or even a campfire in the distance.

There was nothing.

I fired another rocket. It roared upward to break open, spilling streams of gold and silver. For the next two hours I fired a rocket every fifteen minutes. By midnight I'd reached the last one.

Michaela slipped her arms 'round me. "Don't let it bother you, Greg. Even if we are alone we can make this work."

The last rocket rose upward. It seemed to ascend right into the canopy of stars. Even when the powder had burned out it still floated upward, as if gravity could no longer restrain it. Then, at last, it burst without a sound. A waterfall of colored lights cascaded gently earthward—vivid blues, reds, silvers, yellows, greens—that seemed for a moment to become part of the night sky.

"That's the last one, Greg." Zak spoke gently. "There's beer in the Jeep. I know I could do with one right now."

The road where the Jeep sat lay just a few yards down the slope. In a moment I'd have to return to it, then head home, knowing I'd failed.

Ben slapped me on the back. "You gave it a good shot, Greg. Even if there's no one else out there we're going to stick together. We can live on the food in the bunker for years. There's enough gas there to . . ."

His voice faded. Way, way to the north, just on the edge of visibility, a spark flickered on the horizon, then slowly faded.

Ben breathed out. "Oh, my . . ."

Zak turned to the south. "Greg, Michaela, look."

Tony grabbed my arm. "And over there, behind you."

Slowly, without fuss, without sound, skyrockets burst one after another on the far horizons. The nearest couldn't have been any less than fifty miles away. But that didn't matter. They were there. They were fired by human hands. And as dozens of rockets rose upward to burst in the sky on that Fourth of July night I knew without question that I was witnessing one of the most beautiful sights I'd ever seen.

And that can't be a bad way to bring this account of what happened to me to an end, can it?

So just keep smiling. Keep hanging on in there. Because together we're going to make it.

VAMPYRRHIC
SIMON CLARK

Leppington is a small town, quiet and unassuming. Yet beneath its streets terrifying creatures stir. Driven by an ancient need, united in their burning hunger, they share an unending craving. They are vampires. They lurk in the dark, in tunnels and sewers . . . but they come out to feed. For untold years they have remained hidden, seen only by their unfortunate victims. Now the truth of their vile existence is about to be revealed—but will anyone believe it? Or is it already too late?

Dorchester Publishing Co., Inc.
P.O. Box 6640
Wayne, PA 19087-8640

_____5031-5
$5.99 US/$7.99 CAN

SIMON CLARK

DARKER

Richard Young is looking forward to a quiet week with his wife and their little daughter. Firing up the barbecue should be the most stressful task he'll face. He has no idea of the hell that awaits him, the nightmare that will begin with an insistent pounding at his door.

The stranger begging to be let in is being hunted. Not by a man or an animal, but by something that cannot be seen or heard, yet which has the power to crush and destroy anything in its path. It is a relentless, pounding force that has existed for centuries and has now been unleashed to terrify, to ravage . . . to kill.

SIMON CLARK

Blood Crazy

Saturday is a normal day. People go shopping. To the movies. Everything is just as it should be. But not for long. By Sunday, civilization is in ruins. Adults have become murderously insane. One by one they become infected with a crazed, uncontrollable urge to slaughter the young—even their own children. Especially their own children.

Will this be the way the world ends, in waves of madness and carnage? What will be left of our world as we know it? And who, if anyone, will survive? Terror follows terror in this apocalyptic nightmare vision by one of the most powerful talents in modern horror fiction. Prepare yourself for mankind's final days of fear.

__4825-6 $5.99 US/$6.99 CAN